THE ELSON READERS

BOOK FIVE

(REVISION OF ELSON GRAMMAR SCHOOL READER, BOOK ONE)

BY

WILLIAM H. ELSON
AUTHOR OF GOOD ENGLISH SERIES

AND

CHRISTINE M. KECK
HEAD UNION JUNIOR HIGH SCHOOL ENGLISH, GRAND RAPIDS, MICHIGAN

LOST CLASSICS BOOK COMPANY
LAKE WALES, FLORIDA

Publisher's Note

Recognizing the need to return to more traditional principles in education, Lost Classics Book Company is republishing forgotten late 19th and early 20th century literature and textbooks to aid parents in the education of their children.

This edition of *The Elson Readers—Book Five* was reprinted from the 1920 copyright edition. The text has been updated and edited only where necessary. Spelling and punctuation have been updated in works of prose, but not in poetry—these things being the prerogative of the poet.

We have included a glossary and pronunciation guide of more than 1380 terms at the end of the book to encourage children to look up words they don't know.

The Elson Readers—Book Five has been assigned a reading level of 1060L. More information concerning this reading level assessment may be attained by visiting www.lexile.com.

Library of Congress Catalog Card Number: 99-68284
ISBN 978-1-890623-19-7

Part of
The Elson Readers
Nine Volumes: *Primer* through *Book Eight*
ISBN 978-1-890623-23-4

On the Cover:
Ali Baba Counted Forty of Them from *The World's Fairy Tale Book*, pub. by G. Harrap & Co. Ltd., London (book illustration) by Monro Scott Orr (b. 1874)
Private Collection/Bridgeman Art Library

William H. Elson

In the early 1930s, William Harris Elson capped off a successful career as an educator and author of textbook readers by creating the "Fun with Dick and Jane" pre-primer readers with co-author William Scott Gray. Dick and Jane, their families, friends, and pets entered the popular culture as symbols of childhood, and the books themselves became synonymous with the first steps in learning to read.

In 1909 *The Elson Grammar School Reader*, the first in a nine-volume series of school readers, appeared to immediate success. *The Elson Readers*, which Lost Classics Book Company is reprinting, were among Elson's earliest creations and go well beyond the scope of the "Dick and Jane" books. Following a carefully planned model that stresses both improving comprehension and developing appreciation for literature, Elson organized the books in a way that built on the understanding and skills taught in earlier volumes.

Assisting Elson on the series were publishing house writers Lura Runkel and Christine Keck. Runkel helped on the primer and the first and second volume, while Keck worked on the fifth through the eighth volume. Obviously both writers were schooled well in Elson's methodology, as the series displays remarkable consistency and accuracy throughout the entire set of books.

Through the eighth grade, or age 13 to 14, each succeeding book in the *Elson Readers* series introduces students to increasingly complex genres and better writers. The result of using the series as intended is better reading skills and comprehension as well as a growing appreciation for good writing. But the books are so thorough that they may be used individually and still advance a student's understanding and appreciation for the types of writing in a particular volume.

Born on November 22, 1854, in Carroll County, Ohio, Elson lived through a tumultuous period, becoming an educator who helped usher in numerous innovations. Although he did not receive his A.B. degree from Indiana University until 1895, he was active as a schoolteacher and as a school administrator for many years before, beginning with his first teaching assignment in 1881. By 1907 he had established the first technical high school in the nation in Cleveland, Ohio, where he served as school superintendent from 1906-12.

Elson's contributions to teaching children to read and appreciate literature included not only the *Elson Readers* but many other series for which he served as primary author or editor, including *Good English* (3 vols., 1916); *Child-Library Readers* (9 vols., 1923-34); and *Elson Junior Literature* (2 vols., 1932). By the time of his death on February 2, 1935, his books had sold over fifty million copies and were in use in 34 countries on every continent.

Besides helping to create the engaging "Fun with Dick and Jane" books, William Harris Elson implemented a developmental approach to learning reading skills that still works extremely well. Lost Classics Book Company's republication of this volume from the *Elson Readers* provides access to a book that will provide children with a delightful and effective learning experience.

David E. Vancil, Ph.D.
Indiana State University

Biographical Dictionary of American Educators. 3 Vols. Edited by John F. Ohles. Westport, CT: Greenwood Press, 1978. Alphabetical entry.

The National Cyclopaedia of American Biography. Volume 26. New York: James T. White & Co., 1937. Pp. 367-68.

Preface

This book is based on the belief that an efficient reader for the fifth grade must score high when tested on five fundamental features: *quality* of literature; *variety* of literature; *organization* of literature; *quantity* of literature; and *definite helps* sufficient to make the text a genuine tool for classroom use.

Quality of Literature

First among these features is the essential that the foundation of the book must be the acknowledged masterpieces of American and British authors. American boys and girls may be depended upon to read current magazines and newspapers, but if they are ever to have their taste and judgment of literary values enriched by familiarity with the classics of our literature, the schools must provide the opportunity. This ideal does not mean the exclusion of well established present-day writers, but it does mean that the *core* of the school reader should be the rich literary heritage that has won recognition for its enduring value. Moreover, these masterpieces must come to the pupil in complete units, not in mere excerpts or garbled "cross-sections"; for the pupil in his school life should gain some real literary possessions.

A study of the contents of *The Elson Reader, Book Five,* will show how consistently its authors have based the book on this sound test of *quality.* The works of the acknowledged "makers" of our literature have been abundantly drawn upon to furnish a foundation of great stories and poems, gripping in interest and well within the powers of a child's appreciation in this grade.

Variety of Literature

Variety is fundamental to a well-rounded course of reading. If the school reader is to provide for all the purposes that a collection of literature for this grade should serve, it must contain material covering at least the following types: (1) literature representing both British and American authors; (2) some of the best modern poetry and prose as well as the literature of the past; (3) important race stories—great epics—and world-stories of adventure; (4) patriotic literature, rich in ideals of home and country, loyalty and service, thrift, cooperation, and citizenship—ideals of which American children gained, during the World War, a new conception that the school reader should perpetuate; (5) literature suited to festival occasions, particularly those celebrated in the schools: Armistice Day, Thanksgiving Day, Christmas, Arbor Day and Bird Day, anniversaries of the birthdays of Lincoln and Washington, as well as of Longfellow and other great American authors; (6) literature of the seasons, nature, and out-of-door life; (7) literature of humor that will enliven the reading and cultivate the power to discriminate between *wholesome* humor—an essential part of life—and *crude* humor, so prevalent in the pupil's outside reading; (8) adventure stories both imaginative and real; (9) literature suited to dramatization, providing real project material.

This book offers a well-rounded course of reading covering all the types mentioned above. Especially by means of groups of stories and poems that portray love of home and its festivals, love of our free country and its flag, and unselfish service to others, this book makes a stirring appeal to good citizenship. Moreover, it will be noted that wholesome ethical ideals pervade the literature throughout.

The literature of a school reader, if it is to do effective work, must be purposefully organized. Sound organization groups into related units the various selections that center about a common theme. This arrangement enables the pupil to see the larger dominant ideas of the book as a whole, instead of looking upon it as a confused scrapbook of miscellaneous selections. Such arrangement also fosters literary comparison by bringing together selections having a common theme or authorship.

Organization of Literature

This book has been so organized as to fulfill these purposes. There are three main parts, each distinguished by unity of theme or authorship. "Part I," leading from a wholesome appreciation of nature, particularly in its American setting, centers mainly about the important themes of patriotism, service, and good citizenship; "Part II" introduces some of the great tales that typify our love of stirring deeds; "Part III" presents some of our greatest American authors at sufficient length to make them stand out to the pupil. Through these grouped selections, together with the accompanying biographies, pupils may come to be familiar with and love some of the great company of writers that have made the name of America known in the world of literature.

Attention is called to three special features that keep the dominant theme of each part clearly in the foreground: (1) "A Forward Look" and "A Backward Look" for each main division and important subdivision emphasize the larger theme, and show how each selection contributes to the group idea (see pages 19, 56, etc.); (2) the notes and questions frequently call the pupil's attention to the relation the selection bears to the main thought (see pages 39, 75, etc.); (3) the three main divisions, and the subordinate groups within each main unit, are made to stand out clearly by illustrations that typify the theme (see pages 18, 21, etc.) and by topical headings that enable the pupil to visualize the group units. By these three means the organization of the book is emphasized, and fundamental ideals are kept dominant.

Quantity of Literature

Obviously, a book that is to supply the pupil with a year's course in literature must be a generous volume. Variety is impossible without quantity, especially where literary wholes rather than mere fragmentary excerpts are offered. Particularly is this true when complete units are included not only for intensive study, but also for extensive reading—longer units, of the so-called "paper classics" type, to be read mainly for the story element. In bulk such units should be as large as the pupil can control readily in rapid silent reading, a kind of reading that increases the power to enjoy with intelligence a magazine or a book.

The Elson Reader, Book Five, is a generous volume in provision for these needs. Its inclusiveness makes possible a proper balance between prose and poetry, between long and short selections, and between material for intensive and extensive reading.

Definite Helps

If the pupil is to gain the full benefit from his reading, certain definite helps must be provided. An efficient reader must score a high test not only on the fundamentals of *quality, variety, organization,* and *quantity* of literature, but also on its *fitness as a tool* for classroom use. The effectiveness of this reader as such a tool may be indicated by the following distinguishing features:

(1) A distinctive introduction, "The Crystal Glass" (see page 13), gives the pupil an illuminating interpretation of the organization and literary content of the volume.

(2) Definite suggestions for developing speed and concentration in silent reading. (See pages 21, 30, 34, 163, etc.)

(3) A comprehensive glossary (pages 399-439) contains the words and phrases that offer valuable vocabulary training, either of pronunciation or meaning. The teacher is free to use the glossary according to the needs of her particular class, but suggestive type words and phrases are listed under "Notes and Questions".

(4) A complete program of study, "How to Gain the Full Benefit from Your Reading" (pages 28, 29), gives a concise explanation of the various helps found in the book.

(5) The helps to study are more than mere notes; they aid in making significant the larger purposes of the literature. These "Notes and Questions" include:

(a) Biographies of the authors that supply data for interpreting the stories and poems; particularly helpful are those of "Part III";

(b) Historical settings, wherever they are necessary to the intelligent understanding of the selection (see pages 94, 105, etc.);

(c) Questions and suggestions that present clearly the main idea, stimulate original discussion and comparison, and bring out modern parallels to the situations found in the selections;

(d) Words of everyday use frequently mispronounced, listed for study under "Discussion" (see page 29, etc.);

(e) Phrases that offer idiomatic difficulty; for convenience in locating these phrases the page and line numbers are indicated.

(f) Projects, individual and social (see page 82).

Contents

PART III. GREAT AMERICAN AUTHORS

SUGGESTIONS FOR AN ORDER OF READING

In the *Elson Readers* selections are grouped according to theme or authorship. Such an arrangement enables the pupil to see the dominant ideas of the book as a whole. This purpose is further aided by "A Forward Look," or introduction, and "A Backward Look," or review, for each main group. The book, therefore, emphasizes certain fundamental ideals, making them stand out clearly in the mind of the pupil. This result can best be accomplished by reading all the selections of a group in the order given, before taking up those of a different group. The order of the groups, however, may be varied to suit school conditions or preferences.

It goes without saying that selections particularly suited to the celebration of special days will be read in connection with such festival occasions. For example, "The First Thanksgiving Day," page 92, will be read immediately before the Thanksgiving holiday, even if the class at that particular time is in the midst of some other main part of the reader. Before assigning a selection out of order, however, the teacher should scrutinize the notes and questions, to make certain that no references are made within these notes to a discussion in "A Forward Look" or to other selections in the group that pupils have not yet read. In case such references are found the teacher may well conduct a brief class discussion to make these questions significant to the pupils.

It is the belief of the authors that the longer selections, such as those found in "Part II," should be read silently and reported on in class. In this way the monotony incident to the reading of such selections aloud in class will be avoided. However, the class will wish to read aloud certain passages from these longer units because of their beauty, their dramatic quality, or the forceful way in which the author has expressed his thoughts. *Class readings* are frequently suggested for this purpose. In this way reading aloud is given purposefulness.

The Crystal Glass

Once upon a time, as the fairy tale has it, there was a mighty magician named Merlin. He was the teacher of the young Prince Arthur, who was one day to become the British king. Merlin was old and wise, and he had the power of prophecy. One of his most wonderful possessions was a magic glass, a globe of crystal into which one might gaze and see distant places as if they were near at hand and see the events of past and future as if they were happening right before his eyes.

No one knows now the whereabouts of this wonder working crystal, or what was its appearance. Very likely it seemed ordinary enough, though a glass of curious shape. Only those who knew how to use it could learn its secrets; for all others it had no power. But the magic that once lay in it has been given to certain books, which, like Merlin's globe, are filled with mysterious power. Such a book you now hold in your hands. If you do not understand how to use it, it will tell you nothing. But if you have this understanding, you have only to look within these pages, and past and present and future will be unfolded to your gaze.

Here is what you will find if you use this book as a Merlin's glass wherein to see the wonders which lie concealed within it.

First of all, you will see the world of animals and birds and flowers and times and seasons—the world of nature. There is a story about a little girl who wanted to see the king to ask of him a favor. But no one could see him unless he was accompanied by some friends, for the king would not trust anyone unless he had proved himself friendly so that people loved to be with him. Now this little girl was very poor and she had no friends. She wandered alone in the forest, and cried because she had no friends. Just at this time she came into the knowledge of a wonderful secret by which she could understand the language of the birds and of all the shy animals of the forest, and as soon as she could understand them and talk with them, they loved her, and the forest was no longer a lonely place but was filled with friends. Some of these friends went with her to the king's palace, and she now had no difficulty. She knew the language of those who lived in the forest, and she was no longer poor and lonely. So in the pages of this book you will learn of the lives of faithful dogs and huge buffaloes, and the brown thrush will sing for you a song full of meaning. The modest violet, the jack in the pulpit, even the four-leaf clovers will tell you stories about the forest and the field, so that wherever you walk you will be surrounded by your friends. The magic glass of Merlin will unseal for you this world of nature.

Merlin's globe also enables you to look into the past and live in it as if it were the present. You will take part in the first Thanksgiving Day. You will learn why the flag of our country is called Old Glory. You will look in upon the boy Lincoln, tired after his hard day's work on the farm, reading by the open fire in his father's cabin. You will see the young Washington bravely helping General Braddock to save his soldiers. So the magic glass of reading will make the early history of our country real to you, and the past will no longer be the past but a part of your present life.

If you wish to live for a time in the fairy realm, where there are buried treasure chests or magic lamps and rings, or if you would like to make a journey to far off lands where are many wonders, you have only to look in this magic glass, and in a twinkling you are whisked away. You find yourself in a strange country where men and women wear curious, flowing garments of many colors, where trees and animals are unfamiliar, and where queer buildings with many towers attract your delighted eyes. The narrow streets are filled with strange life. You see a boy with eyes that seem to be looking on strange things. He is talking with an evil-looking man who bends over him, pointing down the street and out into the open country at the other end of the town. And presently the boy goes with the stranger, and you follow, for it is Aladdin and the magician, and you wish to know the adventure that is to come.

After this, Ali Baba and the cave of buried treasure and the forty thieves and Morgiana, the shrewd slave girl, and the jars of oil will all appear in the magic glass, and another series of marvelous adventures will be disclosed to you. And then again, you come to a rich man's home, and before it, gazing enviously at it, is a poor tramp. Go up the steps with him and look upon the feast within the house. There is a queer table filled with food of strange form. And there is the rich man, Sindbad the Sailor, and you may listen if you will to his stories of travel to marvelous lands. Thus you travel to the mysterious East, without effort. You take part in wonderful adventures, without danger. Your magic glass is the window through which a world of fairy magic gleams vividly.

At another time you look, and the glass shows an English scene. It is the greenwood, somewhat out from London. Never were trees so green, or flowers so fresh and gay, or birds so filled with joy. You listen, and a gay fellow sings,

> Under the greenwood tree
> Who loves to lie with me,
> And tune his merry note
> Unto the sweet bird's throat,

Come hither! come hither! come hither!
    Here shall he see
    No enemy
But winter and rough weather.

Presently you hear the sound of a horn deep in the forest, to be followed soon by the coming of a merry crowd. Here is the prince of outlaws, clad in Lincoln green and followed by a score of lusty fellows, and at once there are songs, and wrestling matches, and merry jests, till your heart is filled with joy. Little John, and the Sheriff of Nottingham, and Friar Tuck, and Robin Hood, and last of all, the king himself—these are the actors in the play that you see through your magic glass. And so it goes through all these stories of adventure—they become a part of your experience, and you live more lives than one.

Last of all, your magic glass, which is this book, and which is always ready to do you service when you call upon it, will introduce you to a group of great Americans who long ago learned these secrets and wrote down what they themselves had seen. A patriot who helped to make our America will tell you several stories of his childhood. A nature-loving poet will tell you about flowers and birds. Another poet will furnish stories about merry times on the farm. A third will tell you legends of the Indians. Once more the world of nature, the world of adventure, and the world of history and legend will open before you, but this time you will learn something also of the men who have lived in our America and have written about it in such a way as to show us that, after all, we need no marvelous Eastern country or desert islands—there is adventure enough and to spare all about us, if we have eyes to see.

And here is the greatest charm of all. It is good to know about this magic glass of reading, so that we shall never want for the joy it can bring. But while we use it, we shall find our sight made pure and strong, so that when we no longer have the crystal globe, we can walk in field and wood, and along our streets, and see, wondering, the beauty of the world in which we live.

Part I

Nature—Humor—Home and Country

Better—a thousand times better—than all the material wealth the world can give is the love for the best books.

A Reading from Homer

THE WORLD OF NATURE

A Forward Look

If we have eyes to see, the world of nature is a fairyland. Further on in this book you will read how Aladdin—a boy who was led by a magician to a cave in which were all kinds of wonderful objects—came upon a garden underground wherein grew trees filled with extraordinary fruit. "Each tree bore fruit of a different color," we are told. "The white were pearls; the sparkling were diamonds; the deep red were rubies; the green, emeralds; the blue, turquoises."

Now with this compare a story about a great American author, Ralph Waldo Emerson. Emerson loved all the forms of nature. He wrote of the bee, of the wild flowers, of the storm, of the snowbird, and of running waters. And in talking of the magic of a river he reminds us of Aladdin's fairy fruits:

> I see thy brimming, eddying stream
> And thy enchantment,
> For thou changest every rock in thy bed
> Into a gem.
> All is opal and agate,
> And at will thou pavest with diamonds.

Now we may suppose that Aladdin often waded through the brook and noticed the shining pebbles and heard the tinkling music of the water as it rippled over stones in the stream. He *noticed* the pebbles, but did not look *at them.* He *heard* the murmur of the waters, but he did not *listen.* But when the magician uttered his magic words, and the earth opened, and Aladdin saw a little ladder leading down into a deep cave, and in that cave found curious trees bearing curious fruits, he was so surprised that he looked more closely, and all that he saw was full of wonder. Now the poet is like the magician. His words open the door of enchantment for us if we care to enter.

For the poets have been lovers of nature, and they help us to see the beauty that lies about us. One of them calls the stars "the forget-me-nots of the angels." Another writes of the song of the brook as it goes dancing and singing down into the river, until we hear the music of the waters in the melody of the poet's verse.

Through such stories and poems of animals and birds and flowers and of the seasons of the year as you will find in the following pages, your magic glass of reading will open up the fairyland of nature.

For magic wonders are not limited to the fairylands that we read about in the *Arabian Nights* or in the tales of *Cinderella* or of the *Sleeping Beauty*. There is the enchantment which put the princess and all her household to sleep for a hundred years until the prince came to release them. There is also the enchantment of the frost, that stills all the life of brook and lake and river, and holds the outdoor world in deep sleep until the breath of spring comes, and releases the prisoners. There is the enchantment which Aladdin controlled by his lamp and his ring, so that at his bidding giant figures appeared to do his will; there is also the enchantment of the snow, of the fire, of the lightning, of the storm; or there is the equally marvelous enchantment by which the rose unfolds from the bud, the apple grows from the blossom, and the robin from the tiny blue egg. Only we must *see* and *listen* when the magicians lead us to the fairy world of nature.

Aladdin had passed the entrance to the magic cave a hundred times and had seen nothing. So men pass the fields and see nothing but the corn and the wheat and the cotton, and in the autumn they see the harvesters gathering the crops of the fields. But the poet looks on these same fields and gathers another crop from them, and this he puts into a song, and this song opens for us the world of nature.

ANIMALS

Turk, the Faithful Dog*

Samuel White Baker

Turk's Failure

When I was a boy, my grandfather frequently told a story concerning a dog which he knew, as an example of true fidelity. This animal was a mastiff that belonged to a friend, Mr. Prideaux, to whom it was a constant companion.

Whenever Mr. Prideaux went out for a walk, Turk was sure to be near his heels. Street dogs would bark and snarl at the giant as his massive form attracted their attention, but Turk seldom noticed them. At night he slept outside his master's door, and no sentry could be more alert upon his watch than the faithful dog.

One day Mr. Prideaux had a dinner party. The dog Turk was present and stretched his huge form upon the hearthrug. It was a cold night in winter, and Mr. Prideaux's friends after dinner began to discuss the subject of dogs. Almost every person had an anecdote to relate, and my own grandfather, being present, had no doubt added his

* See "Suggestions for Silent Reading," page 163.

mite to the collection, when Turk suddenly awoke from a sound sleep and, having stretched himself, walked up to his master's side and rested his large head upon the table.

"Ha, ha, Turk!" exclaimed Mr. Prideaux, "you must have heard our arguments about the dogs, so you have put in an appearance."

"And a magnificent animal he is!" remarked my grandfather; "but although a mastiff is the largest of dogs, I do not think it is as sensible as many others."

"As a rule you are right," replied his master, "because they are generally chained up as watchdogs, and have not the intimate association with human beings which is so great an advantage to housedogs; but Turk has been my constant companion from the first month of his life, and his intelligence is very remarkable. He understands most things that I say, if they are connected with himself; he will often lie upon the rug with his large eyes fixed upon me, and he will frequently become aware that I wish to go out; at such times he will fetch my hat, cane, or gloves, whichever may be at hand, and wait for me at the front door. He will take a letter to several houses of my acquaintance, and wait for a reply, and he can perform a variety of actions that would imply a share of reason seldom possessed by other dogs."

A smile upon several faces was at once noticed by Mr. Prideaux, who immediately took a guinea from his pocket, and said to his dog, "Here, Turk! They won't believe in you! Take this guinea to No. — Street, to Mr. —, and bring me a receipt."

The dog wagged his huge tail with pleasure, and the guinea having been placed in his mouth, he hastened toward the door; this being opened, he was admitted through the front entrance to the street. It was a miserable night. The wind was blowing the sleet and rain against the windows, and the gutters were running with muddy water; nevertheless, Turk had started upon his mission in the howling gale, while the front door was once more closed against the blast.

The party were comfortably seated around the fire, much interested in the success or failure of the dog's adventure.

"How long will it be before we may expect Turk's return?" inquired a guest.

"The house to which I have sent him is about a mile and a half distant; therefore, if there is no delay when he barks for admission at the door, and my friend is not absent from home, he should return in about three-quarters of an hour with a receipt. If, on the other hand, he cannot gain admission, he may wait for any length of time," replied his master.

Some among the company supported the dog's chances of success, while others were against him. The evening wore away; the allotted time was exceeded, and a whole hour had passed, but no dog had returned. Nevertheless, his master was still hopeful.

"I must tell you," said Mr. Prideaux, "that Turk frequently carries notes for me, and as he knows the house well, he certainly will not make a mistake. Perhaps my friend may be dining out, in which case Turk will probably wait for a longer time."

Two hours passed; the storm was raging. Mr. Prideaux himself went to the front door, which flew open before a fierce gust the instant that the lock was turned. The gutters were clogged with masses of half-melted snow. "Poor Turk!" muttered his master, "this is indeed a wretched night for you. Perhaps they have kept you in the warm kitchen, and will not allow you to return in such fearful weather."

When Mr. Prideaux returned to his guests, he could not conceal his disappointment. "Ha!" exclaimed one, "with a guinea in his mouth, he has probably gone into some house of entertainment where dogs are supplied with dinner and a warm bed, instead of shivering in a winter's gale!"

Jokes were made at the absent dog's expense, but his master was anxious and annoyed. Poor Turk's reputation had suffered severely.

It was long past midnight; the guests had departed, the storm was raging, and violent gusts occasionally shook the house. Mr. Prideaux was alone in his study, and he poked the fire until it blazed and roared up the chimney.

"What can have become of that dog?" exclaimed his master to himself, now really anxious. "I hope they kept him; most likely they would not send him back upon such a dreadful night."

Mr. Prideaux's study was close to the front door, and his attention was suddenly directed to a violent shaking and scratching. In an instant he ran into the hall and unlocked the entrance door. A mass of filth and mud entered. This was Turk!

The dog was shivering with wet and cold. His usually clean coat was thick with mire, as though he had been dragged through deep mud. He wagged his tail when he heard his master's voice, but appeared dejected and ill. The dog was taken downstairs and immediately placed in a large tub of hot water, in which he was accustomed to be bathed. It was now discovered that in addition to mud and dirt, which almost concealed his coat, he was besmeared with blood! Mr. Prideaux sponged his favorite with warm water, and, to his surprise, he saw wounds of a serious nature. The dog's throat was badly torn, his back and breast were deeply bitten, and there could be no doubt that he had been worried by a pack of dogs.

He was now washed clean and was being rubbed dry with a thick towel while he stood upon a blanket before the fire. "Why, Turk, old boy, what has been the matter? Tell us all about it, poor old man!" exclaimed his master.

The dog was now thoroughly warmed, and he panted with the heat of the kitchen fire. He opened his mouth, and the guinea which he had received in trust dropped on the kitchen floor!

"There is some mystery in this," said Mr. Prideaux, "which I will try to discover tomorrow. He has been set upon by strange dogs, and rather than lose the guinea, he has allowed himself to be half killed without once opening his mouth in self-defense! Poor Turk!" continued his master, "you must have lost your way, old man, in the darkness and storm; most likely confused after the unequal fight. What an example you have given us in being faithful to a trust!"

Turk was wonderfully better after his warm bath. He lapped up a large bowl of good thick soup mixed with bread, and in half an hour was comfortably asleep upon his thick rug by his master's bedroom door.

The Mystery Explained

Upon the following morning the storm had cleared away, and a bright sky had succeeded to the gloom of the preceding night. Immediately after breakfast Mr. Prideaux, accompanied by his dog (which was, although rather stiff, not much the worse for the rough treatment he had received), started for a walk toward the house to which he had directed Turk upon the previous evening.

He was anxious to discover whether his friend had been absent, as he believed that the dog might have been waiting for admittance, and had been perhaps attacked by some dogs in the neighborhood.

The master and Turk had walked for nearly a mile, and had just turned the corner of a street, when, as they passed a butcher's shop, a large brindled mastiff rushed from the shop door and flew at Turk.

"Call your dog off!" shouted Mr. Prideaux to the butcher, who watched the attack with impudent satisfaction. "Call him off, or my dog will kill him!" continued Mr. Prideaux.

The usually docile Turk had rushed to meet his assailant with a fury that was extraordinary. With a growl like that of a lion he quickly seized his foe by the throat, and in a fierce struggle of only a few seconds he threw the brindled dog upon his back. It was in vain that Mr. Prideaux tried to call him off. He never for an instant relaxed his hold, but with the strength of a wild beast of prey Turk shook the head of the butcher's dog to the right and left. The butcher attempted to interfere, and lashed him with a huge whip.

"Stand clear! Fair play! Don't you strike my dog!" shouted Mr. Prideaux. "Your dog was the first to attack!" Mr. Prideaux seized Turk by his collar, while the butcher was endeavoring to release his dog from the deadly grip.

At length Mr. Prideaux's voice and action appeared for a moment to create a calm, and he held back his dog.

Turk's flanks were heaving with the intense exertion and excitement of the fight, and he strained to escape from his master's hold to attack once more his enemy. At length, by kind words and the caress of the well-known hand, his fury was calmed down.

"Well, that's the most curious adventure I've ever had with a dog!" exclaimed the butcher, who was now completely crestfallen. "Why, that's the very dog! That's the very dog that came by my shop late last night in the howling storm, and my dog Tiger went at him and tousled him up completely. I never saw such a cowardly cur; he wouldn't show any fight, although he was pretty near as big as a donkey; and there my dog Tiger nearly ate half of him, and dragged the other half about the gutter, till he looked more like an old doormat than a dog; and I thought he must have killed him; and here he comes out as fresh as paint today."

"What do you say?" asked Mr. Prideaux. "Was it your dog that worried my poor dog last night, when he was upon a message of trust? My friend, let me inform you of the fact that my dog had a guinea in his mouth to carry to my friend, and rather than drop it, he allowed himself to be half killed by your savage Tiger. Today he has proved his courage, and your dog has discovered his mistake. This is the guinea that he dropped from his mouth when he returned to me after midnight, beaten and distressed!" said Mr. Prideaux, much excited. "Here, Turk, old boy, take the guinea again, and come along with me! You have had your revenge, and have given us all a lesson." His master gave him the guinea in his mouth, and they continued their walk.

It appeared, upon Mr. Prideaux's arrival at his friend's house, that Turk had never been there; probably after his defeat he had become so confused that he lost his way in the heavy storm, and had at length regained the road home some time after midnight, in the condition already described.

How to Gain the Full Benefit from Your Reading

The reading of this story, besides giving you pleasure, has no doubt given you a new idea of the faithfulness often shown by dogs. But if you are to get the full benefit from any story or poem in this reader, you will need to pause long enough to notice certain things that will give you a better understanding of it.

The Crystal Glass, **A Forward Look,** and **A Backward Look**. First, you should read and discuss in class "The Crystal Glass" (pages 13-16) and study the Table of Contents, to gain a general idea of the book as a whole. Next, you should notice that each story and poem is a part of some special group that treats of some one big idea such as "Nature," "Home and Country," etc. Each selection will have a fuller meaning for you if you understand how it helps to bring out the big idea of this group. Before reading the stories in any group you should read and discuss in class the "Forward Look" (see page 19) that precedes them. And after you have read all the selections in a group, you will enjoy a pleasant class period discussing the "Backward Look" (see page 56)—taking stock, as it were, of the joy and benefit gained from your reading.

In addition, each selection is followed by "Notes and Questions" that contain some or all of the following features:

Biography. First, it is always desirable to learn something about the author. When you read, for example, on page 29, that Samuel White Baker gave the best years of his life to a study of animals, you feel that his story of the dog's faithfulness is well worth reading.

Discussion. Next, if you will read the story so carefully that you can answer the questions given under the topic Discussion (see page 29), you will probably find it easier to understand certain incidents. For example, you hear much about the word "service" in these days when millions of American soldiers have been serving their country so nobly. But perhaps when you think of the answer to the third question on page 29 you will see more clearly than before that "service" and "faithfulness" are qualities that are shown not only on the battlefield but in humble walks of life—sometimes even by animals.

Glossary. One of the benefits that should result from reading is the learning of new words. At the end of the Discussion on page 29 you will find a list of words the meaning of which you are to look up in the glossary and a second list that you should find out how to pronounce. Many of these words you may feel certain you know how to pronounce correctly. But perhaps you have been mispronouncing some of them. Look up in the glossary the words listed under question 9, and you may find that you have been mispronouncing *calm*, *hearth*, or *extraordinary*. When you are looking up words in the pronunciation lists, be sure that you understand the meaning, also.

Besides the individual words that you do not understand, you will sometimes read a phrase, or group of words, used in some special sense. The most striking are listed under the topic "Phrases for Study." Look them up in the Glossary, for you will often find the hardest passage of the reading lesson made easy by the explanation of a single phrase.

NOTES AND QUESTIONS

Biography. Samuel White Baker (1821-1893) was an English engineer and author. At the age of twenty-four he went to Ceylon, where he soon became known as an explorer and hunter of big game. With his wife he later explored the region of the Nile River. He is the author of *True Tales for My Grandsons*, from which "Turk, the Faithful Dog" is taken.

Discussion. 1. How does this story prove the intelligence of Turk? 2. How does it prove his fidelity? 3. Here are two qualities that every man should desire to possess. Do you think many men, set upon by robbers, would act as bravely and as faithfully as Turk? Give reasons for your answer. 4. What do you know of the author? 5. *Class readings*: The conversation between Mr. Prideaux and the butcher, page 26, line 9, to page 27, line 26 (2 pupils). 6. *Outline for testing Silent reading.* Tell the story in your own words, using these topics: (a) Turk's adventure; (b) how the mystery was explained. 7. You will enjoy reading "Cap," the Red Cross dog (in *Stories for Children*, Faulkner). 8. Find in the glossary the meaning of: alert; mission; dejected; besmeared; brindled; docile; relaxed; crestfallen. 9. *Pronounce*: hearthrug, anecdote, guinea, toward, extraordinary, calm.

Phrases for Study

(Numbers in heavy type refer to pages; numbers in light type to lines.)

intimate association, **22**, 12
imply a share of reason, **22**, 23
supported the dog's chances, **23**, 18
of a serious nature, **25**, 1
received in trust, **25**, 10
succeeded to the gloom, **25**, 26

OUR UNINVITED GUEST*

ERNEST HAROLD BAYNES

"Jimmy," our young black bear, was known to every child in the neighborhood. If a children's vote had been taken for the most popular animal in the county, I believe that Jimmy would have been unanimously elected. If the grown people had held the election, however, it is certain that there would have been some votes against him.

For example, when Mr. W——, one of our neighbors, came home very late one night, got into bed in the dark, and unwittingly kicked a bear cub that had climbed in at a window earlier in the evening, of course he had his toes nipped. That man would never have voted for Jimmy.

Neither would the farmer's wife he met one evening coming from the barn with a pail of new milk. The weather was warm, Jimmy was thirsty, and he was particularly fond of new milk. So he stood on his hind legs, threw his arms around the pail, and sucked up half the contents before the good woman had recovered from her astonishment.

But with the children he was a great favorite. He was one of them, and they understood him. Like them he was full of fun and mischief, and he would play as long as anyone cared to play with him.

One Christmas we gave a children's party, and perhaps a score of girls and boys came to spend the evening. As it was not possible to make Jimmy understand about the party, he went to bed early, as usual, and was asleep in his own den under the porch long before the first guests arrived. He was not forgotten by his little friends, however, and "Where's Jimmy?" was the first question

* See "Suggestions for Silent Reading," page 163.

asked by almost every child as he came in. But there was so much to chatter about, and there were so many games to play, that absent comrades—even Jimmy—were soon out of mind.

At last supper was ready, and all the children trooped into the dining room and took their places at the long table.

For a little while everyone was so busy that there was little to be heard except the clatter of forks and spoons and plates. I stood at the end of the room, enjoying the fun. For the moment, my eyes were on a small boy who seemed to be enjoying himself even more than the rest. He was making more noise than anyone else, and at the same time performing remarkable sleight-of-mouth tricks with a large piece of cake and a plate of ice cream. Suddenly, I saw his face change. His laugh was cut in two, his smile faded, the remains of the cake fell to his plate, and a spoonful of ice cream, on its way to his open mouth, remained suspended in the air. He was facing a window, and as I followed his gaze, I saw a hairy black face, with a tawny muzzle and a pair of small shining black eyes, looking eagerly into the room. It was the bear cub, whose slumbers had been disturbed by the noise, and who had come to see what it was all about.

In an instant the room was in an uproar. All the children left the table at once, and crowded around the window yelling—"Jimmy!" "It's Jimmy!" "Let him in!" "Don't you do it!" "Keep him out!" "Open the window!" "Give him some cake!" One little boy, with a piece of cake in his hand, raised the window just a little. That was enough for Jimmy; he thrust his strong muzzle under the sash, raised it with one jerk of his head, and came tumbling into the room. How those children yelled and scattered! While they all thought it good fun to have the cub at the party, none of them knew just what he would do, and some, especially among the younger ones, were decidedly nervous. A small girl hid behind the window curtains, two little boys scurried upstairs and peeped through the banisters, and another, by means of a chair, scrambled to the top of a sideboard. But Jimmy had his own ideas about a party. His first interest was in the supper table. Standing up on his hind legs, he placed his forepaws on the cloth. Just in front of him was a plate with some apple jelly on it. One sweep of his long tongue and the plate was almost as clean as if it had been washed. A dish of blancmange was the next to be gobbled up, and then a boy rather bolder than the rest made an attempt to save the cake. He seized the intruder by the skin of his neck, but except for a loud, grumbling protest, the bear paid no attention to him. He walked right along, pulling the boy with him, and one slice of cake after another disappeared down the black throat. The little girl behind the curtains, seeing that Jimmy did not intend to hurt anyone, came from her hiding place to try to help the boy who was holding him. Now this little girl had been eating strawberry jam, and as little girls sometimes do, had left some of it on her lips. The moment she touched him, Jimmy turned, and seeing and smelling the jam, he caught the child in his short forearms, and in spite of her screams, licked her face all over before letting her go. Then he reached for the sugar basin, lifted it from the table with his paws, and sat down on his haunches to devour the contents.

By this time the children who had been nervous were quite at their ease again and gathered round to see him eat the sugar. In a few moments he had satisfied his hunger and was ready to play. First of all he acted as if he had lost his wits or as if he wanted to "show off," which is about the same thing. He rolled over on his back, turned somersaults, and batted the chairs and the table legs with his paws. The children got down on the floor to romp with him, and together they had a merry time.

When they were all up on their feet again, Jimmy arose and stood perfectly straight on his hind legs. Then he picked out a girl about his own height and took a step toward her, raising his paws as though inviting her to a boxing match. The girl accepted the challenge, and as she was strong, she held her own very well for a time. But as Jimmy warmed up to his work, he became very rough and swung his heavy paws as hard as he could. At last he gave his playmate a stinging slap on the side of her face, and she decided not to play any more. And as I thought that Jimmy had had about enough fun for one evening, I opened the door, and he galloped off to his den under the porch.

NOTES AND QUESTIONS

Biography. Ernest Harold Baynes (1868-1925), the naturalist author, lived in Meriden, New Hampshire. He was the author of the interesting book, *Wild Bird Guests,* and of "Our Animal Allies" (in *Harper's Magazine,* January, 1921). During World War One, Mr. Baynes was in France, studying the part that birds and animals played in helping to win the war. Wherever he went he organized bird clubs, in order to protect our wild birds.

Discussion. 1. Why was Jimmy not popular with the farmer's wife? 2. Why do you think the children liked the bear? 3. Do you think they would have enjoyed the party more, or less, if there had been no "uninvited guest"? 4. *Class readings:* The description of the supper, page 31, line 7, to page 32, line 26. 5. *Outline for testing silent reading.* Tell the story of the "Uninvited Guest," using these topics: (a) the bear and how he was liked; (b) the bear's actions at the children's party; (c) the boxing match. 6. You will find interesting stories in *Bear Stories Retold from St. Nicholas,* Carter, and in *The Biography of a Grizzly,* Seton. 7. Find in the glossary the meaning of: unanimously, unwittingly, sleight-of-mouth, tawny, muzzle, intruder. 8. *Pronounce:* blancmange, haunches.

HUNTING THE AMERICAN BUFFALO*

THEODORE ROOSEVELT

In the fall of 1889 I heard that a very few bison were still left around the head of Wisdom River. Thither I went and hunted faithfully; there was plenty of game of other kinds, but of bison not a trace did we see. Nevertheless, a few days later that same year I came across these great wild cattle at a time when I had no idea of seeing them.

It was, as nearly as we could tell, in Idaho, just south of the Montana boundary line, and some twenty-five miles west of the line of Wyoming. We were camped high among the mountains, with a small pack train. On the day in question we had gone out to find moose, but had seen no sign of them, and had then begun to climb over the higher peaks with an idea of getting sheep. The old hunter who was with me was, very fortunately, suffering from rheumatism, and he therefore carried a long staff instead of his rifle; I say fortunately, for if he had carried his rifle, it would have been impossible to stop his firing at such game as bison, nor would he have spared the cows and calves.

About the middle of the afternoon we crossed a low, rocky ridge, and saw at our feet a basin, or round valley, of singular beauty. Its walls were formed by steep mountains. At its upper end lay a small lake, bordered on one side by a meadow of emerald green. The lake's other side marked the edge of the frowning pine forest which filled the rest of the valley. Beyond the lake the ground rose in a pass much frequented by game in bygone days, their trails lying along it in thick zigzags, each gradually fading out after a few

* See "Suggestions for Silent Reading," page 163.

hundred yards, and then starting again in a little different place, as game trails so often seem to do.

We bent our steps toward these trails, and no sooner had we reached the first than the old hunter bent over it with a sharp exclamation of wonder. There in the dust, apparently but a few hours old, were the hoof marks of a small band of bison. They were headed toward the lake. There had been half a dozen animals in the party: one a big bull and two calves.

We immediately turned and followed the trail. It led down to the little lake, where the beasts had spread and grazed on the tender, green blades, and had drunk their fill. The footprints then came together again, showing where the animals had gathered and walked off in single file to the forest. Evidently they had come to the pool in the early morning, and after drinking and feeding had moved into the forest to find some spot for their noontide rest.

It was a very still day, and there were nearly three hours of daylight left. Without a word my silent companion, who had been scanning the whole country with hawk-eyed eagerness, took the trail, motioning me to follow. In a moment we entered the woods, breathing a sigh of relief as we did so; for while in the meadow we could never tell that the buffalo might not see us, if they happened to be lying in some place with a commanding lookout.

It was not very long before we struck their daybeds, which were made on a knoll, where the forest was open, and where there was much down timber. After leaving the daybeds the animals had at first fed separately around the grassy base and sides of the knoll, and had then made off in their usual single file, going straight to a small pool in the forest. After drinking they had left this pool and traveled down toward the mouth of the basin, the trail leading along the sides of the steep hill, which were dotted by open glades. Here we moved with caution, for the sign had grown very fresh, and the animals had once more scattered and begun feeding. When the trail led across the glades, we usually skirted them so as to keep in the timber.

At last, on nearing the edge of one of these glades, we saw a movement among the young trees on the other side, not fifty yards away. Peering through some thick evergreen bushes, we speedily made out three bison, a cow, a calf, and a yearling, grazing greedily on the other side of the glade. Soon another cow and calf stepped out after them. I did not wish to shoot, waiting for the appearance of the big bull which I knew was accompanying them.

So for several minutes I watched the great, clumsy, shaggy beasts as they grazed in the open glade. Mixed with the eager excitement of the hunter was a certain half melancholy feeling as I gazed on these bison, themselves part of the last remnant of a nearly vanished race. Few, indeed, are the men who now have, or evermore shall have, the chance of seeing the mightiest of American beasts in all his wild vigor.

At last, when I had begun to grow very anxious lest the others should take alarm, the bull likewise appeared on the edge of the glade and stood with outstretched head, scratching his throat against a young tree, which shook violently. I aimed low, behind his shoulder, and pulled the trigger. At the crack of the rifle all the bison turned and raced off at headlong speed. The fringe of young pines beyond and below the glade cracked and swayed as if a whirlwind were passing, and in another moment the bison reached the top of a steep incline, thickly strewn with boulders and dead timber. Down this they plunged with reckless speed; their surefootedness was a marvel. A column of dust obscured their passage, and under its cover they disappeared in the forest, but the trail of the bull was marked by splashes of frothy blood, and we followed it at a trot. Fifty yards beyond the border of the forest we found the black body stretched motionless. He was a splendid old bull, still in his full vigor, with large, sharp horns, and heavy mane and glossy coat; and I felt the most exulting pride as I handled and examined him, for I had procured a trophy such as can fall henceforth to few hunters indeed.

NOTES AND QUESTIONS

Biography. Theodore Roosevelt (1858-1919), twenty-sixth president of the United States, was born in New York City. As a boy he was frail of body, but overcame this handicap by regular exercise and outdoor life. He was always interested in animals and birds and particularly in hunting game in the Western plains and mountains. In 1884 Roosevelt bought two cattle ranches in North Dakota, where for two years he lived and entered actively into Western life and spirit. Two of the books in which he has recorded his Western experiences are *The Deer Family* and *The Wilderness Hunter,* from the latter of which "Hunting the American Buffalo" is taken.

Discussion. 1. What makes this story "exciting," or "thrilling"? 2. How does the writer let you know his feelings? 3. What proof of Roosevelt's good sportsmanship is found in the second paragraph on page 34? 4. *Class reading:* From page 35, line 3, to page 36, line 13. 5. *Outline for testing silent reading.* Tell the story briefly, using these topics: (a) the discovery; (b) the pursuit; (c) the first view; (d) the end of the story. 6. Find in the glossary the meaning of: daybeds; glade; skirted; yearling; trophy. 7. *Pronounce:* bison, boundary, frequented, knoll, melancholy, remnant, incline, strewn.

Phrases for Study

pack train, **34**, 10
frowning pine forest, **34**, 25
much frequented, **34**, 26
thick zigzags, **34**, 28
hawk-eyed eagerness, **35**, 20
commanding lookout, **35**, 25
down timber, **35**, 28
obscured their passage, **37**, 1

BIRDS AND THEIR SONGS

The Birds and I

Liberty H. Bailey

The springtime belongs to the birds and me. We own it. We know when the mayflowers and the buttercups bloom. We know when the first frogs peep. We watch the awakening of the woods. We are wet by the warm April showers. We go where we will, and we are companions. Every tree and brook and blade of grass is ours; and our hearts are full of song.

There are boys who kill the birds, and girls who want to catch them and put them into cages, and there are others who steal their eggs. The birds are not partners with them; they are only servants. Birds, like people, sing for their friends, not for their masters. I am sure that one cannot think much of the springtime and the flowers if his heart is always set upon killing or catching something. We are happy when we are free, and so are the birds.

The birds and I get acquainted all over again every spring. They have seen strange lands in the winter, and all the brooks and woods have been covered with snow. So we run and romp together, and find all the nooks and crannies which we had half forgotten since October. The birds remember the old places. The wrens pull the sticks from the old hollow rail and seem to be wild with joy to see the place again. They must be the same wrens that were here last year, for strangers could not make so much fuss over an old rail. The bluebirds and wrens look into every crack and corner for a place in which to build, and the robins and chipping sparrows explore every tree in the old orchard.

If the birds want to live with us, we should encourage them. The first thing to do is to leave them alone. Let them be as free from danger and fear as you and I. Take the hammer off the old gun, give pussy so much to eat that she will not care to hunt for birds, and keep away the boys who steal eggs and who carry slingshots and throw stones. Plant trees and bushes about the borders of the place, and let some of them, at least, grow into tangles; then, even in the backyard, the wary catbird may make its home.

NOTES AND QUESTIONS

Biography. Liberty Hyde Bailey (1858-1954) has written many books on nature and outdoor life. He was chairman of the Commission on Country Life, appointed by President Theodore Roosevelt.

Discussion. 1. Why does the author say that the springtime belongs to "the birds and me"? 2. When may we say the birds are our partners and when our servants? 3. What different ways of dealing with birds are spoken of? Which way does the writer prefer? 4. How can you encourage the birds to live near you? 5. What do you gain if you persuade them to do this? Find an answer to this question in the poems that follow. 6. What birds come to trees near your home? 7. How are birds helpful to mankind? 8. You will find interesting stories and pictures of birds in *The Burgess Bird Book for Children,* Burgess. 9. Find in the glossary the meaning of: acquainted; explore; wary. 10. *Pronounce:* partners; again.

THE BROWN THRUSH

LUCY LARCOM

There's a merry brown thrush sitting up in a tree
He's singing to me! he's singing to me!
And what does he say, little girl, little boy?
"Oh, the world's running over with joy!
Don't you hear? Don't you see?
Hush! Look! In my tree
I'm as happy as happy can be!"

And the brown thrush keeps singing—"A nest do you see,
And five eggs, hid by me in the juniper-tree?
Don't meddle! don't touch! little girl, little boy,
Or the world will lose some of its joy.
Now I'm glad! Now I'm free!
And I always shall be,
If you never bring sorrow to me."

So the merry brown thrush sings away in the tree,
To you and to me, to you and to me;
And he sings all the day, little girl, little boy—
"Oh, the world's running over with joy;
But long it won't be,
Don't you know, don't you see,
Unless we're as good as can be?"

NOTES AND QUESTIONS

Biography. Lucy Larcom (1826-1893) was the daughter of a sea captain. During twenty years of teaching school, she wrote many charming poems for children.

Discussion. 1. Who is supposed to be speaking in the first two lines? 2. Who asks the question in the third line? 3. Who answers the question? 4. Find the answer to the question in the first stanza. 5. Why is the little bird so happy? 6. What will make him unhappy? 7. How can you help to make the world "run over with joy"? 8. You will enjoy hearing "Songs of Our Native Birds" and "How Birds Sing," Victor records by Kellogg.

Sing On, Blithe Bird

William Motherwell

I've plucked the berry from the bush, the brown nut from the tree,
But heart of happy little bird ne'er broken was by me.
I saw them in their curious nests, close couching, slyly peer
With their wild eyes, like glittering beads, to note if harm were near;
I passed them by, and blessed them all; I felt that it was good
To leave unmoved the creatures small whose home was in the wood.

And here, even now, above my head, a lusty rogue doth sing;
He pecks his swelling breast and neck, and trims his little wing.
He will not fly; he knows full well, while chirping on that spray,
I would not harm him for a world, or interrupt his lay.
Sing on, sing on, blithe bird! and fill my heart with summer gladness;
It has been aching many a day with measures full of sadness!

NOTES AND QUESTIONS

Biography. William Motherwell (1797-1835), a Scotch poet and journalist, was born in Glasgow, where he lived and died. In 1830 he became editor of the *Glasgow Courier.* He wrote a volume of local ballads, and many of his poems were published in magazines and newspapers.

Discussion. 1. To what does the poet compare the eyes of the birds? 2. Find the lines that tell why the bird is not afraid of the poet. 3. How do you think the birds know their friends? 4. What happiness does the poet get because of his kindness to the birds? 5. Read the lines that another poet who loved birds has written about his love for them:

He prayeth well who loveth well
Both man and bird and beast.

He prayeth best who loveth best
All things both great and small;
For the dear God Who loveth us,
He made and loveth all.

6. You will find helpful suggestions in the illustrated Farmers' Bulletins, *Bird Houses and How to Build Them,* and *How to Attract Birds,* sent free by the Department of Agriculture, Washington, D.C. 7. In the Forward Look, on pages 19 and 20, you were told that the poets and wise story writers of nature help us to see the beauty that lies in the great outdoor world. Mention instances of help that you have received from the stories and poems you have read in this group. 8. Find in the glossary the meaning of: peer, glittering, trims, spray, blithe, measures.

Phrases for Study

close couching, **41**, 3
note if harm were near, **41**, 4
leave unmoved, **41**, 6
lusty rogue, **41**, 7
knows full well, **41**, 9
interrupt his lay, **41**, 10

FLOWERS

The Violet and the Bee

John Bannister Tabb

"And pray, who are you?"
Said the Violet blue
To the Bee, with surprise,
At his wonderful size,
In her eyeglass of dew.
"I, madam," quoth he,
"Am a publican Bee,
Collecting the tax
Of honey and wax.
Have you nothing for me?"

NOTES AND QUESTIONS

Biography. Reverend John B. Tabb (1845-1909), a Southern poet, was born near Richmond, Virginia. All his life he was interested in birds, flowers, and outdoor life. When the Civil War began, he joined the Southern army, although he was a mere lad of sixteen. After the war he became a clergyman and a teacher.

Discussion. 1. What did the Violet ask the Bee? 2. What surprised the Violet? 3. What is the Violet's "eyeglass of dew"? 4. Find in the glossary the meaning of: quoth, publican, tax.

Four-Leaf Clovers*

Ella Higginson

I know a place where the sun is like gold,
And the cherry blooms burst with snow;
And down underneath is the loveliest nook,
Where the four-leaf clovers grow.

One leaf is for hope, and one is for faith,
And one is for love, you know;
But God put another in for luck
If you search, you will find where they grow.

But you must have hope, and you must have faith;
You must love and be strong; and so,
If you work, if you wait, you will find the place
Where the four-leaf clovers grow.

NOTES AND QUESTIONS

Biography. Ella Higginson (1862-1940), an American writer, lived in Bellingham, on Puget Sound, Washington. She won a prize of five hundred dollars, offered by a magazine for the best short story.

Discussion. 1. To whom is the four-leaf clover supposed to bring good luck? 2. Which do you think will give greater happiness, to earn something by hard work or to gain it by chance? Why do you think so? 3. What does the poem say we must have? 4. What does the poem say we must do? 5. If we have all these things and do all these things, shall we need to hunt for the four-leaf clover to bring us good fortune? Why? 6. Commit the poem to memory.

---

* From *When the Birds Go North Again,* by Ella Higginson.

Jack in the Pulpit

Clara Smith

Jack in the pulpit
    Preaches today,
Under the green trees
    Just over the way.
Squirrel and song-sparrow,
    High on their perch,
Hear the sweet lily-bells
    Ringing to church.
Come hear what his reverence
    Rises to say
In his low, painted pulpit
    This calm Sabbath day.

Meek-faced anemones,
    Drooping and sad;
Great yellow violets,
    Smiling out glad;
Buttercups' faces,
    Beaming and bright;
Clovers with bonnets,
    Some red and some white;
Daisies, their white fingers
    Half-clasped in prayer;
Dandelions, proud of
    The gold of their hair;
Innocents, children
    Guileless and frail,

Meek little faces
    Upturned and pale;
Wildwood geraniums,
    All in their best,
Languidly leaning,
    In purple gauze dressed
All are assembled
    This sweet Sabbath day
To hear what the priest
    In his pulpit will say.

So much for the preacher;
    The sermon comes next
Shall we tell how he preached it
    And where was his text?
Alas! like too many
    Grown-up folks who play
At worship in churches
    Man-builded today,
We heard not the preacher
    Expound or discuss;
But we looked at the people,
    And they looked at us.
We saw all their dresses
    Their colors and shapes,
The trim of their bonnets,
    The cut of their capes;
We heard the wind-organ,
    The bee, and the bird,
But of Jack in the pulpit
    We heard not a word!

NOTES AND QUESTIONS

Biography. Clara Smith is not a well-known writer, but her poem, "Jack in the Pulpit," is full of beauty. The rhythm is as pleasing as the picture is charming

Discussion. 1. What time of year is described in this poem? 2. Who make up the congregation when Jack in the Pulpit preaches? 3. How does the poet make the flowers seem like people? 4. How many of the flowers described in this poem are familiar to you? 5. Which flower is most beautifully described? Find the lines that give the description. 6. Why are we not told about the sermon? 7. What was the congregation doing during the sermon? 8. What did they see? What did they hear? 9. Find in the glossary the meaning of: drooping; beaming; gauze; assembled; text; worship; expound. 10. *Pronounce:* anemones; guileless; languidly.

Phrases for Study

his reverence, **45**, 9
painted pulpit, **45**, 11
all in their best, **46**, 4
man-builded today, **46**, 18

TIMES AND SEASONS

September

Helen Hunt Jackson

The goldenrod is yellow;
    The corn is turning brown;
The trees in apple orchards
    With fruit are bending down.

The gentian's bluest fringes
    Are curling in the sun;
In dusky pods the milkweed
    Its hidden silk has spun.

The sedges flaunt their harvest
    In every meadow-nook;
And asters by the brookside
    Make asters in the brook.

From dewy lanes at morning
The grapes' sweet odors rise;
At noon the roads all flutter
With yellow butterflies.

By all these lovely tokens
September days are here,
With summer's best of weather,
And autumn's best of cheer.

NOTES AND QUESTIONS

Biography. Helen Hunt Jackson (1831-1885) was an American poet and novelist. She was born in Amherst, Massachusetts, where her father was a professor in Amherst College, but she spent much of her life in California. She married a banker in Colorado Springs, Colorado, where she lived for a few years. Her poems are very beautiful, and "September" and "October's Bright Blue Weather" are especially good pictures of these autumn months. Every child should know these poems by heart.

Discussion. 1. What is meant by the harvest of the sedges? 2. How are the "asters in the brook" made? 3. Which lines in the last stanza tell us what September brings? 4. What things mentioned in this poem have you seen? 5. Read again what is said on pages 19 and 20 about the poet as a magician. What beauty of nature does the poet show you in the following lines?

And asters by the brookside
Make asters in the brook.

6. Find in the glossary the meaning of: sedges, flaunt, flutter. 7. *Pronounce:* gentian, dusky.

Phrases for Study

dusky pods, **48**, 7
hidden silk has spun, **48**, 8
lovely tokens, **49**, 5
best of cheer, **49**, 8

October's Bright Blue Weather

Helen Hunt Jackson

O sun and skies and clouds of June
And flowers of June together,
Ye cannot rival for one hour
October's bright blue weather;

When loud the bumblebee makes haste,
Belated, thriftless vagrant,
And goldenrod is dying fast,
And lanes with grapes are fragrant;

When gentians roll their fringes tight,
To save them for the morning,
And chestnuts fall from satin burs
Without a sound of warning;

When on the ground red apples lie
In piles like jewels, shining,
And redder still on old stone walls
Are leaves of woodbine twining;

When all the lovely wayside things
Their white-winged seeds are sowing,
And in the fields, still green and fair,
Late aftermaths are growing;

When springs run low, and on the brooks,
In idle, golden freighting,
Bright leaves sink noiseless in the hush
Of woods, for winter waiting;

When comrades seek sweet country haunts,
By twos and twos together,
And count like misers hour by hour
October's bright blue weather.

O sun and skies and flowers of June,
Count all your boasts together,
Love loveth best of all the year
October's bright blue weather.

NOTES AND QUESTIONS

For **Biography** see page 49.

Discussion. 1. What comparison is made in the first stanza between June and October? 2. Why is the bumblebee described as "loud"? 3. Compare the description of the goldenrod in this poem with the description of the goldenrod in "September." 4. Compare the description of the apples in this poem with the description of the apples in "September." 5. Find the line that tells why the "gentians roll their fringes tight." 6. What is the color of the woodbine leaves? 7. What are the "wayside things" usually called? 8. What do good comrades like to do in October? 9. Why are we sorry to have October go? 10. Find in the glossary the meaning of: fragrant, twining, aftermath, haunts. 11. *Pronounce:* rival, vagrant, freighting.

Phrases for Study

rival for one hour, **50**, 3
belated, thriftless vagrant, **50**, 6
satin burs, **50**, 11
idle, golden freighting, **51**, 2
hush of woods, **51**, 3
count like misers, **51**, 7
count all your boasts, **51**, 10

NOVEMBER

ALICE CARY

The leaves are fading and falling;
The winds are rough and wild;
The birds have ceased their calling
But let me tell you, my child,

Though day by day, as it closes,
Doth darker and colder grow,
The roots of the bright red roses
Will keep alive in the snow.

And when the winter is over,
The boughs will get new leaves,
The quail come back to the clover,
And the swallow back to the eaves.

The robin will wear on his bosom
A vest that is bright and new,
And the loveliest wayside blossom
Will shine with the sun and dew.

The leaves today are whirling;
The brooks are all dry and dumb
But let me tell you, my darling,
The spring will be sure to come.

There must be rough, cold weather,
And winds and rains so wild;
Not all good things together
Come to us here, my child.

So, when some dear joy loses
Its beauteous summer glow,
Think how the roots of the roses
Are kept alive in the snow.

NOTES AND QUESTIONS

Biography. Alice Cary (1820-1871), an American poet, was born in Cincinnati. She and her sister, Phoebe, wrote many beautiful poems and sketches. They removed to New York City and lived together there. "November" is one of Alice Cary's most widely known poems.

Discussion. 1. What signs of autumn are mentioned in the first stanza? 2. What signs of the coming winter are mentioned in the second stanza? 3. Where have the birds gone? 4. What is meant by the word "here" in line 4, above? 5. Why are the brooks "dry and dumb" in November? 6. Is this true in all parts of the country? 7. What are we told about the spring in "October's Bright Blue Weather"? 8. What will happen when the winter is over? 9. Where does the swallow build his nest? 10. What wonder of nature, about which you read on pages 19 and 20, does the second stanza tell you? 11. How can the snow help keep the roots alive? 12. In what stanza is this thought repeated? 13. Find in the glossary the meaning of: fading, quail, eaves.

Phrases for Study

ceased their calling, **52**, 3
vest that is bright, **52**, 14
wayside blossom, **52**, 15
beauteous summer glow, **53**, 6

TODAY

THOMAS CARLYLE

Lo, here hath been dawning
Another blue day;
Think, wilt thou let it
Slip useless away?

Out of Eternity
This new day is born;
Into Eternity,
At night, will return.

Behold it aforetime
No eye ever did;
So soon it forever
From all eyes is hid.

Here hath been dawning
Another blue day;
Think, wilt thou let it
Slip useless away?

NOTES AND QUESTIONS

Biography. Thomas Carlyle (1795-1881) was a great Scotch writer of essays and history. He lived in Edinburgh and later in London.

Discussion. 1. Find the lines that explain why the day is called a "new day." 2. Find the lines which remind us that the day will pass quickly. 3. The poet tells us in the first stanza to "think"; what does he want us to think about? 4. Find the same lines in another stanza. Why did the poet repeat these words? 5. Read the short story that follows, and tell whether Titus and the poet have the same idea of a "useless" day.

The Roman emperor, Titus, won the love of all his people by his kindness and generosity to those who were in trouble. One night at supper, remembering that he had not helped anyone that day, he exclaimed, "My friends, I have lost a day!"

Phrases for Study

blue day, **54**, 2

behold it aforetime, **54**, 9

THE NIGHT HAS A THOUSAND EYES

FRANCIS BOURDILLON

The night has a thousand eyes,
And the day but one;
Yet the light of the bright world dies
With the dying sun.

The mind has a thousand eyes,
And the heart but one;
Yet the light of a whole life dies
When love is done.

NOTES AND QUESTIONS

Biography. Francis William Bourdillon (1852-1921), an English poet, lived at Buddington, England. He attended college at Oxford. Few poets have written more beautiful lines than his "The Night Has a Thousand Eyes."

Discussion. 1. What are the eyes of the night? 2. What is the eye of the day? 3. How many eyes does the poet say the mind has? 4. How many eyes does he say the heart has? 5. In which line are we told what the eye of the heart is? 6. On page 20 you read that the poet is a magician whose words open for us the fairyland of nature. What have the words of this poet done for you? 7. Memorize the poem.

THE WORLD OF NATURE

A Backward Look

As you look backward over the animal stories you have read in this group, which did you enjoy most? Which story would be the most interesting to tell to a younger brother or sister? Which do you like better, stories in which animals are the actors, or stories about the hunting of animals?

Which one of the poems about birds has lines in it that sound like the bird's song? Which author makes you feel most keenly his love for birds? Which one tells you of pleasures that birds enjoy? Make a program for Arbor and Bird Day from selections found or suggested in this group.

In the "Notes and Questions" you have found a number of suggestions for outside reading. Did you find in the school library or public library any of the books that are mentioned in the different biographies? In your class, who has read Baker's *True Tales for My Grandsons,* or other selections mentioned in the biographies or elsewhere? What progress have you made in silent reading?

If you were making a blackboard calendar for each of the months—September, October, and November—what stanzas in each of the three poems on these months would give you ideas for decoration? Select a stanza from these poems as a motto for each of your calendars. November teaches Alice Cary a truth which she passes on to us; what is this truth?

On pages 19 and 20 you read that the world of nature is a fairyland, and that the poets help us to see the beauty that lies about us. Perhaps now when you look up into a starry sky you say to yourself almost without thinking, "The night has a thousand eyes—." What other poems have revealed beauties of nature to you?

STORIES IN LIGHTER VEIN

A Forward Look

Here is matter for your entertainment. Several interesting persons will appear and will show you that no small part of the joy of reading consists in the merry tales that you may find in books. One of the English poets somewhere calls upon the spirits of fun and joy, a cheerful nymph and her companions, to drive dull care away. This poet, John Milton by name, wrote many poems and prose works on very serious matters. He lived in a serious time, the time when many Englishmen were leaving their native country and emigrating to America in order that they might find a freedom that was denied to them at home.

But even under these circumstances, sympathizing with those who went into exile for freedom, and studying night and day how he could himself advance the cause of liberty, John Milton was too great a man to believe that life is altogether serious and earnest. Humor and jesting and wholesome fun have a part in every life; they are no more to be neglected than the spices in a Thanksgiving pie. So the poet called upon the cheerful nymph and her attendants to help him see the brighter side of life, the fun that there is in foolishness, and the health that comes with a hearty laugh. Here is what he wrote:

> Haste thee, Nymph, and bring with thee
> Jest and youthful Jollity,
>
> Come, and trip it, as you go,
> On the light, fantastic toe.

Now let us imagine that we, also, are inviting these kindly spirits of mirth. Our lives are serious, too. We have arithmetic to learn, or we have a composition to write. People expect us to do all sorts of things that take our time, and of course we want to do these things. But here comes Laughter holding both his sides, a fat old gentleman who makes you feel merry the moment you set eyes on him. And Father Laughter first introduces the Baron Munchausen, who will tell some of his marvelous experiences. We are not compelled to believe all of them. Perhaps Father Laughter wanted to take a sly dig or two at the yarns some travelers tell when they get home. By this means the story illustrates one of the great sources of humor—monstrous exaggeration. It also shows what a foolish thing it is to be a boaster. Most people, at one time or another, are tempted to brag about their deeds, their possessions, or their smartness. If they would only think of Baron Munchausen, they would flee from this temptation.

After this comes a story about the blind men and the elephant. Here Father Laughter gets his way with you by making you see how absurd were the guesses about the elephant made by men who knew only the animal's trunk or his tusks, or his tail. And here, too, after you have laughed heartily at the foolish fellows who were so positive that they knew everything when they knew nothing, you begin to see the danger in what are called "snap judgments." "Look at these ridiculous fellows," says Father Laughter, "and consider how silly it is to jump to a conclusion unless you have all the facts."

You will agree that Father Laughter's next performer, Darius Green, is especially interesting in these days when men fly across the Atlantic or from New York to San Francisco. Darius seems to have been the first "bird-man," and though he was absurd enough, he reminds one of the fact that many useful inventions that now add to our comfort were prepared for by men who seemed to their friends and acquaintances crazy enough.

But this is introduction aplenty; there's really no need to keep you any longer from getting acquainted with Father Laughter and the antics he likes to play.

Adventures of Baron Munchausen

R. E. Raspe

The Savage Boar

Baron Munchausen had feasted his friends right well, and after supper he leaned back in his chair and said, "So you want me to tell you of my adventures in the past." His guests eagerly urged him on, and he began his story.

"Once, when I was returning from a hunt, with an empty gun (having used all my ammunition), a raging wild boar rushed at me. Well, you know how unpleasant such an encounter may be, so I am sure none of you will think me a coward for hastily climbing the nearest tree; it was a young birch which could hardly bear my weight. The boar made a dash for the tree, but was a moment too late, for I had just drawn my legs out of his reach. But so violent was his rush that his tusks went through the trunk of the tree and projected an inch through the other side. I slid down the tree, picked up a stone the size of my fist, and riveted down the projecting points of the tusks. You can imagine what a narrow escape I had when I tell you that the beast weighed five tons—a good deal for a wild boar."

A Narrow Escape

"At another time, when I was hunting in Ceylon, I was terrified to see a gigantic lion approaching, with the evident intention of devouring me. My gun was only loaded with bird-shot, and I had no other about me. The savage animal shook his head several times, uttered a loud roar, and prepared to spring. I turned to flee, and—my flesh creeps even now at the recollection of it—there, on the bank of a river that lay behind me, was a huge crocodile with his terrible jaws open ready to swallow me!

"Imagine, gentlemen, the horror of my situation—before me the lion, behind me the crocodile, on my left a rushing torrent, and on the right an abyss full of poisonous snakes! I gave myself up for lost, and fell to the ground in an almost fainting condition, expecting nothing better than to meet with a horrible death from one or the other of these terrible animals.

"After waiting a few seconds I heard a violent noise, different from any that had fallen on my ears before. I ventured to raise my head, and what do you think had happened?

"The lion had, in his eagerness, jumped clean over me into the crocodile's jaws; the head of the one stuck in the throat of the other, and they were struggling to free themselves. I quickly sprang to my feet, drew out my hunting knife, and with one blow severed the lion's head. Then, with the butt end of my gun, I rammed the head farther into the throat of the crocodile, and destroyed him by suffocation. The hide of the crocodile, which was exactly forty feet in length, I had stuffed, and it now forms one of the chief attractions in the museum at Amsterdam, where the superintendent relates the story to all spectators, with harrowing additions.

"One of these is that the lion jumped right through the crocodile, but as soon as the head appeared, Monsieur the Famous Baron (as he is pleased to call me) cut it off, and three feet of the crocodile's tail as well, whereupon the crocodile turned round, snatched the knife out of my hand, and swallowed it so greedily that it pierced his heart and killed him!

"I need not tell you how annoyed I was by these exaggerations. In this age of doubt, people who do not know me might possibly be led to disbelieve the real facts when they are mixed up with such absurd inventions."

How the Baron Saved Gibraltar

"Some years later I made a voyage to Gibraltar to visit my old friend, General Elliott. He received me with joy and took me for a stroll along the ramparts to examine the operations of the enemy. I had brought with me an excellent telescope, which I had purchased in Rome. Looking through it, I saw that the enemy were about to discharge a thirty-six pound cannon at the very spot where we were standing. I rushed toward our nearest cannon, a forty-eight pounder, and placed it exactly facing that of the enemy. I watched carefully till I saw the Spanish gunner apply a match to the touchhole, and then I, too, gave the word 'Fire.'

"Both reports rang out at the same instant, and the two cannon balls met halfway with amazing force. Ours, being the heavier, caused the enemy's ball to recoil with such violence as to kill the man who had discharged it. It then passed through the masts of three ships which lay in a line behind each other, and flew across the Straits of Gibraltar some miles into Africa. Our own ball, after repelling the other, proceeded on its way, dismounted the very cannon which had just been used against us, and forced it into the hold of the ship, where it fell with so much force as to break its way through the bottom. The ship immediately filled and sank, with about a thousand Spanish sailors and a large number of soldiers on board, who were all drowned.

"You can see for yourselves that this strange tale must be true, however improbable it sounds, or else how could it possibly have happened?"

NOTES AND QUESTIONS

A long time ago a book called *The Travels of Baron Munchausen* was written by Rudolph Erich Raspe. The tales told in this book were so extravagant that the name *Munchausen* is often applied to boasters. The author pretends that the stories are all strictly true.

Discussion. 1. What extravagant statements do you find in the story "The Savage Boar"? In "A Narrow Escape"? In "How the Baron Saved Gibraltar"? 2. Which of the incidents mentioned do you think is the most ridiculous? 3. What do you think of the proof given by the author to prove the truthfulness of the last story? 4. Which of the sources of humor mentioned on page 58 does this story illustrate? 5. Find in the glossary the meaning of: boar, encounter, tusks, riveted, gigantic, abyss, severed, whereupon, exaggerations, ramparts, touchhole, recoil, repelling, dismounted, hold. *6. Pronounce:* Munchausen, projected, harrowing, Monsieur.

Phrases for Study

evident intention, **60**, 5
horror of my situation, **60**, 13
gave myself up for lost, **60**, 16
harrowing additions, **61**, 4
age of doubt, **61**, 13
absurd inventions, **61**, 15
operations of the enemy, **61**, 19
Straits of Gibraltar, **62**, 2

The Blind Men and the Elephant

John G. Saxe

It was six men of Indostan
To learning much inclined,
Who went to see the elephant
(Though all of them were blind),
That each by observation
Might satisfy his mind.

The first approached the elephant,
And happening to fall
Against his broad and sturdy side,
At once began to bawl:
"God bless me! but the elephant
Is very like a wall!"

The second, feeling of the tusk,
Cried, "Ho! what have we here
So very round and smooth and sharp?
To me 'tis mighty clear
This wonder of an elephant
Is very like a spear!"

The third approached the animal,
And happening to take
The squirming trunk within his hands,
Thus boldly up and spake:
"I see," quoth he, "the elephant
Is very like a snake!"

The fourth reached out his eager hand,
And felt about the knee.
"What most this wondrous beast is like
Is mighty plain," quoth he;
"'Tis clear enough the elephant
Is very like a tree!"

The fifth, who chanced to touch the ear,
Said: "E'en the blindest man
Can tell what this resembles most;
Deny the fact who can,
This marvel of an elephant
Is very like a fan!"

The sixth no sooner had begun
About the beast to grope,
Than, seizing on the swinging tail,
That fell within his scope,
"I see," quoth he, "the elephant
Is very like a rope!"

And so these men of Indostan
Disputed loud and long,
Each in his own opinion
Exceeding stiff and strong,
Though each was partly in the right,
And all were in the wrong!

NOTES AND QUESTIONS

Biography. John Godfrey Saxe (1816-1887), an American poet, was born in Vermont. He is best known by his humorous poems, of which "The Blind Men and the Elephant" is most widely read.

Discussion. 1. How could blind men "see" the elephant? 2. To what did each compare the elephant? 3. Explain the comparison each made. 4. Why is comparison a common way of describing objects? 5. Point out instances of its use by other authors in this book. 6. Why were these blind men all "in the wrong"? 7. How far was each "in the right"? 8. What makes this poem humorous? 9. What may we learn from this story? 10. Find in the glossary the meaning of: learning, observation, approached, wonder, resembles, marvel, grope, disputed, stiff. 11. *Pronounce:* sturdy, wondrous, scope.

Phrases for Study

much inclined, **63**, 2
satisfy his mind, **63**, 6
eager hand, **64**, 1
within his scope, **64**, 16

Darius Green and His Flying-Machine

John Townsend Trowbridge

If ever there lived a Yankee lad,
Wise or otherwise, good or bad,
Who, seeing the birds fly, didn't jump
With flapping arms from stake or stump,
Or, spreading the tail
Of his coat for a sail,
Take a soaring leap from post or rail,
And wonder why
He couldn't fly,
And flap and flutter and wish and try—
If ever you knew a country dunce
Who didn't try that as often as once,
All I can say is, that's a sign
He never would do for a hero of mine.

An aspiring genius was D. Green;
The son of a farmer—age fourteen.
His body was long and lank and lean
Just right for flying, as will be seen;
He had two eyes, each bright as a bean,
And a freckled nose that grew between,
A little awry—for I must mention
That he had riveted his attention
Upon his wonderful invention,
Twisting his tongue as he twisted the strings,
Working his face as he worked the wings,
And with every turn of gimlet and screw
Turning and screwing his mouth round, too,
Till his nose seemed bent
To catch the scent,
Around some corner, of new-baked pies,
And his wrinkled cheeks and his squinting eyes
Grew puckered into a queer grimace,
That made him look very droll in the face,
And also very wise.

And wise he must have been, to do more
Than ever a genius did before,
Excepting Daedalus of yore
And his son Icarus, who wore
Upon their backs
Those wings of wax
He had read of in the old almanacs.
Darius was clearly of the opinion
That the air is also man's dominion,
And that, with paddle or fin or pinion,
We soon or late
Shall navigate

The azure as now we sail the sea.
The thing looks simple enough to me;
And if you doubt it,
Hear how Darius reasoned about it.

"Birds can fly,
An' why can't I?
Must we give in,"
Says he with a grin,
" 'T the bluebird an' phoebe
Are smarter'n we be?
Jest fold our hands an' see the swaller
An' blackbird an' catbird beat us holler?
Does the leetle, chatterin', sassy wren,
No bigger'n my thumb, know more than men?
Jest show me that!
Er prove't the bat
Has got more brains than's in my hat,
An' I'll back down, an' not till then!"

He argued further: "Ner I can't see
What's th' use o' wings to a bumblebee,
Fer to git a livin' with, more'n to me;
Ain't my business
Importanter'n his'n is?
That Icarus
Was a silly cuss
Him an' his daddy, Daedalus.
They might 'a' knowed wings made o' wax
Wouldn't stan' sun-heat an' hard whacks;
I'll make mine o' luther,
Er suthin' er other."

And he said to himself, as he tinkered and planned:
"But I ain't goin' to show my hand
To mummies that never can understand
The fust idee that's big an' grand.
They'd 'a' laft an' made fun
O' Creation itself afore 'twas done!"
So he kept his secret from all the rest,
Safely buttoned within his vest;
And in the loft above the shed
Himself he locks, with thimble and thread
And wax and hammer and buckles and screws,
And all such things as geniuses use;
Two bats for patterns, curious fellows!
A charcoal-pot and a pair of bellows;
An old hoop-skirt or two, as well as
Some wire and several old umbrellas;
A carriage-cover, for tail and wings;
A piece of harness; and straps and strings;
And a big strong box,
In which he locks
These and a hundred other things.

His grinning brothers, Reuben and Burke
And Nathan and Jotham and Solomon, lurk
Around the corner to see him work—
Sitting cross-legged, like a Turk,
Drawing the waxed end through with a jerk,
And boring the holes with a comical quirk
Of his wise old head, and a knowing smirk.
But vainly they mounted each other's backs,
And poked through knot-holes and pried through cracks;
With wood from the pile and straw from the stacks
He plugged the knot-holes and calked the cracks;

And a bucket of water, which one would think
He had brought up into the loft to drink
When he chanced to be dry,
Stood always nigh,
For Darius was sly!
And whenever at work he happened to spy
At chink or crevice a blinking eye,
He let a dipper of water fly.
"Take that! an' ef ever ye get a peep,
Guess ye'll ketch a weasel asleep!"
And he sings as he locks
His big strong box:
"The weasel's head is small an' trim,
An' he is leetle an' long an' slim,
An' quick of motion an' nimble of limb,
An' ef yeou'll be
Advised by me,
Keep wide awake when ye're ketchin' him!"

So day after day
He stitched and tinkered and hammered away,
Till at last 'twas done—
The greatest invention under the sun!
"An' now," says Darius, "hooray fer some fun!"

'Twas the Fourth of July,
And the weather was dry,
And not a cloud was on all the sky
Save a few light fleeces, which here and there,
Half mist, half air,
Like foam on the ocean went floating by;
Just as lovely a morning as ever was seen
For a nice little trip in a flying-machine.

Thought cunning Darius: "Now I shan't go
Along 'ith the fellers to see the show.
I'll say I've got sich a terrible cough!
An' then, when the folks 'ave all gone off,
I'll hev full swing
For to try the thing'
An' practyse a leetle on the wing."

"Ain't goin' to see the celebration?"
Says Brother Nate. "No; botheration!
I've got sich a cold—a toothache—I—
My gracious!—feel's though I should fly!"

Said Jotham, "Sho!
Guess ye better go."
But Darius said, "No!
Shouldn't wonder 'f yeou might see me, though,
'Long 'bout noon, ef I git red
O' this jumpin', thumpin' pain 'n my head."

For all the while to himself he said:
"I'll tell ye what!
I'll fly a few times around the lot,
To see how 't seems; then soon's I've got
The hang o' the thing, ez likely's not,
I'll astonish the nation,
And all creation,
By flyin' over the celebration!
Over their heads I'll sail like an eagle;
I'll balance myself on my wings like a sea-gull;
I'll dance on the chimbleys; I'll stan' on the steeple;
I'll flop up to winders an' scare the people!

I'll light on the libbe'ty-pole, an' crow;
An' I'll say to the gawpin' fools below,
'What world's this 'ere
That I've come near?'
Fer I'll make 'em believe I'm a chap f'm the moon!
An' I'll try a race 'ith their ol' bulloon."
He crept from his bed;
And, seeing the others were gone, he said,
"I'm a gittin' over the cold 'n my head."
And away he sped
To open the wonderful box in the shed.

His brothers had walked but a little way
When Jotham to Nathan chanced to say,
"What on airth is he up to, hey?"
"Don'o'—the' 's suthin' er other to pay,
Er he wouldn't 'a' stayed to hum today."
Says Burke, "His toothache's all 'n his eye!
He never'd miss a Fo'th-o'-July
Ef he hedn't got some machine to try.
Le's hurry back an' hide in the barn,
An' pay him fer tellin' us that yarn!"
"Agreed!" Through the orchard they creep back,
Along by the fences, behind the stack,
And one by one, through a hole in the wall,
In under the dusty barn they crawl,
Dressed in their Sunday garments all;
And a very astonishing sight was that,
When each in his cobwebbed coat and hat
Came up through the floor like an ancient rat.
And there they hid;
And Reuben slid

The fastenings back, and the door undid.
"Keep dark!" said he
"While I squint an' see what the' is to see."

As knights of old put on their mail
From head to foot
An iron suit,
Iron jacket and iron boot,
Iron breeches, and on the head
No hat, but an iron pot instead,
And under the chin the bail
(I believe they called the thing a helm);
And the lid they carried they called a shield;
And, thus accoutered, they took the field,
Sallying forth to overwhelm
The dragons and pagans that plagued the realm—
So this modern knight
Prepared for flight,
Put on his wings and strapped them tight;
Jointed and jaunty, strong and light;
Buckled them fast to shoulder and hip—
Ten feet they measured from tip to tip!
And a helm had he, but that he wore,
Not on his head like those of yore,
But more like the helm of a ship.

"Hush!" Reuben said,
"He's up in the shed!
He's opened the winder—I see his head!
He stretches it out
An' pokes it about,
Lookin' to see 'f the coast is clear,
An' nobody near;
Guess he don'o' who's hid in here!

He's riggin' a spring-board over the sill!
Stop laffin', Solomon! Burke, keep still!
He's a climbin' out now—of all the things!
What's he got on? I van, it's wings!
An' that 'tother thing? I vum, it's a tail!
An' there he sets like a hawk on a rail!
Steppin' careful, he travels the length
Of his spring-board, and teeters to try its strength.
Now he stretches his wings, like a monstrous bat;
Peeks over his shoulder, this way an' that,
Fer to see 'f the' 's anyone passin' by;
But the' 's on'y a ca'f an' a goslin' nigh.
They turn up at him a wonderin' eye,
To see—the dragon! he's goin' to fly!
Away he goes! Jimminy! what a jump!
Flop—flop—an' plump
To the ground with a thump!
Flutt'rin' an' flound'rin', all in a lump!"

As a demon is hurled by an angel's spear,
Heels over head, to his proper sphere
Heels over head, and head over heels,
Dizzily down the abyss he wheels
So fell Darius. Upon his crown,
In the midst of the barnyard, he came down,
In a wonderful whirl of tangled strings,
Broken braces and broken springs,
Broken tail and broken wings,
Shooting-stars, and various things!
Away with a bellow fled the calf,
And what was that? Did the gosling laugh?
'Tis a merry roar
From the old barn-door,

And he hears the voice of Jotham crying,
"Say, D'rius! how de yeou like flyin'?"
Slowly, ruefully, where he lay,
Darius just turned and looked that way,
As he stanched his sorrowful nose with his cuff.
"Wal, I like flyin' well enough,"
He said; "but the' ain't sich a thunderin' sight
O' fun in 't when ye come to light."

MORAL

I just have room for the moral here,
And this is the moral: Stick to your sphere
Or if you insist, as you have the right,
On spreading your wings for a loftier flight,
The moral is: Take care how you light.

NOTES AND QUESTIONS

Biography. John Townsend Trowbridge (1827-1916), an American writer, lived in Cambridge. He and Lucy Larcom were for a time editors of *Our Young Folks' Magazine.* Trowbridge first saw a flying machine sixty years after he wrote "Darius Green and His Flying-Machine." He was then eighty-three years old.

Discussion. 1. What did Darius Green believe that men would soon be able to do? 2. What did Darius determine to use as material for his machine? 3. Why did he not tell his brothers what he was trying to do? 4. When did he plan to try his machine? 5. Find the lines that tell what he imagined he would do. 6. Find the lines that tell what he really did. 7. What did he say was the unpleasant part of flying? 8. Mention some inventions that people once thought were as impossible as the boys thought this flying-machine was. 9. Mention some inventors at whom people once laughed but who are now honored. 10. In what way does the author make his story humorous? 11. Notice Darius's language on pages 67 and 68. The writer shows by such words that Darius was not a well-educated boy. Are persons often judged by the way they talk? 12. In Wildman's *Famous Leaders of Industry,* you will find interesting facts about Orville and Wilbur Wright. You will enjoy reading *The Boys' Airplane Book,* Collins. 13. Report any current news on airplane development, airplane mail routes, etc., that you can find. 14. Find in the glossary the meaning of: soaring, lank, gimlet, yore, pinion, tinkered, mummies, quirk, smirk, crevice, weasel, cunning, ancient, helm, ruefully. 15. *Pronounce:* Darius, aspiring, genius, awry, grimace, droll, Daedalus, Icarus, almanacs, phoebe, calked, breeches, accoutered, pagans, jaunty, stanched.

Phrases for Study

aspiring genius, **66**, 1
riveted his attention, **66**, 8
Daedalus of yore, **66**, 23
man's dominion, **66**, 29
navigate the azure, **66**, 32
beat us holler, **67**, 12
like a Turk, **68**, 25
knights of old, **72**, 4
thus accoutered, **72**, 13
plagued the realm, **72**, 15
his proper sphere, **73**, 20
stick to your sphere, **74**, 10

Birthday Greetings

C. L. Dodgson ("Lewis Carroll")

Christ Church, Oxford
October 13, 1875

My dear Gertrude:

I never give birthday *presents,* but you see I do sometimes write a birthday *letter;* so, as I've just arrived here, I am writing this to wish you many and many a happy return of your birthday tomorrow. I will drink your health, if only I can remember, and if you don't mind—but perhaps you object? You see, if I were to sit by you at breakfast, and to drink your tea, you wouldn't like *that,* would you? You would say "Boo! hoo! Here's Mr. Dodgson's drunk all my tea, and I haven't any left!" So I am very much afraid, next time Sybil looks for you, she'll find you sitting by the sad sea-wave, and crying "Boo! hoo! Here's Mr. Dodgson has drunk my health, and I haven't got any left!" And how it will puzzle Dr. Maund, when he is sent for to see you! "My dear Madam, I'm very sorry to say your little girl has got *no health at all!* I never saw such a thing in my life!" "Oh, I can easily explain it!" your mother will say. "You see she would go and make friends with a strange gentleman, and yesterday he drank her health!" "Well, Mrs. Chataway," he will say, "the only way to cure her is to wait till his next birthday, and then for *her* to drink *his* health."

And then we shall have changed healths. I wonder how you'll like mine! Oh, Gertrude, I wish you wouldn't talk such nonsense!

Your loving friend,
Lewis Carroll

NOTES AND QUESTIONS

Biography. Charles Lutwidge Dodgson (1832-1898), better known by his pen name, "Lewis Carroll," was an English author. He was the son of a clergyman. For four years he attended the famous school at Rugby, after which he entered college at Oxford. He became an excellent scholar and mathematician and was appointed a lecturer on mathematics at Oxford University, a position that he held for many years. His keen sympathy with the imagination of children and their sense of fun led him to tell of the adventures of Alice, in a book called *Alice's Adventures in Wonderland.* This book made Lewis Carroll's name famous. His delightful humor is well illustrated in his letter of "Birthday Greetings" to Gertrude Chataway.

Discussion. 1. What is usually meant by "drink your health"? 2. What play on the meaning of these words gives a humorous turn to them? 3. What remedy does the author suggest the doctor will prescribe for Gertrude? 4. What does the author call this humor? 5. The author was a serious man, yet he believed in the value of wholesome fun. Of what great poet did you read, on page 57, who also believed in the value of a hearty laugh?

Phrases for Study

many a happy return, **76**, 6

sad sea-wave, **76**, 14

The Wind and the Moon

George Macdonald

Said the Wind to the Moon, "I will blow you out.
You stare in the air
Like a ghost in a chair,
Always looking what I am about.
I hate to be watched; I will blow you out."

The Wind blew hard, and out went the Moon.
So, deep on a heap
Of clouds, to sleep
Down lay the Wind, and slumbered soon
Muttering low, "I've done for that Moon."

He turned in his bed; she was there again.
On high in the sky,
With her one ghost eye,
The Moon shone white and alive and plain.
Said the Wind, "I will blow you out again."

The Wind blew hard, and the Moon grew dim.
"With my sledge and my wedge
I have knocked off her edge.
If only I blow tight fierce and grim,
The creature will soon be dimmer than dim."

He blew and he blew, and she thinned to a thread.
"One puff more's enough
To blow her to snuff!
One good puff more where the last was bred,
And glimmer, glimmer glum will go the thread."

He blew a great blast, and the thread was gone;
In the air nowhere
Was a moonbeam bare;
Far off and harmless the shy stars shone;
Sure and certain the Moon was gone!

The Wind he took to his revels once more;
        On down, in town,
        Like a merry-mad clown,
He leaped and hallooed with whistle and roar
"What's that?" The glimmering thread once more.

He flew in a rage—he danced and blew;
But in vain was the pain
Of his bursting brain;
For still the broader the moon-scrap grew,
The broader he swelled his big cheeks and blew.

Slowly she grew—till she filled the night,
        And shone on her throne
        In the sky alone,
A matchless, wonderful, silvery light,
Radiant and lovely, the queen of the night.

Said the Wind: "What a marvel of power am I!
        With my breath, good faith,
        I blew her to death
First blew her away right out of the sky—
Then blew her in; what a strength am I!"

But the Moon she knew nothing about the affair,
        For, high in the sky,
        With her one white eye,
Motionless, miles above the air,
She had never heard the great Wind blare.

NOTES AND QUESTIONS

Biography. George Macdonald (1824-1905), a Scotch poet, wrote many entertaining poems and stories for children. "The Wind and the Moon" is a good illustration of the fact that he knew how to interest boys and girls.

Discussion. 1. Why did the wind want to blow out the moon? 2. What natural changes in the shape of the moon take place each month? 3. What really caused it to disappear? 4. What did the wind do when he thought he had succeeded? 5. Find the lines that tell how the wind felt when he saw the moon grow broader and bigger. 6. Find the lines which tell that the moon did not know that the wind was blowing. 7. What qualities does this story give to the wind? 8. Do you know any person who has these qualities? 9. The poet aims in this poem to amuse us; by what means does he do this? 10. Find in the glossary the meaning of: muttering, sledge, wedge, grim, matchless, blare. 11. *Pronounce:* revels, hallooed, radiant.

Phrases for Study

thinned to a thread, **78**, 16	took to his revels, **79**, 1
where the last was bred, **78**, 19	filled the night, **79**, 11

STORIES IN LIGHTER VEIN

A Backward Look

Why is it good for us, even in the midst of serious work, to read humorous stories from time to time? An interesting anecdote is told of Abraham Lincoln that shows how he would have answered this question. One day when the Civil War was at its height, President Lincoln opened his cabinet meeting by saying, "Gentlemen, I am going to read you something that will make you laugh." He then read a chapter from a humorous book, laughing heartily as he read. When he saw that none of the members of his cabinet joined in the laughter, he said with a sigh, "Gentlemen, why don't you laugh? With the fearful strain that is put on me day and night, if I did not laugh once in a while I should die; and you need this medicine as much as I do." What did you read in the Forward Look on page 57 about another serious-minded man who believed that wholesome humor is a "medicine"?

Which selection in this group gave you the heartiest laugh? Often some sensible truth is taught through a little nonsense. Of which selections is this particularly true? It is interesting to stop for a moment and think just why certain stories make us laugh. One story is humorous because of its wild exaggeration; another because it makes us see how ridiculous it is to be a boaster or to be conceited or to jump at conclusions; and still another because it has an interesting little play upon words. What is the source of humor in "The Savage Boar," "A Narrow Escape," "How the Baron Saved Gibraltar," "The Blind Men and the Elephant," "Birthday Greetings," "The Wind and the Moon"?

How does the present day newspaper furnish fun for its readers? Which newspaper cartoons do you look at regularly, and which are your favorites? Bring to class examples of cartoons, and then divide the collection into three groups—those that you think drive home a truth, those that you think are funny and clever, and those that you think are merely silly. Prepare an exhibit for "Cartoon Day" in your school, selecting the material from these examples. Clip and bring to class newspaper jokes that you and your family particularly enjoyed. Recommend to your classmates humorous stories that you have read in *The Junior Red Cross News, Life, St. Nicholas, The Youth's Companion,* or in some other magazine.

In previous pages you have found occasional suggestions for problems similar to those of the preceding paragraph. Like suggestions will be found later in the book. The working out of these problems and reporting on them in class will add greatly to the value and pleasure of your reading.

Some of these suggested problems are: (a) *Silent Reading*—Making a report showing comparisons month by month of individual and class progress in silent reading; (b) *Books I Have Read*—Reviewing a favorite book, giving title, author, time and scene of story, principal characters, and a brief outline of the story, with readings of the selected passages that will give your classmates most pleasure; (c) *Magazine Reading*—Reporting monthly on current numbers of magazines, telling your classmates what you have found that is interesting; in this way you will help each other to become acquainted with a number of magazines; (d) *Newspaper Reading*—Reporting current events, and showing in the newspapers that you read the place of general news, of editorials, society news, sports, the joke column, cartoons, advertisements, etc.; (e) *Dramatizing*—Planning and presenting before your class some selection or some incident from a selection that you think will make an interesting play; (f) *Good Citizenship*—Making a list of the suggestions you find in this reader that help you to be a useful home member and a good citizen, and preparing a program from selections in this book for "Citizenship Day" in your school.

Which of the problems that you have worked out did you find most interesting?

HOME AND COUNTRY

A Forward Look

One of the most famous stories in American literature tells about a man who spoke of his country with sneers and insults and acted in such a way that he was forbidden ever to set foot on American soil again. So he became a wanderer. He saw how men from other countries looked upon their homelands with pride and affection, and how his countrymen loved America better even than their lives. He came to be known as "the man without a country," and he lived a wretched and lonely life. At last he came to the hour of death, and he wrote these words for all Americans to think about if the temptation should ever come to speak scornfully of their country:

"If you are ever tempted to say a word or to do a thing that shall put a bar between you and your country, pray God in His mercy to take you that instant home to His own heaven. Stick by your family, boy; forget you have a self, while you do everything for them. Think of your home, boy; write and send, and talk about it. Let it be nearer and nearer to your thoughts, the farther you have to travel from it; and rush back to it when you are free. And for your country, boy"—and the words rattled in his throat—"and for that flag"—and he pointed to the ship—"never dream a dream but of serving her as she bids you, though the service carry you through a thousand hells. No matter what happens to you, no matter who flatters you or who abuses you, never look to another flag, never let a night pass but you pray God to bless that flag. Remember, boy, that behind all these men you have to do with, behind officers, and government, and people even, there is the Country Herself, your Country, and that you belong to Her as you belong to your mother. Stand by Her, boy, as you would stand by your mother."

Such was the dying message of "the man without a country" to the Americans of his time; such is his message to us. When we were at war, it was to be expected that all men would answer the call of patriotism. But now that peace has come, it is not so easy to forget self in a loyalty to our country and its flag. It is easy to be on guard when we know that an armed enemy is close by, it is not easy when the enemy is hidden, and the guns are silent. These hidden enemies of our country do not fight in armies; they are the bad citizens who are scattered about; often you do not realize who they are.

Generally these bad citizens, who are enemies of our country, possess one or all of the following characteristics:

In the first place, they have no love for home and its festivals. Now, our nation is a collection of homes. The government was formed to protect these homes. The good citizen is a lover of his native soil, a lover of his home, a lover of Thanksgiving and Independence Day and Christmas. These festivals bind men more closely together, make them one, join them to their native land. But there are many bad citizens, enemies of America, who seek to destroy these influences that lead men to work together to make the community a better place in which to live.

Second, the history of the United States, the stories of the founding of our nation, the stories about our flag and its defenders, have no interest for these bad citizens. You remember how mother used to tell you stories about when she was a little girl, and how these stories made you love her the more. It is the same with the stories about the days when our country was young: how the young George Washington showed the kind of man he was, or how the young Abraham Lincoln struggled to fit himself to become a leader of men. Through these stories we learn what the flag really means and what it has cost, and we love our country as we love our mother. But the enemy, the bad citizen, laughs at these things. He just thinks of himself. He thinks he has a right to do as he likes because this is, he says, "a free country." He doesn't think that he owes anything to Washington and Jefferson and Lincoln, or to those who kept the flag at the masthead when it was in peril.

And the third test of a man's loyalty to our country is met only if he has the true feeling of democracy in his heart. This feeling of democracy means *service,* willingness to help others. The man or woman who thinks only of his own good time or his own fortune is a bad citizen.

You see, it is this way. In olden times men had no part in the government unless they were born into a high place in society. The ordinary man did as he was told, went to the wars at the king's pleasure, and paid taxes that often took all he could save. He had little opportunity to make money or collect property. If he did, very probably the king would hear of it and would take away from him all that he had saved. But America was founded with a different idea of these matters. Here men got together and set up the kind of government they wished. They taxed themselves in order to support this government. They worked together to drive away hostile Indians, to kill wild beasts to conquer the forests, to plant their crops, to make their lives safe and happy. In this cooperation, or working together, in government and in all the ways of living we find the spirit of democracy.

This spirit has made America what it is today. It has opened up farms, built railways and ships and great industries, built also mighty cities, and made laws for the protection of property and life. All this men have done through the cooperation that means democracy.

If any man thinks that this freedom gives him the right to trample on others, he is no better than one of the wicked kings of former times. If he thinks that under this freedom he may devote himself wholly to the selfish gain of wealth without giving a share of his money, his time, and his skill to making his community a better place to live in and his nation stronger and more secure, he cheats his fellows, because he takes, without making any return, the blessings that the founders and defenders of the Republic established with their lives.

In the old stories the youth who was ready to be made a knight had to do certain things. He had to take the vow of knighthood, that he would lead a pure and blameless life. He had to render a service to someone in distress. And he had to watch, his arms beside him, through a night.

You boys and girls, lovers of America, her defenders if need be, her guardians in the years to come, must also watch by your arms. These arms are not riot guns and bayonets; they belong to your heart and mind. They are three in number: the love of home, the inheritance of freedom, and the will to work with others. The first is a foundation to make strong your heart; the second is a bulwark to make safe your life; the third is a sword wherewith to slay the enemies of the Republic.

This foundation in the love of home, this bulwark of our inheritance of freedom, and this sword of unselfish service are subjects often dealt with by great writers. In the pages that follow you will find pieces selected in order to bring out these ideas. You should read each of these selections not only for itself but also as a member of the group to which it belongs, and you should try to get the central idea that unites all the pieces that make up the group. Thus, little by little, you will come to see how your joy in Thanksgiving, the thrill that Old Glory can give you, and the service that you can render to someone else, are all related to each other. To defend home and country by being a good citizen is to be your mission in life. It is more important than a successful career or than great personal happiness. For both your career and your happiness will depend upon the way in which you, and the other boys and girls of America, thousands upon thousands, keep watch by these arms, keep faith with home and country.

HOME AND ITS FESTIVALS

Home, Sweet Home

John Howard Payne

'Mid pleasures and palaces though we may roam,
Be it ever so humble, there's no place like home!
A charm from the sky seems to hallow us there,
Which, seek through the world, is ne'er met with elsewhere.
Home, Home, sweet, sweet Home!
There's no place like Home! there's no place like Home!

An exile from home, splendor dazzles in vain;
Oh! give me my lowly thatched cottage again!
The birds, singing gayly, that came at my call
Give me them—and the peace of mind dearer than all!
Home, Home, sweet, sweet Home!
There's no place like Home! there's no place like Home!

How sweet 'tis to sit 'neath a fond father's smile,
And the cares of a mother to soothe and beguile!
Let others delight mid new pleasures to roam,
But give me, oh, give me, the pleasures of home!
Home, Home, sweet, sweet Home!
There's no place like Home! there's no place like Home!

To thee I'll return, overburdened with care;
The heart's dearest solace will smile on me there;
No more from that cottage again will I roam;
Be it ever so humble, there's no place like home.
Home, Home, sweet, sweet Home!
There's no place like Home! there's no place like Home!

NOTES AND QUESTIONS

Biography. John Howard Payne (1792-1852) was born in New York City. He became an actor and also a writer of plays and operas. He died at Tunis, Africa, to which place he had been sent as United States consul. When Jenny Lind, the celebrated Swedish singer, visited the United States in 1850, she sang in Washington before a large audience. John Howard Payne sat in one of the boxes, and at the close of her wonderful concert the singer turned toward the box in which the poet sat, and sang "Home, Sweet Home" with so much sweetness and power that many in the audience cried like children.

Discussion. 1. What words in the first stanza are repeated in the refrain, or chorus? 2. What is it that the poet says "hallows," or blesses, us when we are in our homes? 3. With what word in the second stanza is "cottage" contrasted? 4. What does the second stanza tell us that the poet had at home and missed afterwards? 5. What is it that really makes home beautiful? 6. What great service do our mothers perform? 7. What does page 84 tell you of the value the love of home is to a nation? 8. Explain the expression "splendor dazzles in vain," line 7, page 87. 9. Find in the glossary the meaning of: humble, hallow, charm, fond, soothe, beguile, roam. 10. *Pronounce:* exile, solace.

The Grapevine Swing

Samuel Minturn Peck

When I was a boy on the old plantation,
Down by the deep bayou—
The fairest spot of all creation
Under the arching blue—
When the wind came over the cotton and corn,
To the long, slim loop I'd spring
With brown feet bare, and a hat-brim torn,
And swing in the grapevine swing.

Swinging in the grapevine swing,
Laughing where the wild birds sing,
I dream and sigh
For the days gone by,
Swinging in the grapevine swing.

Out—o'er the water lilies bonny and bright,
Back—to the moss-green trees;
I shouted and laughed with a heart as light
As a wild rose tossed by the breeze.
The mocking bird joined in my reckless glee;
I longed for no angel's wing;
I was just as near heaven as I wanted to be,
Swinging in the grapevine swing.

Swinging in the grapevine swing,
Laughing where the wild birds sing—
Oh to be a boy
With a heart full of joy,
Swinging in the grapevine swing!

I'm weary at noon, I'm weary at night,
    I'm fretted and sore of heart,
And care is sowing my locks with white
    As I wend through the fevered mart.
I'm tired of the world with its pride and pomp,
    And fame seems a worthless thing.
I'd barter it all for one day's romp,
    And a swing in the grapevine swing.

    Swinging in the grapevine swing,
    Laughing where the wild birds sing—
        I would I were away
        From the world today,
    Swinging in the grapevine swing.

NOTES AND QUESTIONS

Biography. Samuel Minturn Peck (1854-1938) was a native of the South. He was born in Tuscaloosa, Alabama, and spent most of his early years in that city. He was gifted in music and became an excellent amateur pianist. His published works include *Cap and Bells, Rhymes and Roses,* and *Rings and Love-Knots,* from which "The Grapevine Swing," one of his most musical poems, is taken.

Discussion. 1. Why does the poet call the old plantation "The fairest spot of all creation"? 2. What does he mean by "the long, slim loop"? 3. For what "days gone by" does the poet sigh? 4. What picture do lines 6, 7, and 8, page 89, give you? 5. What tells you that the swing was near the bayou? 6. What is compared to the wild rose? 7. Why do you think the poet would "barter it all for one day's romp"? 8. Find in the glossary the meaning of: creation, bonny, reckless, fretted, wend, pomp, fame. 9. *Pronounce:* bayou, arching, laughing.

Phrases for Study

arching blue, **89**, 4
moss-green trees, **89**, 15
sore of heart, **90**, 2
care is sowing, **90**, 3
fevered mart, **90**, 4
barter it all, **90**, 7

LULLABY OF AN INFANT CHIEF

SIR WALTER SCOTT

O hush thee, my babie! thy sire was a knight,
Thy mother a lady, both lovely and bright;
The woods and the glens, from the towers which we see,
They are all belonging, dear babie, to thee.

O fear not the bugle, though loudly it blows;
It calls but the warders that guard thy repose;
Their bows would be bended, their blades would be red,
Ere the step of a foeman draws near to thy bed.

O hush thee, my babie! the time soon will come
When thy sleep shall be broken by trumpet and drum;
Then hush thee, my darling, take rest while you may,
For strife comes with manhood, and waking with day.

NOTES AND QUESTIONS

Biography. Sir Walter Scott (1771-1832) was born in Scotland. He was a famous novelist and poet. When a child, he learned the Scottish legends and ballads, and later he wove them into his writings.

Discussion. 1. What things mentioned in the first stanza show that the baby has great possessions? 2. How would the warders protect the baby? 3. What word could be used instead of "blades"? 4. What will this baby have to do when he becomes a man? 5. What will the trumpet and drum mean to him then? 6. How can you tell that this baby lived a long time ago? 7. Find in the glossary the meaning of: sire, knight, lady, glens, towers.

Phrases for Study

calls but the warders, **91**, 6
guard thy repose, **91**, 6
sleep shall be broken, **91**, 10
strife comes with manhood, **91**, 12

The First Thanksgiving Day

Margaret Junkin Preston

"And now," said the Governor, gazing abroad on the piled-up store
Of the sheaves that dotted the clearings and covered the meadows o'er,
"'Tis meet that we render praises because of this yield of grain;
'Tis meet that the Lord of the harvest be thanked for His sun and rain.

"And, therefore, I, William Bradford (by the grace of God today,
And the franchise of this good people), Governor of Plymouth, say,
Through virtue of vested power—ye shall gather with one accord,
And hold, in the month of November, thanksgiving unto the Lord.

"He hath granted us peace and plenty, and the quiet we've sought so long;
He hath thwarted the wily savage, and kept him from wrack and wrong;
And unto our feast the Sachem shall be bidden, that he may know
We worship his own Great Spirit, Who maketh the harvests grow.

"So shoulder your matchlocks, masters—there is hunting of all degrees;
And, fishermen, take your tackle, and scour for spoils the seas;
And, maidens and dames of Plymouth, your delicate crafts employ
To honor our First Thanksgiving, and make it a feast of joy!

"We fail of the fruits and dainties—we fail of the old home cheer;
Ah, these are the lightest losses, mayhap, that befall us here;
But see, in our open clearings, how golden the melons lie;
Enrich them with sweets and spices, and give us the pumpkin-pie!"

So, bravely the preparations went on for the autumn feast;
The deer and the bear were slaughtered; wild game from the greatest to least
Was heaped in the colony cabins; brown home-brew served for wine,
And the plum and the grape of the forest, for orange and peach and pine.

At length came the day appointed; the snow had begun to fall,
But the clang from the meeting-house belfry rang merrily over all,
And summoned the folk of Plymouth, who hastened with glad accord
To listen to Elder Brewster as he fervently thanked the Lord.

In his seat sate Governor Bradford; men, matrons, and maidens fair,
Miles Standish and all his soldiers, with corselet and sword, were there;
And sobbing and tears and gladness had each in its turn the sway,
For the grave of the sweet Rose Standish o'ershadowed Thanksgiving Day.

5 And when Massasoit, the Sachem, sate down with his hundred braves,
And ate of the varied riches of gardens and woods and waves,
And looked on the granaried harvest—with a blow on his brawny chest,
He muttered, "The good Great Spirit loves His white children best!"

NOTES AND QUESTIONS

Biographical and Historical Note. Margaret J. Preston (1820-1897) was one of the leading poets of the South. She wrote many poems and sketches. "The First Thanksgiving Day" gives a good picture of the life in the old Pilgrim days.

The Pilgrims landed at Plymouth on December 21, 1620. During the long, hard winter fifty-one of the one hundred Pilgrims died, among them being Rose Standish, wife of Captain Miles Standish. As soon as spring came, the colonists planted their fields, and by the end of summer a plentiful harvest was gathered in. When provisions and fuel had been laid in for the winter, Governor Bradford appointed a day of thanksgiving. Venison, wild fowl, and fish were easy to obtain. We are told, "there was great store of wild turkeys, of which they took many." For three days a great feast was spread, and Massasoit, the Indian sachem, or chief, and many of his people enjoyed it with the colonists.

Discussion. 1. When did the events related in this story take place? 2. Who was the governor of Plymouth at this time? 3. What proclamation did he make? 4. What did the governor say that God had done for the colony? 5. Who did he say should be invited to the feast? 6. What meat did the Pilgrims have at their first Thanksgiving dinner? 7. What fruits did they have for the feast? 8. What fruit is meant by "pine" in line 12, page 93? 9. What did the colonists do "with glad accord" before they sat down to their feast? 10. Find the lines that tell what Massasoit said when he ate of the feast. 11. Why is it a good thing for America to have a day set apart each year for us to give thanks for our blessings? 12. Find in the glossary the meaning of: store, sheaves, clearings, wrack, dames, mayhap, befall, slaughtered, appointed, summoned, fervently, sate, braves, brawny. 13. *Pronounce:* therefore, franchise, wily, sachem, pumpkin, matrons, corselet, Massasoit, granaried.

Phrases for Study

'tis meet, **92**, 3
franchise of this good people, **92**, 6
virtue of vested power, **92**, 7
with one accord, **92**, 7
thwarted the wily savage, **92**, 10
Great Spirit, **92**, 12
shoulder your matchlocks, **93**, 1
of all degrees, **93**, 1
scour for spoils, **93**, 2
delicate crafts employ, **93**, 3
fail of the fruits, **93**, 5
home-brew served for wine, **93**, 11
each in its turn the sway, **94**, 3
o'ershadowed Thanksgiving Day, **94**, 4
varied riches, **94**, 6

A VISIT FROM ST. NICHOLAS

CLEMENT C. MOORE

'Twas the night before Christmas, when all through the house
Not a creature was stirring, not even a mouse.
The stockings were hung by the chimney with care,
In hopes that St. Nicholas soon would be there.
The children were nestled all snug in their beds,
While visions of sugarplums danced through their heads;
And mamma in her kerchief, and I in my cap,
Had just settled our brains for a long winter's nap—

When out on the lawn there arose such a clatter,
I sprang from my bed to see what was the matter.
Away to the window I flew like a flash,
Tore open the shutters, and threw up the sash;
The moon on the breast of the new-fallen snow
Gave a luster of midday to objects below;
When what to my wondering eyes should appear
But a miniature sleigh and eight tiny reindeer,
With a little old driver, so lively and quick,
I knew in a moment it must be St. Nick.
More rapid than eagles his coursers they came,
And he whistled, and shouted, and called them by name:
"Now, Dasher! now, Dancer! now, Prancer and Vixen!
On, Comet! on, Cupid! on, Donder and Blitzen!—
To the top of the porch, to the top of the wall,
Now, dash away, dash away, dash away, all!"
As dry leaves that before the wild hurricane fly,
When they meet with an obstacle, mount to the sky,
So, up to the housetop the coursers they flew,
With a sleigh full of toys—and St. Nicholas, too.
And then, in a twinkling, I heard on the roof
The prancing and pawing of each little hoof.
As I drew in my head, and was turning around,
Down the chimney St. Nicholas came with a bound;
He was dressed all in fur from his head to his foot,
And his clothes were all tarnished with ashes and soot.
A bundle of toys he had flung on his back,
And he looked like a peddler just opening his pack.
His eyes, how they twinkled! his dimples, how merry!
His cheeks were like roses, his nose like a cherry;
His droll little mouth was drawn up like a bow,
And the beard on his chin was as white as the snow.
The stump of a pipe he held tight in his teeth,

And the smoke, it encircled his head like a wreath.
He had a broad face, and a little round belly
That shook when he laughed, like a bowl full of jelly.
He was chubby and plump—a right jolly old elf;
And I laughed when I saw him, in spite of myself.
A wink of his eye and a twist of his head
Soon gave me to know I had nothing to dread.
He spoke not a word, but went straight to his work,
And filled all the stockings; then turned with a jerk,
And laying his finger aside of his nose,
And giving a nod, up the chimney he rose.
He sprang to his sleigh, to his team gave a whistle,
And away they all flew like the down of a thistle.
But I heard him exclaim, ere they drove out of sight,
"Happy Christmas to all, and to all a good night."

NOTES AND QUESTIONS

Biography. Clement C. Moore (1779-1863) was an American poet and author. He lived in New York City, where for many years he was engaged in educational work.

Discussion. 1. What picture do the first eight lines of this poem give you? 2. Does this picture seem real to you? 3. Of what were the children dreaming? 4. What word do you use instead of sugarplums? 5. What picture do you find in lines 7-10, page 96? 6. What is the next picture? Find the lines that make it. 7. To what is the swiftness of the reindeer compared? 8. What words show how lightly the reindeer flew through the air? 9. Find the lines that picture St. Nicholas after he came down the chimney. 10. Which of all the pictures in the entire poem can you see most distinctly? 11. Which do you like best? 12. What did you read in "A Forward Look," pages 83-86, about the value of the home festivals? What does a love of these festivals do for us? What should we lose if we did not celebrate them? 13. Find in the glossary the meaning of: clatter; coursers; hurricane, obstacle, twinkling, tarnished, encircled, elf. 14. *Pronounce:* miniature, tiny, chimney, droll.

OUR COUNTRY AND ITS FLAG

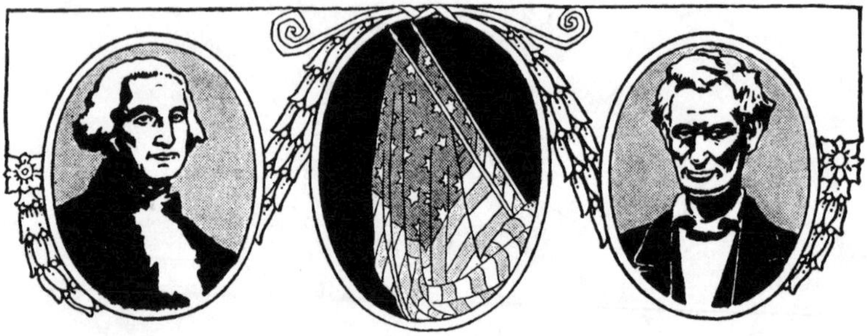

The Land of Liberty

(Author Unknown)

I love my country's pine-clad hills,
Her thousand bright and gushing rills,
    Her sunshine and her storms;
Her rough and rugged rocks, that rear
Their hoary heads high in the air
    In wild, fantastic forms.

I love her rivers, deep and wide,
Those mighty streams that seaward glide
    To seek the ocean's breast;
Her smiling fields, her pleasant vales,
Her shady dells, her flow'ry dales,
    The haunts of peaceful rest.

I love her forests, dark and lone,
For there the wild bird's merry tone
  I hear from morn till night;
And there are lovelier flowers, I ween,
Than e'er in Eastern lands were seen,
  In varied colors bright.

Her forests and her valleys fair,
Her flowers that scent the morning air—
  All have their charms for me;
But more I love my country's name,
Those words that echo deathless fame,
  "The Land of Liberty."

NOTES AND QUESTIONS

Discussion. 1. What parts of our country are noted for pine forests? 2. What things about America call forth the love of the poet? 3. Does he have all parts of America in mind, or some part that he knows well? 4. What name does he give America? Why does this "echo deathless fame"? 5. Name one of the "mighty streams that seaward glide." 6. What does the poet say makes the forests beautiful? 7. This poem is similar in many ways to the national hymn, "America." Compare it with the words of the hymn in as many ways as you can. 8. Commit to memory the last three lines of the poem. 9. Why is our country called "The Land of Liberty"? 10. Find in the glossary the meaning of: gushing, rills, rugged, rear, vales, dells, lone, ween. 11. *Pronounce:* hoary, fantastic, haunts, echo.

Phrases for Study

pine-clad hills, **98**, 1
fantastic forms, **98**, 6
seaward glide, **98**, 8
ocean's breast, **98**, 9
smiling fields, **98**, 10
flow'ry dales, **98**, 11
Eastern lands, **99**, 5
deathless fame, **99**, 11

The Flag of our Country

Charles Sumner

There is the national flag. He must be cold indeed who can look upon its folds, rippling in the breeze, without pride of country. If he be in a foreign land, the flag is companionship and country itself, with all its endearments.

Its highest beauty is in what it symbolizes. It is because it represents all, that all gaze at it with delight and reverence.

It is a piece of bunting lifted in the air; but it speaks sublimely, and every part has a voice. Its stripes of alternate red and white proclaim the original union of thirteen states to maintain the Declaration of Independence. Its stars of white on a field of blue proclaim that union of states constituting our national constellation, which receives a new star with every new state. The two together signify union past and present.

The very colors have a language which was officially recognized by our fathers. White is for purity, red for valor, blue for justice; and all together, bunting, stripes, stars, and colors, blazing in the sky, make the flag of our country to be cherished by all our hearts, to be upheld by all our hands.

NOTES AND QUESTIONS

Biography. Charles Sumner (1811-1874), an American statesman and orator, was born in Boston, Massachusetts. He became United States senator in 1851. "The Flag of Our Country" is taken from an address delivered in 1867 at Cooper Institute in New York.

Discussion. 1. Each paragraph in this selection has a separate message. Does the first paragraph fit America only, or could an Englishman say the same thing about his national flag, and a Frenchman of his? What then is the thing that *any* flag represents to the citizen of the country to which he belongs? 2. What facts peculiar to America does the second paragraph give you? 3. How many stripes has the flag? 4. How many stars were in the first American flag? How many are there now? 5. What is meant by "union past and present"? 6. "White is for purity"—in what way does this express the ideals of the founders of our country? 7. How does it express the motives that led the United States to enter the World War? 8. If we had desired to gain new territory by fighting in this war, would the flag have been honored? 9. How does the quality of justice appear in the course of America in the war? 10. What *injustice* did our soldiers and sailors fight against? 11. Find in the glossary the meaning of: rippling, reverence, bunting, proclaim, original, maintain, constituting, valor, cherished. 12. *Pronounce:* symbolizes, sublimely, alternate, constellation.

Phrases for Study

he must be cold, **100**, 1
all its endearments, **100**, 4
speaks sublimely, **100**, 8
every part has a voice, **100**, 9
national constellation, **100**, 13
signify union, **100**, 15
officially recognized, **100**, 16
blazing in the sky, **100**, 19

The Name of Old Glory

James Whitcomb Riley

Old Glory! say, who,
By the ships and the crew,
And the long, blended ranks of the gray and the blue—
Who gave you, Old Glory, the name that you bear
With such pride everywhere
As you cast yourself free to the rapturous air
And leap out full-length, as we're wanting you to?
Who gave you that name, with the ring of the same,

And the honor and fame so becoming to you?
Your stripes stroked in ripples of white and of red,
With your stars at their glittering best overhead—
By day or by night
Their delightfulest light
Laughing down from their little square heaven of blue!
Who gave you the name of Old Glory?—say, who—
Who gave you the name of Old Glory?

The old banner lifted, and faltering then,
In vague lisps and whispers fell silent again.

Old Glory, the story we're wanting to hear
Is what the plain facts of your christening were;
For your name—just to hear it,
Repeat it, and cheer it, 's a tang to the spirit
As salt as a tear;
And seeing you fly and the boys marching by,
There's a shout in the throat and a blur in the eye
And an aching to live for you always—or die,
If, dying, we still keep you waving on high.
And so, by our love
For you, floating above,
And the scars of all wars and the sorrows thereof,
Who gave you the name of Old Glory, and why
Are we thrilled at the name of Old Glory?

Then the old banner leaped, like a sail in the blast,
And fluttered an audible answer at last.

And it spake, with a shake of the voice, and it said:
"By the driven snow-white and the living blood-red
Of my bars, and their heaven of stars overhead—

By the symbol conjoined of them all, skyward cast,
As I float from the steeple, or flap at the mast,
Or droop o'er the sod where the long grasses nod—
My name is as old as the glory of God.
. . . So I came by the name of Old Glory."

NOTES AND QUESTIONS

Biography. James Whitcomb Riley (1852-1916) was a native of Indiana. Most of his life was spent in Indianapolis, where he lived on the quiet Lockerbie Street which he celebrated in one of his poems. He is called "The Hoosier Poet." He wrote several volumes of poems, the first being *The Old Swimmin' Hole and 'Leven More Poems.* The school children of Indiana celebrated Riley's birthday on October 7, 1911, and have each year since made this a festival day.

Discussion. 1. It is said that the name "Old Glory" was given the flag by Captain William Driver, of the brig *Charles Doggett,* in 1831. Why is this a good name for the American flag? 2. The first stanza describes the beauty of the flag. What words or lines tell you about the *appearance* of Old Glory? Which words or lines tell you about the *personality* (pride, freedom, joy) of the flag? 3. What is meant by "long, *blended* ranks of the gray and the blue"? 4. What response does the flag seem to make? 5. The second stanza gives the effect produced by the flag upon the poet. Where is he? How does he feel? 6. In the last stanza, compare what is said about the parts of the flag and their meaning with what Mr. Sumner told you in the preceding selection. 7. Find in the glossary the meaning of: faltering, thrilled, blast, driven, symbol. 8. *Pronounce:* rapturous, christening, audible.

Phrases for Study

blended ranks, **101**, 3
cast yourself free, **101**, 6
ring of the same, **101**, 8
fame so becoming to you, **102**, 1
stroked in ripples, **102**, 2
at their glittering best, **102**, 3
square heaven of blue, **102**, 6
vague lisps, **102**, 10
tang to the spirit, **102**, 14
blur in the eye, **102**, 17
scars of all wars, **102**, 22
conjoined of them all, **103**, 1
skyward cast, **103**, 1
droop o'er the sod, **103**, 3

The Star-Spangled Banner

Francis Scott Key

O say, can you see, by the dawn's early light,
What so proudly we hailed at the twilight's last gleaming?
Whose broad stripes and bright stars, through the perilous fight,
O'er the ramparts we watched were so gallantly streaming;
And the rockets' red glare, the bombs bursting in air,
Gave proof through the night that our flag was still there;
O say, does that Star-Spangled Banner yet wave
O'er the land of the free and the home of the brave?

On that shore dimly seen through the mists of the deep,
Where the foe's haughty host in dread silence reposes,
What is that which the breeze, o'er the towering steep,
As it fitfully blows, now conceals, now discloses?
Now it catches the gleam of the morning's first beam
In full glory reflected now shines in the stream;
'Tis the Star-Spangled Banner; O long may it wave
O'er the land of the free and the home of the brave!

And where are the foes who so vauntingly swore
That the havoc of war and the battle's confusion
A home and a country should leave us no more?
Their blood has washed out their foul footsteps' pollution.
No refuge could save the hireling and slave
From the terror of flight, or the gloom of the grave;
And the Star-Spangled Banner in triumph doth wave
O'er the land of the free and the home of the brave!

O thus be it ever, when freemen shall stand
Between their loved homes and the war's desolation;
Blest with victory and peace, may the heav'n-rescued land
Praise the Power that hath made and preserved us a nation!
Then conquer we must, for our cause it is just,
And this be our motto, "In God is our trust";
And the Star-Spangled Banner in triumph shall wave
O'er the land of the free and the home of the brave!

NOTES AND QUESTIONS

Biographical and Historical Note. Francis Scott Key (1780-1843), a native of Maryland, was a lawyer and poet. His patriotic poem, "The Star-Spangled Banner," which has become the national anthem, made him famous.

The incidents referred to in this poem occurred during the War of 1812. In August, 1814, a strong force of British entered Washington and burned the Capitol, the White House, and many other public buildings. On September 13 the British admiral moved his fleet into position to attack Fort McHenry, near Baltimore. The bombardment of the fort lasted all night, but the fort was so bravely defended that the flag was still floating over it when morning came.

Just before the bombardment began, Francis Scott Key was sent to the admiral's frigate to arrange for an exchange of prisoners, and was told to wait until the bombardment was over. All night he watched the fort, and by the first rays of morning light he saw the Stars and Stripes still waving. Then, in his joy and pride, he wrote the stirring words of the song which is now known and loved by all Americans—"The Star-Spangled Banner."

Discussion. 1. What lines in the poem are explained by the historic note above? 2. The poem expresses the love and reverence felt by patriots when the flag is endangered by the attacks of armed men in war. What is said on page 84 about the danger to our country in a time of peace? From what people? Can you do anything to prevent this danger? 3. Where was the reflection of the flag seen? 4. What is the meaning of "thus" in line 1, page 105? 5. What land is the "heav'n-rescued land"? 6. What does the poet mean when he speaks of the "Power that hath made and preserved us a nation," line 4, page 105? 7. Find the words that must be our country's motto. 8. Do you think this national song cheered the American soldiers in the last two World Wars? 9. Explain why you think the picture on page 98 aptly illustrates "Our Country and Its Flag." 10. Find in the glossary the meaning of: dawn, gleaming, host, discloses, beam, triumph. 11. *Pronounce:* haughty, vauntingly, pollution, hireling, desolation.

Phrases for Study

proudly we hailed, **104**, 2
gallantly streaming, **104**, 4
Star-Spangled, **104**, 7
mists of the deep, **104**, 9
dread silence reposes, **104**, 10
fitfully blows, **104**, 12
catches the gleam, **104**, 13
full glory reflected, **104**, 14
havoc of war, **104**, 18
foul footsteps' pollution, **104**, 20

The Boyhood of Lincoln*

Elbridge S. Brooks

The future president of the United States was eight years old when he spent the winter with his father, mother, and sister in the "half-faced camp" on Pigeon Creek.

It was indeed rough living in the Lincoln home on Little Pigeon Creek. When he was "good and ready," the father, Thomas Lincoln, set about building a better shelter for his family than the forlorn "half-faced camp." The new building was not such a great improvement; but it was more like a house. It was a rough cabin of logs, without door, window, or floor. But it seemed so much better than the shanty in which they had been living that Abraham felt quite princely.

---

* See "Suggestions for Silent Reading," page 163.

His life was lonely enough in that wilderness; but, before many months, he had company. His Uncle and Aunt Sparrow and his boy cousin, Dennis Hanks, came from Kentucky to try their luck in Indiana. Abraham's father gave them the old "half-faced camp" as a home, and so the Lincolns had near neighbors.

But before the winter set in, there came sad days to both houses. A terrible sickness—what we call an epidemic—visited that section of Indiana. Many people died from it, and among these were first, Uncle and Aunt Sparrow, and then Mrs. Lincoln, the mother of Abraham.

It was a poor kind of housekeeping they had in that shiftless home on Little Pigeon Creek after the mother of the home had been taken away. Sarah, the eldest child, was only twelve; Abraham was but ten, and little Dennis Hanks was eight. Sarah tried to keep house; and her father, in his careless way, tried to help her. But about all they could do was to keep from going hungry. Deer meat broiled on the coals of the wood fire, ash-cakes made of cornmeal, with now and then a slab of pork, was their only bill of fare. About all the pleasure Abraham found, when he was not trying to keep from being cold and hungry, was in his books.

How many do you think he had? Just three: the Bible, *Aesop's Fables*, and *The Pilgrim's Progress*. Think of that, you boys and girls who have more books than you can read and for whom the printing presses are always hard at work. The boy knew these three books almost by heart. He could repeat whole chapters of the Bible, many parts of *The Pilgrim's Progress*, and every one of Aesop's fables; and he never forgot them.

Thomas Lincoln knew that the uncomfortable state of affairs in his log cabin could not long continue or his home, such as it was, would go to ruin. So one day he bade the children good-bye and told them he was going back to Kentucky on a visit. He was away for three weeks; but when he returned from his Kentucky visit in December, 1819, he brought back a new wife to look after his home and be a mother to his motherless children.

Mrs. Lincoln seemed to take an especial liking to the little ten-year-old Abraham. She saw something in the boy that made her feel sure that a little guidance would do wonders for him. Having first made him clean and comfortable, she next made him intelligent, bright, and good. She managed to send him to school for a few months. The little log schoolhouse, close to the meeting house, to which the traveling schoolmaster would come to give four weeks' schooling, was scarcely high enough for a man to stand straight in; it had holes for windows and greased paper to take the place of glass. But in such a place Abraham Lincoln "got his schooling" for a few weeks only in "reading, writing, and ciphering"; here he was again and again head of his class; and here he "spelled down" all the big boys and girls in the exciting contests called "spelling matches."

He became a great reader. He read every book and newspaper he could get hold of, and if he came across anything in his reading that he wished to remember, he would copy it on a shingle, because writing paper was scarce, and either learn it by heart or hide the shingle away until he could get some paper to copy it on.

Lamps and candles were almost unknown in his home, and Abraham, flat on his stomach, would often do his reading, writing, and ciphering in the firelight, as it flashed and flickered on the big hearth of his log cabin home.

One day Abraham found that a man for whom he sometimes worked owned a copy of Weems's *Life of Washington.* This was a famous book in its day. Abraham borrowed it at once. When he was not reading it, he put it away on a shelf—a clapboard resting on wooden pins. There was a big crack between the logs behind the shelf, and one rainy day the *Life of Washington* fell into the crack and was soaked almost into pulp. Young Abraham went at once to the owner of the book and, after telling him of the accident, promised to "work the book out."

The old farmer kept him so strictly to his promise that he made him "pull fodder" for the cattle three days as payment for the book. And that is the way that Abraham Lincoln bought his first book. For he dried the *Life of Washington* and put it in his "library." What boy or girl of today would like to buy books at such a price?

NOTES AND QUESTIONS

Biography. Elbridge S. Brooks (1846-1902) was a native of Massachusetts. He was always interested in stories of history, for his mother descended from the Monroes, who fought bravely at Lexington. He was for a time one of the editors of *St. Nicholas.*

Discussion. 1. What were the hardships suffered by the young Lincoln in the Indiana wilderness? 2. What do you learn about Lincoln's reading? About his school life? 3. What was the first book Lincoln owned, and how did he get it? 4. What do you suppose Lincoln learned from the life of Washington? 5. How did Lincoln fix in his memory things that he wished to remember? 6. What characteristics of the boy help to explain why he afterwards became such a great man? 7. You will enjoy reading *The True Story of Lincoln,* from which this selection is taken. 8. Find in the glossary the meaning of: forlorn, shanty, princely, wilderness, epidemic, shiftless, ash-cakes, slab, guidance, ciphering, clapboard, pulp. *9. Pronounce:* Aesop, bade.

Phrases for Study

half-faced camp, **106**, 3
uncomfortable state, **107**, 31
traveling schoolmaster, **108**, 13
spelled down, **108**, 19
work the book out, **109**, 7
pull fodder, **109**, 9

Washington with General Braddock

Elbridge S. Brooks

The king of England and his advisers determined to make a stand in America against the French. So they sent over two regiments of British troops under command of a brave soldier whose name was Braddock, and told him to get what help he could in Virginia and drive out the French.

General Braddock came to Virginia with his splendid looking fighting men. When he had studied the situation there, one of the first things he did was to ask Colonel George Washington of Mount Vernon to come with him as one of his chief assistants. Washington at once accepted. He saw that now the king of England "meant business," and that if General Braddock were as wise as he was brave, the trouble in the Ohio country might be speedily ended and the French driven out.

But when he had joined General Braddock, he discovered that that brave but obstinate leader thought that battles were to be fought in America just the same as in Europe, and that soldiers could be marched against such forest fighters as the French and Indians as if they were going on a parade. Washington did all he could to advise caution. It was of no use, however. General Braddock said that he was a soldier and knew how to fight, and that he did not wish for any advice from these Americans who had never seen a real battle.

At last everything was ready, and in July, 1755, the army, led by General Braddock, marched off to attack Fort Duquesne, which the French had built at Pittsburgh.

---

*See "Suggestions for Silent Reading," page 163.

Washington had worked so hard to get things ready that he was sick in bed with fever when the soldiers started; but without waiting to get well, he hurried after them and caught up with them on the ninth of July, at a ford on the Monongahela, fifteen miles from Fort Duquesne.

The British troops, in full uniform, and in regular order as if they were to drill before the king, marched straight on in splendid array. Washington thought it the most beautiful show he had ever seen; but he said to the general: "Do not let the soldiers march into the woods like that. The Frenchmen and the Indians may even now be hiding behind the trees ready to shoot us down. Let me send some men ahead to see where they are, and let some of our Virginians who are used to fighting in the forest go before to clear them away." But General Braddock told him to mind his own business, and marched on as gallantly as ever.

Suddenly, just as they reached a narrow part of the road, where the woods were all about them, the Frenchmen and Indians who were waiting for them behind the great trees and underbrush opened fire upon the British troops, and there came just such a dreadful time as Washington had feared. But even now Braddock would not give in. His soldiers must fight as they had been drilled to fight in Europe; and when the Virginians who were with him tried to fight as they had been accustomed to, he called them cowards and ordered them to form in line.

It was all over very soon. The British soldiers, fired upon from all sides and scarcely able to see where their enemies were, became frightened, huddled together, and made all the better marks for the bullets of the French and Indians hiding among the trees and bushes. Then General Braddock fell from his horse, mortally wounded; his splendidly drilled redcoats broke into panic, turned, and ran away; and only the coolness of Washington and the Virginia forest fighters who were with him saved the entire army from being cut to pieces.

Washington fought like a hero. Two horses that he rode were killed while he kept in the saddle; his coat was shot through and through, and it seemed as if he would be killed any moment. But he kept on fighting, caring nothing for danger. He tried to turn back the fleeing British troops; he tried to bring back the cannon, and when the gunners ran away, he leaped from his horse and aimed and fired the cannon himself. Then with his Virginians, that Braddock had so despised as soldiers, he protected the rear of the retreating army, carried off the dying general and, cool and collected in the midst of all the terrible things that were happening, saved the British army from slaughter, buried poor General Braddock in the Virginia woods, and finally brought back to the settlements what was left of that splendid army of the king. He was the only man in all that time of disaster who came out of the fight with glory and renown.

NOTES AND QUESTIONS

For **Biography**, see page 109.

Discussion. 1. Tell what you can of the contest for territory in America between the French and the English. 2. Who was General Braddock and for what was he sent to America? 3. Compare Washington and General Braddock in as many ways as you can. 4. Why did Washington do all he could to help General Braddock in spite of the fact that he knew Braddock was not acting wisely? 5. How did Washington gain glory from the engagement? 6. What are you told on page 84 about the value to us of studying the lives of great Americans? What do you owe to Washington and Lincoln? 7. Find in the glossary the meaning of: advisers, situation, caution, ford, array, gallantly, huddled, collected, disaster, renown. 8. *Pronounce:* Duquesne, Monongahela, mortally wounded.

SERVICE

Somebody's Mother

(Author Unknown)

The woman was old and ragged and gray
And bent with the chill of the winter's day.
The street was wet with the recent snow,
And the woman's feet were aged and slow.

She stood at the crossing and waited long
Alone, uncared for, amid the throng
Of human beings who passed her by,
Nor heeded the glance of her anxious eye.

Down the street with laughter and shout.
Glad in the freedom of "school let out,"
Came the boys like a flock of sheep,
Hailing the snow piled white and deep.

Past the woman so old and gray
Hastened the children on their way,
Nor offered a helping hand to her,
So meek, so timid, afraid to stir,
Lest the carriage wheels or the horses' feet
Should crowd her down in the slippery street.

At last came one of the merry troop,
The gayest laddie of all the group;
He paused beside her and whispered low,
"I'll help you across if you wish to go."

Her aged hand on his strong young arm
She placed, and so, without hurt or harm,
He guided her trembling feet along,
Proud that his own were firm and strong.

Then back again to his friends he went,
His young heart happy and well content.
"She's somebody's mother, boys, you know,
For all she's aged and poor and slow;

"And I hope some fellow will lend a hand
To help my mother, you understand,
If ever she's poor and old and gray,
When her own dear boy is far away."

And "somebody's mother" bowed low her head
In her home that night, and the prayer she said
Was, "God be kind to the noble boy
Who is somebody's son and pride and joy."

NOTES AND QUESTIONS

Discussion. 1. Here is a story about a boy who saw a chance to do a service and did it; how was he different from his companions? 2. What were they interested in? 3. Wasn't he also eager to do what they did? 4. Why did he stop and help the old woman? 5. How did the woman feel toward the boy? 6. How do you think his own mother would have felt if she had seen him? 7. Why is this incident a splendid example of service? How was this boy doing his part as a good citizen?

The Leak in the Dike

Phoebe Cary

The good dame looked from her cottage
    At the close of the pleasant day,
And cheerily called to her little son
    Outside the door at play:
"Come, Peter, come! I want you to go,
    While there is light to see,
To the hut of the blind old man who lives
    Across the dike, for me;
And take these cakes I made for him
    They are hot and smoking yet;
You have time enough to go and come
    Before the sun is set."

And Peter left the brother
    With whom all day he had played,
And the sister who had watched their sports
    In the willow's tender shade;
And told them they'd see him back before
    They saw a star in sight,

Though he wouldn't be afraid to go
In the very darkest night!
For he was a brave, bright fellow
With eye and conscience clear;
He could do whatever a boy might do,
And he had not learned to fear.

And now with his face all glowing
And eyes as bright as the day
With the thoughts of his pleasant errand,
He trudged along the way;
And soon his joyous prattle
Made glad a lonesome place
Alas! if only the blind old man
Could have seen that happy face!
Yet he somehow caught the brightness
Which his voice and presence lent;
And he felt the sunshine come and go
As Peter came and went.

And now as the day was sinking,
And the winds began to rise,
The mother looked from her door again,
Shading her anxious eyes,
And saw the shadows deepen
And birds to their homes come back,
But never a sign of Peter
Along the level track.
But she said: "He will come at morning,
So I need not fret or grieve
Though it isn't like my boy at all
To stay without my leave."

But where was the child delaying?
    On the homeward way was he;
And across the dike while the sun was up
    An hour above the sea;
He was stopping now to gather flowers,
    Now listening to the sound,
As the angry waters dashed themselves
    Against their narrow bound.
"Ah! well for us," said Peter,
    "That the gates are good and strong,
And my father tends them carefully.
    Or they would not hold you long!
You're a wicked sea," said Peter;
    "I know why you fret and chafe;
You would like to spoil our lands and homes;
    But our sluices keep you safe."

But hark! through the noise of waters
    Comes a low, clear, trickling sound;
And the child's face pales with terror,
    And his blossoms drop to the ground.
He is up the bank in a moment,
    And, stealing through the sand,
He sees a stream not yet so large
    As his slender childish hand.
'Tis a leak in the dike! He is but a boy,
    Unused to fearful scenes;
But, young as he is, he has learned to know
    The dreadful thing that means.

A leak in the dike! The stoutest heart
    Grows faint that cry to hear.

And the bravest man in all the land
    Turns white with mortal fear,
For he knows the smallest leak may grow
    To a flood in a single night;
And he knows the strength of the cruel sea
    When loosed in its angry might.

And the boy! he has seen the danger
    And, shouting a wild alarm,
He forces back the weight of the sea
    With the strength of his single arm!
He listens for the joyful sound
    Of a footstep passing nigh;
And lays his ear to the ground, to catch
    The answer to his cry.
And he hears the rough winds blowing,
    And the waters rise and fall,
But never an answer comes to him
    Save the echo of his call.

So, faintly calling and crying
    Till the sun is under the sea,
Crying and moaning till the stars
    Come out for company,
He thinks of his brother and sister,
    Asleep in their safe warm bed;
He thinks of his father and mother,
    Of himself as dying—and dead;
And of how, when the night is over,
    They must come and find him at last;
But he never thinks he can leave the place
    Where duty holds him fast.

The good dame in the cottage
    Is up and astir with the light
For the thought of her little Peter
    Has been with her all the night.
And now she watches the pathway,
    As yester eve she had done:
But what does she see so strange and black
    Against the rising sun?
Her neighbors are bearing between them
    Something straight to her door;
Her child is coming home, but not
    As he ever came before!

"He is dead!" she cries; "my darling!"
    And the startled father hears.
And comes and looks the way she looks,
    And fears the thing she fears;
Till a glad shout from the bearers
    Thrills the stricken man and wife
"Give thanks, for your son has saved our land,
    And God has saved his life!"
So, there in the morning sunshine
    They knelt about the boy;
And every head was bared and bent
    In tearful, reverent joy.

NOTES AND QUESTIONS

Biography. Phoebe Cary (1824-1871) was an American poet. She was born in Cincinnati and lived with her sister, Alice, in New York City. She wrote many poems of beauty and charm, but none is more widely read than "The Leak in the Dike."

Note. A large part of Holland consists of meadow land so low and flat that the sea would overflow it during high tide if it were not protected, partly by natural sand hills but more by a wonderful system of diking. The dikes are long mounds, or thick walls of earth and stone, broad at the base and gradual in slope.

Discussion. 1. What purpose do the dikes of Holland serve? 2. There were no Boy Scouts in those days, but here is a story of a boy who would have been a good member of the Scouts. Why? 3. What service did Peter's mother call him to render? 4. Had he done such things before? 5. How did the blind man think of Peter? 6. How did Peter find the danger? 7. What would many boys have done? 8. How did he stop the leak in the dike? 9. What would have happened if he had grown afraid or tired? 10. Peter saw a duty to be performed and was brave enough to do it, though it was not easy, and might have cost him his life. What were the results of his quick wit and courage? 11. How was Peter doing his part as a good citizen? 12. Find in the glossary the meaning of: prattle, presence, anxious, trickling, stoutest, save, astir, yester, stricken. 13. *Pronounce:* chafe, sluices, loosed.

Phrases for Study

narrow bound, **117**, 8
mortal fear, **118**, 2
sun is under the sea, **118**, 20
duty holds him fast, **118**, 30

Casabianca

Felicia Dorothea Hemans

The boy stood on the burning deck
Whence all but him had fled;
The flame that lit the battle's wreck
Shone round him o'er the dead.

Yet, beautiful and bright he stood,
As born to rule the storm
A creature of heroic blood,
A proud, though childlike, form.

The flames rolled on—he would not go
Without his father's word;
That father, faint in death below,
His voice no longer heard.

He called aloud: "Say, father, say
If yet my task is done!"
He knew not that the chieftain lay
Unconscious of his son.

"Speak, father!" once again he cried,
"If I may yet be gone!"
And but the booming shots replied,
And fast the flames rolled on.

Upon his brow he felt their breath,
And in his waving hair,
And looked from that lone post of death
In still, yet brave, despair;

And shouted but once more aloud,
"My father! must I stay?"
While o'er him fast, through sail and shroud,
The wreathing fires made way.

They wrapped the ship in splendor wild,
They caught the flag on high,
And streamed above the gallant child
Like banners in the sky.

There came a burst of thunder sound—
The boy—oh! where was he?
Ask of the winds that far around
With fragments strewed the sea—

With mast, and helm, and pennon fair,
That well had borne their part;
But the noblest thing which perished there
Was that young, faithful heart!

NOTES AND QUESTIONS

Biographical and Historical Note. Felicia Hemans (1793-1835), an English poet, was born in Liverpool, but spent much of her life in North Wales. "Casabianca" and "The Landing of the Pilgrims" are her best known poems.

The hero of this poem was the son of Louis Casabianca, the captain of *L'Orient,* the flagship of the fleet that carried Napoleon Bonaparte and his army to Egypt. The incident narrated in this poem occurred during the Battle of the Nile. The powder magazine exploded, the ship was burned, and the captain and his son perished.

Discussion. 1. How did it happen that the boy was alone on the "burning deck"? 2. Find two lines in the third stanza that tell how the boy showed his faithfulness and his "heroic blood." 3. Why is his father called the "chieftain"? 4. What did the boy ask his father? 5. Why did he remain in such great danger when he might have saved himself? 6. What was it that "wrapped the ship in splendor wild"? 7. What made the "burst of thunder sound"? 8. What things are mentioned as fragments which "strewed the sea"? 9. Why is it good for us to read such a poem as this? 10. What service did Casabianca do for all of us? 11. Find in the glossary the meaning of: chieftain, unconscious, booming, despair, fragments, pennon. 12. *Pronounce:* heroic, shroud, helm.

Phrases for Study

born to rule the storm, **120**, 6
heroic blood, **120**, 7
lone post of death, **121**, 15
wreathing fires, **121**, 20
splendor wild, **121**, 21
borne their part, **122**, 6

Tubal Cain

Charles Mackay

Old Tubal Cain was a man of might
In the days when the earth was young;
By the fierce red light of his furnace bright
The strokes of his hammer rung;
And he lifted high his brawny hand
On the iron glowing clear,
Till the sparks rushed out in scarlet showers,
As he fashioned the sword and spear.
And he sang, "Hurrah for my handiwork!
Hurrah for the spear and sword!
Hurrah for the hand that shall wield them well!
For he shall be king and lord."

To Tubal Cain came many a one,
As he wrought by his roaring fire.
And each one prayed for a strong steel blade,
As the crown of his desire;
And he made them weapons, sharp and strong,
Till they shouted loud in glee,
And gave him gifts of pearls and gold,
And spoils of forest free.
And they sang, "Hurrah for Tubal Cain,
Who hath given us strength anew!
Hurrah for the Smith! hurrah for the fire!
And hurrah for the metal true!"

But a sudden change came o'er his heart
    Ere the setting of the sun,
And Tubal Cain was filled with pain
    For the evil he had done.
He saw that men, with rage and hate,
    Made war upon their kind;
That the land was red with the blood they shed
    In their lust for carnage, blind.
And he said, "Alas, that ever I made,
    Or that skill of mine should plan,
The spear and the sword for men whose joy
    Is to slay their fellow-man!"

And for many a day old Tubal Cain
    Sat brooding o'er his woe;
And his hand forbore to smite the ore,
    And his furnace smoldered low;
But he rose at last with a cheerful face
    And a bright, courageous eye,
And bared his strong right arm for work,
    While the quick flames mounted high;
And he sang, "Hurrah for my handiwork!"
    And the red sparks lit the air—
"Not alone for the blade was the bright steel made"—
    And he fashioned the first plowshare.

And men, taught wisdom from the past.
    In friendship joined their hands,
Hung the sword in the hall, the spear on the wall,
    And plowed the willing lands;
And sang, "Hurrah for Tubal Cain!
    Our stanch good friend is he;

And, for the plowshare and the plow,
    To him our praise shall be.
But, while oppression lifts its head,
    Or a tyrant would be lord,
Though we may thank him for the plow,
    We'll not forget the sword."

NOTES AND QUESTIONS

Biography. Charles Mackay (1814-1889) was a Scotch poet. For some years he was editor of the *Glasgow Argus,* and afterwards he became editor of the *Illustrated London News.* During the Civil War he was the special correspondent of the *London Times* at New York. He wrote many poems of interest to young people.

Historical Note. Tubal Cain was one of the sons of Lamech, a descendant of Cain. He was an "instructor of every artificer in brass and iron," that is, he was the first smith. All that we really know of his history is given in the fourth chapter of Genesis.

Discussion. 1. What did Tubal Cain first make on his forge? 2. Why did he think that his work was good? 3. What did men say about him? 4. How did Tubal Cain feel when he saw what men were doing with the products of his forge? 5. What did he do then? 6. What made his face "cheerful" at last? 7. Is it better to make instruments of war or tools for industry? 8. Why was Tubal Cain happy when he made plows? 9. Was he working for money, or for service? 10. Explain the last four lines. 11. Find in the glossary the meaning of: fashioned, handiwork, wrought, anew, lust, brooding, forbore, plowshare. 12. *Pronounce:* hurrah, wield, carnage, smoldered, stanch.

Phrases for Study

man of might, **123**, 1
earth was young, **123**, 2
crown of his desire, **123**, 16
spoils of forest free, **123**, 20
metal true, **123**, 24
upon their kind, **124**, 6
whose joy is to slay, **124**, 11
smite the ore, **124**, 15
taught wisdom from the past, **124**, 25
willing lands, **124**, 28
oppression lifts its head, **125**, 3
tyrant would be lord, **125**, 4

The Inchcape Rock

Robert Southey

No stir in the air, no stir in the sea;
The ship was still as she could be;
Her sails from Heaven received no motion;
Her keel was steady in the ocean.

Without either sign or sound of their shock,
The waves flowed over the Inchcape Rock;
So little they rose, so little they fell,
They did not move the Inchcape Bell.

The holy Abbot of Aberbrothok
Had placed that bell on the Inchcape Rock;
On a buoy in the storm it floated and swung,
And over the waves its warning rung.

When the rock was hid by the surge's swell,
The mariners heard the warning bell;
And then they knew the perilous rock
And blessed the Abbot of Aberbrothok.

The sun in heaven was shining gay;
All things were joyful on that day;
The sea-birds screamed as they wheeled around,
And there was joyance in their sound.

The buoy of the Inchcape Bell was seen,
A darker speck on the ocean green;

Sir Ralph the Rover walked his deck,
And he fixed his eye on the darker speck.

He felt the cheering power of spring;
It made him whistle, it made him sing;
His heart was mirthful to excess,
But the Rover's mirth was wickedness.

His eye was on the Inchcape float;
Quoth he, "My men, put out the boat
And row me to the Inchcape Rock,
And I'll plague the Abbot of Aberbrothok."

The boat is lowered, the boatmen row,
And to the Inchcape Rock they go;
Sir Ralph bent over from the boat,
And he cut the bell from the Inchcape float.

Down sank the bell, with a gurgling sound;
The bubbles rose and burst around;
Quoth Sir Ralph, "The next who comes to the Rock
Won't bless the Abbot of Aberbrothok!"

Sir Ralph the Rover sailed away;
He scoured the seas for many a day;
And now grown rich with plundered store,
He steers his course for Scotland's shore.

So thick a haze o'erspreads the sky
They cannot see the sun on high;
The wind hath blown a gale all day;
At evening it hath died away.

On the deck the Rover takes his stand;
So dark it is they see no land.
Quoth Sir Ralph, "It will be lighter soon,
For there is the dawn of the rising moon."

"Canst hear," said one, "the breakers roar?
For methinks we should be near the shore."
"Now where we are I cannot tell,
But I wish I could hear the Inchcape Bell."

They hear no sound; the swell is strong;
Though the wind hath fallen, they drift along
Till the vessel strikes with a shivering shock
"O Christ! it is the Inchcape Rock!"

NOTES AND QUESTIONS

Biographical and Historical Note. Robert Southey (1774-1843) was an English poet. From 1813 until his death he was Poet Laureate of England.

Bell Rock, or Inchcape, is a reef of red sandstone near the Firth of Tay, on the east coast of Scotland. At the time of the spring tides part of the reef is uncovered to the height of four feet. Because so many vessels were wrecked upon these rocks the Abbot of Aberbrothok is said to have placed a bell there, "fixed upon a tree or timber, which rang continually, being moved by the sea."

Discussion. 1. What picture do you see when you read the first stanza? The second stanza? 2. This story tells about a man who failed. You have read about Peter's heroism and the lives he saved, about the service a schoolboy rendered to a poor old woman, about a blacksmith who joyously made the tools by which men raised fruit and grain for food, and about a boy who was faithful to orders, even though it cost his life. Here you see how men sometimes try to make of no effect all the good deeds that others perform. 3. The Abbot of Aberbrothok was a man who lived up to the ideal of service; how did he do this, and why did men bless him? 4. Ralph the Rover was a pirate; why did he destroy the bell? 5. All the others in the stories you have read, boys and men, thought less of themselves than of others; of what did Ralph think? 6. Is a merchant who raises the price of food as high as he can, who makes huge profits while others suffer or starve, any better than Ralph the Rover? 7. What test of loyalty to our country, mentioned on page 85, would prove such a man to be a "bad citizen"? 8. Ralph was a free man—what did "liberty" mean to him? 9. What happened to Ralph the Rover? 10. Find in the glossary the meaning of: keel, abbot, perilous, joyance, breakers, methinks. 11. *Pronounce:* buoy, mariners, excess, scoured.

Phrases for Study

sound of their shock, **126**, 5
surge's swell, **126**, 13
cheering power of spring, **127**, 3
mirthful to excess, **127**, 5
plague the Abbot, **127**, 10
plundered store, **127**, 21

My Boyhood on the Prairie*

Hamlin Garland

The cabin faced a level plain with no tree in sight. A mile away to the west stood a low stone house, and immediately in front of us opened a half-section of unfenced sod. To the north, as far as I could see, the land billowed like a russet ocean, with scarcely a roof to fleck its lonely spread. I cannot say that I liked or disliked it. I merely marveled at it; and while I wandered about the yard, the hired man scorched some cornmeal mush in a skillet, and this, with some butter and gingerbread, made up my first breakfast in Mitchell County.

For a few days my brother and I had little to do other than to keep the cattle from straying, and we used our leisure in becoming acquainted with the region round about.

To the south the sections were nearly all settled upon,

---

* See "Suggestions for Silent Reading," page 163.

for in that direction lay the county town; but to the north and on into Minnesota rolled the unplowed sod, the feeding ground of the cattle, the home of foxes and wolves, and to the west, just beyond the highest ridges, we loved to think the bison might still be seen.

The cabin on this rented farm was a mere shanty, a shell of pine boards, which needed reinforcing to make it habitable, and one day my father said, "Well, Hamlin, I guess you'll have to run the plow team this fall. I must help neighbor Button reinforce the house, and I can't afford to hire another man."

This seemed a fine commission for a lad of ten, and I drove my horses into the field that first morning with a manly pride which added an inch to my stature. I took my initial "round" at a "land" which stretched from one side of the quarter section to the other, in confident mood. I was grown up!

But alas! My sense of elation did not last long. To guide a team for a few minutes as an experiment was one thing—to plow all day like a hired hand was another. It was not a chore; it was a job. It meant moving to and fro hour after hour, day after day, with no one to talk to but the horses. It meant trudging eight or nine miles in the forenoon and as many more in the afternoon, with less than an hour off at noon. It meant dragging the heavy implement around the corners, and it meant also many shipwrecks; for the thick, wet stubble often threw the share completely out of the ground, making it necessary for me to halt the team and jerk the heavy plow backward for a new start.

Although strong and active, I was rather short, even for a ten-year-old, and to reach the plow handles I was obliged to lift my hands above my shoulders; and so with the guiding lines crossed over my back and my worn straw hat bobbing just above the cross brace I must have made a comical figure. At any rate nothing like it had been seen in the neighborhood; and the people on the road to town, looking across the field, laughed and called to me, and neighbor Button said to my father in my hearing, "That chap's too young to run a plow," a judgment which pleased and flattered me greatly.

Harriet cheered me by running out occasionally to meet me as I turned the nearest corner, and sometimes Frank consented to go all the way around, chatting breathlessly as he trotted along behind. At other times he brought me a cookie and a glass of milk, a deed which helped to shorten the forenoon. And yet plowing became tedious.

The flies were savage, especially in the middle of the day, and the horses, tortured by their lances, drove badly, twisting and turning in their rage. Their tails were continually getting over the lines, and in stopping to kick their tormentors they often got astride the traces, and in other ways made trouble for me. Only in the early morning or when the sun sank low at night were they able to move quietly along their way.

The soil was the kind my father had been seeking, a smooth, dark, sandy loam, which made it possible for a lad to do the work of a man. Often the share would go the entire "round" without striking a root or a pebble as big as a walnut, the steel running steadily with a crisp, crunching, ripping sound which I rather liked to hear. In truth, the work would have been quite tolerable had it not been so long drawn out. Ten hours of it, even on a fine day, made about twice too many for a boy.

Meanwhile I cheered myself in every imaginable way. I whistled. I sang. I studied the clouds. I gnawed the beautiful red skin from the seed vessels which hung upon the wild rose bushes, and I counted the prairie chickens as they began to come together in winter flocks, running through the stubble in search of food. I stopped now and again to examine the lizards unhoused by the share, and I measured the little granaries of wheat which the mice and gophers had deposited deep under the ground, storehouses which the plow had violated. My eyes dwelt enviously upon the sailing hawk and on the passing of ducks. The occasional shadowy figure of a prairie wolf made me wish for Uncle David and his rifle.

On certain days nothing could cheer me. When the bitter wind blew from the north, and the sky was filled with wild geese racing southward with swiftly hurrying clouds, winter seemed about to spring upon me. The horses' tails streamed in the wind. Flurries of snow covered me with clinging flakes, and the mud "gummed" my boots and trouser legs, clogging my steps. At such times I suffered from cold and loneliness—all sense of being a man evaporated. I was just a little boy, longing for the leisure of boyhood.

Day after day, through the month of October and deep into November, I followed that team, turning over two acres of stubble each day. I would not believe this without proof, but it is true! At last it grew so cold that in the early morning everything was white with frost, and I was obliged to put one hand in my pocket to keep it warm, while holding the plow with the other; but I didn't mind this so much, for it hinted at the close of autumn. I've no doubt facing the wind in this way was excellent discipline, but I didn't think it necessary then, and my heart was sometimes bitter and rebellious.

My father did not intend to be severe. As he had always been an early riser and a busy toiler, it seemed perfectly natural and good discipline that his sons should also plow and husk corn at ten years of age. He often told of beginning life as a "bound boy" at nine, and these stories helped me to perform my own tasks without whining.

At last there came a morning when by striking my heel upon the ground I convinced my boss that the soil was frozen. "All right," he said, "you may layoff this forenoon."

NOTES AND QUESTIONS

Biography. Hamlin Garland (1860-1940) was born in Wisconsin. His father was a farmer-pioneer, who was always eager to be on the border line of the farming country; consequently, he moved from Wisconsin to Minnesota, from Minnesota to Iowa, and from Iowa to Dakota. The hope of cheaper land, better soil, and bigger crops led him on.

When Hamlin Garland turned his attention to literature, he decided to write truthfully of the western farmer's life and its great hardships in pioneer days, as well as its hopes and joys. In *A Son of the Middle Border*, an autobiography, from which "My Boyhood on the Prairie" is taken, he has given a most interesting record of experiences in the development of the Middle West. Mitchell County, where this scene is laid, is in Iowa.

Discussion. 1. Describe the boy's new home. 2. What work did the boy have to do? 3. In what spirit did he start the plowing? 4. Why did his "sense of elation" soon disappear? 5. Was his task harder than that of Peter or of the boy who helped "Somebody's Mother"? 6. Must a boy do some marvelous thing to be a hero? 7. How did the boy try to keep himself in good cheer? 8. On page 19 you are told that if you have eyes to see, "the world of nature is a fairyland." Why do you think this boy had "eyes to see"? Find your answer by reading the last two lines on page 131 and the first paragraph on page 132. 9. What made him wish for freedom? 10. *Class reading:* Page 131, line 8, to the end of the story. 11. *Outline for testing silent reading.* Tell the story briefly, using these topics: (a) the region and the cabin; (b) what plowing meant to a boy; (c) how the boy was cheered. 12. Find in the glossary the meaning of: marveled, scorched, skillet, ridges, reinforcing, habitable, commission, stature, implement, stubble, share, cross brace, judgment, tormentors, tolerable, unhoused, deposited, clogging, evaporated. 13. *Pronounce:* chore, tedious, loam, imaginable, gopher, leisure.

Phrases for Study

billowed like a russet ocean, **129**, 4
fleck its lonely spread, **129**, 5
county town, **130**, 1
initial round, **130**, 15
confident mood, **130**, 16
sense of elation, **130**, 18
guiding lines, **130**, 33
tortured by their lances, **131**, 15
astride the traces, **131**, 18
go the entire round, **131**, 24
plow had violated, **132**, 7
bound boy, **133**, 3

Woodman, Spare That Tree

George P. Morris

Woodman, spare that tree!
    Touch not a single bough;
In youth it sheltered me,
    And I'll protect it now.
'Twas my forefather's hand
    That placed it near his cot;
There, woodman, let it stand;
    Thy ax shall harm it not;

That old familiar tree,
    Whose glory and renown
Are spread o'er land and sea
    And wouldst thou hack it down?
Woodman, forbear thy stroke!
    Cut not its earth-bound ties;
Oh, spare that aged oak
    Now towering to the skies.

When but an idle boy,
    I sought its grateful shade;
In all their gushing joy,
    Here, too, my sisters played.
My mother kissed me here;
    My father pressed my hand
Forgive this foolish tear,
    But let that old oak stand!

My heart-strings round thee cling,
    Close as thy bark, old friend!
Here shall the wild-bird sing,
    And still thy branches bend.
Old tree! the storm still brave!
    And, woodman, leave the spot;
While I've a hand to save,
    Thy ax shall harm it not.

NOTES AND QUESTIONS

Biography. George P. Morris (1802-1864) was born in Philadelphia. He was an editor and a poet and was connected with a number of newspapers in New York City.

Discussion. 1. To whom is the poet speaking in these verses? 2. What does he wish to prevent? 3. Why is the tree dear to him? 4. Whom does he remember seeing under the tree? 5. What did they do there? 6. How will the poet protect the tree? 7. How does the American Forestry Association protect trees? 8. Why should trees be cared for and protected? 9. Why do we celebrate Arbor Day? 10. Find in the glossary the meaning of: forefather, renown, towering, heart-strings.

Phrases for Study

near his cot, **134**, 6
forbear thy stroke, **134**, 13
earth-bound ties, **134**, 14
storm still brave, **135**, 13

THE AMERICAN BOY

THEODORE ROOSEVELT

What we have a right to expect of the American boy is that he shall turn out to be a good American man. Now the chances are strong that he won't be much of a man unless he is a good deal of a boy. He must not be a coward or a weakling, a bully, a shirk, or a prig. He must work hard and play hard. He must be clean-minded and clean-lived, and able to hold his own against all comers. It is only on these conditions that he will grow into the kind of American man of whom America can be really proud.

No boy can afford to neglect his work, and, with a boy, work as a rule means study. A boy should work, and should work hard, at his lessons—in the first place, for the sake of what he will learn, and in the next place, for the sake of the effect upon his own character of resolutely settling down to learn it. Shiftlessness, slackness, indifference in studying are almost certain to mean inability to get on in other walks of life. I do not believe in mischief-doing in school hours, or in the kind of animal spirits that results in making bad scholars; and I believe that those boys who take part in rough, hard play outside of school will not find any need for horseplay in school. While they study they should study just as hard as they play football. It is wise to obey the homely old adage, "Work while you work; play while you play."

A boy needs both physical and moral courage. Neither can take the place of the other. A coward who will take a blow without returning it is a contemptible creature; but, after all, he is hardly as contemptible as the boy who dares not stand up for what he deems right against the sneers of his companions who are themselves wrong.

There is no need to be a prig. There is no need for a boy to preach about his own conduct and virtue. If he does, he will make himself ridiculous. But there is need that he should practice decency; that he should be clean and straight, honest and truthful, gentle and tender, as well as brave.

The boy can best become a good man by being a good boy—not a goody-goody boy, but just a plain good boy. "Good," in the largest sense, should include whatever is fine, straightforward, clean, brave, and manly. The best boys I know—the best men I know—are good at their studies or their business, fearless and stalwart, hated and feared by all that is wicked, incapable of submitting to wrong-doing, and equally incapable of being aught but tender to the weak and helpless. A healthy-minded boy should feel hearty contempt for the coward, and even more hearty indignation for the boy who bullies girls or small boys, or tortures animals.

Of course the effect that a thoroughly manly, thoroughly straight and upright boy can have upon the companions of his own age, and upon those who are younger, is incalculable. He cannot do good work if he is not strong and does not try with his whole heart and soul to count in any contest; and his strength will be a curse to himself and to everyone else if he does not have thorough command over himself and over his own evil passions, and if he does not use his strength on the side of decency, justice, and fair dealing.

In short, in life, as in a football game, the principle to follow is: Hit the line hard; don't foul and don't shirk, but hit the line hard! —*Abridged*

NOTES AND QUESTIONS

For **Biography**, see page 37.

Discussion. 1. This selection sums up all the stories of service that you have been reading. You will get most out of it if you will think back over these stories and use them as illustrations of what Mr. Roosevelt tells you is his ideal of the American boy. What examples, in these stories, can you find to illustrate the sentence, "He must not be a coward or a weakling. . . He must work hard and play hard"? 2. Illustrate, from the story of Lincoln, what Mr. Roosevelt says about study. What was Lincoln's attitude toward study? What is yours? Did Lincoln's studies have the effect on his character that Mr. Roosevelt speaks about? 3. What story illustrates the sentence, "There is need that he should practice decency; that he should be clean and straight, honest and truthful, *gentle and tender*, as well as brave"? 4. How does the story about life on the prairie illustrate the paragraph that begins, "The boy can best become a good man by being a good boy"? What is the difference between being "a good boy" and "a goody-goody boy"? 5. Was Ralph the Rover a brave man or a coward? 6. Apply the principle stated by Mr. Roosevelt at the end of the selection to the story about Washington and Braddock to the story about the boy on the prairie. 7. Can you relate an instance in which a manly boy had a good influence upon another boy or upon his companions? 8. Do you think the football slogan given in the last sentence on page 137 is a good principle of life? Memorize the slogan. 9. This selection is taken from *The Strenuous Life*; it first appeared in *St. Nicholas,* May, 1900. 10. Find in the glossary the meaning of: shirk, prig, resolutely, indifference, inability, horseplay, deems, indignation, bullies. 11. *Pronounce:* adage, neither, contemptible, ridiculous, stalwart, incapable; aught, incalculable.

Phrases for Study

against all comers, **136**, 7
walks of life, **136**, 17
animal spirits, **136**, 18
homely old adage, **136**, 23
physical and moral courage, **136**, 25
practice decency, **137**, 6
in the largest sense, **137**, 11
aught but tender, **137**, 16

HOME AND COUNTRY

A Backward Look

As you gazed through your Crystal Glass of Reading at the selections in Part 1, you saw reflected now pictures of home and now again a picture of that early Thanksgiving Day when Pilgrim and Indian sat down together to the "varied riches of gardens and woods and waves." When you heard Massasoit say at the feast, "The Good Spirit loves His white children best," you wondered about the truth of his statement and, as you thought about it, perhaps Abraham Lincoln came to mind. What do you think Lincoln, if he had been alive at that time, might have answered the Indian chief? The poems about home might be called memory-pictures of home. Why do you think older people remember with so much fondness their childhood homes? Imagine yourself telling your grandchildren about the home of your youth and about your home pleasures. What things would you mention? Why is it a good thing for a nation to have its people love their homes and the festival days like Christmas and Thanksgiving?

And now a turn of the Crystal Glass reveals a glorious flag, floating protectingly over us. How you love to look upon its starry folds. When statesmen and poets tell you of the meaning of Old Glory you realize that there is good reason for your pride and your love. What did Charles Sumner tell you about the meaning of the stars and the stripes and the colors of the flag? What did James Whitcomb Riley tell you about how Old Glory got its name? What were the circumstances under which Francis Scott Key wrote "The Star-Spangled Banner"? What are some of the things you can do to show your respect for the Flag?

What are some of the things you remember about Lincoln's boyhood? How does his method of memorizing compare with yours? The young George Washington showed remarkable bravery as Braddock's chief assistant. What other fine quality did he show? How may these stories about Washington and Lincoln help you to be a worthy citizen of the country they helped to found and preserve?

We admire all people who are helpful to others, but when in giving service, some forget about themselves and even sacrifice themselves for others, we regard these as heroes. Peter, in "The Leak in the Dike," and the boy in "Somebody's Mother" forgot about themselves in their service to others; one disregarded danger to himself, and the other the possible jeers of his playmates. Do you know of any instances of service in your school? It is fine to serve obediently under the command of superiors as did the young Casabianca, but it is even finer to think quickly in an emergency and to do what should be done when there is no one at hand to give orders. Who gave Peter his orders? Tubal Cain belongs to a group of men who have served their fellow men by useful inventions. Mention some other inventors and tell how they have helped mankind. Hamlin Garland gave you a glimpse of the pioneer's service to our country. What names of pioneers in your locality are honored for their service in the early days? What ideas of being useful home members did you get from Hamlin Garland and Theodore Roosevelt? How does the habit of being useful in the home fit one for being a good citizen? American boys and girls have many opportunities for service in the home, in the school, and in their other relations. Have you done any piece of service, in an organized way, in your school? Does your school belong to the Junior Red Cross, and does it try to follow the motto, "Go forth to serve"?

When you look back upon all that you have read of home and country, you no doubt come to the conclusion that "the man without a country" summed it all up when he said, "Stick to your family...Think of your home...And for your country and for your flag, never dream but of serving her."

From selections found in this book prepare a program for Washington's birthday.

Part II

Stories of Adventure

Hush! Again a forest and somebody up in a tree—not Robin Hood,...but an Eastern king with a glittering scimitar and turban...It is the setting-in of the bright Arabian Nights.

Oh, now all common things become uncommon and enchanted to me. All lamps are wonderful; all rings are talismans...Trees are for Ali Baba to hide in; beefsteaks are to throw down into the Valley of Diamonds that the precious stones may stick to them and be carried by the eagles to their nests, whence the traders, with loud cries, will scare them.

Charles Dickens

The Boyhood of Raleigh

STORIES OF ADVENTURE

A Forward Look

When something out of the ordinary happens to you, you call it an adventure. Perhaps you came very near getting drowned in the swimming pool, or you found a purse with some money and some queer treasures in it, or you met a very curious old man, or you caught a rabbit after an exciting chase, or you went on a long journey and saw many wonderful things. If you have had such an experience, you like to tell about it to your friends, and if you have not, you like to hear the stories told by people who have had some thrilling adventure of their own.

From the earliest times to the present the man who has had some unusual experience to tell about has been a favorite. We are eager to hear such stories; they make life seem more interesting and varied. Nowadays we read such stories in books and magazines; we are not dependent upon hearing them from the lips of those who have lived lives of adventure. But centuries ago, before there were books and newspapers, when any journey away from home, even for a few miles, was filled with peril, the traveler who could tell of marvelous things, or the weaver of tales who had a vivid imagination so that he could tell about things that seemed really true, found eager hearers. Among the French, stories about Roland, the wonderful knight who fought in the wars of the Emperor Charlemagne, were known by every boy and girl. The English had King Arthur, and Saint George, and Robin Hood.

Besides these legends about a national hero, there are many collections of stories that have grown up among the common people. One of the oldest of these collections of tales is that known as the *Arabian Nights.* For hundreds of years these stories were told in the tents of the desert or in the gay bazaars of the cities of the East. About the time of the discovery of America they were written down and became known as the *Arabian Nights Entertainment,* or the tales of a thousand and one nights. We are told that there was once a cruel king who planned to slay all the women in his kingdom. His wife determined to tell him such wonderful stories that he would give up his cruel purpose. So she told him of enchanted gardens, of caves filled with treasure, of palaces built in a night, and of many other things. He was so eager to hear these stories that a thousand and one nights passed before he could escape from the spell that she laid upon him. By this time he was so much in love with her that he withdrew his wicked order. You may see how marvelous were these tales by reading the stories of Aladdin, of Ali Baba, and of Sindbad the Sailor. Perhaps when you have finished them you will not wonder that the king found the thousand and one nights so happy that he lost his desire to carry out his cruel purpose.

Next, you are introduced to one of the most popular of English heroes, Robin Hood. Many old ballads and tales, older than the first American colony, have come down to us with these stories of the famous outlaw. The stories are very different from those of the *Arabian Nights.* They have no treasure caves or magic lamps or voyages to strange countries in them. They tell of contests in archery, for which the English were famous; of wrestling and swimming matches; of outlaws and dwellers in the greenwood. Because he was their champion against unjust taxation and oppressive laws, Robin Hood was the idol of the common people. They made up games about him, in which old and young took part. Wandering minstrels sang about him. "Lincoln green," the color of the clothing worn by Robin and his followers, was a favorite with all foresters. Why Robin was so loved you may determine for yourselves by reading the stories of Robin Hood given in the pages that follow.

In *Gulliver's Travels* we pass from stories like the *Arabian Nights* and "Robin Hood," which grew up among the common people, to a story composed by a single author who wrote out his material and then had it printed in order that all might enjoy it. We do not know who wrote the story of Ali Baba or the adventures of Robin Hood, but we know all about Jonathan Swift, the great English writer who tells us the story of Gulliver's adventures among the little people, or Lilliputians. Gulliver also had wonderful experiences among a race of giants and in a land where the citizens were horses that were more intelligent than men.

Somewhat different from all the other tales in this part of our book is the story of Robinson Crusoe, written by Daniel Defoe about two hundred years ago and here condensed for your enjoyment. There was, in Defoe's time, a sailor, Alexander Selkirk by name, who was left by his shipmates on an island and who lived by himself for four years before he attracted the attention of a passing ship. This suggested the idea of *Robinson Crusoe* to Defoe, but he has greatly expanded the story. Crusoe lived on his lonely island for twenty-seven years. During this time he learned how to make tools, to build his house, to cultivate his farm, to prepare to defend himself against an enemy's attack, and to civilize barbarous people.

In its original form each of the stories in this group makes a good-sized book. While some incidents and many details have been omitted here in order to shorten and simplify the stories, the main plot and all the most interesting incidents are given.

The world is full of stories of adventure; these are only samples of the joyful experiences that you may have through your power to read. And you boys and girls are more fortunate than those who lived in the time of Aladdin, or even those who lived in the time of Robin Hood or Robinson Crusoe, for they had no books at all, or only a few, and if they had any, these books were poorly printed, with very ugly illustrations, not at all like the wonderful books that you may have at will.

But of all the stories that might have been selected, the ones placed before you have been chosen for two reasons. First of all, they are interesting, and are to be read for pure enjoyment. And next, these stories leave with you certain ideas that are well worthwhile. Aladdin and Ali Baba, the heroes of the Arabian Nights stories, who became rich through their strange adventures, helped their neighbors with their wealth. Robin Hood, too, helped the poor oppressed people of his time, though he did many things that would be wrong today. Robinson Crusoe's lonely life on a desert island shows us how much we depend upon the work of those about us. And Captain Gulliver, in the midst of his wonderful adventures, always kept in mind the ideas of justice and honor.

So in all these stories there is a sense of justice and responsibility. Nowadays—at least in America—men are free. Buried treasure is as hard to find as ever, but it can be found. The man who works hard, who seizes opportunities, who builds up a business or runs a farm, can find his treasure. The government will protect him; we no longer need to use the methods of Robin Hood to get justice. The important question is whether the Ali Babas and Aladdins of our day will feel just such responsibility to others as you find recorded in these stories, and whether the desire to help the unfortunate is as strong in our free America as it was in the heart of Robin Hood.

STORIES FROM THE ARABIAN NIGHTS

ALADDIN, OR THE WONDERFUL LAMP*

Aladdin was the son of Mustapha, a poor tailor in one of the rich provinces of China. When the boy was old enough to learn a trade, his father took him into his own workshop. But Aladdin, being but an idle fellow, loved play more than work, and spent his days playing in the public streets with other boys as idle as himself.

His father died while he was yet very young; but Aladdin still continued his foolish ways, and his mother was forced to spin cotton night and day in order to keep herself and her boy.

When Aladdin was about fifteen years old, he was one day playing in the streets with some of his companions. A stranger who was going by stopped and looked at him. This stranger was a famous African magician, who, having need of the help of some ignorant person, no sooner beheld Aladdin than he knew by his whole manner and appearance that he was a person of small prudence and very fit to be made a tool of. The magician inquired of some persons standing near, the name and character of

* See "Suggestions for Silent Reading," page 163.

Aladdin, and the answers proved to him that he had judged rightly of the boy.

The stranger, pressing in among the crowd of lads, clapped his hand on Aladdin's shoulder, and said, "My good lad, are you not the son of Mustapha, the tailor?"

"Yes, sir," said Aladdin; "but my father has been dead this long time."

"Alas!" cried he, "what unhappy news! I am your father's brother, child. I have been many years abroad; and now that I have come home in the hope of seeing him, you tell me he is dead!" And all the while tears ran down the stranger's cheeks, and his bosom heaved with sighs. Then, pulling out a purse, he gave Aladdin two pieces of gold, saying, "Take this, my boy, to your mother. Tell her that I will come and see her tonight, and sup with her."

Pleased with the money, Aladdin ran home to his mother. "Mother," said he, "have I an uncle?" His mother told him he had not, whereupon Aladdin pulled out his gold and told her that a man who said he was his father's brother was coming to sup with her that very evening. Full of bewilderment, the good woman set out for the market, where she bought provisions, and was busy preparing the supper when the magician knocked at the door. He entered, followed by a porter who brought all kinds of delicious fruits and sweetmeats for their dessert.

As soon as they sat down to supper, he gave Aladdin's mother an account of his travels, saying that for forty years he had been away from home, in order to see the wonders of distant countries. Then, turning toward Aladdin, he asked his name. "I am called Aladdin," said he. "Well, Aladdin," said the magician, "what business do you follow?"

At this question Aladdin hung down his head, and was not a little abashed when his mother made answer: "Aladdin is an idle fellow; his father strove all he could to teach him his trade, but could not succeed; and since his death, in spite of all I can say to him, he does nothing but idle away his time in the streets, so that I despair of his ever coming to any good." With these words the poor woman burst into tears, and the magician, turning to Aladdin, said: "This is not well, Nephew; you must think of helping yourself and getting your livelihood. I will help you as far as I may. What think you—shall I take a shop and furnish it for you?" Aladdin was overjoyed at the idea, for he thought there was very little labor in keeping a shop, and he told his uncle this would suit him better than anything else.

"I will take you with me tomorrow," said the magician, "clothe you as handsomely as the best merchants in the city, and then we will open a shop."

Aladdin's mother thanked him very heartily and begged Aladdin to behave so as to prove himself worthy of the good fortune promised by his kind uncle.

Next day the stranger called for Aladdin as he had promised and led him to a merchant's, where clothes for all sorts of people were sold. Then he caused Aladdin to try on the handsomest suits, and choosing the one Aladdin preferred, he paid the merchant for it at once. The pretended uncle then took Aladdin to visit the bazaars, the khans where the foreign merchants were, and the most splendid mosques, and gave him a merry feast in the evening.

The next morning Aladdin got up and dressed himself very early, so impatient was he to see his uncle. Presently he saw him coming, and ran to meet him. The magician greeted him very kindly. "Come, my good boy," he said with a smile. "I will today show you some very fine things."

He then led him through some beautiful gardens with great houses standing in the midst of them. Aladdin did nothing but exclaim at their beauty, and so his uncle by degrees led him on farther and farther into the country.

"We shall now," said he to Aladdin, "go no farther, for I shall here show you some extraordinary wonders that no one besides yourself will ever have seen. I am now going to strike a light, and do you, in the meantime, collect all the dry sticks and leaves that you can find, in order to make a fire."

There were so many pieces of dry sticks scattered about this place that Aladdin collected more than enough by the time his uncle had struck a light. The magician then set them on fire, and as soon as they were in a blaze he threw a certain perfume, that he had ready in his hand, upon them. A dense smoke arose, while the magician spoke some mysterious words. At the same instant the ground shook slightly, and, opening in the spot where they stood, showed a square stone about a foot and a half across, with a brass ring in the center.

Aladdin was frightened out of his wits and was about to run away, when the magician suddenly gave him a box on the ear so violent as to beat him down and very nearly to knock some of his teeth out. Poor Aladdin, with tears in his eyes and trembling in every limb, got up. "My dear uncle," he cried, "what have I done to deserve so severe a blow?" "I have good reasons for it," replied the magician. "Do you but obey me, and you will not repent of it. Underneath that stone is a great hidden treasure, which will make you richer than many kings if you will be attentive to what I shall say to you."

Aladdin had now got the better of his fright. "Well," said he, "what must I do? Tell me; I am ready to obey you in everything!" "Well said!" replied the magician; "come to me, then; take hold of this ring, and lift up the stone."

To Aladdin's surprise the stone was raised without any trouble, and then he could see a small opening three or four feet deep, at the bottom of which was a little door, with steps to go down still lower. "You must now," said the magician, "go down into this cavern, and when you have come to the bottom of the steps, you will see an open door which leads into three great halls. In each of these you will see, on both sides of you, four bronze vases as large as tubs, full of gold and silver, but you must not touch any of it.

"When you get to the first hall, bind your robe around you. Then go to the second without stopping, and thence in the same manner to the third. Above all, be very particular not to go near the walls or even to touch them with your robe; for if any part of your dress should chance to touch them, your instant death will be the consequence. At the far end of the third hall there is a door which leads to a garden planted with beautiful trees, all of which are full of fruit. Go straight forward, and follow a path which you will see. This will bring you to the bottom of a flight of fifty steps, at the top of which there is a terrace.

"There you will see a niche and in it a lighted lamp. Take the lamp and extinguish it. Then throw out the wick and the liquid that is within, and put the lamp in your bosom. If you should wish very much to gather any of the fruit in the garden, you may do so; and there is nothing to prevent your taking as much as you please."

When the magician had given these directions to Aladdin, he took off a ring which he had on one of his fingers and put it on his pretended nephew, telling him at the same time that it was to secure him against every evil that might otherwise happen to him. "Go, my child," he said; "descend boldly; we shall now both of us become immensely rich for the rest of our lives."

ALADDIN FINDS THE WONDERFUL LAMP

Aladdin jumped willingly into the opening and went down to the bottom of the steps. He found the three halls exactly as the magician had said. These he passed through with the greatest care, keeping in mind his uncle's warning. He went on to the garden, and mounted to the terrace without stopping. There in a niche was the lamp, which he seized, and after he had thrown out the oil which it contained, he put it in his bosom.

This done, he returned to the garden. The trees here were all full of the most extraordinary fruit. Never before had he seen fruits of so many different colors. The white were pearls; the sparkling and transparent were diamonds; the deep red were rubies; the paler, a particular sort of ruby called balas; the green, emeralds; the blue, turquoises; the violet, amethysts; those tinged with yellow, sapphires. All were of the largest size, and finer than were ever seen before in the whole world. Aladdin was not yet of an age to know their value, and thought they were all only pieces of colored glass.

However, the variety, brilliancy, and extraordinary size of each sort tempted him to gather some of each; and he took so many of every color that he filled both his pockets, as well as the two new purses the magician had bought for him at the time he made him a present of his new suit.

Since his pockets were already full, he fastened the two purses on each side of his girdle, and also wrapped some of the gems in its folds, as it was of silk and made very full. In this manner he carried his treasures so that they could not fall out. He did not forget to fill even his bosom quite full, between his robe and his shirt.

Laden in this manner with the most immense treasure,

though ignorant of its value, Aladdin made haste through the three halls, in order that he might not make his uncle wait too long. Having passed through them with the same caution as before, he began to ascend the steps he had come down, and reached the entrance of the cave, where the magician was impatiently waiting.

When Aladdin saw his uncle, he called to him, "Help me up!" "My dear boy," replied the magician, "you had better first give me the lamp, as that will only hinder you." "It is not at all in my way," said Aladdin, "and I will give it to you when I am out." The magician still persevered in wishing to get the lamp before he helped Aladdin out of the cave; but the boy had so covered it with the fruit of the trees that he absolutely refused to give it. The wicked magician was in the greatest despair at the obstinate resistance the boy made and fell into the most violent rage.

He then threw some perfume on the fire and had hardly spoken two magic words before the stone, which served to shut up the entrance to the cavern, returned of its own accord to the place, with all the earth over it, exactly in the same state as it was when the magician and Aladdin first arrived there.

When Aladdin found himself buried alive, he called aloud a thousand times to his uncle, telling him he was ready to give him the lamp. But all his cries were useless, and, having no other means of making himself heard, he remained in perfect darkness.

Finally he went down to the bottom of the stairs, intending to go toward the light in the garden, where he had been before. But the walls, which had been opened by enchantment, were now shut by the same means. The poor boy felt all around him several times, but could not discover the least opening. He then redoubled his cries and tears and sat down upon the step of his dungeon, without the least hope of ever seeing the light of day again.

For two days Aladdin remained in this state, without either eating or drinking. On the third day, feeling that his death was near, he clasped his hands in prayer and said in a loud tone of voice, "There is no strength or power but in the great and high heavens." In this act of joining his hands he happened, without thinking of it, to rub the ring which the magician had put upon his finger.

Instantly a genius of enormous figure and horrid countenance rose out of the earth. This genius, who was so extremely tall that his head touched the roof, addressed these words to Aladdin: "What do you wish? I am ready to obey you as your slave, both I and the other slaves of the ring." Weak and terrified, and scarcely daring to hope, Aladdin cried, "Whoever you are, take me, if you are able, out of this place!" No sooner had his lips formed the words than he found himself on the outside of the cave, at the very spot where the magician had left him. Almost unable to believe his good fortune, he arose trembling, and seeing the city in the distance, made his way back by the same road over which he had come. Such a long weary road he found it to his mother's door that when he reached it he was fainting from hunger and fatigue.

His mother, whose heart had been almost broken by his long absence, received him joyfully and refreshed him with food. When he had regained his strength, he told her all and showed her the lamp and the colored fruits and the wonderful ring on his finger. His mother thought little of the jewels, as she was quite ignorant of their value; so Aladdin put them all behind one of the cushions of the sofa on which they were sitting.

Next morning when Aladdin awoke, his first thought

was that he was very hungry and would like some breakfast. "Alas, my child," said his mother, "I have not a morsel of bread to give you. Last night you ate all the food in the house. However, I have a little cotton of my own spinning. I will go and sell it and buy something for our dinner."

"Keep your cotton, Mother, for another time," said Aladdin, "and give me the lamp which I brought with me yesterday. I will go and sell that, and the money will serve us for breakfast and dinner too; perhaps also for supper."

Aladdin's mother took the lamp from the place where she had put it. "Here it is," she said to her son; "but it is very dirty; if I were to clean it a little, perhaps it might sell for something more." She then took some water and a little fine sand with which to clean it. But she had scarcely begun to rub the lamp, when a hideous and gigantic genius rose out of the ground before her, and cried with a voice as loud as thunder, "What do you wish? I am ready to obey you as your slave, both I and the other slaves of the lamp."

Aladdin's mother was much terrified, but Aladdin, who had seen the genius in the cavern, did not lose his presence of mind. Seizing the lamp, he answered in a firm voice, "I am hungry; bring me something to eat." The genius disappeared and returned a moment later with a large silver basin, which he carried on his head. In it were twelve covered dishes of the same material, filled with the most delicious meats, and six loaves as white as snow upon as many plates, and in his hand he carried two silver cups. All these the genius placed upon the table and instantly vanished.

When Aladdin's mother had recovered from her fright, they both sat down to their meal in the greatest delight imaginable, for never before had they eaten such delicate meats or seen such splendid dishes.

The remains of this feast provided them with food for

some days, and when it was all gone, Aladdin sold the silver dishes one by one for their support. In this way they lived happily for several years, for Aladdin had been sobered by his adventure, and now behaved with the greatest wisdom and prudence. He took care to visit the principal shops and public places, speaking only with wise and prudent persons; and in this way he gathered much wisdom, and grew to be a courteous and handsome youth.

Aladdin Weds the Princess

One day Aladdin told his mother that he intended to ask the sultan to give him his daughter in marriage.

"Truly, my son," said his mother, "you seem to have forgotten that your father was but a poor tailor; and indeed I do not know who will dare to go and speak to the sultan about it." "You yourself must," said he, decidedly. "I!" cried his mother, in the greatest surprise; "I go to the sultan! Not I, indeed; I will take care that I am not joined to such folly. You know very well that no one can make any demand of the sultan without bringing a rich present, and where shall such poor folk as we find one?"

Thereupon Aladdin told his mother that while talking with the merchants in the bazaar he had learned to know the value of their gems, and for a long time he had known that nothing which the merchants had in their shops was half so fine as those jewels he had brought home from the enchanted cave. So his mother took them from the drawer where they had been hidden and put them in a dish of fine porcelain.

Aladdin's mother, now sure that such a gift was one that could not fail to please the sultan, at last agreed to do everything her son wished. She took the porcelain dish with its precious contents and folded it up in a very fine linen cloth. She then took another, less fine, and tied the four corners of it together, that she might carry it without trouble. This done, she took the road toward the palace of the sultan.

Trembling, she told the sultan of her son's boldness and begged his mercy for Aladdin and for herself. The sultan heard her kindly; then before giving any answer to her request, he asked her what she had with her so carefully tied up in a linen cloth. Aladdin's mother unfolded the cloths and humbly laid the jewels before him.

It is impossible to express the surprise which this monarch felt when he saw before him such a quantity of the most precious, perfect, and brilliant jewels, the size of which was greater than any he had ever seen before. For some moments he gazed at them, speechless. Then he took the present from the hand of Aladdin's mother and exclaimed, in a transport of joy, "Ah! how very beautiful, how very wonderful they are!"

Then turning to his grand vizier, he showed him the gems and talked privately to him for some minutes. At last he said to Aladdin's mother: "My good woman, I will indeed make your son happy by marrying him to the princess, my daughter, as soon as he shall send me forty large basins of massive gold, quite full of the same varieties of precious stones which you have already presented me with, brought by an equal number of black slaves, each of whom shall be led by a white slave, young, well-made, handsome, and richly dressed. These are the conditions upon which I am ready to give him the princess, my daughter. Go, my good woman, and I will wait till you bring me his answer."

Full of disappointment, Aladdin's mother made her way home, and told her son the sultan's strange wish. But Aladdin only smiled, and when his mother had gone out, he took the lamp and rubbed it. Instantly the genius appeared, and Aladdin commanded him to lose no time in bringing the present which the sultan had wished for. The genius only said that his commands should be at once obeyed and then disappeared.

In a very short time the genius returned with forty black slaves, each carrying upon his head a large golden basin of great weight, full of pearls, diamonds, rubies, and emeralds, quite as fine as the jewels that Aladdin's mother had given the sultan. Each basin was covered with a cloth of silver, embroidered with flowers of gold. There were also forty white slaves, as Aladdin had commanded. All these slaves with their golden basins entirely filled the house, which was but small, as well as the court in front and the garden behind it.

Aladdin's mother now came back and almost fainted when she saw this great crowd and all its magnificence. Aladdin desired her at once to follow the procession of slaves to the palace and present to the sultan the dowry of the princess.

The astonishment of the sultan at the sight of all these riches is hardly to be imagined. After gazing upon the slaves with their shining heaps of jewels, he said to Aladdin's mother, "Go, my good woman, and tell your son that I am waiting with open arms to embrace him!"

Aladdin was so delighted with this news that he could hardly answer his mother, and, hastening to his chamber, he shut the door. Once more he summoned the genius, who brought to him garments that shone like the sun. The genius also brought him a splendid charger and twenty slaves to march on either side of him on the way to the sultan's palace, all holding purses of gold to scatter among the people.

If there had been a crowd before, there was ten times as great a one now to watch Aladdin as he rode to the sultan's palace and to pick up the gold pieces which were showered by his slaves as he went. The sultan came down from his throne to greet him, and all was feasting and joy in the palace.

After the feast the judge drew up a contract of marriage between Aladdin and the beautiful princess. As soon as this was done, the sultan asked Aladdin if he wished to remain in the palace and complete all the ceremonies that day. "Sire," he replied, "however impatient I may be to have entire possession of all your majesty's bounties, I beg you to permit me to wait until I shall have built a palace to receive the princess in, that shall be worthy of her; and for this purpose I request that you will have the goodness to point out a suitable place for it near your own, that I may always be ready to pay my court to your majesty. I will then neglect nothing to get it finished with all possible diligence."

"My son," answered the sultan, "take the open space before my palace; but remember that, to have my happiness complete, I cannot see you united too soon to my daughter." Having said this, he again embraced Aladdin, who now took leave of the sultan as if he had been brought up and had spent all his life at court.

As soon as Aladdin reached home, he again summoned the genius and commanded him to build instantly the most gorgeous palace ever seen, on the spot of ground given by the sultan. Early the next morning the genius appeared. "Sir," said he, "your palace is finished; see if it is as you wish."

Words cannot paint the astonishment of the sultan and all his household at seeing this gorgeous palace shining in the place which only the day before had been empty and bare. The princess, too, rejoiced much at the sight. Her marriage with Aladdin was held the same day, and their happiness was the greatest that heart could wish.

Aladdin Loses and Regains the Lamp

For some months they lived thus, Aladdin showing great kindness to the poor, and pleasing all by his generosity.

About this time his old enemy, the African magician, found out by some of his magic arts that Aladdin was alive and enormously rich instead of being, as he had supposed, dead in the enchanted cave. He was filled with rage, and, vowing to destroy Aladdin, he immediately set out for China. There he learned that Aladdin had gone hunting and was not expected home for three or four days.

The magician bought a dozen shining new lamps, put them in a basket, and set out for Aladdin's palace. As he came near it he cried, "Who will change old lamps for new?"

When he came under the princess's windows, one of her slaves said, "Come, let us see if the old fool means what he says; there is an ugly old lamp lying on the cornice of the hall of four-and-twenty windows; we will put a new one in its place, if the old fellow is really in earnest." The princess having given permission, one of the slaves took the lamp to the magician, who willingly gave her the best he had among his new ones.

As soon as night arrived, the magician summoned the genius of the lamp and commanded him to transport him, the palace, and the princess to the remotest corner of Africa.

The confusion and grief of the sultan were terrible when he found the palace vanished and his daughter lost. The people ran in fear through the streets, and the soldiers were sent in search of Aladdin, who had not yet returned.

Aladdin was soon found and dragged before the sultan like a criminal. He would have been beheaded had not the sultan been afraid to enrage the people. "Go, wretch!" cried the sultan; "I grant thee thy life; but if ever thou appearest before me again, death shall overtake thee, unless in forty days thou bringest me tidings of my daughter."

Aladdin, wretched and downfallen, left the palace, not knowing whither to turn his steps. At length he stopped at a brook to bathe his eyes, which smarted with the tears he had shed. As he stooped, his foot slipped, and, catching hold of a piece of rock to save himself from falling, he pressed the magician's ring, which he still wore on his finger, and the genius of the ring appeared before him, saying, "What would you have?" "Oh, Genius," cried Aladdin, "bring my palace back without delay."

"What you command," replied the genius, "is not in my power; you must call the genius of the lamp."

"Then I command you," said Aladdin, "to transport me to the place where now it stands." Instantly Aladdin found himself beside his own palace, which stood in a meadow not far from a strange city; and the princess was then walking in her own chamber, weeping for her loss. Happening to come near to the window, she saw Aladdin under it, and making a sign to him to keep silence, she sent a slave to bring him in. The princess and her husband having kissed each other and shed many tears, Aladdin said, "Tell me, my princess, what has become of an old lamp which I left on the cornice of the hall of four-and-twenty windows?"

The princess then told how her slave had exchanged it for a new one, and said that the tyrant in whose power she was, always carried that very lamp in his bosom. Aladdin was then sure that this person was no other than his old enemy, the African magician.

After talking a long while, they hit upon a plan for getting back the lamp. Aladdin went into the city in the disguise of a slave and bought a powder. Then the princess invited the magician to sup with her. As she had never before shown him the least kindness, he was delighted and came. While they were at table, she ordered a slave to bring two cups of wine, one of which she had prepared by mixing in the powder. After pretending to taste the one she held in her hand, she asked the magician to change cups, as was the custom in China. He joyfully seized the goblet and, drinking it all at a draft, fell senseless on the floor.

Aladdin was at hand to snatch the lamp from his bosom. Hastily rubbing it, he summoned the genius, who instantly transported the palace and all it contained back to the place whence they had come.

Some hours after, the sultan, who had risen at break of day to mourn for his daughter, went to the window to look at the spot which he expected to see empty and vacant, and there to his unspeakable joy he saw Aladdin's palace shining in its place. He summoned his guards and hastened to embrace his daughter; and during a whole week nothing was heard but the sound of drums, trumpets, and cymbals, and there were all kinds of music and feasting, in honor of Aladdin's return with the princess.

Some time after this, the sultan died, and Aladdin and the princess ascended the throne. They reigned together many years and left many noble sons and daughters at their death.

Suggestions for Silent Reading

Some stories and poems must be read thoughtfully in order to gain the author's full meaning; such reading cannot be done rapidly. In other selections, the meaning can be grasped easily, and the reading can be rapid; in such cases we read mainly *for the story,* holding in mind the various incidents as the plot unfolds. Throughout this book certain stories, particularly those of "Part II," may well be read silently and reported on in class. The following suggestions will help you to gain power in silent reading:

(a) Time yourself by the clock as you read each story suggested for silent reading; what was your reading speed per page?

(b) Test your ability to get the thought quickly from the printed page (1) by noting how many of the questions that develop the main thoughts, under Discussion, you can answer after one reading, and (2) by telling the substance of the story from an outline. Sometimes this guiding outline is prepared for you, as in question 19, below; sometimes you are asked to prepare it. This outline may also be used at the close of the lesson as a guide in retelling the story. You may have to read parts of the story again to be able to answer all these questions and to give the substance of the story fully. Notice that the rapid silent readers in your class generally gain and retain more facts than the slow readers do. Try steadily to increase your speed in silent reading.

To supplement and give balance to the lessons in silent reading, certain passages notable for their beauty, their force, or their dramatic quality, are listed, under *Class readings,* to be read aloud.

NOTES AND QUESTIONS

Discussion. 1. What kind of boy was Aladdin? 2. What caused the magician to notice him? 3. What did the magician do to make Aladdin and his mother like him? 4. How did he force Aladdin to obey him? 5. What did Aladdin see when he raised the stone? 6. What directions did the magician give Aladdin before he descended the steps? 7. Explain the magician's anxiety to get the lamp before he helped Aladdin up from the cavern. 8. How was Aladdin rescued from the cavern? 9. How did he discover the power of his lamp? 10. What effect did his good fortune have upon him? 11. What use did Aladdin make of the fruit he had gathered? 12. How did Aladdin persuade his mother to see the sultan? 13. Why did the sultan permit Aladdin to marry his daughter? 14. How and where was Aladdin's palace built? 15. Where had Aladdin left the lamp when he went on his hunting trip? 16. How did the magician gain possession of it? 17. How did Aladdin regain the lamp? 18. *Class readings:* Page 156, line 9, to page 160, line 4 (5 pupils). 19. *Outline for testing silent reading.* Tell in your own words the story of Aladdin, using the following topics: (a) the boyhood of Aladdin; (b) Aladdin's pretended uncle; (c) the visit to the cave; (d) Aladdin's return to his mother; (e) Aladdin and the princess. 20. Find in the glossary the meaning of: province, prudence, bewilderment, abashed, extinguish (pp. 147-151), transparent, enchantment, dungeon, genius (pp. 152-155), sultan, magnificence, bounties (pp. 156-159), cornice, transport (p. 160). 21. *Pronounce:* dessert, nephew, niche (pp. 147-151), fatigue, hideous, imaginable (pp. 152-156), porcelain, vizier, gorgeous (pp. 156-159).

Ali Baba and the Open Sesame*

In an old town of Persia there lived two brothers, Cassim and Ali Baba.

Cassim married a wife who owned a fine shop, a warehouse, and some land; he thus found himself quite at his ease and soon became one of the richest men in the town.

Ali Baba, on the other hand, had a wife no better off than himself and lived in a very poor house. He supported his family by cutting wood in the forest and carrying it on his asses to sell about the town.

One day Ali Baba went to the forest and had very nearly finished cutting as much wood as his asses could carry, when he saw high in the air a thick cloud of dust, which seemed to be coming toward him. He gazed at it for a long time, until he saw a company of men on horseback, riding so fast that they were almost hidden by the dust.

* See "Suggestions for Silent Reading," page 163.

Although that part of the country was not often troubled by robbers, Ali Baba thought that these horsemen looked like evil men. Therefore, without thinking at all what might become of his asses, his first and only care was to save himself. So he climbed up quickly into a large tree, the branches of which spread out so close and thick that from the midst of them he could see everything that passed, without being seen.

The robbers rode swiftly up to this very tree and there alighted. Ali Baba counted forty of them and saw that each horseman took the bridle off his horse and hung over its head a bag filled with barley. Then they took their traveling bags, which were so heavy that Ali Baba thought they must be filled with gold and silver.

With his bag on his shoulder, the captain of the thieves came close to the rock, at the very spot where the tree grew in which Ali Baba had hidden himself. After the rascal had made his way through the shrubs that grew there, he cried out, "Open Sesame!" so that Ali Baba distinctly heard the words. No sooner were they spoken than a door opened in the rock. The captain and all his men passed quickly in, and the door closed again.

There they stayed for a long time. Ali Baba was compelled to wait in the tree with patience, as he was afraid some of them might come out if he left his hiding place.

At length the door opened, and the forty thieves came out. After he had seen all the troop pass out before him, the captain exclaimed, "Shut Sesame!" Each man then bridled his horse and mounted. When the captain saw that all were ready, he put himself at their head, and they rode off as they had come.

Ali Baba did not come down from the tree at once because he thought they might have forgotten something and be obliged to come back, and that he should thus be caught. He watched them as long as he could, nor did he leave the tree for a long time after he had lost sight of them. Then, recalling the words the captain had used to open and shut the door, he made his way through the bushes to it and called out, "Open Sesame!" Instantly the door flew wide open!

Ali Baba expected to find only a dark cave and was very much astonished at seeing a fine large chamber, dug out of the rock, and higher than a man could reach. It received its light from a hole in the top of the rock. In it were piled all sorts of rare fruits, bales of rich merchandise, silk stuffs and brocades, and great heaps of money, both silver and gold, some loose, some in large leather bags. The sight of all these things almost took Ali Baba's breath away.

But he did not hesitate long as to what he should do. He went boldly into the cave, and as soon as he was there, the door shut; but since he knew the secret by which to open it, this gave him no fear. Leaving the silver, he turned to the gold which was in the bags, and when he had gathered enough for loading his three asses, he brought them to the rock, loaded them, and so covered the sacks of gold over with wood that no one could suspect anything. This done, he went to the door, and had no sooner said the words, "Shut Sesame," than it closed.

And now Ali Baba took the road to the town; and when he got home, he drove his asses into the yard and shut the gate with great care. He threw off the wood that hid the gold and carried the bags into the house, where he laid them down in a row before his wife, who was sitting upon a couch.

When he had told the whole story of the cave and the

forty thieves, he emptied the sacks, making one great heap of gold that quite dazzled his wife's eyes.

His wife began to rejoice in this good fortune, and was going to count over the money that lay before her, piece by piece.

"What are you going to do?" said he. "Why, you would never finish counting them. I will dig a pit to bury it in; we have no time to lose."

"It is right, though," replied the wife, "that we should know about how much there may be. I will go and borrow a small grain measure, and while you are digging the pit, I will find how much there is."

So the wife of Ali Baba set off and went to her brother-in-law, Cassim, who lived a short way from her house. Cassim was away from home, so she begged his wife to lend her a measure for a few minutes. "That I will with pleasure," said Cassim's wife. She went to seek a measure but knowing how poor Ali Baba was, she was curious to know what sort of grain his wife wanted to measure; so she put some tallow on the bottom of the measure in such a way that no one would notice it.

The wife of Ali Baba returned home and placing the measure on the heap of gold, filled it over and over again, till she had measured the whole. Ali Baba by this time had dug the pit for it, and while he was burying the gold, his wife went back with the measure to her sister-in-law, but without noticing that a piece of gold had stuck to the bottom of it.

The wife of Ali Baba had scarcely turned her back, when Cassim's wife looked at the bottom of the measure and was astonished to see a piece of gold sticking to it. "What!" said she, "Ali Baba measures his gold! Where can the wretch have got it?" When her husband, Cassim, came home, she said to him, "Cassim, you think you are rich, but Ali Baba must have far more wealth than you; he does not count his gold as you do; he measures it." Then she showed him the piece of money she had found sticking to the bottom of the measure—a coin so ancient that the name of the prince engraved on it was unknown to her.

Far from feeling glad at the good fortune which his brother had met with, Cassim grew so jealous of Ali Baba that he passed almost the whole night without closing his eyes. The next morning before sunrise he went to him. "Ali Baba," said he, harshly, "you pretend to be poor and miserable and a beggar, and yet you measure your money." Here Cassim showed him the piece of gold his wife had given him. "How many pieces," added he, "have you like this, that my wife found sticking to the bottom of the measure yesterday?"

Cassim Visits the Cave

From this speech Ali Baba knew that Cassim, and his wife also, must suspect what had happened. So, without showing the least sign of surprise, he told Cassim by what chance he had found the retreat of the thieves and where it was; and offered, if he would keep the secret, to share the treasure with him.

"This I certainly expect," replied Cassim in a haughty tone; "otherwise I will inform the police of it."

Ali Baba, led rather by his good nature than by fear, told him all, even to the words he must pronounce, both on entering the cave and on quitting it. Cassim made no further inquiries of Ali Baba; he left him, determined to seize the whole treasure, and set off the next morning before break of day with ten mules laden with large hampers which he proposed to fill. He took the road which Ali Baba had pointed out and arrived at the rock and the tree; on looking for the door, he soon discovered it. When he cried, "Open Sesame!" the door obeyed; he entered, and it closed again.

Greedy as Cassim was, he could have passed the whole day in feasting his eyes with the sight of so much gold, but he remembered that he had come to take away as much as he could. He therefore filled his sacks, and coming to the door, he found that he had forgotten the secret words, and instead of saying, "Open Sesame" he said, "Open Barley." So the door, instead of flying open, remained closed. He named various other kinds of grain; all but the right one were called upon, and still the door did not move.

The thieves returned to their cave toward noon, and when they were within a short distance of it and saw the mules belonging to Cassim laden with hampers, standing about the rock, they were a good deal surprised. They drove away the ten mules, which took to flight in the forest. Then the captain and his men, with their sabers in their hands, went toward the door and said, "Open Sesame!" At once it flew open.

Cassim, who from the inside of the cave heard the horses trampling on the ground, did not doubt that the thieves had come, and that his death was near. Resolved, however, on one effort to escape and reach some place of safety, he placed himself near the door ready to run out as soon as it should open. The word "Sesame" was scarcely pronounced when it opened, and he rushed out with such violence that he threw the captain to the ground. He could not, however, escape the other thieves, who slew him on the spot.

On entering the cave the thieves found, near the door, the sacks which Cassim had filled, but they could not imagine how he had been able to get in.

The wife of Cassim, in the meantime, was in the greatest uneasiness when night came and her husband did not return. After waiting as long as she could, she went in the utmost alarm to Ali Baba, and said to him, "Brother, I believe you know that Cassim has gone to the forest; he has not yet come back, although it is almost morning. I fear some accident may have befallen him."

Ali Baba did not wait for entreaties to go and seek for Cassim. He immediately set off with his three asses and went to the forest. As he drew near the rock, he was astonished to see that blood had been shed near the cave. When he reached the door, he said, "Open Sesame!" and it opened.

He was shocked to see his brother's body in the cave. He decided to carry it home and placed it on one of his asses, covering it with sticks to conceal it. The other two asses he quickly loaded with sacks of gold, putting wood over them as before. Then, commanding the door to close, he took the road to the city, waiting in the forest till nightfall, that he might return without being observed. When he got home, he left the two asses that were laden with gold for his wife to unload; and having told her what had happened, he led the other ass to his sister-in-law's.

Ali Baba knocked at the door, which was opened to him by Morgiana, who was a female slave, clever and full of invention. "Morgiana," said he, "the first thing I have to ask you is to keep a deep secret! This packet contains the body of your master, and we must bury him as if he had died a natural death. Let me speak to your mistress, and hearken what I say to her."

Morgiana went to call her mistress, and Ali Baba then told her all that had happened before his arrival with the body of Cassim. "Sister," added he, "here is a sad affliction for you, but we must contrive to bury my brother as if he had died a natural death; and then we shall be glad to offer you a shelter under our own roof."

The widow of Cassim reflected that she could not do better than consent. She therefore wiped away her tears and suppressed her mournful cries, and thereby showed Ali Baba that she accepted his offer.

Ali Baba left her in this frame of mind, and Morgiana went out with him to an apothecary's there. She knocked at the shop door, and when it was opened, asked for a particular kind of lozenge of great effect in dangerous illness. The apothecary gave her the lozenge, asking who was ill in her master's family. "Ah!" exclaimed she with a deep sigh, "it is my worthy master, Cassim himself. He can neither speak nor eat!"

Meanwhile, as Ali Baba and his wife were seen going backwards and forwards to the house of Cassim, in the course of the day, no one was surprised on hearing in the evening the piercing cries of his widow and Morgiana, which announced his death.

And so the body of Cassim was prepared for its burial, which took place the next day, attended by Ali Baba and Morgiana.

As for his widow, she remained at home to lament and weep with her neighbors, who, according to the usual custom, repaired to her house during the ceremony of the burial, and joining their cries to hers, filled the air with sounds of woe. Thus the manner of Cassim's death was so well hidden that no one in the city knew anything about it.

The Robbers Seek Revenge on Ali Baba

But let us now leave Ali Baba and Morgiana, and return to the forty thieves. When they came back to their cave, they found the body of Cassim gone, and with it much of their treasure. "We are discovered," said the captain, "and we shall be lost if we are not very careful. All that we can at present tell is that the man whom we killed in the cave knew the secret of opening the door. But he was not the only one; another must have found it out too. Having slain one, we must not let the other escape. Well, the first thing to be done is that one of you should go to the city in the dress of a traveler and try to learn who the man we killed was."

The thief who agreed to carry out this plan, having disguised himself so that no one could have told who he was, set off at night and entered the city just at dawn.

By asking questions in the town he discovered that a body had been prepared for burial at a certain house. Having found the house, the thief marked the door with chalk and returned to the forest.

Very soon after this, Morgiana had occasion to go out and saw the mark which the thief had made on the door of Ali Baba's house. "What can this mark mean?" thought she; "has anyone a spite against my master, or has it been done only for fun? In any case, it will be well to guard against the worst that may happen." She therefore took some chalk, and as several of the doors, both above and below her master's, were alike, she marked them in the same manner and then went in without saying anything of what she had done either to her master or mistress.

The thief in the meantime arrived at the forest and related the success of his journey. They all listened to him with great delight, and the captain, after praising him, said, "Comrades, we have no time to lose; let us arm ourselves and depart, and when we have entered the city, which we had best do separately, let us all meet in the great square, and I will go and find out the house with the chalk mark."

Thus the thieves went in small parties of two or three to the city without causing any suspicion. The thief who had been there in the morning then led the captain to the street in which he had marked the house of Ali Baba. When they reached the first house that had been marked by Morgiana, he pointed it out, saying that was the one. But as they continued walking on, the captain saw that the next door was marked in the same manner. At this the thief was quite confused and knew not what to say, for they found four or five doors more with the same mark.

The captain, who was in great anger, returned to the square and told the first of his men whom he met to tell the rest that they had lost their labor, and that nothing remained but to return to the forest.

When they had reached the forest, the captain declared the mistaken thief deserving of death, and he was at once killed by his companions.

Next day another thief, in spite of this, determined to succeed where the other had failed. He went to the city, found the house, and marked the door of it with red. But, a short time after, Morgiana went out and saw the red mark and did not fail to make a similar red mark on the neighboring doors.

The thief when he returned to the forest boasted of his success, and the captain and the rest repaired to the city with as much care as before, and the captain and his guide went immediately to the street where Ali Baba resided; but the same thing occurred as before.

Thus they were obliged to return again to the forest disappointed. The second thief was put to death as a punishment for deceiving them.

Next time the captain himself went to the city and found the house of Ali Baba. But not choosing to amuse himself by making marks on it, he examined it so well, not only by looking at it, but by passing before it several times, that at last he was certain he could not mistake it.

Thereupon he returned to the forest and told the thieves he had made sure of the house, and had made a plan such that at last he was certain he could not mistake it.

And first he ordered them to divide into small parties and go into the neighboring towns and villages and buy nineteen mules and thirty-eight large leather jars to carry oil, one of which must be full, and all the others empty.

In the course of two or three days the thieves returned, and the captain made one of his men enter each jar, armed as he thought necessary. Then he closed the jars as if each were full of oil, leaving, however, a small slit open to admit air.

Things being thus disposed, the mules were laden with the thirty-seven thieves, each concealed in a jar, and the jar that was filled with oil; whereupon the captain took the road to the city at the hour that had been agreed and arrived about an hour after sunset. He went straight to the house of Ali Baba, where he found Ali Baba at the door, enjoying the fresh air after supper. "Sir," said he, "I have brought oil from a great distance to sell tomorrow at the market, and I do not know where to go to pass the night; if it would not occasion you much trouble, do me the favor to take me in."

Although Ali Baba had seen in the forest, the man who now spoke to him and had even heard his voice, yet he had no idea that this was the captain of the forty robbers, disguised as an oil merchant. "You are welcome," said he, and took him into the house and his mules into the stable.

THE OIL MERCHANT IN THE HOME OF ALI BABA

Ali Baba, having told Morgiana to see that his guest wanted nothing, added, "Tomorrow before daybreak I shall go to the bath. Make me some good broth to take when I return." After giving these orders, he went to bed.

In the meantime, the captain of the thieves, on leaving the stable, went to give his people orders what to do. Beginning with the first jar, and going through the whole number, he said to each, "When I shall throw some pebbles from my chamber, do not fail to rip open the jar from top to bottom with the knife you have, and to come out; I shall be with you soon after." The knives he spoke of were sharpened for the purpose. This done, he returned, and Morgiana took a light and led him to his chamber. Not to cause any suspicion, he put out the light and lay down in his clothes, to be ready to rise as soon as he had taken his first sleep.

Morgiana did not forget Ali Baba's orders; she prepared his linen for the bath and gave it to Abdalla, Ali Baba's slave, who had not yet gone to bed. Then she put the pot on the fire to make the broth, but while she was skimming it, the lamp went out. There was no more oil in the house, and she had no candle. She did not know what to do. She wanted a light to see to skim the pot and mentioned it to Abdalla. "Take some oil," said he, "out of one of the jars in the court."

Morgiana accordingly took the oil can and went into the court. As she drew near the first jar, the thief who was concealed within said in a low voice, "Is it time?"

Any other slave except Morgiana, in the first moment of surprise at finding a man in the jar instead of some oil, would have made a great uproar. But Morgiana collected her thoughts, and without showing any emotion assumed the voice of the captain, and answered, "Not yet, but presently." She approached the next jar, and the others in turn, making the same answer to the same question, till she came to the last, which was full of oil.

Morgiana by this means discovered that her master, who supposed he was giving a night's lodging to an oil merchant only, had afforded shelter to thirty-eight robbers, including the pretended merchant, their captain. She quickly filled her oil can from the last jar and returned to the kitchen; and after having put some oil in her lamp and lighting it, she took a large kettle and went again into the court to fill it with oil from the jar. This done, she brought it back again, put it over the fire, and made a great blaze under it with a quantity of wood; for the sooner the oil boiled, the sooner her plan would be carried out. At length the oil boiled. She then took the kettle and poured into each jar, from the first to the last, enough boiling oil to kill the robbers.

This being done without any noise, she returned to the kitchen with the empty kettle and shut the door. She put out the large fire she had made up for this purpose and left only enough to finish boiling the broth for Ali Baba. She then blew out the lamp and remained perfectly silent, determined not to go to bed until she had watched what would happen from a window which overlooked the court.

Morgiana had waited scarcely a quarter of an hour when the captain of the robbers awoke. He got up, and opening the window, looked out. All was dark and silent; he gave the signal by throwing the pebbles, many of which fell on the jars, as the sound plainly proved. He listened, but heard nothing that could lead him to suppose his men obeyed the summons. He became uneasy at this delay and threw some pebbles down a second time, and even a third. They all struck the jars, yet nothing moved, and he became frightened.

He went down into the court in the utmost alarm; and going up to the first jar, he was going to ask if the robber contained in it was asleep. As soon as he drew near, he smelled a strong scent of hot and burning oil coming out of the jar. From this he feared that his wicked plan had failed. He went to the next jar, and to each in turn, and discovered that all his men were dead. Terrified at this, he jumped over the garden gate, and going from one garden to another by getting over the walls, he made his escape.

Before daybreak, Ali Baba, followed by his slave, went out and repaired to the bath, totally ignorant of the surprising events that had taken place in his house during his sleep. Morgiana had not thought it necessary to wake him, particularly as she had no time to lose while she was engaged in her perilous enterprise, and it was useless to disturb him after she had averted the danger.

When he returned from the bath, the sun being risen, Ali Baba was surprised to see the jars of oil still in their places; he inquired the reason of Morgiana, who let him in, and who had left everything as it was, in order to show it to him.

"My good master," said Morgiana to Ali Baba's question, "may God preserve you and all your family. You will soon know the reason, if you will take the trouble to come with me." Ali Baba followed Morgiana, and when she had shut the door, she took him to the first jar and bade him look in and see if it contained oil. He did as she desired; and seeing a man in the jar, he hastily drew back and uttered a cry of surprise. "Do not be afraid," said she; "the man you see there will not do you any harm; he will never hurt either you or anyone else again, for he is now a corpse."

"Morgiana!" exclaimed Ali Baba, "what does all this mean? Do explain this mystery." "I will explain it," replied Morgiana, "but pray be cautious, and do not awaken the curiosity of your neighbors to learn what it is of the utmost importance that you should keep secret and concealed. Look first at all the other jars."

Ali Baba examined all the rest of the jars, one after the other, from the first till he came to the last, which contained the oil, and he noticed that its oil was nearly all gone. This done, he stood, sometimes casting his eyes on Morgiana, then looking at the jars, yet without speaking a word, so great was his surprise. At length he said, "And what has become of the merchant?"

"The merchant," replied Morgiana, "is just as much a merchant as I am. I can tell you who he is."

She then described the marks made upon the door and the way in which she had copied them, adding: "You see this is a plot contrived by the thieves of the forest, whose troop, I know not how, seems to be diminished by two. But be that as it may, it is now reduced to three at most. This proves that they are determined on your death, and you will do right to be on your guard against them, so long as you are certain that even one of the robbers remains."

Ali Baba, full of gratitude for all he owed her, replied, "I will reward you as you deserve before I die. I owe my life to you, and from this moment I give you your liberty and will soon do still more for you."

Morgiana's Great Courage and Reward

Meanwhile the captain of the forty thieves had returned to the forest full of rage and determined to revenge himself on Ali Baba.

Next morning, he awoke at an early hour, put on a merchant's dress, and returned to the city, where he took a lodging in a khan. Then he bought a horse, which he made use of to convey to his lodging several kinds of rich stuffs and fine linens, bringing them from the forest at various times. In order to dispose of these wares, he took a shop and established himself in it. This shop was exactly opposite to that which had been Cassim's and was now occupied by the son of Ali Baba.

The captain of the thieves, who had taken the name of Cogia Houssam, soon succeeded in making friends with the son of Ali Baba, who was young and good-natured. He often invited the youth to sup with him and made him rich gifts.

When Ali Baba heard of it, he resolved to make a return for this kindness to Cogia Houssam, little thinking that the pretended merchant was really the captain of the thieves. So one day he asked Cogia Houssam to do him the honor of supping and spending the evening at his house. "Sir," replied Cogia, "I am grateful for your kindness, but I must beg you to excuse me, and for a reason which I am sure you will think sufficient. It is this: I never eat of any dish that has salt in it; judge, then, of the figure I should make at your table." "If this be your only reason," replied Ali Baba, "it need not prevent your coming to supper with me. The bread which is eaten in my house does not contain any salt; and as for the meat and other dishes, I promise you there shall be none in those which are served before you."

So Ali Baba went into the kitchen and desired Morgiana not to put any salt in the meat she was going to serve for supper, and also to prepare two or three dishes of those that he had ordered without any salt.

Morgiana obeyed, though much against her will; and she felt some curiosity to see this man who did not eat salt. When she had finished and Abdalla had prepared the table, she helped him in carrying the dishes. On looking at Cogia Houssam, she instantly recognized the captain of the robbers, in spite of his disguise; and looking at him more closely, she saw that he had a dagger hidden under his dress. "I am no longer surprised," said she to herself, "that this villain will not eat salt with my master; he is his enemy, and means to murder him! But I will prevent the villain!"

When the supper was ended, the captain of the thieves thought that the time for revenging himself on Ali Baba had come. "I will make them both drink much wine," thought he, "and then the son, against whom I bear no malice, will not prevent my plunging my dagger into the heart of his father, and I shall escape by way of the garden, as I did before, while the cook and the slave are at their supper in the kitchen."

Instead, however, of going to supper, Morgiana did not allow him time to carry out his wicked plans. She dressed herself as a dancer, put on a headdress suitable to that character and wore round her waist a fancy girdle of gilt, to which she fastened a dagger made of the same metal. Her face was hidden by a very handsome mask. When she had so disguised herself, she said to Abdalla, "Take your tabor, and let us go and entertain our master's guest, who is the friend of his son, as we do sometimes by our performances."

Abdalla took his tabor and began to play, as he walked before Morgiana and entered the room. Morgiana followed him, making a low curtsy, and performed several dances with equal grace and agility. At length she drew out the dagger, and dancing with it in her hand, she surpassed all she had yet done, by her light movements and high leaps; sometimes presenting the dagger as if to strike and at others holding it to her own bosom as if to stab herself.

At length, as if out of breath, she took the tabor from Abdalla with her left hand, and holding the dagger in her right, she held out the tabor to Ali Baba, who threw a piece of gold into it. Morgiana then held the tabor out to his son, who did the same. Cogia Houssam, who saw that she was coming to him next, had already taken his purse from his bosom and was putting his hand in it, when Morgiana, with great courage, suddenly plunged the dagger into his heart.

Ali Baba and his son, terrified at this action, uttered a loud cry: "Wretch!" exclaimed Ali Baba, "what hast thou done? Thou hast ruined me and my family forever."

"What I have done," replied Morgiana, "is not for your ruin, but for your safety." Then opening Cogia Houssam's robe to show Ali Baba the poniard which was concealed under it, "See," continued she, "the cruel enemy you had to deal with; examine him, and you will recognize the pretended oil merchant and the captain of the forty thieves! Do you now see why he refused to eat salt with you? Can you require a stronger proof of his treachery?"

Ali Baba, who now saw all that he owed to Morgiana for having thus saved his life a second time, cried, "Morgiana, I gave you your liberty and at the same time promised to do more for you at some future time. This time has come, and I present you to my son as his wife."

A few years after, Ali Baba had the marriage of his son and Morgiana celebrated with great feasting.

After the marriage, Ali Baba decided to visit again the cave of the forty thieves. On reaching it he repeated the word, "Open Sesame." At once the door opened, and he entered the cave and found that no one had been in it from the time that Cogia Houssam had opened his shop in the city. He therefore knew that the whole troop of thieves was killed, and that he was the only person in the world who knew the secret of the cave.

From that time Ali Baba and his son, whom he took to the cave and taught the secret of how to enter it, enjoyed its riches with moderation and lived in great happiness and comfort to the end of their long lives.

NOTES AND QUESTIONS

Discussion. 1. How did Ali Baba make his living? 2. When did he first see the robber band? 3. What words did the captain say to gain entrance to the cave? 4. Why did Ali Baba wish to see the cave? 5. How did he plan to hide his gold after he returned home? 6. What aroused the suspicions of his brother? 7. How did Cassim feel toward Ali Baba when he heard the story? 8. What did Cassim plan to do? 9. Why could not Cassim open the door after it closed upon him? 10. Why did Ali Baba wish to conceal the fact that Cassim was killed by the robbers? 11. Why could not the robbers find Ali Baba's house after it had been marked with chalk? 12. What plan did the captain of the robbers determine upon in order to have revenge upon Ali Baba? 13. How did Morgiana discover the plot and prevent it from being carried out? 14. How did Ali Baba reward her? 15. How did the captain manage to win the friendship of Ali Baba? 16. What was his object in doing this? 17. The captain would not eat salt in Ali Baba's house because, according to an old Eastern custom, the use of salt at a meal was a sign of friendship and loyalty. How did Morgiana save Ali Baba's life? 18. Who is the cleverest person in the story? 19. Did Ali Baba have a right to take the treasure from the robbers and keep it? Why? 20. *Class readings:* Select passages to be read aloud in class. 21. *Outline for testing silent reading.* Tell in your own words the story of Ali Baba, using the following topics: (a) the adventure in the forest; (b) Ali Baba's return; (c) the fate of Cassim; (d) Morgiana's plans; (e) how the thieves were caught; (f) how Ali Baba used his good fortune. 22. Find in the glossary the meaning of: bridled, recalling, astonished, merchandise (pp. 165-166), retreat, hampers, resolved, uneasiness, utmost, invention, packet, reflected, suppressed, ceremony (pp. 168-171), related, confused (pp. 172-173), presently, enterprise, contrived, diminished (pp. 176-178); prevent; gilt; surpassed; moderation (pp. 179-182). 23. *Pronounce:* Ali Baba, sesame, brocades (pp. 164-166), inquiries, hearken, affliction, apothecary, lozenge, burial (pp. 168-171), comrades (p. 173), averted, corpse (pp. 177-178), Cogia Houssam, villain, curtsy, agility, poniard (pp. 179-181).

Phrases for Study

feasting his eyes, **169**, 5
full of invention, **170**, 25
natural death, **170**, 29
repaired to her house, **171**, 27
had occasion to go out, **172**, 20
lost their labor, **173**, 18
thus disposed, **174**, 21
wanted nothing, **175**, 5
collected her thoughts, **176**, 3
rich stuffs, **179**, 7
bear no malice, **180**, 21
suitable to that character, **180**, 28

Sindbad the Sailor*

In the reign of the caliph Harun-al-Rashid there lived in Baghdad a poor porter called Hindbad. One day he was carrying a heavy burden from one end of the town to the other. Being weary, he took off his load and sat upon it, near a large mansion.

He knew not who owned the mansion, but he went to the servants and asked the name of the master. "How," replied one of them, "do you live in Baghdad, and know

---

* See "Suggestions for Silent Reading" page 163.

not that this is the house of Sindbad the sailor, that famous voyager, who has sailed round the world?"

The porter said, loud enough to be heard, "Almighty Creator of all things, consider the difference between Sindbad and me! I work faithfully every day and suffer hardships and can scarcely get barley bread for myself and family, while happy Sindbad spends riches and leads a life of continual pleasure. What has he done to obtain a lot so agreeable? And what have I done to deserve one so wretched?"

While the porter was thus complaining, a servant came out of the house and said to him, "Sindbad, my master, wishes to speak to you. Come in."

The servants took him into a great hall, where a number of people sat around a table covered with all sorts of savory dishes. At the upper end was a tall, grave gentleman, with a long white beard, and behind him stood a number of officers and servants, all ready to attend his pleasure. This person was Sindbad. Hindbad, whose fear was increased at the sight of so many people and of so great a feast, saluted the company tremblingly. Sindbad bade him draw near, and seating him at his right hand, served him himself.

Now, Sindbad had heard the porter complain, and this it was that led him to have the man brought in. When the repast was over, Sindbad spoke to Hindbad, asked his name and business, and said: "I wish to hear from your own mouth what it was you said in the street."

Hindbad replied, "My lord, I confess that my weariness put me out of humor and made me utter some foolish words, which I beg you to pardon." "Do not think I am so unjust," resumed Sindbad, "as to blame you. But you are mistaken about me, and I wish to set you right. You think that I have gained without labor and trouble the ease and plenty which I now enjoy. But make no mistake; I did not reach this happy condition without suffering for several years more trouble of body and mind than can well be imagined. Yes, gentlemen," he added, speaking to the whole company, "I assure you that my sufferings have been so extraordinary that they would make the greatest miser lose his love of riches; and I will, with your leave, tell of the dangers I have overcome, which I think will not be uninteresting to you."

THE FIRST VOYAGE OF SINDBAD THE SAILOR

He then told the following story:

"My father was a wealthy merchant, much respected by everyone. He left me a large fortune, which I wasted in wild living. I then remembered Solomon's saying, 'A good name is better than precious ointment,' and resolved to walk in my father's ways. I therefore made arrangements to go on a voyage with some merchants.

"After touching at many places where we sold or exchanged goods, we were becalmed near a small island which looked like a green meadow. The captain permitted some of us to land, but while we were eating and drinking, the island began to shake, and he called to us to return to the ship. What we thought was an island was really the back of a sea monster. I had just time to catch hold of a piece of wood, when the island disappeared into the sea.

"The captain, thinking I was drowned, resolved to make use of a favorable gale, which had just risen, to continue his voyage. I was tossed by the waves all that day and night, but the next day I was thrown upon an island. I was very feeble, but I crept along and found a spring of water, which did much to restore my strength.

"After this I went farther into the island and saw a man watching some horses that were feeding nearby. He was much surprised to see me and led me to a cave where there were several other men. They told me they were grooms of the Maharaja, ruler of the island, and that every year they brought his horses to this uninhabited place for pasturage.

"Next morning they returned to the capital of the island, taking me with them. They presented me to the Maharaja, who ordered his people to care for me. The capital has a fine harbor, where ships arrive daily from all parts of the world, and I hoped soon to have a chance to return to Baghdad.

"One day the ship arrived in which I had sailed from home. I went to the captain and asked for my goods. 'I am Sindbad,' I said, 'and those bales marked with his name are mine.' At first the captain did not know me, but after looking at me closely, he cried, 'Heaven be praised for your happy escape. These are your goods; take them and do what you please with them.'

"I made a present of my choicest goods to the Maharaja, who asked me how I came by such rarities. When I told him, he was much pleased and gave me many valuable things in return. After exchanging my goods for aloes, sandalwood, camphor, nutmegs, cloves, pepper, and ginger, I sailed for home and at last reached Baghdad with goods worth one hundred thousand sequins."

Sindbad stopped here and ordered the musicians to proceed with their concert. When it was evening, Sindbad gave the porter a purse of one hundred sequins and told him to come back the next day to hear more of his adventures.

Hindbad put on his best robe the next day and

returned to the bountiful traveler, who welcomed him heartily. When all the guests had arrived, dinner was served and continued a long time. When it was ended, Sindbad said, "Gentlemen, hear now the adventures of my second voyage. They deserve your attention even more than those of the first."

THE SECOND VOYAGE OF SINDBAD THE SAILOR

"I planned, after my first voyage, to spend the rest of my days at Baghdad, but I grew weary of an idle life, and put to sea a second time, with merchants I knew to be honorable. We embarked on board a good ship and set sail. We traded from island to island, and exchanged goods with great profit.

"One day we landed on an island covered with fruit trees, but we could see neither man nor animal. We walked in the meadows and along the streams that watered them. While some gathered flowers and others fruits, I took my wine and provisions and sat down near a stream between two high trees, which formed a thick shade. I made a good meal and afterwards fell asleep. I cannot tell how long I slept, but when I awoke, the ship was gone.

"In this sad condition, I was ready to die with grief. I was sorry that I had not been satisfied with the profits of my first voyage, that might have been enough for me all my life. But my repentance came too late. At last I took courage and, not knowing what to do, climbed to the top of a lofty tree and looked about on all sides to see if I could discover anything that could give me hope. Toward the sea I could see nothing but sky and water; but looking over the land, I beheld something white, and, coming down, I took what provisions I had left and went toward it, the distance being so great that I could not tell what it was.

"As I came nearer, I thought it was a white dome, of great height and size; and when I came up to it, I touched it and found it to be very smooth. I went around to see if it was open on any side, but saw it was not, and that there was no climbing up to the top, as it was so smooth. It was at least fifty paces around.

"By this time the sun was about to set, and all of a sudden the sky became as dark as if it had been covered with a thick cloud. I was much astonished at this sudden darkness, but much more when I found it was caused by a bird of monstrous size that came flying toward me.

"I remembered that I had often heard sailors speak of a wonderful bird called the roc, and saw that the great dome which I so much admired must be its egg. The bird alighted, and sat over the egg.

"As I saw it coming, I crept close to the egg, so that I had before me one of the legs of the bird, which was as big as the trunk of a tree. I tied myself strongly to it with my turban, hoping that the roc next morning would carry me out of this desert island.

"After passing the night in this condition, the bird flew away as soon as it was daylight and carried me so high that I could not see the earth. It afterwards descended so swiftly that I lost my senses. But when I found myself on the ground, I speedily untied the knot and had scarcely done so when the roc, having taken up a serpent in its bill, flew away.

"The spot where it left me was surrounded by mountains that seemed to reach above the clouds and so steep that there was no chance of getting out of the valley. When I compared this place with the desert island from which the roc had brought me, I found that I had gained nothing by the change.

"As I walked through this valley, I saw it was strewn with diamonds, some of which were of a surprising size.

"I had never believed what I had heard sailors tell of the valley of diamonds and of the tricks used by merchants to obtain jewels from that place; but now I found that they had stated nothing but the truth. For the fact is that the merchants come to this valley when the eagles have young ones and throw great joints of meat into the valley; the diamonds, upon whose points they fall, stick to them; the eagles pounce upon those pieces of meat and carry them to their nests on the rocks to feed their young; the merchants at this time run to the nests, drive off the eagles, and take away the diamonds that stick to the meat.

"I had thought the valley must surely be my grave, but now I took courage and began to plan a way to escape.

"Collecting the largest diamonds and putting them into the leather bag in which I used to carry my provisions, I took the largest of the pieces of meat, tied it close around me, and then lay down upon the ground, face downwards, the bag of diamonds being made fast to my girdle.

"I had scarcely placed myself in this position when one of the eagles, having taken me up with the piece of meat to which I was fastened, carried me to his nest on the top of the mountain. The merchants frightened the eagles, and when they had forced them to quit their prey, one of them came to the nest where I was. He was much alarmed when he saw me; but, recovering himself, instead of asking how I came thither, began to quarrel with me, and asked why I stole his goods.

"'You will treat me,' replied I, 'with more politeness when you know me better. Do not be uneasy; I have diamonds enough for you and myself, more than all the other merchants together. Whatever they have they owe to chance, but I selected for myself in the bottom of the valley those which you see in this bag.'

"I had scarcely done speaking when the other merchants came crowding about us, much astonished to see me, but more surprised when I told them my story.

"They took me to their camp, and there, when I opened my bag, they were surprised at the beauty of my diamonds and confessed that they had never seen any of such size and perfection.

"I prayed the merchant who owned the nest to which I had been carried, for every merchant had his own nest, to take as many for his share as he pleased. He, however, took only one, and that, too, the least of them; and when I pressed him to take more, he said, 'No, I am very well satisfied with this gem, which is valuable enough to save me the trouble of making any more voyages and will bring as great a fortune as I desire.'

"The merchants had thrown their pieces of meat into the valley for several days; and each of them being satisfied with the diamonds that had fallen to his lot, we left the place and traveled near high mountains, where there were serpents of great length, which we had the fortune to escape.

"We took shipping at the first port we reached and touched at the isle of Roha, where the trees grow that yield camphor.

"I pass over many other things peculiar to this island, lest I should weary you. Here I exchanged some of my diamonds for merchandise. From here we went to other islands, and at last, having touched at several trading towns of the continent, we landed at Bussorah and from there I proceeded to Baghdad. There I gave presents to the poor and lived honorably upon the vast riches I had gained with so many terrible hardships and so many great perils."

Thus Sindbad ended the story of the second voyage, gave Hindbad another hundred sequins, and invited him to come the next day to hear more of his adventures.

THE THIRD VOYAGE OF SINDBAD THE SAILOR

On the third day the porter again repaired to the house in which he had heard such wonderful tales. After the dinner was finished, the host began once more to tell of his travels.

"I soon grew weary of a life of idleness and embarked with some merchants on another long voyage. One day we were overtaken by a storm, which drove us out of our course, and we were obliged to cast anchor near an island. As soon as we landed, we were surrounded by savage dwarfs, who took possession of our ship and sailed away.

"Left without means of escape from the island, we determined to explore it, in hope of finding food and shelter. We had not advanced far, however, when we discovered that this island was inhabited by giants, more savage than the dwarfs who had first attacked us. We knew that we could not remain on the island, and so we went back to the shore and planned how we might escape.

"When night came, we made rafts, each large enough to carry three men, and as soon as it was light we put to sea with all the speed we could. The giants saw us as we pushed out and, rushing down to the water's edge, threw great stones, which sank all the rafts except the one upon which I was.

"All that day and night we were tossed by the waves, but the next morning we were thrown upon an island, where we found delicious fruit which satisfied our hunger. Beautiful as this island was, we found ourselves in danger as great as any we had escaped. My two companions were killed by serpents, and I was almost in despair, when I saw a ship in the distance. By shouting and waving my turban I attracted the attention of the crew, and a boat was sent for me.

"As soon as I saw the captain, I knew him to be the man who, in my second voyage, had left me on the island. 'Captain,' said I, 'I am Sindbad, whom you left on the island.'

"'Heaven be praised,' said the captain; 'I am glad that my careless act did not cause your death. These are your goods, which I always took care to preserve.'

"We continued at sea for some time and touched at many islands, where I traded for cloves, cinnamon, and other spices. At last I returned to Baghdad with so much wealth that I knew not its value. I gave a great deal to the poor and bought another estate."

Thus Sindbad finished the story of his third voyage. He gave another hundred sequins to Hindbad and invited him to dinner the next day.

The Fourth Voyage of Sindbad the Sailor

After dinner on the fourth day the merchant once more began to tell of his adventures.

"After I had rested from the dangers of my third voyage, my love for trade and adventure again took hold of me. I provided a stock of goods and started on another voyage.

"We had sailed a great way when we were overtaken by a storm, and the ship was wrecked. I clung to a plank and was carried by the current to an island; here I found fruit and spring water, which saved my life. The next day I started to explore the island and, seeing some huts, I went toward them. The people who lived in these huts were savages, and they took me prisoner. I was in such fear of them that I could not eat, and at last I became sick.

"After that they did not watch me so closely, and I found a chance to escape. I traveled seven days, living upon coconuts, which served me for food and drink. On the eighth day I met some people gathering pepper, and I told them my story. They treated me with great kindness and took me with them when they sailed home.

"On arriving in their own country they presented me to their king, who commanded his people to take care of me, and soon I was looked upon as a native rather than a stranger. I was not, however, satisfied to remain away from my own home and planned to escape and return to Baghdad.

"One day I saw a ship approaching the place where I was. I called to the crew, and they quickly sent a boat and took me on board. We stopped at several islands and collected great stores of costly goods. After we had finished our traffic, we put to sea again and at last arrived at Baghdad. I gave large sums to the poor and enjoyed myself with my friends in feasts and amusements."

Here Sindbad made a present of one hundred sequins to Hindbad, whom he requested to return the next day to dine with him and hear the story of his fifth voyage.

THE FIFTH VOYAGE OF SINDBAD THE SAILOR

The story of the fifth day was as follows:

"All the misfortunes I had undergone could not cure me of my desire to make new voyages. I therefore had a ship built and, taking with me several merchants, I started on my fifth voyage.

"We touched at a desert island, where we found a roc's egg. We could see that the young bird had begun to break the shell with his beak. The merchants who were with me broke the shell with hatchets and killed the young roc. Scarcely had they done this when the parent birds flew down with a frightful noise. We hurried to the ship and set sail as speedily as possible. But the great birds followed us, each carrying a rock between its claws. When they came directly over our ship, they let the rocks fall, and the ship was crushed and most of the passengers killed.

"I caught hold of a piece of the wreck and swam to an island. Here I found fruit and streams of fresh, pure water. After resting and eating some of the fruit, I determined to find out who lived upon the island.

"I had not walked far when I saw an old man sitting on the bank of a stream. He made signs to me to carry him over the brook, and as he seemed very weak, I took him upon my back and carried him across. When we reached the other side, the old man threw his legs around my neck and squeezed my throat until I fainted. But he kept his seat and kicked me to make me stand up. He made me carry him all that day and at night lay down with me, still holding fast to my neck.

"This continued for some time, and I grew weaker every day. One day, feeling sure that I could not escape, he began to laugh and sing and move around on my back. This was my opportunity, and, using all my strength, I threw him to the ground, where he lay motionless.

"Feeling very thankful at my escape, I went down to the beach and saw a ship at anchor there. The crew were very much surprised when I told my adventure. 'You are the first,' they said, 'who ever escaped from the old man of the sea after falling into his power.'

"We soon put out to sea and after a few days arrived at a great city. One of the merchants invited me to go with him and others to gather coconuts. The trunks of the coconut trees were lofty and very smooth, and I saw many apes among the branches. It was not possible to climb the trees, but the merchants, by throwing stones, provoked the apes to throw the coconuts at us, and by this trick we collected enough coconuts to load our ship.

"We then set sail and touched at other islands, where I exchanged my coconuts for pepper and wood of aloes. I also hired divers, who brought me up pearls that were very large and perfect. When I returned to Baghdad, I made vast sums from my pepper, precious woods, and pearls. I gave the tenth of my gains to charity, as I had done on my return from other voyages."

Sindbad here ordered one hundred sequins to be given to Hindbad and requested him to dine with him the next day to hear the account of his next voyage.

The Sixth Voyage of Sindbad the Sailor

When dinner was finished on the sixth day, Sindbad spoke as follows:

"After a year's rest I prepared for a sixth voyage, notwithstanding the entreaties of my friends, who did all in their power to keep me at home. I traveled through several provinces of Persia and the Indies and then embarked on a long voyage, in the course of which the ship was carried by a rapid current to the foot of a high mountain, where she struck and went to pieces.

"We managed to save most of our provisions and our goods, but it was impossible to climb the mountain or to escape by the sea. We were obliged to remain upon the strip of shore between the mountain and the sea. At last our provisions were exhausted, and my companions died, one after the other. Then I determined to try once more to find a way of escape.

"A river ran from the sea into a dark cavern under an archway of rock. I said to myself, 'If I make a raft and float with the current, it will doubtless carry me to some inhabited country.' I made a very solid raft and loaded it with bales of rich goods from the wreck, and rubies, emeralds, and other precious stones which covered the mountain.

"As soon as I entered the cavern, I found myself in darkness and I floated on, I knew not where. I must have fallen asleep, for when I opened my eyes I was on the bank of a river, and a great many people were around me. They spoke to me, but I did not understand their language. I was so full of joy at my escape from death that I said aloud in Arabic, 'Close thine eyes, and while thou art asleep, Heaven will change thy evil fortune into good fortune.'

"One of the men, who understood Arabic, said, 'Brother, we are inhabitants of this country and water our fields from this river. We saw your raft, and one of us swam out and brought it here. Pray, tell us your history.'

"After they had given me food, I told them my story, and then they took me to their king. I told the king my adventures; and when my raft was brought in, I showed him my rich goods and precious stones. I saw that my jewels pleased him, and I said, 'Sire, I am at Your Majesty's service, and all that I have is yours.' He answered, with a smile, 'Sindbad, I will take nothing from you; far from lessening your wealth, I mean to increase it.'

"I prayed the king to allow me to return to my own country, and he granted me permission in the most honorable manner. He gave me a rich present and a letter for the Commander of the Faithful, our sovereign, saying to me, 'I pray you, give this present and this letter to the caliph Harun-al-Rashid.'

"The letter was written on the skin of a certain animal of great value, very scarce, and of a yellowish color. The characters of this letter were of azure, and the contents as follows:

"'The king of the Indies, before whom march one hundred elephants, who lives in a palace that shines with one hundred thousand rubies, and who has in his treasury twenty thousand crowns enriched with diamonds, to Caliph Harun-al-Rashid—

"'Though the present we send you be small, receive it, however, as a brother and a friend, in consideration of the hearty friendship which we bear for you, and of which we are willing to give you proof. We send you this letter as from one brother to another. Farewell.'

"The present consisted of one single ruby made into a cup, about half a foot high and an inch thick, filled with round pearls large and beautiful; the skin of a serpent, whose scales were as bright as an ordinary piece of gold, and had the power to preserve from sickness those who lay upon it; quantities of the best wood of aloes and camphor; and, lastly, a wonderful robe covered with jewels of great beauty.

"The ship set sail, and after a successful voyage we landed at Bussorah, and from there I went to the city of Baghdad, where the first thing I did was to go to the palace of the caliph.

"Taking the king's letter, I presented myself at the gate of the Commander of the Faithful and was conducted to the throne of the caliph. I presented the letter and gift. When he had finished reading, he asked me if that ruler were really as rich as he represented himself in his letter.

"I said, 'Commander of the Faithful, I can assure Your Majesty he does not stretch the truth. I bear him witness. Nothing is more worthy of admiration than the splendor of his palace. When the king appears in public, he has a throne fixed on the back of an elephant, and rides betwixt two ranks of his ministers and favorites, and other people of his court. Before him, upon the same elephant, an officer carries a golden lance in his hand, and behind him there is another who stands with a rod of gold, on the top of which is an emerald half a foot long and an inch thick.

"'He is attended by one thousand men, clad in cloth of gold and mounted on elephants richly decked. The officer who is before him cries from time to time in a loud voice, "Behold the great monarch, the powerful sultan of the Indies, the monarch greater than Solomon and the powerful Maharaja." After he has pronounced these words, the officer behind the throne cries in his turn, "This monarch, so great and so powerful, must die, must die, must die." And the officer before replies, "Praise be to Him alone who liveth forever and ever."'

"The caliph was much pleased with my account, and sent me home with a rich present."

Here Sindbad commanded another hundred sequins to be paid to Hindbad and begged his return on the morrow to hear of his last voyage.

The Last Voyage of Sindbad the Sailor

On the seventh day, after dinner, Sindbad told the story of his last voyage:

"On my return home from my sixth voyage, I had entirely given up all thoughts of again going to sea; for, not only did my age now require rest, but I was resolved to run no more such risks as I had encountered, so that I thought of nothing but to pass the rest of my days in peace.

"One day, however, an officer of the caliph inquired for me. 'The caliph,' said he, 'has sent me to tell you that he must speak with you.' I followed the officer to the palace, where, being presented to the caliph, I saluted him, throwing myself at his feet.

"'Sindbad,' said he to me, 'I stand in need of your service; you must carry my answer and present to the king of the Indies.'

"This command of the caliph was to me like a clap of thunder. 'Commander of the Faithful,' I replied, 'I am ready to do whatever Your Majesty shall think fit to command, but I beg you most humbly to consider what I have undergone. I have also made a vow never to leave Baghdad.'

"The caliph insisted, and I finally told him that I was willing to obey. He was pleased and gave me one thousand sequins for the expenses of my journey.

"I prepared for my departure in a few days. As soon as the caliph's letter and present were delivered to me, I went to Bussorah, where I embarked, and had a safe voyage. Having arrived at the capital of the Indies, I was shown to the palace with much pomp, when I prostrated myself on the ground before the king.

"'Sindbad,' said the king, 'you are welcome; I have many times thought of you; I bless the day on which I see you once more.' I thanked him for his kindness, and delivered the gifts from my master.

"The caliph's present was a complete suit of cloth of gold, fifty robes of rich stuff, a hundred of white cloth, the finest of Cairo, Suez, and Alexandria; a vessel of agate, more broad than deep, an inch thick, and half a foot long, the bottom of which was carved to represent a man with one knee on the ground, who held a bow and arrow, ready to discharge at a lion. He sent him also a rich tablet, which, according to tradition, had belonged to the great Solomon.

"The king of the Indies was highly gratified at the caliph's mark of friendship. A little time after this I asked leave to depart and with much difficulty obtained it. The king, when he dismissed me, made me a very splendid present. I embarked for Baghdad, but had not the good fortune to arrive there so speedily as I had hoped.

"Three or four days after my departure we were attacked by pirates, who seized upon our ship, because it was not a vessel of war. Some of the crew fought back, which cost them their lives. But myself and the rest, who were not so rash, the pirates saved, and carried into a distant island, where they sold us.

"I fell into the hands of a rich merchant, who, as soon as he bought me, took me to his house, treated me well, and clad me handsomely as a slave. Some days after, he asked me if I understood any trade. I answered that I was no mechanic, but a merchant, and that the pirates who sold me had robbed me of all I had.

"'Tell me,' he said, 'can you shoot with a bow?' I answered that the bow was one of my exercises in my youth.

"Then my master told me to climb into a tree and shoot at the elephants as they passed and let him know as soon as I killed one, in order that he might get the tusks. I did as he told me, and as I was successful the first day, he sent me day after day, for two months.

"One morning the elephants surrounded my tree, and the largest pulled up the tree with his trunk and threw it on the ground. Then, picking me up, he laid me on his back and carried me to a hill almost covered with the bones and tusks of elephants. I knew that this must be the burial place of the elephants, and they had brought me here to show me that I could get vast quantities of ivory without killing any more elephants.

"I went back to the city and told my master all that had happened. He was overjoyed at my escape from death and the riches which I had obtained for him. As a reward for my services he set me free and promised to send me home as soon as the trade winds brought the ships for ivory.

"A ship arrived at last, and my master loaded one half of it with ivory for me. When we reached a port on the mainland, I landed my ivory and set out for home with a caravan of merchants. I was a long time on the journey, but was happy in thinking that I had nothing to fear from the sea or from pirates. At last I arrived at Baghdad, and the caliph loaded me with honors and rich presents."

Sindbad here finished the story of his seventh and last voyage. Then addressing himself to Hindbad, he said, "Well, friend, did you ever hear of any person who had suffered as much as I have?"

Hindbad kissed Sindbad's hand and said, "Sir, my afflictions are not to be compared with yours. You not only deserve a quiet life, but are worthy of all the riches you possess. May you live happily for a long time."

Sindbad ordered him to be paid another hundred sequins and told him to give up carrying burdens and to eat henceforth at his table, for he wished him to remember that he would always have a friend in Sindbad the Sailor.

NOTES AND QUESTIONS

Discussion. 1. Why did Sindbad tell the story of his voyages? 2. What was the effect of these stories upon Hindbad? 3. If Hindbad had desired to become as rich as Sindbad, what should he have done, and what price would he have paid? 4. Why did Sindbad give money to his guest at the end of each story? 5. Did he do other good deeds with his money? 6. In each of these three long stories, of Aladdin, Ali Baba, and Sindbad the sailor, what do you learn about the duty of men who have by chance or by their own hard work succeeded in acquiring riches? 7. How many voyages did Sindbad make to satisfy his love of adventure? 8. Which voyage was undertaken to please someone else? 9. Mention some things that Sindbad sold at great profit. 10. Where are these articles most used or valued? 11. Why was it so difficult to travel by water at the time Sindbad lived? 12. What do we learn about Sindbad's character from the story of his voyages? 13. What do we learn about Sindbad's character from his treatment of Hindbad? 14. What parts of the story show that people in Sindbad's time knew very little about geography? 15. Which of Sindbad's seven voyages is the most interesting to you? 16. What have you learned of Eastern customs from this story? 17. On page 146 you were told why we read adventure stories of this kind; show why you think *The Arabian Nights* stories have the two values mentioned. 18. *Class readings:* Select passages to be read aloud. 19. *Outline for testing silent reading.* Tell in your own words the story of each of the voyages of Sindbad, using the topic headings given in the book. If possible, try to tell these stories to some child who cannot read them. 20. *The Arabian Nights* by Wiggin and Smith was illustrated by the famous American artist, Maxfield Parrish; you will enjoy looking at these pictures. 21. Find in the glossary the meaning of: mansion, grave, humor (pp. 183-184), ointment, sandalwood (pp. 185-186), repentance, turban, shipping (pp. 187-190), traffic (p. 193), azure (p. 197). 22. *Pronounce:* caliph, Harun-al-Rashid, savory, repast (pp. 183-184), becalmed, Maharaja, rarities, aloes, sequin (pp. 185-186), roc, desert (p. 188), Arabic, sovereign (pp. 196-197), tradition (p. 200).

Phrases for Study

attend his pleasure, **184**, 18
bountiful traveler, **187**, 1
Commander of the Faithful, **197**, 1
trade winds **201**, 13

The Story of Robin Hood*

The Home of Robin in Sherwood Forest

Many hundreds of years ago, when the Plantagenets were kings, England was so covered with woods that a squirrel was said to be able to hop from tree to tree from the Severn to the Humber.

It must have been very different looking from the country we travel through now; but still there were roads that ran from north to south and from east to west, for the use of those who wished to leave their homes, and at certain times of the year these roads were thronged with people. Pilgrims going to some holy shrine passed along, merchants taking their wares to court, abbots and bishops ambling by on palfreys to bear their part in the king's council and, more frequently still, a solitary knight seeking adventures.

Besides the broad roads there were small tracks and little green paths, and these led to clumps of low huts, where dwelt the peasants, charcoal-burners, and plowmen,

* See "Suggestions for Silent Reading," page 163.

while here and there some larger clearing than usual told that the house of a yeoman was near.

Now and then as you passed through the forest you might ride by a splendid abbey and catch a glimpse of monks in long black or white gowns, fishing in the streams and rivers that abound in this part of England, or casting nets in the fish ponds which were in the midst of the abbey gardens. Or you might chance to see a castle with round turrets and high battlements, circled by strong walls, and protected by a moat full of water.

This was the sort of England into which the famous Robin Hood was born. We know very little about him, who he was, or where he lived, except that for some reason he had offended the king, who had declared him an outlaw, so that any man might kill him and never pay a penalty for it.

But, outlaw or not, the poor people loved him and looked on him as their friend, and many a stout fellow came to join him and led a merry life in the greenwood, with moss and fern for bed, and for meat the king's deer, which it was death to slay.

Peasants of all sorts, tillers of the land, yeomen, and, as some say, knights, went on their ways freely, for of them Robin took no toll; but rich men with moneybags well filled trembled as they drew near to Sherwood Forest—who was to know whether behind every tree there did not lurk Robin Hood or some of his men?

The Coming of Little John

One day Robin was walking alone in the wood and reached a river which was spanned by a very narrow bridge, over which one man only could pass. In the middle stood a stranger, and Robin bade him go back and let him go over. "I am no man of yours," was all the answer Robin got, and in anger he drew his bow and fitted an arrow to it.

"Would you shoot a man who has no arms but a staff?" asked the stranger in scorn, and with shame Robin laid down his bow and unbuckled an oaken stick at his side. "We will fight till one of us falls into the water," he said, and fight they did, till the stranger planted a blow so well that Robin rolled over into the river.

"You are a brave soul," said he, when he had waded to land; and he blew a blast with his horn which brought fifty good fellows, clad in green, to the little bridge.

"Have you fallen into the river, that your clothes are wet?" asked one, and Robin made answer, "No, but this stranger, fighting on the bridge, got the better of me and tumbled me into the stream."

At this, the foresters seized the stranger and would have ducked him, had not their leader bade them stop and begged the stranger to stay with them and make one of themselves. "Here is my hand," replied the stranger, "and my heart with it. My name, if you would know it, is John Little."

"That must be altered," cried Will Scarlett; "we will call a feast, and henceforth, because he is full seven feet tall and round the waist at least an ell, he shall be called Little John."

And thus it was done, but at the feast Little John, who always liked to know exactly what work he had to do, put some questions to Robin Hood. "Before I join hands with you, tell me first what sort of life this is you lead. How am I to know whose goods I shall take, and whose I shall leave? Whom shall I beat, and whom shall I refrain from beating?"

And Robin answered: "Look that you harm not any tiller of the ground, nor any yeoman of the greenwood—no, nor any knight or squire, unless you have heard him ill spoken of. But if rich men with moneybags come your way, see that you spoil *them,* and mark that you always hold in your mind the High Sheriff of Nottingham."

This being settled, Robin Hood declared Little John to be second in command to himself among the brotherhood of the forest, and the new outlaw never forgot to hold in his mind the High Sheriff of Nottingham, who was the bitterest enemy the foresters had.

Robin Hood, however, had no liking for a company of idle men about him, so he at once sent off Little John and Will Scarlett to the great road known as Watling Street with orders to hide among the trees and wait till some adventure might come to them. If they took captive earl or baron, abbot or knight, he was to be brought unharmed back to Robin Hood.

But all along Watling Street the road was bare; white and hard it lay in the sun, without the tiniest cloud of dust to show that a rich company might be coming; east and west the land lay still.

Little John's First Adventure

At length, just where a side path turned into the broad highway, there rode a knight, and a sorrier man than he never sat a horse on a summer day. One foot only was in the stirrup; the other hung carelessly by his side. His head was bowed, the reins dropped loose, and his horse went on as he would. At so sad a sight the hearts of the outlaws were filled with pity, and Little John fell on his knees and bade the knight welcome in the name of his master.

"Who is your master?" asked the knight.

"Robin Hood," answered Little John.

"I have heard much good of him," replied the knight, "and will go with you gladly."

Then they all set off together, tears running down the knight's cheeks as he rode. But he said nothing; neither was anything said to him. And in this wise they came to Robin Hood.

"Welcome, Sir Knight," cried he, "and thrice welcome, for I waited to break my fast till you or some other had come to me."

"God save you, good Robin," answered the knight; and after they had washed themselves in the stream, they sat down to dine off bread and wine, with flesh of the king's deer, and swans and pheasants. "Such a dinner have I not had for three weeks and more," said the knight. "And if I ever come again this way, good Robin, I will give you as fine a dinner as you have given me."

"I thank you," replied Robin; "my dinner is always welcome; still, I am none so greedy but I can wait for it. But before you go, pay me, I pray you, for the food which you have had. It was never the custom for a yeoman to pay for a knight."

"My bag is empty," said the knight, "save for ten shillings only."

"Go, Little John, and look in his wallet," said Robin, "and, Sir Knight, if in truth you have no more, not one penny will I take; nay, I will give you all that you shall need."

So Little John spread out the knight's mantle, and opened the bag, and therein lay ten shillings and naught besides.

"What tidings, Little John?" cried his master.

"Sir, the knight speaks truly," said Little John.

"Then fill a cup of the best wine and tell me, Sir Knight, whether it is your own ill doings which have brought you to this sorry pass."

"For a hundred years my fathers have dwelt in the forest," answered the knight, "and four hundred pounds might they spend yearly. But within two years, misfortune has befallen me, and my wife and children also."

"How did this evil come to pass?" asked Robin.

"Through my own folly," answered the knight, "and because of the great love I bore my son, who would never be guided of my counsel and slew, ere he was twenty years old, a knight of Lancaster and his squire. For their deaths I had to pay a large sum, which I could not raise without giving my lands in pledge to a rich man at York. If I cannot give him the money by a certain day, they will be lost to me forever."

"What is the sum?" asked Robin. "Tell me truly."

"It is four hundred pounds," said the knight.

"And what will you do if you lose your lands?" asked Robin again.

"Hie myself over the sea," said the knight, "and bid farewell to my friends and country. There is no better way open to me."

As he spoke, tears fell from his eyes, and he turned to depart. "Good day, my friend," he said to Robin; "I cannot pay you what I should—" But Robin held him fast. "Where are your friends?" asked he.

"Sir, they have all forsaken me, since I became poor, and they turn away their heads if we meet upon the road, though when I was rich they were ever in my castle."

When Little John and Will Scarlett and the rest heard this, they wept for very shame and fury, and Robin bade them fill a cup of the best wine and give it to the knight.

"Have you no one who would stay surety for you?" said he.

"None," answered the knight; "there is no one who will stay surety for me."

"You speak well," said Robin, "and you, Little John, go to my treasure chest and bring me thence four hundred pounds. And be sure you count it truly."

So Little John went, and Will Scarlett, and they brought back the money.

"Sir," said Little John, when Robin had counted it and found it no more and no less, "look at his clothes, how thin they are! You have stores of garments, green and scarlet, in your coffers—no merchant in England can boast the like. I will measure some out with my bow." And thus he did.

"Master," spoke Little John again, "there is still something else. You must give him a horse, that he may go as beseems his quality to York."

"Take the gray horse," said Robin, "and put a new saddle on it, and take likewise a good palfrey and a pair of boots, with gilt spurs on them. And as it would be a shame for a knight to ride by himself on this errand, I will lend you Little John as squire—perchance he may stand you in yeoman's stead."

"When shall we meet again?" asked the knight.

"This day twelve months," said Robin, "under the greenwood tree."

The Knight Wins Back His Lands

Then the knight rode on his way, with Little John behind him, and as he went he thought of Robin Hood and his men and blessed them for the goodness they had shown toward him.

"Tomorrow," he said to Little John, "I must be in the city of York, for if I am so much as a day late, my lands are lost forever; and though I were to bring the money, I should not be allowed to redeem them."

Now the man who had lent the money, as well as the knight, had been counting the days, and the next day he said to his friends, "This day year there came a knight and borrowed of me four hundred pounds, giving his lands as surety. If he come not to pay his debt before midnight, they will be mine forever."

"It is full early yet," said one; "he may still be coming."

"He is far beyond the sea and suffers from hunger and cold," said the rich man. "How is he to get here?"

"It were a shame," said another, "for you to take his lands. And you do him much wrong if you drive such a hard bargain."

"He is dead or hanged," said a third, "and you will have his lands."

So they went to the high justiciar, whose duty it would be to declare the knight's lands forfeited if he did not pay the money.

"If he come not this day," cried the rich man, rubbing his hands, "the lands will be mine."

"He will not come," said the justiciar, but he knew not that the knight was already at the outer gate, and Little John with him.

"Welcome, Sir Knight," said the porter. "The horse that you ride is the noblest that ever I saw. Let me lead it and the steed of your companion to the stable, that they may have food and rest."

"They shall not pass these gates," answered the knight sternly, and he entered the hall alone.

"I have come back, my lord," he said, kneeling down

before the rich man, who had just returned from court.

"Have you brought my money?"

"I have come to pray you to give me more time," said the knight.

"The day was fixed and cannot be gainsaid," answered the justiciar, who was sitting at meat with others in the hall.

The knight begged the justiciar to be his friend and help him, but he refused.

"Give me one more chance to get the money and free my lands," prayed the knight. "I will serve you day and night till I have four hundred pounds to redeem them."

But the rich man only vowed that the money must be paid that day or the lands be forfeited.

Then the knight stood up straight and tall.

"You are not courteous," he said, "to make a knight kneel so long. But it is well to prove one's friends against the hour of need."

Then he looked the rich man full in the face, and the man felt uneasy and hated the knight more than ever.

"Out of my hall, false knight," he cried, pretending to a courage he did not feel.

But the knight answered him, "Never was I false, and that I have shown in justs and in tourneys."

"Give him two hundred pounds more," said the justiciar to the rich man, "and keep the lands yourself."

"No," cried the knight, "not if you offered me a thousand pounds would I do it. No one here shall be heir of mine." Then he strode up to a table and emptied out four hundred pounds. "Take your gold which you lent to me a year agone," he said. "Had you but received me civilly, I would have paid you something more."

Then he passed out of the hall singing merrily and rode

back to his house, where his wife met him at the gate.

He went forth full merrily singing,
As men have told in tale;
His lady met him at the gate,
At home in Wierysdale.

"Welcome, my lord," said his lady;
"Sir, lost is all your good."
"Be merry, Dame," said the knight,
"And pray for Robin Hood."

Then he told how Robin Hood had befriended him, and how he had redeemed his lands, and finished his tale by praising the outlaw. "But for his kindness," he said, "we had been beggars."

After this the knight dwelt at home, looking after his lands and saving his money carefully, till the four hundred pounds lay ready for Robin Hood. Then he bought a hundred bows and a hundred arrows, and every arrow was an ell long, and had a head of silver and peacock's feathers. And clothing himself in white and red, and with a hundred men in his train, he set off to Sherwood Forest.

On the way he passed an open space near a bridge where there was a wrestling, and the knight stopped and looked, for he himself had taken many a prize in that sport. Here the prizes were such as to fill any man with envy: a fine horse, saddled and bridled, a great white bull, a pair of gloves, and a ring of bright, red gold.

There was not a yeoman present who did not hope to win one of them. But when the wrestling was over, the yeoman who had beaten them all was a man who kept apart from his fellows and was said to think much of himself.

Therefore the men grudged him his skill and set upon him with blows and would have killed him had not the knight, for love of Robin Hood, taken pity on him, while his followers fought with the crowd and would not suffer them to touch the prizes a better man had won.

When the wrestling was finished, the knight rode on, and there under the greenwood tree, in the place appointed, he found Robin and his merry men waiting for him, according to the tryst that they had fixed last year.

"God save thee, Robin Hood,
  And all this company."
"Welcome be thou, gentle knight,
  And right welcome to me.

"Hast thou thy land again?" said Robin;
  "Truth then tell thou me."
"Yea, 'fore God," said the knight,
  "And for it thank I God and thee.

"Have here four hundred pounds,
  The which you lent to me;
And here are also twenty marks
  For your courtesie."

But Robin would not take the money. A miracle had happened, he said, and it had been paid to him, and shame would it be for him to take it twice over.

Then he noticed for the first time the bows and arrows which the knight had brought and asked what they were. "A poor present to you," answered the knight; and Robin, who would not be outdone, sent Little John once more to his treasury and bade him bring forth four hundred pounds, which were given to the knight.

After that they parted in much love; and Robin prayed the knight if he were in any strait to let him know at the greenwood tree, and while there was any gold there he should have it.

How Little John Became the Sheriff's Servant

Meanwhile, the High Sheriff of Nottingham proclaimed a great shooting match in a broad open space, and Little John was minded to try his skill with the rest. He rode through the forest, whistling gaily to himself, for well he knew that not one of Robin Hood's men could send an arrow as straight as he, and he felt little fear of anyone else.

When he reached the trysting place, he found a large company assembled, the sheriff with them, and the rules of the match were read out: where they were to stand, how far the mark was to be, and that three tries should be given to every man.

Some of the shooters shot near the mark; some of them even touched it; but none but Little John split the slender wand of willow with every arrow that flew from his bow.

At this sight the Sheriff of Nottingham swore that Little John was the best archer that ever he had seen, and asked him who he was and where he was born, and vowed that if he would enter his service he would give twenty marks a year to so good a bowman.

Little John, who did not wish to confess that he was one of Robin Hood's men and an outlaw, said his name was Reynold Greenleaf, and that he was in the service of a knight, whose leave he must get before he became the servant of any man.

This was given heartily by the knight whose lands had been saved by the kindness of Robin Hood, and Little John bound himself to the sheriff for the space of twelve months and was given a good white horse to ride on whenever he went abroad. But for all that, he did not like his bargain, and made up his mind to do the sheriff, who was hated of the outlaws, all the mischief he could.

His chance came on a Wednesday, when the sheriff always went hunting, and Little John lay in bed till noon, or till he grew hungry. Then he got up and told the steward that he wanted some dinner. The steward answered that he should have nothing till the sheriff came home; so Little John grumbled and left him, and sought out the butler.

Here he was no more successful than before; the butler just went to the buttery door and locked it, and told Little John that he would have to make himself happy till his lord returned.

Rude words mattered nothing to Little John, who was not accustomed to be balked by trifles; so he gave a mighty kick, which burst open the door, and then ate and drank as much as he would, and when he had finished all there was in the buttery, he went down into the kitchen.

Now the sheriff's cook was a strong man and a bold one and had no mind to let another man play the king in his kitchen; so he gave Little John three smart blows, which were returned heartily. "Thou art a brave man and hardy," said Little John, "and a good fighter withal. I have a sword; take you another, and let us see which is the better man of us twain."

The cook did as he was bid, and for two hours they fought, neither of them harming the other. "Fellow," said Little John at last, "you are one of the best swordsmen that I ever saw—and if you could shoot as well with the bow, I would take you back to the merry greenwood, and

Robin Hood would give you twenty marks a year and two changes of clothing."

"Put up your sword," said the cook, "and I will go with you. But first we will have some food in my kitchen and carry off a little of the gold and silver that is in the sheriff's treasure house."

They ate and drank till they wanted no more, and they broke the locks of the treasure house and took of the silver as much as they could carry, and of the gold, three hundred pounds and more, and departed unseen by anyone to Robin in the forest.

"Welcome! Welcome!" cried Robin, when he saw them; "a welcome, too, to the fair yeoman you bring with you. What tidings from Nottingham, Little John?"

"The proud sheriff greets you and sends you by my hand his cook and his silver vessels and three hundred pounds and three also."

Robin shook his head, for he knew better than to believe Little John's tale. "It was never by his good will that you brought such treasure to me," he answered; and Little John, fearing that he might be ordered to take it back again, slipped away into the forest to carry out a plan that had just come into his head.

He ran straight on for five miles, till he came up with the sheriff, who was still hunting, and flung himself on his knees before him.

"Reynold Greenleaf," cried the sheriff, "what are you doing here, and where have you been?"

"I have been in the forest, where I saw a fair hart of a green color and seven score deer feeding hard by."

"That sight would I see too," said the sheriff.

"Then follow me," answered Little John, and he ran back the way he came, the sheriff following on horseback, till they turned a corner of the forest and found themselves in Robin Hood's presence. "Sir, here is the masterhart," said Little John.

Still stood the proud sheriff;
    A sorry man was he.
"Woe be to you, Reynold Greenleaf;
    Thou hast betrayed me!"

"It was not my fault," answered Little John, "but the fault of your servants, master; for they would not give me my dinner." So he went away to see to the supper.

It was spread under the greenwood tree, and they sat down to it, hungry men all. But when the sheriff saw himself served from his own dishes, his appetite went from him.

"Take heart, man," said Robin Hood, "and think not we will poison you. For charity's sake, and for the love of Little John, your life shall be granted you. Only for twelve months you shall dwell with me and learn what it is to be an outlaw."

To the sheriff this punishment was worse to bear than the loss of gold, or silver dishes, and earnestly he begged Robin Hood to set him free vowing he would prove himself the best friend that ever the foresters had.

Neither Robin nor any of his men believed him; but he swore that he would never seek to do them harm, and that if he found any of them in evil plight he would deliver them out of it. With that Robin let him go.

How Robin Met Friar Tuck

In many ways life in the forest was dull in the winter, and often the days passed slowly; but in summer, when the leaves were green, and flowers and ferns covered all the woodland, Robin Hood and his men would come out of their warm resting places, like the rabbits and the squirrels, and would play, too. Races they ran to stretch their legs, or leaping matches were arranged, or they would shoot at a mark. Anything was pleasant when the grass was soft once more under their feet.

"Who of you can kill a hart five hundred paces off?" So said Robin to his men one bright May morning; and they went into the wood and tried their skill, and in the end it was Little John who brought down the hart, to the great joy of Robin Hood.

"I would ride my horse a hundred miles to find one who could match with thee," he said to Little John; and Will Scarlett, who was perhaps rather jealous of this mighty deed, answered with a laugh, "There lives a friar in Fountains Abbey who would beat both him and you."

Now Robin Hood did not like to be told that any man could shoot better than himself or his foresters; so he swore lustily that he would neither eat nor drink till he had seen that friar. Leaving his men where they were, he put on a coat of mail and a steel cap, took his shield and sword, slung his bow over his shoulder, and filled his quiver with arrows. Thus armed, he set forth to Fountains Dale.

By the side of the river a friar was walking, armed like Robin, but without a bow. At this sight Robin jumped from his horse, which he tied to a thorn, and called to the friar to carry him over the water, or it would cost him his life.

The friar said nothing, but hoisted Robin on his broad back and marched into the river. Not a word was spoken till they reached the other side, when Robin leaped lightly down, and was going on his way. Then the friar stopped him. "Not so fast, my fine fellow," said he. "It is my turn now, and you shall take me across the river, or woe will betide you."

So Robin carried him, and when they had reached the side from which they had started, he set down the friar and jumped for the second time on his back and bade him take him whence he had come. The friar strode into the stream with his burden, but as soon as they got to the middle he bent his head, and Robin fell into the water. "Now you can sink or swim, as you like," said the friar, as he stood and laughed.

Robin Hood swam to a bush of golden broom and pulled himself out of the water; and while the friar was scrambling out, Robin fitted an arrow to his bow and let fly at him. But the friar quickly held up his shield, and the arrow fell harmless.

"Shoot on, my fine fellow; shoot on all day if you like," shouted the friar; and Robin shot till his arrows were gone, but always missed his mark. Then they took their swords, and at four of the afternoon they were still fighting.

By this time, Robin's strength was wearing, and he felt he could not fight much more. "A boon, a boon!" cried he. "Let me but blow three blasts on my horn, and I will thank you on my bended knees for it."

The friar told him to blow as many blasts as he liked, and in an instant the forest echoed with his horn; it was but a few minutes before half a hundred yeomen were racing over the lea. The friar stared when he saw them; then, turning to Robin, he begged of him a boon also; and leave being granted, he gave three whistles, which were followed by the noise of a great crashing through the trees, as fifty great dogs bounded toward him.

"Here's a dog for each of your men," said the friar, "and

I myself for you;" but the dogs did not listen to his words, for two of them rushed at Robin and tore his mantle of Lincoln green from off his back. His men were kept busy defending themselves, for every arrow shot at a dog was caught and held in the creature's mouth.

Robin's men were not used to fighting with dogs and felt they were getting beaten. At last Little John bade the friar call off his dogs, and as he did not do so, he let fly some arrows, which this time left half a dozen dead on the ground.

"Hold, hold, my good fellow," said the friar, "till your master and I can come to a bargain," and when the bargain was made, this was how it ran: that the friar was to forswear Fountains Abbey and join Robin Hood, and that he should be paid a golden noble every Sunday throughout the year, besides a change of clothes on each holy day.

This friar had kept Fountains Dale
Seven long years or more;
There was neither knight, nor lord, nor earl
Could make him yield before.

But now he became one of the most famous members of Robin Hood's men under the name of Friar Tuck.

How Robin Hood and Little John Fell Out

One Whitsunday morning, when the sun was shining and the birds singing, Robin Hood called to Little John to come with him into Nottingham to church. As was their custom, they took their bows, and on the way Little John proposed that they should shoot a match, with a penny for a wager.

Robin, who held that he shot better than any other man living, laughed in scorn and told Little John that he should have three tries to his master's one, which John without more ado accepted.

But Robin soon repented both of his offer and his scorn, for Little John speedily won five shillings, whereat Robin became angry and smote Little John with his hand.

Little John was not the man to bear being treated so, and he told Robin roundly that he would never more own him for master and straightway turned back into the wood.

At this, Robin was ashamed of what he had done, but his pride would not suffer him to say so; and he continued his way to Nottingham and entered the Church of St. Mary, not without secret fears, for the sheriff of the town was ever his enemy. However, there he was, and there he meant to stay.

He knelt down in the sight of all the people; but none knew him save one man only, and he stole out of church and ran to the sheriff and bade him come quickly and take his foe.

The sheriff was not slow to do what he was bidden, and, calling his men to follow him, he marched to the church. The noise they made in entering caused Robin to look round. "Alas, alas," he said to himself, "now miss I Little John."

But he drew his two-handed sword and laid about him in such wise that twelve of the sheriff's men lay dead before him. Then Robin found himself face to face with the sheriff and gave him a fierce blow, but his sword broke on the sheriff's head, and he had shot away all his arrows. So the men closed round him and bound his arms.

Ill news travels fast, and not many hours had passed before the foresters heard that their master was in prison. They wept and moaned and wrung their hands and seemed to have gone suddenly mad, till Little John bade them pluck up their hearts and help him deal with the sheriff.

The next morning Little John hid himself and waited with a comrade till he saw a messenger riding along the road, carrying letters from the sheriff to the king, telling him of the capture of Robin Hood.

"Whence come you?" asked Little John, going up to the messenger, "and can you give us tidings of an outlaw named Robin Hood, who was taken prisoner yesterday?"

"You may thank me that he is taken," said the rider, "for I laid hands on him."

"I thank you so much that I and my friend will bear you company," said Little John, "for in this forest are many wild men who own Robin Hood for leader, and you ride along this road at the peril of your life."

They went on together, talking the while, when suddenly Little John seized the horse by the head and pulled down the rider.

"He was my master," said Little John,
"That you have brought to bale;
Never shall you come at the king
For to tell him that tale."

Then taking the letters, Little John carried them to the king.

When they arrived at the palace in the presence of the king, Little John and his companion fell on their knees and held out the letters. "God save you, my liege lord," they said, and the king unfolded the letters and read them.

Then he handed his own seal to Little John and ordered

him to bear it to the sheriff and bid him without delay bring Robin Hood unhurt into his presence. "There never was yeoman in Merry England that I longed so sore to see," he said.

The king also ordered his treasurer to give the messengers twenty pounds each and made them yeomen of the crown.

Little John took the king's seal to the sheriff, who made him and his companion welcome because they came from the king. He set a feast for them, and after he had eaten he fell asleep. Then the two outlaws stole softly to the prison. They overpowered the guard and, taking the keys, hunted through the cells until they found Robin Hood. Little John whispered to his master to follow him, and they crept along till they reached the lowest part of the city wall, from which they jumped and were safe and free.

"Now, farewell," said Little John; "'I have done you a good turn for an ill." "Not so," answered Robin Hood; "I make you master of my men and me." But Little John would hear nothing of it. "I only wish to be your comrade, and thus it shall be," he replied.

"Little John has beguiled us both," said the king, when he heard of the adventure.

How the King Visited Robin Hood

Now the king had no mind that Robin Hood should do as he willed and called his knights to follow him to Nottingham, where they would lay plans how best to take captive the outlaw. Here they heard sad tales of Robin's misdoings, and how of the many herds of wild deer that had roamed the forest, in some places scarce one deer remained. This was the work of Robin Hood and his merry men, on whom the king swore vengeance with a great oath.

"I would I had this Robin Hood in my hands," cried he, "and an end should soon be put to his doings." So spake the king; but an old knight, full of days and wisdom, answered him and warned him that the task of taking Robin Hood would be a sore one, and best let alone.

The king, who had seen the vanity of his hot words the moment that he had uttered them, listened to the old man and resolved to bide his time until perchance someday Robin should fall into his power.

All this time, and for six weeks later that he dwelt in Nottingham, the king could hear nothing of Robin, who seemed to have vanished into the earth with his merry men, though one by one the deer were vanishing, too.

At last one day a forester came to the king and told him that if he would see Robin he must come with him and take five of his best knights. The king eagerly sprang up to do his bidding, and the six men, clad in monks' clothes, mounted their palfreys and rode merrily along, the king wearing an abbot's broad hat over his crown, and singing as he passed through the greenwood.

Suddenly, at the turn of a path Robin and his archers appeared before them.

"By your leave, Sir Abbot," said Robin, seizing the king's bridle, "you will stay a while with us. Know that we are yeomen, who live upon the king's deer, and other food have we none. Now you have abbeys and churches and gold in plenty; therefore give us some of it, in the name of holy charity."

"I have no more than forty pounds with me," answered the king, "but sorry I am it is not a hundred, for you should have it all."

So Robin took the forty pounds and gave half to his men and then told the king he might go on his way. "I thank you," said the king, "but I would have you know that our liege lord has bid me bear you his seal and pray you to come to Nottingham."

At this message Robin bent his knee.

> "I love no man in all the world
> So well as I do my king,"

he cried, "and Sir Abbot, for thy tidings, which fill my heart with joy, today thou shalt dine with me, for love of my king."

Then he led the king into an open place, and Robin took a horn and blew it loud, and at its blast seven score of young men came speedily to do his will.

"They are quicker to do his bidding than my men are to do mine," said the king to himself.

Speedily the foresters set out the dinner, roasts of venison and loaves of white bread, and Robin and Little John served the king. "Make good cheer," said Robin, "Abbot, for charity, and then you shall see what sort of life we lead, so that you may tell our king."

When he had finished eating, the archers took their bows and hung rose garlands up with a string, and every man was to shoot through the garland. If he failed, he should have a buffet on the head from Robin.

Good bowmen as they were, few managed to stand the test. Little John and Will Scarlett and Much all shot wide of the mark, and at length no one was left in but Robin himself and Gilbert of the Wide Hand. Then Robin fired his last bolt, and it fell three fingers from the garland. "Master," said Gilbert, "you have lost; stand forth and take your punishment, as was agreed."

"I will take it," answered Robin, "but, Sir Abbot, I pray you that I may suffer it at your hands."

The king hesitated. "It does not become me," he said, "to smite such a stout yeoman," but Robin bade him smite on and spare him not; so he turned up his sleeve, and gave Robin such a lusty buffet on the head that he lost his feet and rolled upon the ground.

"There is pith in your arm," said Robin. "Come, shoot a main with me." And the king took up a bow, and in so doing his hat fell back, and Robin saw his face.

"My lord the king of England, now I know you well," cried he; and he fell on his knees, and all the outlaws with him. "Mercy I ask, my lord the king, for all my brave foresters and me."

"Mercy I grant," then said the king; "and therefore I came hither, to bid you and your men leave the greenwood and dwell in my court with me."

"So shall it be," answered Robin; "I and my men will come to your court and see how your service liketh us."

ROBIN AT COURT

"Have you any green cloth," asked the king, "that you could sell to me?" and Robin brought out thirty yards and more, and clad the king and his men in coats of Lincoln green. "Now we will all ride to Nottingham," said he, and they went merrily, shooting by the way.

The people of Nottingham saw them coming and trembled as they watched the dark mass of Lincoln green drawing near over the fields. "I fear lest our king be slain," whispered one to another; "and if Robin Hood gets into the town, there is not one of us whose life is safe," and every man, woman, and child made ready to flee.

The king laughed out when he saw their fright and

called them back. Right glad were they to hear his voice, and they feasted and made merry. A few days later the king returned to London, and Robin dwelt in his court for twelve months. By that time he had spent a hundred pounds, for he gave largely to the knights and squires he met, and great renown he had for his open-handedness.

But his men, who had been born under the shadow of the forest, could not live amid streets and houses. One by one they slipped away, till only Little John and Will Scarlett were left. Then Robin himself grew homesick, and at the sight of some young men shooting he thought upon the time when he was accounted the best archer in all England and went straightway to the king and begged for leave to go on a pilgrimage.

"I may not say you nay," answered the king; "seven nights you may be gone and no more." And Robin thanked him and that evening set out for the greenwood.

It was early morning when he reached it at last and listened thirstily to the notes of singing birds, great and small.

"It seems long since I was here," he said to himself; "it would give me great joy if I could bring down a deer once more," and he shot a great hart, and blew his horn, and all the outlaws of the forest came flocking round him. "Welcome," they said, "our dear master, back to the greenwood tree," and they threw off their caps and fell on their knees before him in delight at his return.

Naught that the king could say would tempt Robin Hood back again, and he dwelt in the greenwood for two and twenty years after he had run away from court. And he was ever a faithful friend, kind to the poor, and gentle to all women.

NOTES AND QUESTIONS

Historical Note. When William the Conqueror became king of England he destroyed many villages and towns to make royal forests in which he might enjoy his favorite sport of hunting. The most famous of the hunting grounds was in Hampshire and was called the New Forest. Hundreds of poor people were driven from their homes and left shelterless that this hunting park might be made. In order to keep up these hunting grounds, William and the kings who followed him made very severe laws for the protection of the deer.

The temptation to shoot these deer must have been very strong, especially to men living near the forest, for the English at that time excelled all other nations in the use of the long bow. In consequence of this, many men killed the king's deer and fled to the woods to escape punishment. There they formed into bands and, knowing the forests so well, were safe from the king's officers. Among these outlaws were many brave and skillful archers, but none was ever more famous than the hero of this story, Robin Hood.

Discussion. 1. Why was Robin Hood obliged to live in the forest? 2. How did he win the friendship of Little John? 3. What did Robin Hood tell him about the Sheriff of Nottingham? 4. Describe the appearance of the knight whom Little John met in the forest. 5. What foods were prepared for the dinner to which Robin Hood invited the knight? 6. How had these provisions been obtained? 7. What story did the knight tell to Robin Hood? 8. How did Robin Hood help him? 9. Where do you think the treasure chest was kept? 10. From whom had this treasure been taken? 11. How did the knight show his gratitude after he regained his lands? 12. Why did the Sheriff of Nottingham want Little John in his service? 13. What thought was constantly in Little John's mind? 14. How did he accomplish his purpose? 15. What explanation did he give to Robin Hood for what he brought from the sheriff's house? 16. How did he induce the sheriff to follow him to the place where Robin Hood was? 17. What punishment did Robin Hood decide upon for the sheriff? Why did he not carry it out? 18. How was Robin Hood captured by the sheriff? 19. What reason do you think the king had for wanting to see Robin Hood? 20. What did he determine to do after Robin Hood's escape? 21. Find words in which Robin Hood expressed his love for his king. 22. What offer did the king make to Robin Hood and his men? Why did the king make them such an offer? 23. Why did Robin dislike living at court? 24. How long did Robin Hood live in the greenwood after he left the court? 25. Under what conditions do you think life in the forest would be pleasant? 26. What were these men obliged to give up when they went into the forest to live? 27. What did they gain by living in the forest? 28. When did Robin Hood show himself generous? 29. When did Robin show himself merciful? 30. What do you think of Little John's treatment of the Sheriff of Nottingham after he had lived in his house? 31. When did Little John show himself a loyal friend? 32. When did he show himself hard and cruel? 33. What things mentioned in this story show that the manners and life of the people in England at this time were rough? 34. What qualities were most admired in men at the time of Robin Hood? 35. What was the reason for this? 36. Make a list showing the good qualities of Robin Hood, such as his courtesy, his justice, his sense of fair play. Mention the incidents that illustrate each characteristic. 37. Show that this story has the two values mentioned in the first paragraph of page 146. 38. Why did Robin dislike the sheriff? 39. Find, from the story, ways in which poor or unfortunate men were oppressed by the laws in those days. 40. Did the laws seem made to give equal justice to all, or unfair advantages to the rich and powerful? 41. How do you think Robin felt about these matters? 42. How did he try to take the side of the poor men who were thus unfairly dealt with by the government? 43. Tell the story of Friar Tuck. 44. Why did the king take such an interest in Robin? Do you think the king was glad to get away from the court? Why? 45. What did he say about the way in which Robin was obeyed by his followers? 46. What does the Forward Look, page 144, tell you about the source of this story? 47. *Class readings:* Little John's first adventure, omitting all but the dialogue, page 206, line 23, to page 209, line 27 (3 pupils); Robin and his archers with the king, page 224, line 25, to page 226, line 19; Robin at the king's court, page 226, line 20, to page 227, line 32. 48. *Outline for testing silent reading.* Tell the story of Robin Hood, using these topics: (a) the home of Robin in Sherwood Forest; (b) the coming of Little John; (C) Little John's first adventure; (d) the knight's recovery of his lands; (e) Little John as the sheriff's servant; (f) Robin's meeting with Friar Tuck; (g) the disagreement between Robin and Little John; (h) the king's visit to Robin Hood; (i) Robin at court. 49. You will enjoy seeing the pictures in the edition of *Robin Hood* illustrated by N. C. Wyeth. 50. Find in the glossary the meaning of: abbey, battlements (p. 204), ell (p. 205), coffers (p. 209), tourneys (p. 211), hart (p. 216), broom, boon, noble (pp. 219-220). 51. *Pronounce:* Plantagenets, palfreys, peasants, yeoman, toll (pp. 203-204), pheasants, naught, hie, surety (pp. 207-209), justiciar, gainsaid, justs, heir, tryst (pp. 210-213), steward, balked (p. 215), lea (p. 219), ado, liege, beguiled (pp. 221-223), buffet (p. 226).

Phrases for Study

king's council, **203**, 12
stout fellow, **204**, 18
took no toll, **204**, 24
break my fast, **207**, 9
sorry pass, **208**, 3
guided of my counsel, **208**, 11
stay surety, **209**, 1
beseems his quality, **209**, 18
stand you in yeoman's stead, **209**, 24
redeem them, **210**, 4
was minded to try, **214**, 7
without more ado, **221**, 2
in such wise, **221**, 26
brought to bale, **222**, 22
shoot a main, **226**, 8
service liketh us, 226, 19

Gulliver's Travels*

Jonathan Swift

Gulliver Sails for the South Sea and is Shipwrecked

My name is Lemuel Gulliver, and my home is in Nottinghamshire. I went to college at Cambridge, where I studied hard, for I knew my father was not rich enough to keep me when I should become a man, and that I must be able to earn my own living.

I decided to be a doctor, but as I had always longed to travel, I learned to be a good sailor as well. When I had succeeded in becoming both doctor and sailor, I married, and with my wife's consent I became surgeon upon a ship and made many voyages. One of these voyages was with Captain Prichard, master of a vessel called the *Antelope,* bound for the South Sea. We set sail from Bristol and started upon our journey very fairly, until there came a violent storm that drove our ship near an island called Van Diemen's Land. The *Antelope* was driven against a rock, which wrecked and split the vessel in half.

* See "Suggestions for Silent Reading," page 163.

Six of the sailors and myself let down one of the small boats and, getting into it, rowed away from the ruined vessel and the dangerous rock. We rowed until we were so tired we could no longer hold the oars; then we were obliged to allow our boat to go as the waves carried it. Suddenly there came another violent gust of wind from the north, and our small boat was at once overturned. I do not know what became of my unfortunate companions, but I fear all must have been drowned. I was a good swimmer, and I swam for my life. I went the best way I could, pushed forward by wind and tide. Sometimes I let my legs drop to see if my feet touched the bottom, and when I was almost overcome and fainting, I found to my great joy that I was out of the deep water and able to walk.

By this time the storm was over. I walked about a mile, until I reached the shore, and when I stood upon land I could not see a sign of any houses or people. I felt very weak and tired; so I lay down upon the grass, which was very short and soft, and soon fell into a sound sleep.

I must have slept all that night, for when I awoke, it was bright daylight. I tried to rise, but found I was not able even to move. I had been lying upon my back, and I found my arms and legs were strongly fastened on each side to the ground; and that my hair, which was long and thick, was also tied to the ground. I felt several slender threads over my body. Fastened in this way, I could only look upwards, and, as the sun came out and shone in my eyes, this was very uncomfortable. I heard a queer noise about me, but could see nothing except the sky.

In a little while I felt something alive moving on my left leg; this thing came gently forward over my breast and almost up to my chin. Bending my eyes downward as much as I could, I saw a tiny human creature, not more than six inches high, with a tiny bow and arrow in his hands. While I gazed in astonishment, forty more of the same kind followed the first. I called out so loud in my amazement that they all ran back in a fright, and I felt them leaping from my sides to the ground. However, they soon returned, and one of them came up so far as to get a full sight of my face. As he looked at me, he held up his hands and cried out in a shrill but distinct voice, "Hekinah degul!" Of course I did not understand what this meant, but from the tone in which it was said I thought it must express admiration for me.

All this time I lay in great uneasiness. At length I struggled to get loose and managed to break the strings and pull up the pegs that fastened my left arm to the ground. Then with a violent tug that caused me much pain I broke the strings that tied down my hair on the left side and was then able to turn my head a trifle.

The little people all ran off before I could seize them, and there was a great deal of shouting in very shrill voices. Then in about an instant I felt quite a hundred arrows shot on my left hand, which pricked me like so many needles. Besides this, another hundred were shot into the air and fell all over my body, and some upon my face. When this shower of arrows was over, I lay groaning with the pain and covering my face with my free hand. I had only just done so in time, for immediately another and larger shower fell upon me, and some of the little people tried to stick their spears into my sides; but luckily I had a leather waistcoat on, which the tiny spears could not pierce.

After this, I thought I had better be still and remain

very quiet till night came. Then I hoped this odd army would leave me and I should be able to set myself free. I was not at all afraid of any number of such small people, once I had the use of my limbs.

GULLIVER IS VISITED BY THE EMPEROR

When they saw I was quiet, they stopped shooting arrows; and, as I was almost starving, I tried to show them I wanted food by putting my finger to my mouth, and looking beseechingly at them, praying them to give me something to eat.

Soon several ladders were put against my sides. Upon these about a hundred of the people mounted and walked toward my mouth, carrying baskets full of meat. This meat was in the same shape as shoulders, legs, and loins of mutton, but smaller than the wings of a lark. It was all well dressed and cooked, and I ate two or three joints at a mouthful and took three loaves at a time, which were no bigger than bullets. The little people gave the food to me as fast as they could, and showed much wonder at the greatness of my appetite.

I must confess I was tempted to pick up those who were running over my body and throw them to the ground. But remembering the shower of arrows and the food they had given me, I felt I was bound in honor not to do them harm. I could not help thinking these tiny creatures were plucky and brave, that they should dare to walk over such a giant as I must seem to them, although one of my hands was free to seize upon them.

After a time there came before me no less a personage than His Imperial Majesty, the emperor of these odd little people. His Majesty mounted my right leg and advanced forward to my face, followed by a dozen of his courtiers.

As he stood looking at my face, he spoke for about ten minutes without any sign of anger, but very gravely and sternly, and often pointing in front of him, toward, as I afterwards found, the capital city.

To this city the people agreed I was to be carried, and it lay about half a mile off. I made signs to the emperor that I wanted to be freed from the cords that bound me to the earth and allowed to rise. But although he understood me well enough, His Majesty shook his head and showed me I must be carried as a prisoner. However, he made other signs that told me I should have meat and drink and was not to be ill-treated. After this the emperor and his train got off my body and went away.

Soon after, I felt a great number of people at my left side; and they loosened the cords that held me, and so let me turn a little upon my right and get more ease in my uncomfortable position.

Then they put some sweet-smelling ointment upon my face and hands, which soon removed the smart of the arrows. Being thus refreshed, I again fell into a deep sleep, which lasted some hours.

These little people were very clever at making all kinds of machines and engines for carrying heavy weights. They built their ships and men-of-war, which were about the length of a large dining table, in the woods where the timber grew and then carried them to the sea upon the machines they made.

They now set to work to prepare the greatest engine they had, which was a frame of wood, raised three inches from the ground, and about as long as one of our bedsteads and nearly as wide across. Five hundred carpenters and engineers got this machine into readiness to carry me to the city. There was loud shouting, as it was brought up to my side; and then came the chief difficulty, which was how to lift me on to it.

Eighty poles were driven into the ground, each pole about as tall as an ordinary ruler. Then the workmen bound my neck, hands, body, and legs in bandages, and to these bandages they fixed hooks with the strongest cords fastened to them. Nine hundred of the strongest men then drew up these cords by pulleys attached to the poles, and thus in about three hours I was raised and slung upon the machine and there tied fast. Fifteen hundred of the emperor's largest horses, each about four inches and a half high, were used to draw me on the machine to the city.

When at last we arrived at the city gates, the emperor and all his court came out to meet us. At the place where we stopped there stood a very old temple, which was the largest in the whole kingdom. The people no longer used it to worship in, and it had been emptied of all its furniture and ornaments. It was in this building the emperor decided I should live. The great gate was about four feet high and two feet wide, and I could easily creep through it. Upon each side of the gate was a small window, just six inches from the ground. To one of these windows the emperor's smith fixed ninety-one chains, like these we use as watch chains in England, and these chains were locked to my left leg by thirty-six padlocks. Just in front of the temple there was a turret five feet high, and the emperor and his principal nobles got upon the top of this turret to be able to look at me as I lay.

So many people crowded from the city to see me, and all mounted upon my body by the help of ladders, that at last the emperor gave an order that no one else must do so, on penalty of death. For this I was very glad, as I was becoming quite worn out.

When the workmen found it was impossible for me to break my chains and get free, they cut all the strings that bound me, and I rose up feeling very strange and sad. The astonishment of the people at seeing me rise was truly great. The chains that held my left leg were two yards long, and that allowed me to walk backwards and forwards and also to creep into the temple and lie down.

GULLIVER IS KEPT A PRISONER AT THE CAPITAL

When I found myself on my feet, I looked about at the surrounding country. It seemed like one big garden, and the fields, which were about the size of an ordinary room, appeared like so many beds of flowers. Then there were the little patches of trees, which made the woods of this tiny country, and the tallest tree among them was not much higher than an Englishman. The little city itself looked like the painted scene in a theater.

As I was extremely tired, I did not stay long to look, but crept into my house and shut the door after me. When I had rested, I came out again and stepped backward and forward as far as my chains allowed. Then the emperor began to ride up to me; but upon seeing me, the horse took fright and nearly threw its rider, which was no wonder, as the poor animal must have thought I was a moving mountain. The prince was an excellent horseman and kept his seat well, while his attendants ran to assist him. Then His Majesty got off his horse and walked up to me and seemed to look at me with great admiration, but did not come near enough for me to touch him. He ordered his cooks to bring me more food and drink, and they brought me the food put into carriages upon wheels, which they pushed forward until I could reach them. I very soon emptied the carriages.

The empress and the young princes, with many other nobles and ladies, all came and gathered round the emperor and watched me while I ate. His Majesty was taller than any of the others; that is to say, he stood about the breadth of my nail above the heads of his people. He was handsome and well made and had an air of great dignity. I heard that he had reigned seven years, and had been victorious, and that he was much respected.

His dress was very plain, except that he had on his head a light helmet made of gold and adorned with jewels and with a plume upon it. He now held his drawn sword in his hand, to defend himself if I should happen to break loose. This sword was about three inches long, and the hilt and case of it were gold, enriched with diamonds.

After about two hours the court went away, and I was left with a guard of soldiers to keep the people from crowding round me. This guard was necessary, for one of the men had the impudence to shoot an arrow at me as I sat upon the ground, and it nearly hit my eye. Then the soldiers ordered the man to be seized and bound and given into my hands to punish. I took him up and made a face as if I were going to eat him. The poor little fellow screamed terribly, and even the soldiers looked very much alarmed when I took out my penknife.

However, I soon put an end to their fears, for I cut the strings that bound my captive and set him gently upon the ground and let him run away. I saw that all the soldiers and people were delighted at this mark of my mercy and gentleness; and I afterwards heard they told the emperor about it, and he was very pleased with me.

When night came, I crept into my shelter again and lay upon the ground to sleep. The next day the emperor gave orders for a bed to be made for me. The workmen brought six hundred beds to my house in carriages and sewed them all together to make one large enough for me to lie upon. They did the same with sheets and blankets, and at the end of two weeks' labor my bed was ready for me.

As the news of my arrival spread over the kingdom, it brought numbers of people to see me. The villages were almost emptied, and those men and women who should have been at work came to the city to gaze at me. At last the emperor gave orders that all who had seen me once were to go to their homes immediately and not come near me again without His Majesty's permission.

The emperor and his court met together to talk over what could be done with me which seemed a very difficult question. They were afraid I might break my chains and do them harm; then they were afraid that I would eat so much that it would cause a famine in the land and there would be no food left for them. Luckily for me, His Majesty remembered the kind way I had treated the man who shot the arrow at me, and because of my good behavior he allowed me to live. Orders were given for each of the villages round the city to send in every morning six cows and forty sheep for my meals, and also bread and wine, for all of which the emperor paid.

I was also given six hundred little men as my servants, and these built their tents upon each side of my door. Then three hundred tailors set to work to make me a suit of clothes like those worn in that country, and six of the most learned men taught me to speak the language. Lastly, the emperor's horses and those of the nobles and soldiers were ridden and exercised before me, until they became quite used to seeing me and would trot quietly past.

Gulliver is Given His Liberty

My quiet and good behavior so pleased the emperor and his court that I began to hope he would soon give me my liberty. I did all I could to make the people like me and lose their fear of me. I would lie down and let five or six of them dance upon my hand, and at last the boys and girls even dared to come and play at hide-and-seek in my hair.

There was one general, named Skyresh, who was my enemy. I had not given him any cause to dislike me, but he did, and it was he who tried to persuade the emperor not to give me my liberty. However, I implored His Majesty so often to set me free that at last he promised to do so, but he first made me swear to certain conditions which were to be read to me. These conditions were as follows:

"His Majesty, the mighty emperor of Lilliput, proposes to the Man-Mountain the following articles, which he must swear to perform:

"First. The Man-Mountain shall not depart from our country without our permission.

"Second. He shall not enter our chief city without our express consent.

"Third. He shall walk only along the principal roads and not over our meadows and fields of corn.

"Fourth. As he walks he must take the greatest care not to trample upon any of our subjects or their horses and carriages, and he must not take any into his hands without their consent.

"Fifth. If we desire to send a message anywhere very quickly, the Man-Mountain shall be obliged to carry the messenger and his horse in his pocket and return with them safe to our court.

"Sixth. He must promise not to join the army of our enemies in the island of Blefuscu, and he must do his utmost to destroy their fleet of ships, which is now preparing to attack us.

"Seventh. The Man-Mountain shall always be ready to help our workmen in lifting heavy weights.

"Eighth. He must walk all round our island and then tell us how many steps round it measures.

"Lastly. The Man-Mountain shall have a daily allowance of food sufficient for 1724 of our subjects.

"All of these conditions he must take a solemn oath to keep. Then he shall be allowed his liberty."

I swore to keep these promises, and my chains were at once unlocked and I was at full liberty. I expressed my gratitude by casting myself at the emperor's feet, but he graciously commanded me to rise, telling me he hoped I would prove a useful servant and deserve all the favors he had conferred upon me.

One morning, about a fortnight after I had obtained my liberty, the principal noble who managed the emperor's private affairs, and whose name was Reldresal, came to my house, attended by only one servant. He asked to speak to me privately, and I readily consented, as he had always shown me much kindness. I offered to lie down so that he could speak into my ear, but he chose to let me hold him in my hand during our conversation.

He told me that the island of Lilliput was threatened with invasion by an army from the island of Blefuscu, which was the next island, and one almost as large and powerful as Lilliput itself. These two islands and their emperors had for some time been engaged in a most obstinate war.

Reldresal told me that His Majesty had just heard that the Blefuscudians had got together a large fleet of warships and were preparing to invade Lilliput. His Majesty said he placed great trust in my power to help them in this trouble and had commanded his officer to lay the case before me.

I told Reldresal to present my humble duty to the emperor and tell him I thought it would hardly be fair for me, as I was a foreigner, to interfere between the two islands. But I said I was quite ready, even at the risk of my life, to defend His Majesty's state and person against all invaders.

The island of Blefuscu was separated from Lilliput by a channel eight hundred yards wide. I had not yet seen it, but after hearing that the emperor of Blefuscu had a fleet of ships upon the water, I kept from going near the coast, as I did not want to be noticed by the enemy. The Blefuscudians did not know of my presence in Lilliput. I told His Majesty, the emperor of Lilliput, that I had a plan by which I could seize all the enemy's ships.

GULLIVER CAPTURES THE BLEFUSCUDIAN FLEET

I had asked the most clever seamen upon the island how deep the channel was, and they told me that in the middle it was about six feet deep, and at the sides it was only four feet. I then walked toward the coast and lay down behind a hillock; here I took out my telescope and looked at the enemy's fleet. It consisted of fifty men-of-war and a great number of smaller vessels. I hurried back to my house and gave orders for a quantity of the strongest rope and bars of iron. The emperor said all my orders were to be carried out. The rope that was brought me was only as thick as our packing thread, and the iron bars were the length and size of a knitting needle. I twisted three lengths of the rope together to make it stronger and three of the iron bars in the same way. I turned up the ends of the bars to form a hook. I fixed fifty hooks to as many pieces of rope, and then I took them all down to the coast.

Here I took off my shoes and stockings and coat and walked into the sea. I waded until I came to the middle of the channel, and, the water being deep there, I was obliged to swim about thirty yards. After this I waded again, and in less than half an hour I arrived at the fleet of the enemy. The Blefuscudians were so frightened when they saw me that they leaped out of their ships and swam to shore.

I then took my hooks and ropes and fastened a hook to the end of each vessel. Then I tied all the ropes together. While I was doing this, the enemy discharged several thousand arrows at me from the shore, and many of the arrows stuck in my face and hands. This hurt me very much and prevented my working quickly. My worst fear was for my eyes, which would certainly have been put out by arrows had I not thought of my spectacles. These I fastened as strongly as I could upon my nose, and, thus protected, I went boldly on, while the arrows struck my glasses without even cracking them.

When I had fastened all my hooks, I took the knot of ropes in my hand and began to pull. But I could not move a single ship, for they were all held fast by their anchors. Therefore I let go the cord, and, taking my knife from my pocket, I cut the cables that held the anchors, at the same time receiving about two hundred arrows from the enemy, in my face and hands. After this, I once more grasped the ropes, and, with the greatest ease, I pulled fifty of their largest vessels after me. The Blefuscudians were confounded with astonishment. They had seen me cut the cables, but thought I only meant to let the ships run adrift; but when they saw me walking off with almost all of the fleet, they set up a tremendous scream of grief and despair.

When I had got out of danger, I stopped to pick out the arrows that were stuck in my hands and face, and I rubbed on some of the ointment the Lilliputians had given me. Then I took off my spectacles and waded on with my cargo. As the tide was then fallen, I did not need to swim through the middle, but was able to walk right into the royal port of Lilliput.

The emperor and all his court stood upon the shore, watching for my return. They saw the ships coming over the water, in the form of a great half-moon, and soon I was able to make the emperor hear my voice. Holding up my rope, I cried aloud, "Long live the most glorious emperor of Lilliput!"

His Majesty received me with great joy and honor and made me a lord of the island upon the spot.

The emperor then wished me to try to bring all the rest of the enemy's ships to Lilliput. And he talked of taking the whole island of Blefuscu and reigning over it himself. I did not think this at all fair, but very selfish and greedy of His Majesty. I tried to tell him so as politely as I could, and said I could not help to bring a free and brave people into slavery. My bold speech made the emperor very angry indeed, and he never forgave me. But most of his best nobles thought the same as I did, although they dared not say so openly.

From this time His Majesty and some of his court began to bear me ill will, which nearly ended in my death. I considered this very mean of the emperor, after my helping him as I did; but like many other people, he became ungrateful when he found he could not get all he wanted. About three weeks after this the emperor of Blefuscu sent messengers with humble offers to make peace; to this the Lilliputians agreed, upon certain terms.

The messengers consisted of six nobles with a train of five hundred men. They were all very grandly and magnificently dressed. After they had spoken to our emperor, they expressed a wish to come to visit me. It seems they were told I had been their friend when the emperor asked me to help him take Blefuscu, and they came to thank me for my justice and generosity. They invited me to visit their island, where I should receive every kindness and hospitality. I thanked their lordships very much and said I should be pleased to come and pay my respects to the emperor of Blefuscu before I returned to my own country.

So the next time I saw our emperor I begged his permission to go to Blefuscu, which he was gracious enough to grant me, although in a very cold manner. I afterwards heard that my request displeased him, and he did not like my making friends of the Blefuscudians.

The Inhabitants of Lilliput—Their Laws and Customs

I am now going to say a few words about the Lilliputians and their laws and customs.

These little people are generally about six inches high, their horses and oxen between four and five inches, their sheep an inch and a half, and their geese about the size of a sparrow. One day I watched a cook pulling the feathers off a lark, which was no bigger than a fly.

Some of their laws are very unlike our English ones, but they are very just all the same. If a man accuses another of any crime, and it is proved that he has told a lie and the man is innocent, then the accuser is severely punished, and the innocent man is rewarded for all the injustice and pain he has suffered. This keeps people from being so ready to tell tales about others.

Then deceit and cunning are considered greater crimes than stealing in Lilliput, for the people say that a man can take means to protect his goods and money, but he cannot prevent another man's deceiving him. And so, if any man makes a promise of importance to another and then breaks it, he is severely punished. Also, if he has any money belonging to another and has promised to take care of it, and then loses it through carelessness or spends any upon himself, he is guilty of a crime. Another law is that not only the guilty should be punished, but that the innocent shall be rewarded. So that whoever shall behave himself well and keep the laws of his country for a whole year, shall receive a sum of money and a favor from the emperor.

When the emperor has some special favor to confer, or position to offer, he does not choose the most clever or learned man to give it to, but picks out the one who has been the best behaved and who is the bravest and truest among his subjects.

Ingratitude among the Lilliputians is considered a capital crime, and anyone who returns evil for good is judged not fit to live.

I am sorry to say that the emperor and his people did not keep these good laws as they should have done, for if they had, His Majesty would never have treated me so badly after I had done my best to help him.

In Lilliput there are large public schools to which parents are bound to send their children. Here they are educated and fitted for some position in life, for no one is allowed to be idle.

All the children are brought up very well indeed and taught to be honorable, courageous, and truthful men and women.

The nurses are forbidden to tell the children foolish or frightening stories, and if they are found to do so, they are soundly whipped and sent to a most lonely part of the country.

And now I will give a further account of my own way of living among these strange little people.

I had made myself a table and chair, as large as I could get out of the biggest tree in the royal park. Two hundred sewing women were employed to make my shirts and the linen for my bed and table. They got the strongest and coarsest linen the island could produce, and even then they were obliged to sew several folds together to make it strong enough for my use. The sewing women took my measure as I lay upon the ground, one standing at my neck and another at my leg, with a strong cord that each held, one at one end and one at the other.

One clever woman fitted me for a shirt by simply taking the width of my right thumb, for she said that twice round the thumb is once round the wrist, and twice round the wrist is once round the neck, and twice round the neck is once round the waist. By this means she was able to fit me exactly.

The three hundred tailors who were employed to make my clothes had another way of measuring me. I knelt down, and they raised a ladder from the ground to my neck; upon this ladder one man mounted and let fall a cord from my collar to the floor, which was the length for my coat. My waist and arms I measured myself. As the largest piece of cloth made in the island was only about the size of a yard of wide ribbon, my clothes looked like a patchwork quilt; only, the cloth was all of the same color.

I had three hundred cooks to prepare my food, and each one cooked me two dishes. When I was ready for my meal, I took up twenty waiters in my hand and placed them upon the table; a hundred more attended on the ground, carrying the dishes. The waiters upon the table drew these things up by cords, as we might draw a bucket from a well.

One joint of meat generally made a mouthful for me, but once I actually had a sirloin of beef so large that I was forced to make three bites of it. I never had another as big. The geese and turkeys also only made a mouthful, and of the small fowl I could take up twenty at a time on my fork.

Gulliver Escapes to Blefuscu

I must now tell my reader of a great plot that had been formed against me in the island of Lilliput.

I was preparing to pay my promised visit to the emperor of Blefuscu, when one day a Lilliputian noble called at my house privately, and at night; and without sending in his name, he asked me to allow him to come in and speak to me.

I went out and picked up his lordship and brought him on to my table. Then I fastened the door of my house and sat down in front of the noble. As I saw he looked very anxious and troubled, I asked him if anything was the matter. At that he begged me to listen to him with patience, as he had much to tell me that concerned my life and honor. I replied that I was all eagerness to hear him, and this is what he told me:

"You must know," said he, "that His Majesty has lately had many private meetings with his nobles about yourself. And two days ago he formed a plan that will do you great injury. You know that Skyresh has always been your mortal enemy, and his hatred grew even more when you so successfully won the ships of the Blefuscudians. He was very jealous and considered you had taken away some of the glory that ought to have been his as an admiral of His Majesty. This lord, with some others who dislike you, has prepared a charge against you of treason and other crimes. Now, because I consider this to be unjust treatment, and because you have always shown me kindness and courtesy, I have risked my life to come here tonight to warn you.

"Skyresh and the other nobles insisted that you should be put to death, and that in the most cruel way: either by setting fire to your house while you slept or by having you shot with poisoned arrows by twenty thousand men. But His Majesty could not be persuaded to do this cruelty and decided to spare your life. Then Reldresal, who has always been your true friend, was asked by the emperor to give his opinion, which he accordingly did.

"He allowed your crimes to be very great, but said that he considered mercy ought to be shown you in return for the services you had rendered the empire. He advised His Majesty to spare your life, but have both your eyes put out. By this means justice would be satisfied, and the loss of your eyes would not take from your bodily strength, so that you could still be useful to us. This proposal of Reldresal was not at all approved by the other lords. Skyresh flew into a great passion and said he wondered

Reldresal could dare to wish to save the life of a traitor. He again accused you of being a traitor and insisted that you should be put to death.

"Still His Majesty refused to consent to your death, but said that, as the court did not consider putting out your eyes was sufficient punishment for your crimes, some other must be thought of.

"Then Reldresal again spoke saying that, as it cost so much to feed you, another way of punishing you would be to give you less and less to eat, until you were gradually starved to death.

"This proposal was agreed upon, but it was decided to keep the plan of starving you a great secret. In three days from now Reldresal will be sent here to read these accusations I have now told to you, and to tell you that His Majesty condemns you to the loss of your eyes. Twenty of His Majesty's surgeons will attend in order to perform the operation, which will be done by shooting very sharp pointed arrows into the balls of your eyes as you lie upon the ground.

"I have now told you all that will happen to you and must leave you to act as you think best. As no one must know I have been here with you now, I must hasten back to the court as secretly as I can."

This his lordship immediately did, leaving me in much doubt and trouble. Knowing the good and just laws of the island of Lilliput, I was much shocked and astonished to find the emperor could so far forget them as to condemn an innocent man to so brutal a punishment. I tried to think what I had better do to save myself. My first idea was to wait quietly and go through with my trial. Then I could plead my innocence and try to obtain mercy. But, upon second thoughts, I saw that this was a dangerous, almost a hopeless, plan, as my enemies at court were so bitter against me.

Then I almost made up my mind to use my own strength, for while I had liberty I knew that I could easily overcome all the Lilliputians and knock the city to pieces with stones. But I put the idea away as unfair and dishonorable, because I had given my oath not to harm the island and its inhabitants. And even though the emperor was so unjust and cruel to me, I did not consider that his conduct freed me from the promise I had made.

At last I formed a plan by which I hoped to save my eyesight and my liberty, and, as things proved, it was a very fortunate plan for me. As I had obtained the emperor's permission to visit the island of Blefuscu, I at once made preparations to go there. I sent a letter to Reldresal telling him I intended to visit Blefuscu, according to the permission I had obtained from His Majesty, and that I was starting that morning. By wading and swimming I crossed the channel and reached the port of Blefuscu.

I found the people there had long expected me, and they appeared very pleased to see me. They lent me two guides to show me the way to the capital city. These men I held in my hands, while they directed me which way to take. Having arrived at the city gate, I put them down and desired them to tell His Majesty, the emperor of Blefuscu, that I was awaiting his commands.

I had an answer in about an hour, which was that His Majesty and the royal family were coming out to receive me.

The emperor and his train then rode out of the palace, and the empress and her ladies also drove up in coaches. They did not seem at all frightened at seeing me. I lay upon the ground to kiss His Majesty's and the empress's hands. I told His Majesty I had come according to my promise and with the consent of the emperor of Lilliput, and that I considered it a great honor to receive the welcome I did. I also begged to offer His Majesty any service I could render him.

I was treated with much kindness and generosity while at Blefuscu; but as there was no place large enough for me to get into, I had to be without house and bed. So I was forced to sleep upon the ground, wrapped in my cloak.

Gulliver Returns to England

Three days after my arrival at Blefuscu, I was walking along the coast when I suddenly caught sight of some object in the sea that looked like a boat overturned. I pulled off my shoes and stockings and waded out into the water. As I drew near the object, I could plainly see that it was a big boat, which, I suppose, must have been driven there by some tempest. Having made this discovery, I hastened back to shore and went to the city to beg His Majesty to lend me twenty of his tallest ships and three thousand sailors, under the command of an admiral.

The emperor gave his consent, and the fleet of ships sailed to the place where I had discovered the boat. I again waded into the water and found that the tide had driven the boat still nearer the shore. The sailors in the ships were all provided with cord, which I had twisted together and made strong. I walked as near the boat as I could, then swam up to it. The sailors threw me the end of the cord, which I fastened to part of the boat and the other end to a man-of-war. Then, getting behind the boat, I swam and pushed it as best I could with one hand until I had got it out of the deep water. Being then able to walk, I rested a few minutes, and then, taking some other ropes,

I fastened all of them to the boat and then to the vessels the emperor had lent me. Then the sailors pulled, and I shoved, and, the wind being favorable, we arrived at the shore of Blefuscu, dragging the boat with us. With the help of two thousand men, with ropes and engines, I was able to turn the boat upon the right side and found it was in quite good condition.

After this I worked hard for many days making paddles for my boat and getting it ready to go to sea in. The people of Blefuscu came and gazed in wonder and astonishment at so immense a vessel. I told the emperor that my good fortune had thrown this boat in my way to carry me to some place from which I might be able to return to my native land. And I begged His Majesty to allow me to have materials with which to fit it up, and also to give me his gracious permission to depart when it was ready. This His Majesty most kindly granted me.

Five hundred workmen were employed to make two sails for my boat under my directions. This had to be done by sewing together thirteen folds of their strongest linen. Then I made rope by twisting together twenty or thirty lengths of the stoutest cord upon the island. After a long search by the seashore I discovered a large stone, which had to serve me for an anchor. I used the fat of three hundred cows for greasing my boat. Then I set to work and cut down some of the largest trees to make into oars and masts. His Majesty's carpenters helped me greatly in smoothing them after I had cut them into shape.

In about a month all was ready, and I sent to tell His Majesty I was going to take my leave.

The emperor and royal family came out of the palace and allowed me to kiss their hands. His Majesty presented me with fifty purses containing two hundred pieces of gold in each, together with his picture at full length. This I immediately put into one of my gloves to keep from being hurt.

I stored my boat with the bodies of a hundred oxen and three hundred sheep, with bread and drink and as much cooked meat as four hundred cooks could provide for me. I also took six live cows and two live bulls, and as many lambs, intending to carry them to England to show them to my friends. To feed these animals I had a good bundle of hay and a bag of corn. I should like to have taken some of the little people with me, but this the emperor would not allow.

Having thus prepared everything as well as I was able, I set sail on the twenty-fourth day of September, 1701, at six in the morning. When I had gone some distance, I saw a small island. I advanced toward it and cast anchor by the shore. I got out of my boat, upon the island, which seemed to be uninhabited, as I could not see a sign of anyone about. After I had eaten a little, I lay down and went to sleep. I slept well and awoke about daybreak.

I finished eating my breakfast before the sun was up; then pulling up my anchor, I once more started upon my journey. I sailed all that day without making any discoveries. But upon the next, at about three o'clock in the afternoon, I saw the white sails of a ship in the distance before me. I hailed her, but could get no answer. I did my utmost to get up to her, and when I had drawn nearer I called again, and this time she heard me and answered.

I cannot express the joy it gave me to feel I had a real chance of getting back to England and the dear ones I had left there. And I was delighted to see that the ship had the English colors flying. When I got up to her, I picked up my cows and sheep and put them into my pocket and got on board the ship. The vessel was an English merchantman returning from Japan, and the captain of it was William Biddle, a very kind and excellent man. There were about fifty men on board the ship, and one was an old comrade of mine, who gave me a good character to the captain. Everyone treated me with great kindness and asked me where I had come from and whither I was going. When I told them about my adventures in Lilliput and Blefuscu, they thought I was mad and raving; whereupon I took my cattle and sheep out of my pockets. Their astonishment was great at the sight of the tiny creatures. I then showed the purses of gold given me by the emperor of Blefuscu and His Majesty's full-length picture. I gave Captain Biddle two of the purses and also a cow and a sheep, with all of which he was much pleased.

We had a very fair voyage to England. I had one misfortune, which was that one of my little sheep died; however, the others lived and ate well. When we landed, I took them safely ashore and put them on a little lawn, where they enjoyed the grass very much. For many years I made a good deal of money by showing my tiny animals to different people, and I finally sold them for six hundred pounds.

NOTES AND QUESTIONS

Biography. Jonathan Swift (1667-1745), a great British writer, was born in Dublin. He was educated at Trinity College, Dublin, and at Oxford University. He became active in political life and wrote attacks upon the government. *Gulliver's Travels*, Swift's most famous work, is full of fun and rich in imaginative pictures.

Discussion. 1. How did Gulliver arrive at the land of the Lilliputians? 2. How was he treated by the inhabitants? What did they call him? 3. How did Gulliver prove that he did not wish to hurt them? 4. What arrangements did they make for his comfort? 5. What rules were set for him when he was given his liberty? 6. How did Gulliver capture the fleet from Blefuscu? 7. What did the emperor of Lilliput wish to do when Gulliver had won the victory? 8. What evil thing about war does this incident show? 9. Can a nation fight a great war without desire to add to its territory? Was this true of the United States in World War One? 10. What was Gulliver's feeling about the proposal of the emperor? Was he right? 11. How did the emperor feel toward him after his refusal? 12. How did Gulliver learn of the plot against him? 13. Why did he not use his strength against his enemies? 14. What did he decide to do? 15. What fortunate discovery did Gulliver make at Blefuscu? 16. How did Gulliver get back to England? 17. Name two or three things that you think he learned on his travels. 18. What are we told about the education of children in Lilliput? 19. Why did the people consider deceit worse than stealing? 20. What did they think of a person who returns evil for good? 21. Name some of the laws of the Lilliputians. Which of these laws do you like, and why? 22. Why were not all the people of Lilliput good when they had such good laws? 23. Compare Gulliver's adventures with those of Baron Munchausen. 24. How does this story differ as to its source from *The Arabian Nights* tales? 25. Show that it has the two values mentioned on page 146. 26. *Class readings:* Select passages to be read aloud in class. 27. *Outline for testing silent reading.* Tell the story briefly in your own words, following the topic headings given in the book. 28. Find in the glossary the meaning of: keep, human (pp. 231-233), engines, bandages, turret (pp. 235-236), carriages (p. 237), merchantmen (p. 255). 29. *Pronounce:* ruined, drowned, waistcoat (pp. 232-233), imperial, courtiers (p. 234), theater, reigned, learned (pp. 237-239), Lilliput, graciously, fortnight (pp. 240-241), Lilliputians (p. 244).

Phrases for Study

express consent, **240**, 22
state and person, **242**, 13
confounded with astonishment, **244**, 4
capital crime, **246**, 28
mortal enemy, **249**, 7
gave me a good character, **255**, 5
fair voyage, **255**, 16

Robinson Crusoe

Daniel Defoe

How I Went to Sea and was Shipwrecked

I was born at York, in England, on the first of March, 1632. From the time that I was quite a young child I had felt a great wish to spend my life at sea, and as I grew, so did this taste grow more and more strong; till at last on September first, 1651, I ran away from my school and home and found my way on foot to Hull, where I soon got a place on board a ship.

Never did any young adventurer's misfortunes begin sooner or continue longer than mine, for when we were far out at sea, some Turks in a small ship came on our track in full chase. After a long pursuit our vessel was captured, and all on board were taken as slaves.

The chief of the Turks took me as his prize to a port which was held by the Moors. There I remained in slavery for several years, and bitterly did I repent my rash act in leaving my good parents in England.

---

* See "Suggestions for Silent Reading," page 163.

At length I found an opportunity to escape to a vessel that was passing by and was kindly received by the captain, who proved to be an English sailor bound on a voyage of trade.

I had not been aboard more than twelve days when a high wind took us off, we knew not where. All at once there was a cry of "Land!" and the ship struck on a bank of sand, in which she sank so deep that we could not get her off. At last we found that we must make up our minds to leave her and get to shore as well as we could. There had been a boat at her stern, but we found it had been torn off by the force of the waves. One small boat was still left on the ship's side, so we got into it.

There we were, all of us, on the wild sea. The heart of each now grew faint, our cheeks were pale, and our eyes were dim, for there was but one hope, and that was to find some bay, and so get in the lee of the land.

The sea grew more and more rough, and its white foam would curl and boil till at last the waves in their wild sport burst on the boat's side, and we were all thrown out.

I could swim well, but the force of the waves made me lose my breath too much to do so. At length one large wave took me to the shore and left me high and dry, though half dead with fear. I got on my feet and made the best of my way for the land; but just then the curve of a huge wave rose up as high as a hill, and this I had no strength to keep from, so it took me back to the sea. I did my best to float on the top and held my breath to do so. The next wave was quite as high and shut me up in its bulk. I held my hands down tight to my sides, and then my head shot out at the top of the waves. This gave me breath, and soon my feet felt the ground.

I stood quite still for a short time, to let the sea run

back from me, and then I set off with all my might to the shore, but yet the waves caught me, and twice more did they take me back, and twice more land me on the shore. I thought the last wave would have been the death of me, for it drove me on a piece of rock, and with such force as to leave me in a kind of swoon. I soon regained my senses and got up to the cliffs close to the shore, where I found some grass out of the reach of the sea. There I sat down, safe on land at last.

I felt so wrapped in joy that all I could do was to walk up and down the coast, now lift up my hands, now fold them on my breast and thank God for all that He had done for me, when the rest of the men were lost. I now cast my eyes round me, to find out what kind of place it was that I had been thus thrown in, like a bird in a storm. Then all the glee I felt at first left me; for I was wet and cold and had no dry clothes to put on, no food to eat, and not a friend to help me.

I feared that there might be wild beasts here, and I had no gun to shoot them with, or to keep me from their jaws. I had but a knife and a pipe.

It now grew dark; and where was I to go for the night? I thought the top of some high tree would be a good place to keep me out of harm's way; and that there I might sit and think of death, for, as yet, I had no hope of life. Well, I went to my tree and made a kind of nest to sleep in. Then I cut a stick to keep off beasts of prey, in case any should come, and fell asleep just as if the branch I lay on had been a bed of down.

When I woke up, it was broad day; the sky, too, was clear and the sea calm. But I saw from the top of the tree that in the night the ship had left the bank of sand and lay but a mile from me. I soon threw off my clothes, took to the sea, and swam up to the wreck. But how was I to get on deck? I had gone twice around the ship, when a piece of rope caught my eye, which hung down from her side so low that at first the waves hid it. By the help of this rope I got on board.

How I Made and Used a Raft

I found that there was a bulge in the ship, and that she had sprung a leak. You may be sure that my first thought was to look around for some food, and I soon made my way to the bin where the bread was kept and ate some of it as I went to and fro, for there was no time to lose. What I stood most in need of was a boat to take the goods to shore. But it was vain to wish for that which could not be had; and as there were some spare yards in the ship, two or three large planks, and a mast or two, I fell to work with these to make a raft.

I put four spars side by side and laid short bits of plank on them, crossways, to make my raft strong. Though these planks would bear my own weight, they were too slight to bear much of my freight. So I took a saw which was on board and cut a mast in three lengths, and these gave great strength to the raft. I found some bread and rice, a Dutch cheese, and some dry goat's flesh.

My next task was to screen my goods from the spray of the sea; and this did not take long, for there were three large chests on board which held all, and these I put on the raft.

"See, here is a prize!" said I out loud (though there was none to hear me); "now I shall not starve." For I found four large guns. But how was my raft to be got to land? I had no sail, no oars; and a gust of wind would make all my store slide off. Yet there were three things which I was glad of—a calm sea, a tide which set in to the shore, and a slight breeze to blow me there.

I had the good luck to find some oars in a part of the ship in which I had made no search till now. With these I put to sea, and for half a mile my raft went well; but soon I found it driven to one side. At length I saw a creek, up which, with some toil, I took my raft.

I saw that there were birds on the isle, and I shot one of them. Mine must have been the first gun that had been heard there since the world was made; for, at the sound of it, whole flocks of birds flew up, with loud cries, from all parts of the wood. The shape of the beak of the one I shot was like that of a hawk, but the claws were not so large.

I now went back to my raft to land my stores, and this took up the rest of the day. What to do at night I knew not, nor where to find a safe place to land my stores on. I did not like to lie down on the ground for fear of beasts of prey, as well as snakes; but there was no cause for these fears, as I have since found. I put the chests and boards round me as well as I could and made a kind of hut for the night.

As there was still a great store of things left in the ship which would be of use to me, I thought that I ought to bring them to land at once; for I knew that the first storm would break up the ship. So I went on board and took good care this time not to load my raft too much.

The first thing I sought for was the tool chest; and in it were some bags of nails, spikes, saws, knives, and such things; but best of all, I found a stone to grind my tools on. There were two or three flasks, some large bags of shot, and a roll of lead; but this last I had not the strength to hoist up to the ship's side, so as to get it on my raft. There were some spare sails too, which I brought to shore.

Now that I had two freights of goods on hand, I made a tent with the ship's sails to stow them in and cut the poles for it from the wood. I now took all the things out of the casks and chests and put the casks in piles round the tent to give it strength; and when this was done, I shut up the door with the boards, spread on the ground one of the beds which I had brought from the ship, laid two guns close to my head, and went to bed for the first time. I slept all night, for I was much in need of rest.

The next day I was sad and sick at heart, for I felt how dull it was to be thus cut off from all the rest of the world! I had no great wish for work; but there was too much to be done for me to dwell long on my sad lot. Each day, as it came, I went off to the wreck to fetch more things; and I brought back as much as the raft would hold.

The last time I went to the wreck the wind blew so hard that I made up my mind to go on board next time at low tide. I found some tea and some gold coin; but as to the gold, it made me laugh to look at it. "O drug!" said I, "thou art of no use to me! I care not to save thee. Stay where thou art till the ship goes down; then go thou with it!"

Still, I thought I might just as well take it; so I put it in a piece of the sail and threw it on deck, that I might place it on the raft. By and by the wind blew from the shore, so I had to hurry back with all speed; for I knew that at the turn of the tide I should find it hard work to get to land at all. But in spite of the high wind I came to my home all safe. At dawn I put my head out and cast my eyes on the sea, when lo! no ship was there!

This great change in the face of things, and the loss of such a friend, quite struck me down. Yet I was glad to think that I had brought to shore all that could be of use to me. I had now to look out for some spot where I could make my home. Halfway up the hill there was a small plain, four or five score feet long and twice as broad; and as it had a full view of the sea, I thought that it would be a good place for my house.

How I Made Myself a Home on the Island

I first dug a trench round a space which took in twelve yards; and in this I drove two rows of stakes, till they stood firm like piles, five and a half feet from the ground. I made the stakes close and tight with bits of rope and put small sticks on the top of them in the shape of spikes. This made so strong a fence that no man or beast could get in.

The door of my house was on top, and I had to climb up to it by steps, which I took in with me, so that no one else might come up by the same way. Close to the back of the house stood a sand rock, in which I made a cave, and laid all the earth that I had dug out of it round my house, to the height of a foot and a half. I had to go out once a day in search of food. The first time, I saw some goats, but they were too shy to let me get near them.

At first I thought that for the lack of pen and ink I should lose all note of time; so I made a large post, in the shape of a cross, on which I cut these words: "I came on shore here on the thirtieth of September, 1659." On the side of this post I made a notch each day, and this I kept up till the last.

I have not yet said a word of my four pets, which were two cats, a dog, and a parrot. You may guess how fond I was of them, for they were all the friends left to me. I brought the dog and two cats from the ship. The dog would fetch things for me at all times, and by his bark, his whine, his growl, and his tricks, he would all but talk to me; yet he could not give me thought for thought.

If I could but have had someone near me to find fault with, or to find fault with me, what a treat it would have been!

I was a long way out of the course of ships; and oh! how dull it was to be cast on this lone spot with no one to love, no one to make me laugh, no one to make me weep, no one to make me think. It was dull to roam day by day from the wood to the shore, and from the shore back to the wood, and feed on my own thoughts all the while.

So much for the sad view of my case; but like most things, it had a bright side as well as a dark one. For here was I safe on land, while all the rest of the ship's crew were lost. True, I was cast on a rough and rude part of the globe, but there were no beasts of prey on it to kill or hurt me. God had sent the ship so near to me that I had got from it all things to meet my wants for the rest of my days. Let life be what it might, there was surely much to thank God for. And I soon gave up all dull thoughts and did not so much as look out for a sail.

My goods from the wreck remained in the cave for more than ten months; I decided then that it was time to put them right, as they took up all the space and left me no room to turn in; so I made my small cave a large one, and dug it out a long way back in the sand rock.

Then I brought the mouth of the cave up to my fence, and so made a back way to my house. This done, I put shelves on each side to hold my goods, which made the cave look like a shop full of stores. To make these shelves was a very difficult task and took a long time; for to make a board I was forced to cut down a whole tree, chop away with my ax till one side was flat, and then cut at the other side till the board was thin enough, when I smoothed it with my adz. But, in this way, out of each tree I would get only one plank. I made for myself also a table and a chair and finally got my castle, as I called it, in good order.

I usually rose early and worked till noon, when I ate my meal; then I went out with my gun, after which I worked once more till the sun had set; and then to bed. It took me more than a week to change the shape and size of my cave. Unfortunately, I made it far too large, for, later on, the earth fell in from the roof; and had I been in it when this took place, I should have lost my life. I had now to set up posts in my cave, with planks on the top of them, so as to make a roof of wood.

How I Supplied My Needs

I had to go to bed at dusk, till I made a lamp of goat's fat, which I put in a clay dish; and this, with a piece of hemp for a wick, made a good light. As I had found a use for the bag which had held the fowls' food on board ship, I shook out from it the husks of grain. This was just at the time when the great rains fell, and in the course of a month, blades of rice and barley sprang up. As time went by, and the grain was ripe, I kept it, and took care to sow it each year; but I could not boast of a crop of grain for three years.

I knew that tools would be my first want and that I should have to grind mine on the stone, as they were blunt and worn with use. But as it took both hands to hold the tool, I could not turn the stone; so I made a wheel by which I could move it with my foot. This was no small task, but I took great pains with it, and at length it was done.

I had now been in the isle twelve months, and I thought it was time to go all round it in search of its woods, springs, and creeks. So I set off, and brought back with me limes and grapes in their prime, large and ripe. I had hung the grapes in the sun to dry, and in a few days' time went to fetch them, that I might lay up a store. The vale on the banks of which they grew was fresh and green, and a clear, bright stream ran through it, which gave so great a charm to the spot as to make me wish to live there.

But there was no view of the sea from this vale, while from my house no ships could come on my side of the isle and not be seen by me; yet the cool, soft banks were so sweet and new to me that much of my time was spent there.

In the first of the three years in which I had grown barley, I had sown it too late; in the next it was spoiled by the drought; but the third year's crop had sprung up well.

Few of us think of the cost at which a loaf of bread is made. Of course, there was no plow here to turn up the earth, and no spade to dig it with, so I made one with wood; but this was soon worn out, and for want of a rake I made use of the bough of a tree. When I had got the grain home, I had to thrash it, part the grain from the chaff, and store it up. Then came the want of sieves to clean it, of a mill to grind it, and of yeast to make bread of it.

If I could have found a large stone, slightly hollow on top, I might, by pounding the grain on it with another round stone, have made very good meal. But all the stones I could find were too soft; and in the end I had to make a sort of mill of hard wood, in which I burned a hollow place, and in that pounded the grain into meal with a heavy stick.

Baking I did by building a big fire, raking away the ashes, and putting the dough on the hot place, covered with a kind of basin made of clay, over which I had heaped the red ashes.

Thus my bread was made, though I had no tools; and no one could say that I did not earn it by the sweat of my brow. When the rain kept me indoors, it was good fun to teach my pet bird Poll to talk; but so mute were all things round me that the sound of my own voice made me start.

My chief wants now were jars, pots, cups, and plates, but I knew not how I could make them. At last I went in search of clay and found a bank of it a mile from my house; but it was quite a joke to see the queer shapes and forms that I made out of it. For some of my pots and jars were too weak to bear their own weight; and they would fall out here, and in there, in all sorts of ways; while some, when they were put in the sun to bake, would crack with the heat of its rays. You may guess what my joy was when at last a pot was made which would stand the fire, so that I could boil the meat for broth.

The next thing to turn my thoughts to was the ship's boat, which lay on the high ridge of sand, where it had been thrust by the storm which had cast me on these shores. But it lay with the keel to the sky, so I had to dig the sand from it and turn it up with the help of a pole. When I had done this, I found it was all in vain, for I had not the strength to launch it. So all I could do now was to make a boat of less size out of a tree; and I found one that was just fit for it, which grew not far from the shore, but I could no more stir this than I could the ship's boat.

"Well," thought I, "I must give up the boat, and with it all my hopes of leaving the isle. But I have this to think of: I am lord of the whole isle; in fact, a king. I have wood with which I might build a fleet, and grapes, if not grain, to freight it with, though all my wealth is but a few gold coins." For these I had no sort of use, and could have found it in my heart to give them all for a peck of peas and some ink, which last I stood much in need of. But it was best to dwell more on what I had than on what I had not.

I now must needs try once more to build a boat, but this time it was to have a mast, for which the ship's sails would be of great use. I made a deck at each end to keep out the spray of the sea, a bin for my food, and a rest for my gun, with a flap to screen it from the wet. More than all, the boat was one of such a size that I could launch it.

My first cruise was up and down the creek, but soon I got bold and made the whole round of my isle. I took with me bread, cakes, a pot full of rice, half a goat, and two greatcoats, one of which was to lie on and one to put on at night. I set sail in the sixth year of my reign. On the east side of the isle there was a large ridge of rocks which lay two miles from the shore, and a shoal of sand lay for half a mile from the rocks to the beach. To get round this point I had to sail a great way out to sea; and here I all but lost my life.

But I got back to my home at last. On my way there, quite worn out with the toils of the boat, I lay down in the shade to rest my limbs and slept. But judge, if you can, what a start I gave when a voice woke me out of my sleep, and spoke my name three times! A voice in this wild place! To call me by name, too! Then the voice said, "Robin! Robin Crusoe! Where are you? Where have you been? How came you here?" But now I saw it all; for at the top of the hedge sat Poll, who did but say the words she had been taught by me.

I now went in search of some goats and laid snares for them, with rice for a bait. I had set the traps in the night, and found they had stood, though the bait was all gone. So I thought of a new way to take them, which was to make a pit and lay sticks and grass on it so as to hide it; and in this way I caught an old goat and some kids. But the old goat was much too fierce for me, so I let him go.

I brought all the young ones home and let them fast a long time, till at last they fed from my hand and were quite tame. I kept them in a kind of park, in which there were trees to screen them from the sun. At first my park was half a mile round; but it struck me that, in so great a space, the kids would soon get as wild as if they had the range of the whole vale, and that it would be as well to give them less room; so I had to make a hedge, which took me three months to plant. My park held a flock of twelve goats, and in two years time there were more than two score.

My dog sat at meals with me and one cat on each side of me, on stools, and we had Poll to talk to us. Now for a word or two as to the dress in which I made a tour round the isle. I could but think how droll it would look in the streets of the town in which I was born.

I usually wore a high cap of goatskin, with a long flap that hung down to keep the sun and rain from my neck, a coat made from the skin of a goat, too, the skirts of which came down to my hips, and the same on my legs, with no shoes, but flaps of the fur round my shins. I had a broad belt of the same around my waist, which drew on with two thongs; and from it, on my right side, hung a saw and an ax; and on my left side a pouch for the shot. My beard had not been cut since I came here. But no more need be said of my looks, for there were few to see me.

HOW I DISCOVERED A FOOTPRINT AND SAVED FRIDAY

A strange sight was now in store for me, which was to change the whole course of my life in the isle.

One day at noon, while on a stroll down to a part of the shore that was new to me, what should I see on the sand but the print of a man's foot! I felt as if I were bound by a spell and could not stir from the spot.

By and by I stole a look around me, but no one was in sight. What could this mean? I went three or four times to look at it. There it was—the print of a man's foot: toes, heel, and all the parts of a foot. How could it have come there?

My head swam with fear; and as I left the spot, I made two or three steps and then took a look around me; then two steps more, and did the same thing. I took fright at the stump of an old tree and ran to my house, as if for my life. How could aught in the shape of a man come to that shore, and I not know it? Where was the ship that brought him? Then a vague dread took hold of my mind that some man, or set of men, had found me out; and it might be that they meant to kill me, or rob me of all I had.

Fear kept me indoors for three days, till the want of food drove me out. At last I was so bold as to go down to the coast to look once more at the print of the foot, to see if it was the same shape as my own. I found it was not so large by a great deal; so it was clear that it was not one of my own footprints and that there were men in the isle.

One day as I went from the hill to the coast, a scene lay in front of me which made me sick at heart. The spot was spread with the bones of men. There was a round place dug in the earth, where a fire had been made, and here some men had come to feast. Now that I had seen this sight, I knew not how to act; I kept close to my home and would scarce stir from it save to milk my flock of goats.

A few days later I was struck by the sight of some smoke, which came from a fire no more than two miles off. From this time I lost all my peace of mind. Day and night a dread would haunt me that the men who had made this fire would find me out. I went home and drew up my steps, but first I made all things round me look wild and rude. To load my gun was the next thing to do, and I thought it would be best to stay at home and hide.

But this was not to be borne long. I had no spy to send out, and all I could do was to get to the top of the hill and keep a good lookout. At last, through my glass, I could see a group of wild men join in a dance round their fire. As soon as they stopped, I took two guns and slung a sword on my side; then with all speed I set off to the top of the hill, once more to have a good view.

This time I made up my mind to go up to the men, but not with a view to kill them, for I felt that it would be wrong to do so. With a heavy load of arms it took me two hours to reach the spot where the fire was; and by the time I got there the men had all gone; but I saw them in four boats out at sea.

Down on the shore there was a proof of what the work of these men had been. The signs of their feast made me sick at heart, and I shut my eyes. I durst not fire my gun when I went out for food on that side of the isle, lest there should be some of the men left who might hear it, and so find me out.

From this time all went well with me for two years, but it was not to last. One day, as I stood on the hill, I saw six boats on the shore. What could this mean? Where were the men who had brought them? And what had they come for? I saw through my glass that there were a score and a half at least on the east side of the isle. They had meat on the fire, round which I could see them dance. They then took a man from one of the boats, who was bound hand and foot; but when they loosed his bonds, he set off as fast as his feet would take him, and in a straight line to my house.

To tell the truth, when I saw all the rest of the men run to catch him, my hair stood on end with fright. In the creek he swam like a fish, and the plunge which he took brought him through it in a few strokes. All the men now gave up the chase but two, and they swam through the creek, but by no means so fast as the slave had done.

Now, I thought, was the time to help the poor man, and my heart told me it would be right to do so. I ran down my steps with my two guns and went with all speed up the hill, and then down by a short cut to meet them.

I gave a sign to the poor slave to come to me and at the same time went up to meet the two men who were in chase of him. I made a rush at the first of these, to knock him down with the stock of my gun, and he fell. I saw the one who was left aim at me with his bow; so, to save my life, I aimed carefully and shot him dead.

The smoke and noise from my gun gave the poor slave who had been bound such a shock that he stood still on the spot, as if he had been in a trance. I gave a loud shout for him to come to me, and I took care to show him that I was a friend, and made all the signs I could think of to coax him up to me. At length he came, knelt down to kiss the ground, and then took hold of my foot and set it on his head. All this meant that he was my slave; and I bade him rise and made much of him.

I did not like to take my slave to my house or to my cave; so I threw down some straw from the rice plant for him to sleep on and gave him some bread and a bunch of dry grapes to eat. He was a fine man with straight, strong limbs, tall and young. His hair was thick, like wool, and black. His head was large and high, and he had bright black eyes. He was of a dark brown hue; his face was round and his nose small, but not flat; he had a good mouth with thin lips, with which he could give a soft smile; and his teeth were as white as snow.

Toward evening I had been out to milk my goats, and when he saw me, he ran to me and lay down on the ground to show me his thanks. He then put his head on the ground and set my foot on his head, as he had done at first. He took all the means he could think of to let me know that he would serve me all his life, and I gave a sign to make him understand that I thought well of him.

The next thing was to think of some name to call him by. I chose that of the sixth day of the week, Friday, as he came to me on that day. I took care not to lose sight of him all that night. When the sun rose, we went up to the top of the hill to look out for the men; but as we could not see them or their boats, it was clear that they had left the isle.

I now set to work to make my man a cap of hare's skin and gave him a goat's skin to wear round his waist. It was a great source of pride to him to find that his clothes were as good as my own.

At night I kept my guns, swords, and bow close to my side; but there was no need for this, as my slave was, in sooth, most true to me. He did all that he was set to do, with his whole heart in the work; and I knew that he would lay down his life to save mine. What could a man do more than that? And oh, the joy to have him here to cheer me in this lone isle!

How Friday Learned My Ways

I did my best to teach him, so like a child he was, to do and feel all that was right. I found him apt and full of fun, and he took great pains to understand and learn all that I could tell him.

One day I sent him to beat out and sift some grain. I let him see me make the bread, and he soon did all the work. I felt quite a love for his true, warm heart, and he soon learned to talk to me. One day I said, "Do the men of your tribe win in fight?" He told me, with a smile, that they did. "Well, then," said I, "how came they to let their foes take you?"

"They run one, two, three, and make go in the boat that time."

"Well, and what do the men do with those they take?"

"Eat them all up."

This was not good news for me, but I went on and said, "Where do they take them?"

"Go to next place where they think."

"Do they come here?"

"Yes, yes, they come here, come else place, too."

"Have you been here with them twice?"

"Yes, come there."

He meant the northwest side of the isle, so to this spot I took him the next day. He knew the place and told me he was there once, and with him twelve men. To let me know this, he placed twelve stones all in a row and made me count them.

"Are not the boats lost on your shore now and then?"

He said that there was no fear, and that no boats

were lost. He told me that up a great way by the moon—that is, where the moon then came up—there dwelt a tribe of white men like me, with beards. I felt sure that they must have come from Spain, to work the gold mines. I put this to him: "Could I go from this isle and join those men?"

"Yes, yes, you may go in two boats."

It was hard to see how one man could go in two boats, but what he meant was a boat twice as large as my own.

To please my poor slave, I gave him a sketch of my whole life; I told him where I was born and where I spent my days when a child. He was glad to hear tales of the land of my birth and of the trade which we kept up, in ships, with all parts of the known world. I gave him a knife and a belt, which made him dance with joy.

One day as we stood on the top of the hill at the east side of the isle, I saw him fix his eyes on the mainland and stand for a long time gazing at it, then jump and sing and call out to me.

"What do you see?" said I.

"O joy!" said he, with a fierce glee in his eyes, "O glad! There see my land!"

Why did he strain his eyes to stare at this land as if he had a wish to be there? It put fears in my mind which made me feel far less at my ease with him. Thought I, if he should go back to his home, he will think no more of what I have taught him and done for him. He will be sure to tell the rest of his tribe all my ways and come back with, it may be, scores of them and kill me and then dance round me, as they did round the men the last time they came on my isle.

But these were all false fears, though they found a place in my mind for a long while; and I was not so kind to him now as I had been. From this time I made it a rule, day by day, to find out if there were grounds for my fears or not. I said, "Do you wish to be once more in your own land?"

"Yes! I be much glad to be at my own land."

"What would you do there? Would you turn wild, and be as you were?"

"No, no, I would tell them to be good, tell them eat bread, grain, milk, no eat man more!"

"Why, they would kill you!"

"No, no, they no kill; they love learn."

He then told me that some white men who had come on their shores in a boat had taught them a great deal.

"Then will you go back to your land with me?"

He said he could not swim so far, so I told him he should help me to build a boat to go in. Then he said, "If you go, I go."

"I go? Why, they would eat me!"

"No, me make them much love you."

Then he told me, as well as he could, how kind they had been to some white men. I brought out the large boat to hear what he thought of it, but he said it was too small. We then went to look at the old ship's boat, which, as it had been in the sun for years, was not at all in a sound state. The poor man made sure that it would do. But how were we to know this? I told him we should build a boat as large as that, and that he should go home in it. He spoke not a word, but was grave and sad.

"What ails you?" said I.

"Why you grieve mad with your man?"

"What do you mean? I am not cross with you."

"No cross? No cross with me? Why send your man home to his own land, then?"

"Did you not tell me you would like to go back?"

"Yes, yes, we both there; no wish self there, if you not there!"

"And what should I do there?"

"You do great deal much good! You teach wild men be good men."

We soon set to work to make a boat that would take us both. The first thing was to look out for some large tree that grew near the shore, so that we could launch our boat when it was made. My slave's plan was to burn the wood to make it the right shape; but as mine was to hew it, I set him to work with my tools, and in two months' time we had made a good, strong boat; but it took a long while to get her down to the shore and float her.

Friday had the whole charge of her; and, large as she was, he made her move with ease and said, "Me think she go there well, though great blow wind!" He did not know that I meant to make a mast and sail. I cut down a young fir tree for the mast, and then I set to work at the sail. It made me laugh to see my man stand and stare, when he came to watch me sail the boat. But he soon gave a jump, a laugh, and a clap of the hands when for the first time he saw the sail jib and fall, now on this side, now on that.

The next thing to do was to stow our boat up in the creek, where we dug a small dock; and when the tide was low, we made a dam to keep out the sea. The time of year had now come for us to set sail, so we got out all our stores to put them into the boat.

THE ENGLISH SHIP AND HOW I SAILED FOR HOME

I was fast asleep in my hutch one morning when my man Friday came running in to me and called aloud, "Master, master, they are come, they are come!" I jumped up and went out, as soon as I could get my clothes on, through my little grove, which, by the way, was by this time grown to be a very thick wood. I went without my arms, which was not my custom; but I was surprised when, turning my eyes to the sea, I saw a boat at about a league and a half distance, standing in for the shore, with a shoulder-of-mutton sail, as they call it, and the wind blowing pretty fair to bring them in; also I saw that they did not come from that side which the shore lay on, but from the south end of the island.

Upon this I hastily called Friday in and bade him lie close, for we did not know yet whether they were friends or enemies. In the next place, I went in to fetch my glass to see what I could make of them; and, having climbed up to the top of the hill, I saw a ship lying at anchor at about two leagues from me, but not above a league and a half from the shore. It seemed to be an English ship, and the boat looked like an English longboat.

They ran their boat on shore upon the beach, at about half a mile from me; which was very happy for me, else they would have landed just at my door, as I may say, and would soon have beaten me out of my castle, and perhaps have plundered me of all I had. When they were on shore, I saw they were Englishmen; there were, in all, eleven men, whereof three of them I found were unarmed, and, as I thought, bound; and when the first four or five of them had jumped on shore, they took those three out of the boat as prisoners; one of the three I could see using the gestures of entreaty and despair; the other two, I could see, lifted up their hands and appeared concerned, but not to such a degree as the first.

I was shocked and terrified at the sight of all this and knew not what the meaning of it could be. Friday called out to me in English, as well as he could, "O master! you see English mans eat prisoner as well as savage mans." "Why, Friday," said I, "do you think they are going to eat them, then?" "Yes," said Friday, "they will eat them." "No, no," said I, "Friday, I am afraid they will murder them indeed; but you may be sure they will not eat them."

I expected every minute to see the three prisoners killed, so I fitted myself up for a battle, though with much caution, knowing that I had to do with another kind of enemy than if I were fighting savages. I ordered Friday also to load himself with arms. I took myself two fowling pieces, and I gave him two muskets. My figure was very fierce; I had my goatskin coat on, with the great cap, a naked sword, two pistols in my belt, and a gun upon each shoulder.

It was my design not to make any attempt till it was dark; but about two o'clock, being the heat of the day, I found, in short, they had all gone straggling into the woods, and, as I thought, had all lain down to sleep. The three poor, distressed men, too anxious for their condition to get any sleep, had, however, sat down under the shelter of a great tree.

I resolved to discover myself to them and learn something of their condition; immediately I marched toward them, my man Friday at a good distance behind me, as formidable for his arms as I, but not making quite so staring a specter-like figure as I did. I came as near them undiscovered as I could, and then, before any of them saw me, I called aloud to them in Spanish, "Who are ye, sirs?"

They gave a start at my voice and at my strange dress and made a move as if they would flee from me. I said, "Do not fear me, for it may be that you have a friend at hand, though you do not think it." "He must be sent from the sky, then," said one of them with a grave look and he took off his hat to me at the same time. "All help is from thence, sir," I said. "But what can I do to aid you? You look as if you had some load of grief on your breast. A moment ago I saw one of the men lift his sword as if to kill you."

The tears ran down the poor man's face as he said, "Is this a god, or is it but a man?" "Have no doubt on that score, sir," said I, "for a god would not have come with a dress like this. No, do not fear—nor raise your hopes too high; for you see but a man, yet one who will do all he can to help you. Your speech shows me that you come from the same land as I do. I will do all I can to serve you. Tell me your case."

"Our case, sir, is too long to tell you while they who would kill us are so near. My name is Paul. To be short, sir, my crew have thrust me out of my ship, which you see out there, and have left me here to die. It was as much as I could do to make them sheathe their swords, which you saw were drawn to slay me. They have set me down in this isle with these two men, my friend here, and the ship's mate."

"Where have they gone?" said I.

"There, in the wood close by. I fear they may have seen and heard us. If they have, they will be sure to kill us all."

"Have they firearms?"

"They have four guns, one of which is in the boat."

"Well, then, leave all to me!"

"There are two of the men," said he, "who are worse than the rest. All but these I feel sure would go back to work the ship."

I thought it was best to speak out to Paul at once, and

I said, "Now if I save your life, there are two things which you must do."

But he read my thoughts and said, "If you save my life, you shall do as you like with me and my ship and take her where you please."

I saw that the two men, in whose charge the boat had been left, had come on shore; so the first thing I did was to send Friday to fetch from it the oars, the sail, and the gun. And now the ship might be said to be in our hands. When the time came for the men to go back to the ship, they were in a great rage; for, as the boat had now no sail or oars, they knew not how to get out to their ship.

We heard them say that it was a strange sort of isle, for sprites had come to the boat to take off the sails and oars. We could see them run to and fro, with great rage, then go and sit in the boat to rest, and then come on shore once more. When they drew near to us, Paul and Friday would fain have had me fall on them at once. But my wish was to spare them and kill as few as possible. I told two of my men to creep on their hands and knees close to the ground so that they might not be seen, and when they got up to the men, not to fire till I gave the word.

They had not stood thus long when three of the crew came up to us. Till now we had but heard their voices, but when they came so near as to be seen, Paul and Friday shot at them. Two of the men fell dead, and they were the worst of the crew, and the third ran off. At the sound of the guns I came up, but it was so dark that the men could not tell if there were three of us or three score.

It fell out just as I wished, for I heard the men ask, "To whom must we yield, and where are they?" Friday told them that Paul was there with the king of the isle, who had brought with him a crowd of men! At this, one of the crew said, "If Paul will spare our lives, we will yield." "Then," said Friday, "you shall know the king's will." Then Paul said to them, "You know my voice; if you lay down your arms, the king will spare your lives."

They fell on their knees to beg the same of me. I took good care that they did not see me, but I gave them my word that they should all live, that I should take four of them to work the ship, and that the rest would be bound hand and foot for the good faith of the four. This was to show them what a stern king I was.

Of course, I soon set them free, and I put them in a way to take my place on the isle. I told them of all my ways, taught them how to mind the goats, how to work the farm, and how to make the bread. I gave them a house to live in, firearms, tools, and my two tame cats—in fact, all that I owned but Poll and my gold.

As I sat on the top of the hill, Paul came up to me. He held out his hand to point to the ship, and with much warmth took me to his arms and said, "My dear friend, there is your ship! For this vessel is all yours, and all that is in her, and so are all of us."

I made ready to go on board the ship, but told the captain I would stay that night to get my things in shape, and asked him to go on board in the meantime and keep things right on the ship.

I cast my eyes to the ship, which rode half a mile off the shore, at the mouth of the creek, and near the place where I had brought my raft to the land. Yes, there she stood, the ship that was to set me free and to take me where I might choose to go. She set her sails to the wind, and her flags threw out their gay stripes in the breeze. Such a sight was too much for me, and I fell down faint with joy.

Friday and Paul then went on board the ship, and Paul took charge of her once more. We did not start that night, but at noon the next day I left the isle—that lone isle, where I had spent so great a part of my life.

When I took leave of this island, I carried on board a great goatskin cap I had made and my parrot; also the money which had lain by me so long useless that it was grown rusty or tarnished, and could hardly pass for gold till it had been a little rubbed and handled. And thus I left the island, the nineteenth of December, as I found by the ship's account, in the year 1686, after I had been upon it seven-and-twenty years, two months, and nineteen days. In this vessel, after a long voyage, I arrived in England the eleventh of June, in the year 1687.

NOTES AND QUESTIONS

Biography. Daniel Defoe (1659-1731), an English author, was born in London. He was well educated and devoted himself chiefly to writing. He was active in political life, and many of his early pamphlets were attacks upon the government. *Robinson Crusoe,* his greatest story, is a world classic. It is founded mainly on the adventures of Alexander Selkirk, who told Defoe about his own experiences as a castaway on an island. Defoe tells his story in simple, direct language, with frequent use of details and illustrations.

Discussion. 1. Why was an ocean voyage so difficult and dangerous at the time when *Robinson Crusoe* was written? 2. Find the lines that describe what you think was the most difficult work undertaken by Robinson Crusoe. 3. What undertaking required the most perseverance? Find lines that show this. 4. At what time did Crusoe show the greatest courage? Find lines that seem to you to prove your answer is correct. 5. What was the greatest disappointment that he had to bear while on the island? 6. What do you think was the greatest happiness he had? 7. Find lines that tell how Robinson Crusoe studied to make something which was very necessary to him. 8. Mention something he made that you have tried to make. 9. How did your result compare with his? What reason can you give for this? 10. This story shows how dependent we are upon the tools, the inventions, and the means of protection that men have devised for making life happy. Crusoe had to make for himself under great difficulties things that we think nothing of. Show from the story how dependent we are upon the cooperation and assistance of others. Imagine the cooperation that has been necessary to give you milk, oranges or bananas, sugar for your dessert, meat for your dinner. What has been done to give you the stove on which your dinner is cooked, the fuel that it burns, the light that you use at night, the telephone that you use? Crusoe had to get along without such assistance. 11. Do you owe anything, any return service, for what you receive and use? If Crusoe's hut had taken fire, what would have happened? What would happen if your home should catch fire? Who would pay for the help given you? If Crusoe had been attacked by robbers, what would have happened? What keeps you safe at night? If Crusoe had wished to go on a long journey, what would have been necessary? Who would help you if you had to take such a journey? 12. Tell a story about your debt to someone for an invention or discovery that makes your life pleasanter or safer. Tell a story about your debt for the sugar you use for your dessert. Tell a story to illustrate what the government does for you. 13. *Class readings:* Select passages to be read aloud in class. *14. Outline for testing silent reading.* Tell the story briefly in your own words, using the topic headings given in the book. 15. You will enjoy seeing the pictures in the edition of *Robinson Crusoe* that is illustrated by N. C. Wyeth. 16. Find in the glossary the meaning of: stern (p. 258), bulge, spikes (pp. 260-261), adz (p. 265), limes, mute, thongs (pp. 266-269), league, fowling piece (pp. 278-279). 17. *Pronounce:* pursuit, swoon (pp. 257-259), spars (p. 260), drought, sieve, launch, cruise, shoal, tour (pp. 266-269), jib (p. 277), gesture, formidable, sheathe, sprites (pp. 278-281).

Phrases for Study

lee of the land, **258**, 17
spare yards, **260**, 13
drug, **262**, 20
give me thought for thought, **264**, 3
whole round of my isle, **268**, 15
bound by a spell, **270**, 6
in sooth, **273**, 30
I found him apt, **274**, 4
standing in for the shore, **278**, 6
appeared concerned, **278**, 30
discover myself to them, **279**, 23
specter-like figure, **279**, 27

STORIES OF ADVENTURE

A Backward Look

Now that you have read all of these tales of adventure, perhaps some evening you will curl up in that big chair in a cozy place and will close your eyes and dream a dream. And in that dream you will see—who knows? Ali Baba and Aladdin in their queer dress, and Sindbad, the rich old sailor, and Captain Lemuel Gulliver, and Robin Hood in his Lincoln green, and Robinson Crusoe with his man Friday. All of them will sit down near you, between you and the fire perhaps, and they will talk to each other about the meaning of all the perils and successes that life brought them. And you will doubtless get the idea from them all that every man, rich or poor, ought to feel some responsibility to others. Ali Baba and Aladdin and Sindbad will tell the company, there in the firelight before your very eyes, how they felt that they owed something to others because of the wealth they had gained. Aladdin became a serious and public spirited man, though as a boy he had been of little worth. Ali Baba and Sindbad helped others and did many good deeds.

Then Robin Hood will join in the conversation. He lived in a time, as you can see from his story, when the poor not only had no chance but were oppressed. Robin tried to do away with some of this injustice. He was an outlaw; he did many things that it would not be right to do today; but he did these things in order to help people who were wretched and who had no chance.

And next, Robinson Crusoe has a word to say. His experience, he tells us, showed him how much we depend on each other. If a man is suddenly cut off from his fellows, has to get his own food or starve, build his own house with his own rude tools or freeze, he finds out how much he owes to the cooperation of thousands of other people.

And finally, Captain Gulliver, who has been listening quietly for a long time, knocks the ashes from his pipe as he gets up to go and says, "You know, it all comes down to this: can a man or a nation stand being rich and strong? You know those Lilliputians, when they conquered the people of Blefuscu, wanted right away to annex the lands of their enemies. They had no right to the lands; they had enough of their own; if I had let them do what they planned, they would have made many people very miserable. But the moment they saw a chance to grab something, they wanted to go right after it. And it makes me wonder about this America that is so much discussed just now. In my day we scarcely knew there was such a country, but you know how strong and prosperous the Americans are, and what a war they can fight, and how many rich men they have. They seem to me to have found that lamp and ring that friend Aladdin once had; everything they touch seems to turn to gold, and they can build a city overnight. I just wonder what they will do with all this power."

And they all shake their heads, as if to say that they wonder, too. And the fire has grown lower and lower, so that you can hardly see the strange forms. And then Father calls to you to wake up and get your lesson or go to bed, and they all vanish at the sound of that voice.

How would you answer Captain Gulliver's question about America? What did America do with its power in World War One? What good American citizens that you know of have used their wealth to found libraries, hospitals, parks, and other public benefits? Show that boys and girls join together in teamwork for the good of all by organizing clubs, Boy Scouts, Camp Fire Girls, Junior Red Cross, etc. Mention kinds of service these organizations give for the good of all. Show that each of the six stories in "Part II" has the two values mentioned in the first paragraph on page 146. Which story did you enjoy most? Which gave you the most worthwhile ideas? What gains have you made in your ability to read silently with speed and understanding?

Part III

Great American Authors

A man lives in the last half of life on the memory of things read in the first half of life.

Samuel Johnson

THE CONGRESSIONAL LIBRARY AT WASHINGTON

GREAT AMERICAN AUTHORS

A Forward Look

When Mother used to tell you a story about when she was a little girl, you were interested only in the story and in the pictures her words called up in your mind. Suppose some older person had been listening while she told one of these tales, and had been interested not alone in the adventure that she was telling about, as you were, but in the way in which she told it. This person, your uncle, let's say, would notice how Mother planned her story so as to keep the very most exciting thing to the last, and how you grew more and more excited about it, and how your eyes shone, and her eyes too, and how without knowing it she was letting him see what kind of people they were in her story, and what kind of little girl she was—very brave, you know—and when at the end you drew a long breath and had that delightful little thrill that you always have at the end of a perfectly wonderful story—after all this, suppose your uncle should look at Mother in a funny kind of way and should say, "Bless me, Sis, I had no idea you were an *author.*"

What would you say? Mother an *author?* Why, an author is a person who writes big books in words that no one can understand, but Mother, she—why, she is *Mother!*

Yet your uncle is right. Mother is an author when she thinks back over her life and picks out something that is interesting, and then tells it in her very most interesting way to please you. If she would only write out that story, and a printer would print it in a book, and in the front of the book you should read "When I Was a Little Girl. By Mother"—that would be a book, and Mother would be a real author.

Now long, long ago, there weren't any books. When Mother told you a story, if you had lived then, you would remember it and would tell it to other people, and after you grew up you would tell it to your children, and when they had grown up, they would tell it to your grandchildren, and so on and on. Who wrote "Cinderella," or "Sleeping Beauty," or the "Three Bears?" You don't know. Nobody knows. They just happened. They were told by mothers to their children and so on and so on, and after centuries, perhaps, when printing had been invented, some printer man thought, like your uncle, that here was a story that ought to be printed and so he made a book of it. But he didn't claim to be the author of it, for he was not.

So, some of the stories you have read in this book do not have any author's name attached to them. And even if they did, you were not thinking, while you were reading, about the man who wrote them. You just thought of the story and whether you liked it or not. Yet no small part of the advantage that you enjoy because you live now, instead of in the days when there were no books, lies in the fact that you can become acquainted with the men and women who have written the stories and poems that you read.

Let's put it this way. In those old days that we have been speaking about, you would have had to depend upon your mother, or some other mother, or some village weaver of tales for your stories. But they were busy, and you couldn't get enough stories to satisfy your appetite. Then one time, let's say, a strange, wandering fellow came to your village. And he had yards and yards of the most wonderful stories to tell. And he went home with you, let's say, and stayed there, and did nothing but tell you stories whenever you wanted them, first thing in the morning, and after school, and bedtime, and all. And he was never too busy. And you learned to know him, what an interesting man he was, and what fine eyes he had, and what a smile that made you smile back before he said a word, and how he loved truth and hated lies, and loved honor and hated shameful things. He was your author, your book, your book of books. And he was as dear to you, in himself, as his stories were.

Now you can have just such a friend, no, you can have a whole company of just such friends, for yourself. How? In books, of course. Only they won't be merely books; they will be friends. Washington Irving, teller of wonderful stories, and Robert Louis Stevenson are there, in those books, and you can learn *them* as well as their stories. And Henry W. Longfellow, writer of stories in verse; and John G. Whittier, writer of poems about barefoot boys and corn huskings; and Benjamin Franklin, a kindly philosopher—there, that word is too hard for you, but it just slipped out, and so you will have to be told that a philosopher is a person who *thinks* about life and its meaning.

That's what all authors are, in a way. That's what makes them authors. They don't just eat and sleep and do their work, whatever it is—they *think* about life. And what they see and think they set down for you. To know them is to know delightful friends who will tell you what everything means and will answer all your questions.

There they are, on your bookshelf. They won't speak to you unless you speak first. If you want to do something else and don't wish to be bothered, they won't bother you. But when you want to talk with them, they are ready. Call upon them often, and you will learn one of the blessedest things about life: the companionship of books.

Some of them, men of our own America, are to be introduced to you in the following pages. From now on you are to do three things. First, you are to listen and enjoy when they tell you what they have to say. Next, you are to begin to do just what your uncle was doing when he listened to Mother telling you that story—you are to see that there is a way to tell something that is good, and that if one has learned this way, like Mother, he is an author. And last, you are to find that these authors are real persons whom you can learn to know. Then you will love them, just as you love Mother, not alone for what they *say*, but for what they *are*.

Benjamin Franklin

Benjamin Franklin (1706-1790) was born in Boston in the early colonial days. While still a boy, he learned the printer's trade, but, having difficulty with his brother, for whom he worked, he went to Philadelphia, where later he became owner and editor of the *Philadelphia Gazette,* the city's leading newspaper. Later he established another periodical, called *Poor Richard's Almanac.*

Franklin was greatly interested in the study of science. He "snatched lightning from the skies" by the use of a key and a kite with a silk string. This experiment led to his invention of the lightning rod, which was soon placed on public and private buildings not only in America but also in England and France. He invented the "Franklin Stove," which is still in use in some places. This is an open stove made in such a way as to economize heat and save fuel. Franklin invented a street lamp which was used for lighting the streets of Philadelphia.

Franklin was bighearted and wished to be of real service to his fellow citizens. He organized a debating club, a night watch, a volunteer fire company, a street cleaning department, and a public library—the first of its kind in America.

His services to the new government that the Americans were just setting up were equally noteworthy. He went to England to represent the colonies and did all that he could to patch up the quarrel between the colonies and the mother country. When all these attempts failed, he gave himself heart and soul to the business of making a new government. He was one of the signers of the Declaration of Independence. Later, as a special minister to France, he delighted Frenchmen by his humor and his common sense, and he even succeeded in securing the promise of the French government to acknowledge the independence of the colonies and to send ships and men to their assistance.

In a letter to a friend in 1779, Franklin tells the story, "The Whistle." "An Ax to Grind" is from his autobiography.

The Whistle

When I was a child seven years old, my friends on a holiday filled my pocket with coppers. I went directly to a shop where they sold toys for children, and, being charmed with the sound of a whistle that I met by the way in the hands of another boy, I voluntarily offered and gave all my money for one. I then ran home and went whistling all over the house, much pleased with my whistle, but disturbing all the family.

My brothers and sisters and cousins, understanding the bargain I had made, told me I had given four times as much for it as it was worth, put me in mind what good things I might have bought with the rest of the money, and laughed at me so much for my folly that I cried with vexation, and the reflection gave me more chagrin than the whistle gave me pleasure.

This, however, was afterwards of use to me, the impression continuing on my mind, so that often when I was tempted to buy some unnecessary thing, I said to myself, "Don't give too much for the whistle," and I saved my money.

As I grew up, came into the world, and observed the actions of men, I thought I met with many, very many, who gave too much for the whistle.

When I saw one too ambitious of court favor, sacrificing his time in attendance on levees—his repose, his liberty, his virtue, and perhaps his friends, to attain it—I have said to myself, "This man gives too much for his whistle."

When I saw another fond of popularity, constantly employing himself in political bustles, neglecting his own affairs, and ruining them by that neglect, "He pays indeed," said I, "too much for his whistle."

If I knew a miser who gave up every kind of comfortable living, all the pleasure of doing good to others, all the esteem of his fellow citizens, and the joys of benevolent friendship, for the sake of accumulating wealth, "Poor man," said I, "you pay too much for your whistle."

When I met with a man of pleasure, sacrificing every laudable improvement of the mind or of his fortune to mere corporeal sensations, and ruining his health in their pursuit, "Mistaken man," said I, "you are providing pain for yourself instead of pleasure; you give too much for your whistle."

If I see one fond of appearance, or fine clothes, fine houses, fine furniture, fine equipages, all above his fortune, for which he contracts debts and ends his career in a prison, "Alas!" say I, "he has paid dear, very dear, for his whistle."

In short, I conceive that a great part of the miseries of mankind are brought upon them by the false estimates they have made of the value of things, and by their giving too much for their whistles.

NOTES AND QUESTIONS

Discussion. 1. Why did Franklin say that he paid too much for his whistle? 2. How was this incident of use to him afterwards? 3. How does it apply to a man too fond of popularity? To the miser? To the man of pleasure? To the one who cares too much for appearance? 4. Can you think of other incidents that illustrate what Franklin had in mind? 5. Extravagance has been called the great fault of Americans. During World War One what efforts were made by our people to correct this fault? Why were the efforts successful? 6. Why is it necessary to continue these efforts now? If all Americans would practice what Franklin advises, what would be the effect on the cost of living, and why? 7. In what ways can you save some of the pennies you might spend foolishly? 8. What do you know about Savings Bonds? About savings accounts? 9. Write a letter to your teacher, proposing that the children in your class save as many pennies as possible for opening savings accounts or for buying Saving Bonds, pointing out some ways in which children may save their pennies; bring in a part of Franklin's story in the most interesting way that you can. 10. Tell what you can about the author. 11. Find in the glossary the meaning of: coppers; voluntarily; vexation; ambitious; esteem; contracts. 12. *Pronounce:* directly; chagrin; sacrificing; levee; accumulating; laudable; equipage.

Phrases for Study

impression continuing, **293**, 16
political bustles, **294**, 12
corporeal sensations, **294**, 22
above his fortune, **294**, 26

AN AX TO GRIND

When I was a little boy, I remember, one cold winter morning, I was accosted by a smiling man with an ax on his shoulder. "My pretty boy," said he, "has your father a grindstone?"

"Yes, sir," said I.

"You are a fine little fellow!" said he. "Will you let me grind my ax on it?"

Pleased with the compliment of "fine little fellow," "Oh, yes, sir," I answered. "It is down in the shop."

"And will you, my man," said he, patting me on the head, "get me a little hot water?"

How could I refuse? I ran and soon brought a kettleful.

"How old are you—and what's your name?" continued he, without waiting for a reply. "I'm sure you are one of the finest lads that I have ever seen. Will you just turn a few minutes for me?"

Tickled with the flattery, like a little fool, I went to work, and bitterly did I rue the day. It was a new ax, and I toiled and tugged till I was almost tired to death. The school bell rang, and I could not get away. My hands were blistered, and the ax was not half ground.

At length, however, it was sharpened, and the man turned to me with, "Now, you little rascal, you've played truant! Scud to school, or you'll rue it!"

"Alas!" thought I, "it was hard enough to turn a grindstone this cold day, but now to be called a little rascal is too much."

It sank deep into my mind, and often have I thought of it since.

NOTES AND QUESTIONS

Discussion. 1. In this story Franklin advises you to be on your guard against flatterers who wish to make use of you in order to gain their own ends. What made Franklin do as the man wanted him to? What do you think of the man? 2. How would you have sought the boy's help? 3. In what way was this incident of use to Franklin afterwards? 4. What is meant when we say of a person that he has "an ax to grind"? 5. How do you think Franklin valued sincerity? 6. How do you value it? 7. Tell the story as the man would have told it to a friend. 8. *Pronounce:* accosted.

William Cullen Bryant

William Cullen Bryant (1794-1878) was born in the rugged hill country of western Massachusetts. From infancy he showed remarkable powers of mind. He could read by the time he was two years old, wrote verses at nine, and when scarcely eighteen wrote his most noted poem, "Thanatopsis," now one of the world's classics. He had a wonderful memory, and it is said he could repeat "by heart" every poem he had written.

Bryant removed to New York, where in 1825 he became editor of the *Evening Post.* Through the remainder of his long life he devoted his energy and great gifts to building up one of the most forceful of American newspapers, but he found time also to study nature and to write so many poems that we now think of him as a poet, not as an editor. He was also a student, and we are indebted to him for some excellent translations from old authors. And, finally, he was a public spirited American, interested in all matters that have to do with the honor of our country. Imagine yourself in New York City during the latter part of the nineteenth century. If you were walking up Broadway almost any morning, your attention would be attracted to a venerable looking man, with heavy, flowing, snow-white hair and beard, whom you would be quite likely to meet swinging along at a vigorous pace. You would not need to be told that this man is our first American poet, with whose verses you are already familiar; and you would probably know, too, that he is also the editor of the *Evening Post* and that, although now past eighty, he is on his way to his office, walking from his home some two miles away, as he has done, rain or shine, for over half a century.

This great man was not too busy with affairs, or too learned, to look for the joy that comes from companionship with nature. Like Irving he chose American subjects taken from his own surroundings: the scenes of his boyhood, the flowers, birds, and hills of his old New England home. He found pleasure in the simplest things, and he wrote about this pleasure in the simplest way. In this simplicity and the variety of his interests his wealth consisted, a treasure that made rich not only the poet who possessed it but all Americans, to whom he left his life and works for an inheritance.

The Yellow Violet

When beechen buds begin to swell,
  And woods the bluebird's warble know,
The yellow violet's modest bell
  Peeps from the last year's leaves below.

Ere russet fields their green resume,
  Sweet flower, I love, in forest bare,
To meet thee, when thy faint perfume
  Alone is in the virgin air.

Of all her train, the hands of Spring
  First plant thee in the watery mold;
And I have seen thee blossoming
  Beside the snow-bank's edges cold.

Thy parent sun, who bade thee view
    Pale skies, and chilling moisture sip,
Has bathed thee in his own bright hue,
    And streaked with jet thy glowing lip.

Yet slight thy form, and low thy seat,
    And earthward bent thy gentle eye,
Unapt the passing view to meet,
    When loftier flowers are flaunting nigh.

Oft, in the sunless April day,
    Thy early smile has stayed my walk,
But 'midst the gorgeous blooms of May
    I passed thee on thy humble stalk.

So they who climb to wealth forget
    The friends in darker fortunes tried.
I copied them—but I regret
    That I should ape the ways of pride.

And when again the genial hour
    Awakes the painted tribes of light,
I'll not o'erlook the modest flower
    That made the woods of April bright.

NOTES AND QUESTIONS

Discussion. 1. When does the poet say the violet makes its appearance? 2. Why is the violet called a "modest" flower? 3. Why does the violet make glad the heart of the poet? When the woods and fields are *full* of flowers, does he notice the violet? 4. What does "alone" add to the meaning of line 8, page 298? 5. What is meant by "her train," line 9, page 298? 6. What are "the hands of Spring"? 7. In what sense is the sun the "parent" of the violet? 8. Why does Bryant say the violet's seat is low? 9. What does the poet say the violet's "early smile" has often done for him? 10. Point out the stanzas in which the poet tells you where he finds the violet; the stanzas in which he tells you about the appearance and character of the flower; the stanzas in which he rebukes himself for passing it by, and makes a promise. 11. Why does Bryant stop to view the violet in April and pass it by in May? 12. With what does the poet compare this treatment of the violet? 13. What does the poet say he regrets? 14. What other flowers come very early in the spring? How do you feel when you see them? 15. Which stanza of the poem do you like best? 16. What other poem on the violet have you read? 17. Tell what you can about the author. 18. Find in the glossary the meaning of: beechen, russet, train, jet, unapt. 19. *Pronounce:* ere, parent, gorgeous, humble, genial.

Phrases for Study

modest bell, **298**, 3
their green resume, **298**, 5
virgin air, **298**, 8
pale skies, **299**, 2
flaunting nigh, **299**, 8
stayed my walk, **299**, 10
in darker fortunes tried, **299**, 14
ape the ways of pride, **299**, 16
genial hour, **299**, 17
painted tribes of light, **299**, 18

THE GLADNESS OF NATURE

Is this a time to be cloudy and sad,
When our Mother Nature laughs around,
When even the deep blue heavens look glad,
And gladness breathes from the blossoming ground?

There are notes of joy from the hangbird and wren,
And the gossip of swallows through all the sky;
The ground squirrel gayly chirps by his den,
And the wilding bee hums merrily by.

The clouds are at play in the azure space,
And their shadows at play on the bright green vale,
And here they stretch to the frolic chase,
And there they roll on the easy gale.

There's a dance of leaves in that aspen bower;
There's a titter of winds in that beechen tree;
There's a smile on the fruit, and a smile on the flower,
And a laugh from the brook that runs to the sea.

And look at the broad-faced sun, how he smiles
On the dewy earth that smiles in his ray,
On the leaping waters and gay young isles;
Ay, look, and he'll smile thy gloom away.

NOTES AND QUESTIONS

Discussion. 1. What season is described here? 2. What are the signs that Nature is glad? How do all these things affect the poet? How do you sometimes feel on a cold, rainy day? 3. What signs of gladness are mentioned in the first two stanzas? 4. Which of these have you seen in springtime? 5. Have you ever seen clouds that seemed to chase one another? 6. What is meant by "a laugh from the brook"? 7. What does the poet say the sun will do for us? 8. Do you think spring is "a time to be cloudy and sad"? Why? 9. Why do city boys and girls like to visit the country? 10. Read again "A Forward Look," pages 19-20, and then point out fancies that Bryant uses in this poem to help us see the beauty and wonder of nature. 11. Commit to memory the stanza that you like best. 12. *Pronounce:* wilding, azure, isles, ay.

Phrases for Study

gladness breathes, **300**, 4
blossoming ground, **300**, 4
gossip of swallows, **300**, 6
azure space, **301**, 1
frolic chase, **301**, 3
aspen bower, **301**, 5
titter of winds, **301**, 6
broad-faced sun, **301**, 9

John Greenleaf Whittier

John Greenleaf Whittier (1807-1892) was born near the town of Haverhill, Massachusetts, not far from Hawthorne's birthplace. He had very little opportunity for education beyond what the district school afforded, for his parents were too poor to send him away to school. His two years' attendance at Haverhill Academy was paid for by his own work at making ladies' slippers for twenty-five cents a pair. He began writing verses almost as soon as he learned to write at all, but his father discouraged this ambition as frivolous, saying it would never give him bread. His family were Quakers, sturdy of stature as of character. He is called "The Quaker Poet."

Whittier led the life of a New England farm boy, used to hard work and few pleasures. His library consisted of practically one book, the family Bible. Later, a copy of Burns's poems was loaned to him by the district schoolmaster. Like Burns he had great sympathy with the humble and the poor. In his poems Whittier described the scenes and told the legends of his own locality. *Home Ballads* and *Songs of Labor,* in which "The Huskers" and "The Corn-Song" appear, are among his most widely read books. They picture country life and the scenes of the simple occupations common in his part of the country. Whittier was intensely patriotic and religious by nature. His happiness lay in his association with his friends, with children, animals, and the outdoor world.

In these respects he was like Bryant, a man who found pleasure in simple things. Like Bryant, also, he was interested in public affairs. Any injustice to the poor he opposed passionately. He wrote many poems in protest against slavery. He wrote, also, ballads of early New England history, and some of our most beautiful religious poetry comes from his pen. His life was less filled with business cares than that of Bryant, but it was equally full of interests that made him happy and a source of help and joy to others.

The Huskers

It was late in mild October, and the long autumnal rain
Had left the summer harvest-fields all green with grass
again;
The first sharp frosts had fallen, leaving all the wood-
lands gay
With the hues of summer's rainbow or the meadow flowers
of May.

Through a thin, dry mist, that morning, the sun rose
broad and red;
At first a rayless disk of fire, he brightened as he sped;
Yet even his noontide glory fell chastened and subdued
On the cornfields and the orchards and softly pictured
wood.

And all that quiet afternoon, slow sloping to the night,
He wove with golden shuttle the haze with yellow light;

Slanting through the painted beeches, he glorified the hill;
And, beneath it, pond and meadow lay brighter, greener still.

And shouting boys in woodland haunts caught glimpses of that sky,
Flecked by the many-tinted leaves, and laughed, they knew not why;
And schoolgirls, gay with aster-flowers, beside the meadow brooks,
Mingled the glow of autumn with the sunshine of sweet looks.

From spire and barn looked westerly the patient weather-cocks;
But even the birches on the hill stood motionless as rocks.
No sound was in the woodlands save the squirrel's dropping shell,
And the yellow leaves among the boughs, low rustling as they fell.

The summer grains were harvested; the stubble-fields lay dry,
Where June winds rolled, in light and shade, the pale green waves of rye;
But still, on gentle hill-slopes, in valleys fringed with wood,
Ungathered, bleaching in the sun, the heavy corn crop stood.

Bent low by autumn's wind and rain, through husks that, dry and sear,
Unfolded from their ripened charge, shone out the yellow ear;

Beneath, the turnip lay concealed in many a verdant fold,
And glistened in the slanting light the pumpkin's sphere of gold.

There wrought the busy harvester, and many a creaking wain
Bore slowly to the long barn-floor its load of husk and grain;
Till broad and red, as when he rose, the sun sank down at last,
And like a merry guest's farewell the day in brightness passed.

And lo! as through the western pines, on meadow, stream, and pond,
Flamed the red radiance of a sky set all afire beyond,
Slowly o'er the eastern sea-bluffs a milder glory shone,
And the sunset and the moonrise were mingled into one!

As thus into the quiet night the twilight lapsed away,
And deeper in the brightening moon the tranquil shadows lay,
From many a brown old farmhouse and hamlet without name,
Their milking and their home-tasks done, the merry huskers came.

Swung o'er the heaped-up harvest, from pitchforks in the mow,
Shone dimly down the lanterns on the pleasant scene below,
The glowing pile of husks behind, the golden ears before,
And laughing eyes and busy hands and brown cheeks glimmering o'er.

Half hidden in a quiet nook, serene of look and heart,
Talking their old times over, the old men sat apart;
While up and down the unhusked pile, or nestling in its shade,
At hide-and-seek, with laugh and shout, the happy children played.

Urged by the good host's daughter, a maiden young and fair,
Lifting to light her sweet blue eyes and pride of soft brown hair,
The master of the village school, sleek of hair and smooth of tongue,
To the quaint tune of some old psalm, a husking-ballad sung.

NOTES AND QUESTIONS

Discussion. 1. What is the difference between the sunshine of October and that of May? 2. Why does it seem to the poet as if the sun wove with golden shuttle the yellow haze? 3. What had the frost done that made the woodlands gay? 4. What words in the second stanza make you feel that the wood was some distance away? 5. To whom does "he" in the third stanza refer? 6. What words in the second stanza explain the word "haze" in the third stanza? 7. What gave the beeches the appearance of being painted? 8. What are the colors of the woods and sky in this poem? What colors are they in the poem, "The Yellow Violet"? Find the words and phrases that tell you. How many times, in this poem, does the poet use the words *golden* and *yellow*, or speak of things that suggest these colors? 9. What do you think was the reason the boys laughed when they looked up to the sky? 10. What "summer grain" is mentioned in line 11, page 304? 11. What crop was still ungathered? 12. Where were the harvesters at work? 13. What was it that set the sky "all afire beyond"? 14. Where did the husking take place? What tells you this? 15. How did the old men spend the evening? 16. What things that we eat depend on the work of the huskers? 17. Tell what you can about the author. 18. Find in the glossary the meaning of: shuttle, spire, sear, verdant, wain, lapsed 19. *Pronounce:* autumnal, chastened, beneath, sphere, wrought, radiance, tranquil, mow, serene, psalm.

Phrases for Study

hues of summer's rainbow, **303**, 4
rayless disk of fire, **303**, 6
brightened as he sped, **303**, 6
glory fell chastened, **303**, 7
softly pictured wood, **303**, 8
slow sloping to the night, **303**, 9
glorified the hill, **304**, 1
sunshine of sweet looks, **304**, 6
looked westerly, **304**, 7
patient weathercocks, **304**, 7
ripened charge, **304**, 16
sphere of gold, **305**, 2
milder glory shone, **305**, 9
mingled into one, **305**, 10
hamlet without name, **305**, 13
golden ears before, **305**, 17
glimmering o'er, **305**, 18
serene of look and heart, **306**, 1

The Corn-Song

Heap high the farmer's wintry hoard!
Heap high the golden corn!
No richer gift has Autumn poured
From out her lavish horn!

Let other lands, exulting, glean
The apple from the pine,
The orange from its glossy green,
The cluster from the vine;

We better love the hardy gift
Our rugged vales bestow,
To cheer us when the storm shall drift
Our harvest-fields with snow.

Through vales of grass and meads of flowers
Our plows their furrows made,
While on the hills the sun and showers
Of changeful April played.

We dropped the seed o'er hill and plain,
Beneath the sun of May,
And frightened from our sprouting grain
The robber crows away.

All through the long, bright days of June
Its leaves grew green and fair,
And waved in hot midsummer's noon
Its soft and yellow hair.

And now, with Autumn's moonlit eves,
Its harvest-time has come;
We pluck away the frosted leaves,
And bear the treasure home.

. . . .

Then shame on all the proud and vain
Whose folly laughs to scorn
The blessing of our hardy grain,
Our wealth of golden corn!

Let earth withhold her goodly root,
Let mildew blight the rye,
Give to the worm the orchard's fruit,
The wheat-field to the fly;

But let the good old crop adorn
    The hills our fathers trod;
Still let us, for his golden corn,
    Send up our thanks to God!

NOTES AND QUESTIONS

Discussion. 1. In "A Forward Look," pages 19-20, you read that poets help you to see beauty in things that might otherwise seem common. The yellow violet is less showy than the chrysanthemum, but the poet writes of the violet. The pineapple, the orange, the grape, seem more interesting than the yellow corn of the fields, but here is a poem about one of the commonest of farm crops. To whom is the poet speaking in the first two stanzas? Point out some of the poet's fancies in this poem. 2. Is all corn "golden"? What other kinds have you seen? 3. Name other gifts autumn brings us. 4. Why is the corn a "hardy gift"? What other words or phrases in the poem suggest the same idea? 5. What do we call the "apple from the pine"? 6. What clusters are picked from vines? 7. In what "other lands" do these fruits grow? 8. Where was Whittier's home? 9. What do you know of the soil and climate of New England? 10. Find the line that tells when we plant the corn. 11. Find the lines that tell when we harvest the corn. 12. What is the "yellow hair" the corn waves in summer? 13. What does the poet mean by "frosted leaves"? 14. What does he think of those who scorn the blessing of the corn? 15. What wish does the poet express in the last stanza? 16. What service did our farmers and boys and girls on the farms perform during World War One? 17. On page 291 you were asked to notice the way in which these American authors have expressed their thoughts. Does Whittier's use of rhyme add to the beauty of his "song" about corn? Point out some of the lines that rhyme. 18. Find in the glossary the meaning of: glean, hardy, meads, furrows, frosted, mildew, adorn. 19. *Pronounce:* hoard, lavish, glossy, root.

Phrases for Study

wintry hoard, **307**, 1
lavish horn, **307**, 4
exulting, glean, **307**, 5
hardy gift, **307**, 9
rugged vales bestow, **307**, 10
changeful April, **308**, 4
folly laughs to scorn, **308**, 18
goodly root, **308**, 21

Washington Irving

Washington Irving (1783-1859) was a native of New York. He led a happy life, rambling in his boyhood about every nook and corner of the city and the adjacent woods, which at that time were not very far to seek. New York, called New Amsterdam in early colonial times, was then the capital of the country, and here the boy grew up happy, seeing many sides of American life, both in the city and country.

Manhattan Island and the region about it, with its commanding position at the entrance to a great inland waterway, was from the first a prize for which the nations from across the sea had contended. Such a mingling of different people must give rise to interesting experiences, and when someone appears who can put the story of those events into a pleasing sketch, then we begin to have real literature. Irving had not only the experience and observation, but the ability to express what he had seen and felt. Therefore, when he grew to manhood and gave his sketches of this region to the world, we had our first real American literature.

Irving is best known as a humorist and a charming storyteller, but he has also written serious and tender works. His life of Washington is a tribute of loving reverence to the great

American for whom he was named. As a boy, Irving was of a rather mischievous turn, a trait which perhaps helped to make him the "first American humorist." Indeed, it has been said that "before Irving there was no laughter in the land." He is called the "Father of American Literature," and also the "gentle humorist." "Capturing the Wild Horse" is taken from *A Tour of the Prairies* and "The Adventure of the Mason" from *The Alhambra.*

Capturing the Wild Horse*

We left the buffalo camp about eight o'clock and had a toilsome march of two hours over ridges of hills covered with a ragged forest of scrub oaks and broken by deep gullies. Among the oaks I observed many of the most diminutive size, some not above a foot high, yet bearing abundance of small acorns.

About ten o'clock in the morning we came to where this line of rugged hills swept down into a valley, through which flowed the north fork of the Red River. A beautiful meadow about half a mile wide, colored with yellow autumnal flowers, stretched for two or three miles along the foot of the hills, bordered on the opposite side by the river, whose bank was fringed with cottonwood trees.

The meadow was finely diversified by groves and clumps of trees, so happily arranged that they seemed as if set out by the hand of art. As we cast our eyes over this fresh and delightful valley, we saw a troop of wild horses quietly grazing on a green lawn about a mile distant to our right, while to our left, at nearly the same distance, were several buffaloes—some feeding, others reposing and ruminating among the high, rich herbage under the shade of a clump

* See "Suggestions for Silent Reading," page 163.

of cottonwood trees. The whole had the appearance of a broad, beautiful tract of pasture land on the estate of some gentleman farmer, with his cattle grazing about the lawns and meadows.

A council of war was now held, and it was determined to profit by the present favorable opportunity and try our hand at the grand hunting maneuver which is called "ringing the wild horse."

This requires a large party of horsemen, well mounted. They extend themselves in each direction, singly, at certain distances apart, and gradually form a ring of two or three miles in circumference, so as to surround the game. This has to be done with extreme care, for the wild horse is the most readily alarmed inhabitant of the prairie, and can scent a hunter at a great distance, if to windward.

The ring being formed, two or three ride toward the horses, which start off in an opposite direction. Whenever they approach the bounds of the ring, however, a huntsman presents himself and turns them from their course. In this way they are checked and driven back at every point and kept galloping round and round this magic circle, until, being completely tired down, it is easy for the hunters to ride up beside them and throw the lariat over their heads. The prime horses of most speed and courage, however, are apt to break through and escape, so that in general it is the second-rate horses that are taken.

Preparations were now made for a hunt of this kind. The packhorses were taken into the woods and firmly tied to trees, lest in a rush of the wild horses they should break away with them. Twenty-five men were then sent, under the command of a lieutenant, to steal along the edge of the valley within the strip of wood that skirted the hills. They were to station themselves about fifty yards apart, within the edge of the woods, and not advance or show themselves until the horses dashed in that direction.

Twenty-five men were sent across the valley to steal in like manner along the river bank that bordered the opposite side and to station themselves among the trees. A third party of about the same number was to form a line stretching across the lower part of the valley, so as to connect the two wings. Beatte and our other half-breed, Antoine, together with the ever officious Tonish, were to make a circuit through the woods, so as to get to the upper part of the valley in the rear of the horses, and to drive them forward into the kind of sack that we had formed, while the two wings should join behind them and make a complete circle.

The flanking parties were quietly extending themselves, out of sight, on each side of the valley, and the rest were stretching themselves like the links of a chain across it, when the wild horses gave signs that they scented an enemy—snuffing the air, snorting, and looking about.

At length they pranced off slowly toward the river and disappeared behind a green bank. Here, had the rules of the chase been observed, they would have been quietly checked and turned back by the advance of a hunter from among the trees. Unluckily, however, we had our wildfire Jack-o'-lantern little Frenchman to deal with.

Instead of keeping quietly up the right side of the valley to get above the horses, the moment he saw them move toward the river he broke out of the thicket of woods and dashed furiously across the plain in pursuit of them, being mounted on one of the led horses belonging to the count. This put an end to all system. The half-breeds and half a score of rangers joined in the chase.

Away they all went over the green bank. In a moment or two the wild horses reappeared and came thundering down the valley, with Frenchman, half-breeds, and rangers galloping and yelling like mad behind them. It was in vain that the line drawn across the valley attempted to check and turn back the fugitives. They were too hotly pressed by their pursuers. In their panic they dashed through the line and clattered down the plain.

The whole troop joined in the headlong chase—some of the rangers without hats or caps, their hair flying about their ears; others with handkerchiefs tied round their heads. The buffaloes, which had been calmly ruminating among the herbage, heaved up their huge forms, gazed for a moment with astonishment at the tempest that came scouring down the meadow, then turned and took to heavy-rolling flight. They were soon overtaken. The mixed throng were pressed together by the sides of the valley, and away they went, pell-mell, hurry-scurry, wild buffalo, wild horse, wild huntsman, with clang and clatter, and whoop and halloo, that made the forests ring.

At length the buffaloes turned into a green brake on the river bank, while the horses dashed up a narrow defile of the hills, with their pursuers close at their heels. Beatte passed several of them, having fixed his eye upon a fine Pawnee horse that had his ears slit, and saddle marks upon his back. He pressed him gallantly, but lost him in the woods.

Among the wild horses was a fine black mare. In scrambling up the defile she tripped and fell. A young ranger sprang from his horse and seized her by the mane and muzzle. Another ranger dismounted and came to his assistance. The mare struggled fiercely, kicking and biting and striking with her fore feet, but a noose was slipped over her head, and her struggles were in vain. It was some time, however, before she gave over rearing and plunging and lashing out with her feet on every side. The two rangers then led her along the valley by two long lariats, which enabled them to keep at a sufficient distance on each side to be out of the reach of her hoofs, and whenever she struck out in one direction, she was jerked in the other. In this way her spirit was gradually subdued.

As to little Tonish, who had marred the whole scene by his rashness, he had been more successful than he deserved, having managed to catch a beautiful cream colored colt about seven months old, which had not strength to keep up with its companions. The little Frenchman was beside himself with joy. It was amusing to see him with his prize. The colt would rear and kick and struggle to get free, when Tonish would take him about the neck, wrestle with him, jump on his back, and cut as many antics as a monkey with a kitten.

Nothing surprised me more, however, than to see how soon these poor animals, thus taken from the unbounded freedom of the prairie, yielded to the control of man. In the course of two or three days the mare and colt went with the led horses and became quite docile.

NOTES AND QUESTIONS

Historical Note. In 1832 Irving made "a tour of the prairies"—that is, of what was then the Far West, beyond the Mississippi, where, he says, "there is neither to be seen the log house of the white man, nor the wigwam of the Indian."

Discussion. 1. What picture do the first three paragraphs give you? 2. Tell how "ringing the wild horse" is accomplished. 3. What preparations did Irving's party make for the hunt? 4. Who broke the rules of the chase? 5. What was the effect of this? 6. Tell all you can learn about Tonish, the little Frenchman. 7. What does Irving say about the ease with which the wild horses were tamed? 8. List the words that give ideas of thrilling action in the paragraph beginning, "The whole troop joined in the headlong chase." What words tell the difference between the buffaloes and the horses in flight? 9. Tell what you can about the author. 10. *Class readings:* Select the passages you like best. 11. *Outline for testing silent reading.* Tell the story in your own words, using the following topics: (a) the scene of action; (b) the method of approach; (c) the preparations; (d) the mistake of Tonish; (e) the excitement of the chase; (f) the two captures. 12. Find in the glossary the meaning of: toilsome, gullies, diversified, circumference, prime, skirted, fugitives, brake, defile. 13. *Pronounce:* diminutive, ruminating, herbage, maneuver, kept, lariat, circuit, reappeared, rangers, handkerchiefs, rearing, marred.

Phrases for Study

swept down into a valley, **311**, 8
fringed with trees, **311**, 13
happily arranged, **311**, 15
hand of art, **311**, 16
council of war, **312**, 5
well mounted, **312**, 9
if to windward, **312**, 15
approach the bounds, **312**, 18
ever-officious Tonish, **313**, 9
flanking parties, **313**, 14
extending themselves, **313**, 14
wildfire Jack-o'-lantern, **313**, 23
thundering down the valley, **313**, 33
hotly pressed, **314**, 4
scouring down the meadow, **314**, 13
heavy-rolling flight, **314**, 14
spirit was gradually subdued, **315**, 6
marred the whole scene, **315**, 7
beside himself with joy, **315**, 12
unbounded freedom, **315**, 18

The Adventure of the Mason*

There was once upon a time a poor mason, or bricklayer, in Granada, who kept all the saints' days and holidays, and Saint Monday into the bargain, and yet with all his devotion he grew poorer and poorer and could scarcely earn bread for his numerous family. One night he was roused from his first sleep by a knocking at his door. He opened it and beheld before him a tall stranger.

* See "Suggestions for Silent Reading," page 163.

"Hark ye, honest friend!" said the stranger. "I have observed that you are a good Christian and one to be trusted. Will you undertake a job this very night?"

"With all my heart, señor, on condition that I am paid accordingly."

"That you shall be; but you must suffer yourself to be blindfolded."

To this the mason made no objection. So, being hoodwinked, he was led by the stranger through various rough lanes and winding passages until they stopped before the portal of a house. The stranger then applied a key, turned a creaking lock, and opened what sounded like a ponderous door. They entered, the door was closed and bolted, and the mason was conducted through an echoing corridor and a spacious hall to an interior part of the building. Here the bandage was removed from his eyes, and he found himself in a court dimly lighted by a single lamp. In the center was the dry basin of an old fountain, under which the stranger requested him to form a small vault, bricks and mortar being at hand for the purpose. He worked all night, but without finishing the job. Just before daybreak the stranger put a piece of gold into his hand, and having again blindfolded him, conducted him back to his dwelling.

"Are you willing," said he, "to return and complete your work?"

"Gladly, señor, provided I am so well paid."

"Well then, tomorrow at midnight I will call again."

He did so, and the vault was completed.

"Now," said the stranger, "you must help me to bring forth the bodies that are to be buried in this vault."

The poor mason's hair rose on his head at these words. He followed the stranger with trembling steps into a retired chamber of the mansion, expecting to behold some ghastly spectacle of death, but was relieved on seeing three or four jars standing in one corner. They were full of money, and it was with great labor that he and the stranger carried them forth and consigned them to their tomb. The vault was then closed, the pavement replaced, and all traces of the work were obliterated. The mason was again hoodwinked and led forth by a route different from that by which he had come. After they had wandered for a long time through a maze of lanes and alleys, they halted. The stranger then put two pieces of gold into his hand. "Wait here," said he, "until you hear the cathedral bell toll. If you uncover your eyes before that time, evil will befall you." So saying, he departed. The mason waited faithfully, amusing himself by weighing the gold pieces in his hand and clinking them against each other. The moment the cathedral bell rang its peals he uncovered his eyes and found himself on the banks of the Xenil, whence he made the best of his way home and reveled with his family for a whole fortnight on the profits of his two nights' work, after which he was as poor as ever.

He continued to work a little and pray a good deal and keep saints' days and holidays from year to year, while his family grew up gaunt and ragged as a crew of gypsies. As he was seated one evening at the door of his hovel, he was accosted by a rich old curmudgeon who was noted for owning many houses and being a griping landlord. The man of money eyed him for a moment from beneath a pair of anxious, shaggy eyes.

"I am told, friend, that you are very poor."

"There is no denying the fact, señor—it speaks for itself."

"I presume then that you will be glad of a job and will work cheap?"

"As cheap, my master, as any mason in Granada."

"That's what I want. I have an old house fallen into decay, which costs me more money than it is worth to keep in repair, for nobody will live in it. So I must patch it up and keep it together at as small expense as possible."

The mason was accordingly conducted to a large deserted house that seemed going to ruin. Passing through several empty halls and chambers, he entered an inner court, where his eye was caught by an old fountain. He paused for a moment, for a dreamy recollection of the place came over him.

"Pray," said he, "who occupied this house formerly?"

"A pest upon him!" cried the landlord. "It was an old miserly fellow who cared for nobody but himself. He was said to be immensely rich. He died suddenly, and nothing could they find but a few ducats in a leathern purse. The worst luck has fallen on me, for since his death the old fellow continues to occupy my house without paying rent. The people pretend to hear the clinking of gold all night in the chamber where the old fellow slept, as if he were counting over his money and sometimes a groaning and moaning about the court. Whether true or false, these stories have brought a bad name on my house, and not a tenant will remain in it."

"Enough," said the mason sturdily. "Let me live in your house rent free until some better tenant appears, and I will put it in repair and quiet the troubled spirit that disturbs it. I am a good Christian and a poor man and am not to be daunted by the devil himself, even though he should come in the shape of a big bag of money!"

The offer of the mason was gladly accepted. He moved with his family into the house and fulfilled all of his engagements. By little and little he restored it to its former state.

The clinking of gold was no more heard at night in the chamber of the defunct tenant, but began to be heard by day in the pocket of the living mason. In a word, he increased rapidly in wealth, to the admiration of all his neighbors, and became one of the richest men in Granada. He gave large sums to the Church—by way, no doubt, of satisfying his conscience—and never revealed the secret of the vault until on his deathbed to his son and heir.

NOTES AND QUESTIONS

Discussion. 1. What condition led the mason to undertake the stranger's task? 2. Why was the mason blindfolded? 3. How long did it take him to complete the vault? 4. What was buried in it? 5. How did the mason find his way home? 6. Was the mason's poverty relieved by the pay he received from the stranger? 7. What work did the grasping landlord propose to the mason? 8. What stories had brought a bad name upon the landlord's house? 9. What was the "dreamy recollection"? 10. How did the mason show his quick wit? 11. Why did he say that he was not afraid of the devil in the shape of a bag of money? 12. What differences do you notice between this story of how the mason came upon great wealth and the stories of Aladdin and Ali Baba? 13. Read again pages 289-291 and tell what makes Irving a real author. Can you tell why you enjoyed this story? 14. *Class reading:* The second part of the story, page 318, line 21, to the end. 15. *Outline for testing silent reading.* Tell the story in your own words, using the following topics: (a) how the mason built the vault in the mysterious house; (b) how he unexpectedly came into possession of this vault many years later. 16. Find in the glossary the meaning of: hoodwinked, vault, maze, cathedral, pest, ducat. 17. *Pronounce:* Granada, señor, ponderous, ghastly, obliterated, route, gaunt, hovel, curmudgeon, daunted.

Phrases for Study

retired chamber, **317**, 32
ghastly spectacle, **317**, 33
crew of gypsies, **318**, 23
griping landlord, **318**, 26
troubled spirit, **319**, 27
former state, **319**, 33
defunct tenant, **320**, 2
by way of satisfying, **320**, 6

Henry Wadsworth Longfellow

Henry Wadsworth Longfellow (1807-1882) was a native of Maine and a graduate of Bowdoin College, in the same class with Nathaniel Hawthorne. Longfellow came of early New England ancestry, his mother being a daughter of General Wadsworth of the Revolutionary War.

After his graduation from college he spent several years abroad and upon his return to America held professorships first in Bowdoin and later in Harvard College. When he moved to Cambridge and began his active work at Harvard, he took up his residence in the historic Craigie House, overlooking the Charles River—a house in which Washington had been quartered for some months when in 1775 he took command of the Continental army.

Longfellow is the poet who has spoken most sincerely and sympathetically to the hearts of the common people and to children. His style is notable for its simplicity and grace. His *Hiawatha* is a national poem that records the picturesque traditions of the American Indian. Its charm and melody are the delight of all children, and in years to come, when the race which it describes has utterly disappeared, we shall value at even higher worth these stories of the romantic past of America and of the brave people who inhabited these mountains and plains before the white man came.

Besides Indian stories, Longfellow wrote many narratives in verse dealing with old legends of America. "The Skeleton in Armor" is an example of the legends about European explorers who came here before the days of Columbus. *Evangeline* and *The Courtship of Miles Standish* are longer poems which find their subjects in early colonial history. He wrote also of legends of Europe and was well acquainted with stories and romances of older civilizations than ours. Equally well-known poems, of a different type, are those in which household joys and sorrows give the theme. Longfellow is the poet of the home life, of simple hopes, of true religious faith. His spirit was the spirit of a child, affectionate, loyal, eager for romance and knightly adventure. He is the "Children's Poet," as the poem "The Children's Hour" helps to show. There were sorrows as well as joys in his life, and this is why we go to him in trouble and why so many people know his poems by heart. Sorrow never took away his faith or made him bitter. He is genial and kindly, the friend of all Americans everywhere.

The Arrow and the Song

I shot an arrow into the air;
It fell to earth, I knew not where;
For, so swiftly it flew, the sight
Could not follow it in its flight.

I breathed a song into the air;
It fell to earth, I knew not where;
For who has sight so keen and strong
That it can follow the flight of song?

Long, long afterwards, in an oak
I found the arrow, still unbroke;
And the song, from beginning to end,
I found again in the heart of a friend.

NOTES AND QUESTIONS

Discussion. 1. What became of the arrow? Of the song? 2. Where was the arrow found? When? 3. Where was the song found? 4. Point out lines that rhyme. 5. What is Longfellow's purpose in this poem? 6. Why is the poet's song compared to the flight of an arrow? 7. A poet once said, "Let me make the songs of a nation, and I care not who makes the laws." What did he mean? 8. What was the song doing "in the heart of a friend"?

Phrases for Study

breathed a song, **322**, 5
flight of song, **322**, 8

THE CHILDREN'S HOUR

Between the dark and the daylight,
When the night is beginning to lower,
Comes a pause in the day's occupations,
That is known as the Children's Hour.

I hear in the chamber above me
The patter of little feet,
The sound of a door that is opened,
And voices soft and sweet.

From my study I see in the lamplight,
Descending the broad hall stair,
Grave Alice, and laughing Allegra,
And Edith with golden hair.

A whisper, and then a silence;
    Yet I know by their merry eyes
They are plotting and planning together
    To take me by surprise.

A sudden rush from the stairway,
    A sudden raid from the hall!
By three doors left unguarded
    They enter my castle wall!

They climb up into my turret
    O'er the arms and back of my chair;
If I try to escape, they surround me;
    They seem to be everywhere.

They almost devour me with kisses;
    Their arms about me entwine;
Till I think of the Bishop of Bingen
    In his Mouse-Tower on the Rhine!

Do you think, O blue-eyed banditti,
    Because you have scaled the wall,
Such an old mustache as I am
    Is not a match for you all?

I have you fast in my fortress,
    And will not let you depart,
But put you down into the dungeon
    In the round-tower of my heart.

And there will I keep you forever,
  Yes, forever and a day,
Till the walls shall crumble to ruin,
  And molder in dust away!

NOTES AND QUESTIONS

Discussion. 1. What is the time "Between the dark and the daylight" usually called? 2. What do you suppose Longfellow had been doing in his study before the children came down to him? 3. What reasons can you give for the "pause in the day's occupations"? 4. Who were the children whom the poet saw "Descending the broad hall stair" to enter his "castle wall"? 5. What were these children whispering about? 6. What does Longfellow mean by his "turret"? 7. To what does he compare the rush made by the children? 8. What wall did they scale in order to reach him? 9. Where does Longfellow say he will put the children now that he has captured them? 10. Which stanza of this poem do you like best? 11. Tell what you know about the life of Longfellow. 12. Find in the glossary the meaning of: raid, match. 13. *Pronounce:* lower, banditti, dungeon.

Phrases for Study

Bishop of Bingen, **324**, 15
scaled the wall, **324**, 18
such an old mustache, **324**, 19
fast in my fortress, **324**, 21
round-tower of my heart, **324**, 24
forever and a day, **325**, 2
molder in dust away, **325**, 4

The Song of Hiawatha

Introduction

Should you ask me, whence these stories,
Whence these legends and traditions,
With the odors of the forest
With the dew and damp of meadows,
With the curling smoke of wigwams,
With the rushing of great rivers,
With their frequent repetitions,
And their wild reverberations,
As of thunder in the mountains,
    I should answer, I should tell you:
"From the forests and the prairies,
From the great lakes of the Northland,
From the land of the Ojibways,
From the land of the Dacotahs,
From the mountains, moors, and fenlands,
Where the heron, the Shuh-shuh-gah,
Feeds among the reeds and rushes.
I repeat them as I heard them
From the lips of Nawadaha,
The musician, the sweet singer."
    Should you ask where Nawadaha
Found these songs, so wild and wayward,
Found these legends and traditions,
    I should answer, I should tell you:
"In the birds'-nests of the forests,
In the lodges of the beaver,
In the hoof-prints of the bison,
In the aerie of the eagle!"

. . . . .

If still further you should ask me,
Saying, "Who was Nawadaha?
Tell us of this Nawadaha,"
I should answer your inquiries
Straightway in such words as follow:
"In the Vale of Tawasentha,
In the green and silent valley,
By the pleasant water-courses,
Dwelt the singer Nawadaha.
Round about the Indian village
Spread the meadows and the cornfields,
And beyond them stood the forest,
Stood the groves of singing pine-trees,
Green in summer, white in winter,
Ever sighing, ever singing.

"There he sang of Hiawatha,
Sang the Song of Hiawatha,
Sang his wondrous birth and being,
How he prayed and how he fasted,
How he lived, and toiled, and suffered,
That the tribes of men might prosper,
That he might advance his people!"
Ye who love the haunts of Nature,
Love the sunshine of the meadow,
Love the shadow of the forest,
Love the wind among the branches,
And the rain-shower and the snowstorm,
And the rushing of great rivers
Through their palisades of pine-trees,
And the thunder in the mountains,

. . . . .

Listen to this Indian Legend,
To this Song of Hiawatha!
Ye whose hearts are fresh and simple,
Who have faith in God and Nature,

. . . . .

Listen to this simple story,
To this Song of Hiawatha!

. . . . .

NOTES AND QUESTIONS

You have now begun to read parts of a long poem about Indian life and tradition. The Indians, like all other races of men, have such songs. Longfellow studied the Indian legends and put them into English verse so that all of us may enjoy them. Such a poem, which is really a collection of ballads or songs about heroes and about the beliefs and superstitions of a race, is often called an epic. Notice that the poet tells you that these stories in verse have the odors of the forest, the curling smoke of wigwams, the rushing of great rivers, and the roar of mountain thunder. This means that such stories are very closely connected with the simple life of a simple people—there is much of their thought about nature, much of their love of the land where they live. Next, notice that he got his knowledge of these songs from a "sweet singer," a minstrel. All simple tribes have had such singers, who went about from place to place telling in verse what the people wanted to hear. There were no books, and boys and girls learned their stories from older people, or from wandering singers. Next, you observe that the theme of the stories is the life of Hiawatha, their great hero. So the Greeks had stories about their hero Ulysses, the early English about Beowulf and King Arthur, the French about Roland. Every great race honors the memory of a hero who lived when the race was young. Many stories cluster about the name of this hero, and poets and minstrels love to sing, and the people to hear, about these great characters. Finally, notice at the end of the poet's "Introduction," two things: First, Hiawatha lived and toiled and suffered that the tribes might prosper, that he might advance his people—thus an epic poem deals with the founding of a people or race. Second, you notice that there is much about God and nature in the poem—the simple religious faith of the people. The hero, his deeds that helped his people, the religion of the tribes—these are the subjects. Find illustrations of these things as you read.

Discussion. 1. Where did these stories come from? Read lines which tell. 2. Name the Great Lakes. 3. Who was Nawadaha? 4. What word tells the sound of the pine trees? 5. Read five lines that tell what the singer sang of Hiawatha. 6. Find in the glossary the meaning of: reverberations; fenlands. 7. *Pronounce:* legends; wigwams; aerie.

Phrases for Study

singing pine-trees, **327**, 13
wondrous birth and being, **327**, 18
tribes of men might prosper, **327**, 21
advance his people, **327**, 22
haunts of Nature, **327**, 23
palisades of pine-trees, **327**, 29

Hiawatha's Childhood

By the shores of Gitche Gumee,
By the shining Big-Sea-Water,
Stood the wigwam of Nokomis,
Daughter of the Moon, Nokomis.
Dark behind it rose the forest,
Rose the black and gloomy pine-trees,
Rose the firs with cones upon them;
Bright before it beat the water,
Beat the clear and sunny water,
Beat the shining Big-Sea-Water.
There the wrinkled, old Nokomis
Nursed the little Hiawatha;
Rocked him in his linden cradle,
Bedded soft in moss and rushes,
Safely bound with reindeer sinews;

Stilled his fretful wail by saying,
"Hush! the Naked Bear will get thee!"
Lulled him into slumber, singing,
"Ewa-yea! my little owlet!
Who is this that lights the wigwam,
With his great eyes lights the wigwam?
Ewa-yea! my little owlet!"
    Many things Nokomis taught him
Of the stars that shine in heaven;

. . . .

Showed the broad, white road in heaven,
Pathway of the ghosts, the shadows,
Running straight across the heavens,
Crowded with the ghosts, the shadows.
    At the door on summer evenings
Sat the little Hiawatha;
Heard the whispering of the pine-trees,
Heard the lapping of the water,
Sounds of music, words of wonder;
"Minne-wawa!" said the pine-trees,
"Mudway-aushka!" said the water.
    Saw the firefly, Wah-wah-taysee,
Flitting through the dusk of evening,
With the twinkle of its candle
Lighting up the brakes and bushes;
And he sang the song of children,
Sang the song Nokomis taught him:
"Wab-wah-taysee, little firefly,
Little, flitting, white-fire insect,
Little, dancing, white-fire creature,
Light me with your little candle,
Ere upon my bed I lay me,
Ere in sleep I close my eyelids!"

Saw the moon rise from the water
Rippling, rounding from the water;
Saw the flecks and shadows on it;
Whispered, "What is that, Nokomis?"
And the good Nokomis answered:
"Once a warrior, very angry,
Seized his grandmother, and threw her
Up into the sky at midnight;
Right against the moon he threw her;
'Tis her body that you see there."
Saw the rainbow in the heaven,
In the eastern sky, the rainbow;
Whispered, "What is that, Nokomis?"
And the good Nokomis answered:
"'Tis the heaven of flowers you see there.
All the wild-flowers of the forest,
All the lilies of the prairie,
When on earth they fade and perish,
Blossom in that heaven above us."
When he heard the owls at midnight,
Hooting, laughing in the forest,
"What is that?" he cried in terror;
"What is that," he said, "Nokomis?"
And the good Nokomis answered:
"That is but the owl and owlet,
Talking in their native language,
Talking, scolding at each other."
Then the little Hiawatha
Learned of every bird its language,
Learned their names and all their secrets
How they built their nests in summer,
Where they hid themselves in winter
Talked with them whene'er he met them,

Called them "Hiawatha's Chickens."
Of all beasts he learned the language,
Learned their names and all their secrets—
How the beavers built their lodges,
Where the squirrels hid their acorns,
How the reindeer ran so swiftly,
Why the rabbit was so timid;
Talked with them whene'er he met them,
Called them "Hiawatha's Brothers."
Then Iagoo, the great boaster,
He the marvelous story-teller,
He the traveler and the talker,
He the friend of old Nokomis,
Made a bow for Hiawatha;
From a branch of ash he made it,
From an oak-bough made the arrows,
Tipped with flint, and winged with feathers,
And the cord he made of deerskin.
Then he said to Hiawatha:
"Go, my son, into the forest,
Where the red deer herd together;
Kill for us a famous roebuck,
Kill for us a deer with antlers!"
Forth into the forest straightway
All alone walked Hiawatha
Proudly, with his bow and arrows;
And the birds sang round him, o'er him,
"Do not shoot us, Hiawatha!"
Sang the robin, the Opechee,
Sang the bluebird, the Owaissa,
"Do not shoot us, Hiawatha!"
Up the oak-tree, close beside him,
Sprang the squirrel, Adjidaumo,

In and out among the branches,
Coughed and chattered from the oak-tree,
Laughed, and said between his laughing,
"Do not shoot me, Hiawatha!"
And the rabbit from his pathway
Leaped aside, and at a distance
Sat erect upon his haunches,
Half in fear and half in frolic,
Saying to the little hunter,
"Do not shoot me, Hiawatha!"
But he heeded not, nor heard them,
For his thoughts were with the red deer;
On their tracks his eyes were fastened,
Leading downward to the river,
To the ford across the river;
And as one in slumber walked he.
Hidden in the alder-bushes,
There he waited till the deer came,
Till he saw two antlers lifted,
Saw two eyes look from the thicket,
Saw two nostrils point to windward,
And a deer came down the pathway,
Flecked with leafy light and shadow.
And his heart within him fluttered,
Trembled like the leaves above him,
Like the birch-leaf palpitated,
As the deer came down the pathway.
Then, upon one knee uprising,
Hiawatha aimed an arrow;
Scarce a twig moved with his motion,
Scarce a leaf was stirred or rustled,
But the wary roebuck started,
Stamped with all his hoofs together,

Listened with one foot uplifted,
Leaped as if to meet the arrow,
Ah! the singing, fatal arrow;
Like a wasp it buzzed and stung him!
Dead he lay there in the forest,
By the ford across the river;
Beat his timid heart no longer.
But the heart of Hiawatha
Throbbed and shouted and exulted,
As he bore the red deer homeward;
And Iagoo and Nokomis
Hailed his coming with applauses.
From the red deer's hide Nokomis
Made a cloak for Hiawatha;
From the red deer's flesh Nokomis
Made a banquet in his honor.
All the village came and feasted;
All the guests praised Hiawatha,
Called him Strong-Heart, Soan-ge-taha!
Called him Loon-Heart, Mahn-go-taysee!

NOTES AND QUESTIONS.

Discussion. 1. What body of water is called Gitche Gumee? 2. Where did the wigwam of Nokomis stand? 3. What is meant by the "beat" of the water? 4. Why does Longfellow call the pine trees "black and gloomy"? 5. Who was Nokomis? 6. Why did she call Hiawatha "my little owlet"? 7. What do we call the "broad, white road in heaven"? 8. What word tells the sound of the water? 9. Read lines that tell what Hiawatha learned of the birds and the beasts. 10. Of what was Hiawatha's bow made? His arrows? The cord? 11. Why was a tip of flint used on the arrows? 12. What is meant by "the ford across the river"? 13. Read lines which tell that Hiawatha was excited when hunting. 14. Find in the glossary the meaning of: linden; frolic; nostrils. 15. *Pronounce:* moss; sinews; warrior; haunches; alder; palpitated; exulted.

Phrases for Study

twinkle of its candle, **330**, 23
native language, **331**, 26
tipped with flint, **332**, 17
winged with feathers, **332**, 17
famous roebuck, **332**, 22
point to windward, **333**, 21
flecked with leafy light, **333**, 23
hailed his coming, **334**, 12

Hiawatha's Friends

Two good friends had Hiawatha,
Singled out from all the others,
Bound to him in closest union,
And to whom he gave the right hand
Of his heart, in joy and sorrow:
Chibiabos, the musician,
And the very strong man, Kwasind.

. . . . .

Most beloved by Hiawatha
Was the gentle Chibiabos,
He the best of all musicians,
He the sweetest of all singers.
Beautiful and childlike was he,
Brave as man is, soft as woman,
Pliant as a wand of willow,
Stately as a deer with antlers.
When he sang, the village listened;
All the warriors gathered round him,
All the women came to hear him;
Now he stirred their souls to passion,
Now he melted them to pity.
From the hollow reeds he fashioned
Flutes so musical and mellow
That the brook, the Sebowisha,

Ceased to murmur in the woodland,
That the wood-birds ceased from singing,
And the squirrel, Adjidaumo,
Ceased his chatter in the oak-tree,
And the rabbit, the Wabasso,
Sat upright to look and listen.
    Yes, the brook, the Sebowisha,
Pausing, said, "O Chibiabos,
Teach my waves to flow in music,
Softly as your words in singing!"
Yes, the bluebird, the Owaissa,
Envious, said, "O Chibiabos,
Teach me tones as wild and wayward,
Teach me songs as full of frenzy!"
    Yes, the robin, the Opechee,
Joyous, said, "O Chibiabos,
Teach me tunes as sweet and tender,
Teach me songs as full of gladness!"
    And the whippoorwill, Wawonaissa,
Sobbing, said, "O Chibiabos,
Teach me tones as melancholy,
Teach me songs as full of sadness!"
    All the many sounds of nature
Borrowed sweetness from his singing;
All the hearts of men were softened
By the pathos of his music;
For he sang of peace and freedom,
Sang of beauty, love, and longing;
Sang of death, and life undying
In the Islands of the Blessed,
In the kingdom of Ponemah,
In the land of the Hereafter.
    Very dear to Hiawatha
Was the gentle Chibiabos,

He the best of all musicians,
He the sweetest of all singers;
For his gentleness he loved him,
And the magic of his singing.
Dear, too, unto Hiawatha
Was the very strong man, Kwasind,
He the strongest of all mortals,
He the mightiest among many;
For his very strength he loved him,
For his strength allied to goodness.
Idle in his youth was Kwasind,
Very listless, dull, and dreamy,
Never played with other children,
Never fished and never hunted;
Not like other children was he.

. . . . .

"Lazy Kwasind!" said his mother,
"In my work you never help me!
In the summer you are roaming
Idly in the fields and forests;
In the winter you are cowering
O'er the firebrands in the wigwam!
In the coldest days of winter
I must break the ice for fishing;
With my nets you never help me!
At the door my nets are hanging,
Dripping, freezing with the water;
Go and wring them, Yenadizze!
Go and dry them in the sunshine!"
Slowly, from the ashes, Kwasind
Rose, but made no angry answer;
From the lodge went forth in silence,
Took the nets, that hung together,
Dripping, freezing at the doorway;

Like a wisp of straw he wrung them,
Like a wisp of straw he broke them,
Could not wring them without breaking,
Such the strength was in his fingers.
"Lazy Kwasind!" said his father,
"In the hunt you never help me;
Every bow you touch is broken,
Snapped asunder every arrow;
Yet come with me to the forest,
You shall bring the hunting homeward."
Down a narrow pass they wandered,
Where a brooklet led them onward,
Where the trail of deer and bison
Marked the soft mud on the margin,
Till they found all further passage
Shut against them, barred securely
By the trunks of trees uprooted,
Lying lengthwise, lying crosswise,
And forbidding further passage.
"We must go back," said the old man;
"O'er these logs we cannot clamber;
Not a woodchuck could get through them,
Not a squirrel clamber o'er them!"
And straightway his pipe he lighted,
And sat down to smoke and ponder.
But before his pipe was finished,
Lo! the path was cleared before him;
All the trunks had Kwasind lifted;
To the right hand, to the left hand,
Shot the pine-trees swift as arrows;
Hurled the cedars light as lances.
"Lazy Kwasind!" said the young men,
As they sported in the meadow;

"Why stand idly looking at us,
Leaning on the rock behind you?
Come and wrestle with the others;
Let us pitch the quoit together!"
Lazy Kwasind made no answer,
To their challenge made no answer,
Only rose, and, slowly turning,
Seized the huge rock in his fingers,
Tore it from its deep foundation,
Poised it in the air a moment,
Pitched it sheer into the river,
Sheer into the swift Pauwating,
Where it still is seen in summer.
Once as down that foaming river,
Down the rapids of Pauwating,
Kwasind sailed with his companions,
In the stream he saw a beaver,
Saw Ahmeek, the King of Beavers,
Struggling with the rushing currents,
Rising, sinking in the water.
Without speaking, without pausing,
Kwasind leaped into the river,
Plunged beneath the bubbling surface,
Through the whirlpools chased the beaver,
Followed him among the islands,
Stayed so long beneath the water
That his terrified companions
Cried, "Alas! good-by to Kwasind!
We shall never more see Kwasind!"
But he reappeared triumphant,
And upon his shining shoulders
Brought the beaver, dead and dripping,
Brought the King of all the Beavers.

And these two, as I have told you,
Were the friends of Hiawatha,
Chibiabos, the musician,
And the very strong man, Kwasind;
Long they lived in peace together,
Spake with naked hearts together,
Pondering much and much contriving
How the tribes of men might prosper.

NOTES AND QUESTIONS

Discussion. 1. What two friends had Hiawatha "Singled out from all the others"? 2. What were they "contriving"? 3. Read lines that tell of Chibiabos. 4. With what is he compared? Read lines that tell. 5. From what did he make his flutes? 6. Read lines that tell how musical they were. 7. What did the brook say to Chibiabos? The bluebird? The robin? 8. Of what did Chibiabos sing? 9. Why did Hiawatha love him more than all others? 10. For what did Hiawatha love Kwasind? 11. What did Kwasind's mother say to him? His father? 12. What is meant by the line, "Every bow you touch is broken"? 13. Read lines that tell of Kwasind and the beaver. 14. Which of Hiawatha's two friends do you like the better? Why? 15. Find in the glossary the meaning of: reeds, frenzy, listless, cowering, clamber, ponder, sported. 16. *Pronounce:* pliant, wand, pathos, allied, asunder, quoit, triumphant.

Phrases for Study

singled out, **335**, 2
bound to him, **335**, 3
pliant as a wand, **335**, 14
stirred their souls to passion, **335**, 19
melted them to pity, **335**, 20
fashioned flutes, **335**, 21
flow in music, **336**, 9
Islands of the Blessed, **336**, 30
magic of his singing, **337**, 4
strength allied to goodness, **337**, 10
bring the hunting homeward, **338**, 10
forbidding further passage, **338**, 19
poised it in the air, **339**, 10
sheer into the river, **339**, 11
shining shoulders, **339**, 31
spake with naked hearts, **340**, 6
pondering much, **340**, 7
much contriving, **340**, 7

HIAWATHA'S SAILING

"Give me of your bark, O Birch-Tree!
Of your yellow bark, O Birch-Tree!
Growing by the rushing river,
Tall and stately in the valley!
I a light canoe will build me,
Build a swift Cheemaun for sailing,
That shall float upon the river,
Like a yellow leaf in autumn,
Like a yellow water-lily!
"Lay aside your cloak, O Birch-Tree!
Lay aside your white-skin wrapper,
For the summer-time is coming,
And the sun is warm in heaven,
And you need no white-skin wrapper!"
Thus aloud cried Hiawatha.

. . . . .

And the tree with all its branches
Rustled in the breeze of morning,
Saying, with a sigh of patience,
"Take my cloak, O Hiawatha!"
With his knife the tree he girdled,
Just beneath its lowest branches;
Just above the roots he cut it,
Till the sap came oozing outward;
Down the trunk, from top to bottom,
Sheer he cleft the bark asunder;
With a wooden wedge he raised it,
Stripped it from the trunk unbroken.
"Give me of your boughs, O Cedar!
Of your strong and pliant branches,
My canoe to make more steady,

Make more strong and firm beneath me!"
Through the summit of the Cedar
Went a sound, a cry of horror,
Went a murmur of resistance;
But it whispered, bending downward,
"Take my boughs, O Hiawatha!"
Down he hewed the boughs of cedar,
Shaped them straightway to a framework;
Like two bows he formed and shaped them,
Like two bended bows together.
"Give me of your roots, O Tamarack!
Of your fibrous roots, O Larch-Tree!
My canoe to bind together,
So to bind the ends together
That the water may not enter,
That the river may not wet me!"
And the Larch, with all its fibers,
Shivered in the air of morning,
Touched his forehead with its tassels,
Said, with one long sigh of sorrow,
"Take them all, O Hiawatha!"
From the earth he tore the fibers,
Tore the tough roots of the Larch-Tree,
Closely sewed the bark together,
Bound it closely to the framework.
"Give me of your balm, O Fir-Tree!
Of your balsam and your resin,
So to close the seams together
That the water may not enter,
That the river may not wet me!
And the Fir-Tree, tall and somber,
Sobbed through all its robes of darkness,
Rattled like a shore with pebbles,

Answered wailing, answered weeping,
"Take my balm, O Hiawatha!"
And he took the tears of balsam,
Took the resin of the Fir-Tree,
Smeared therewith each seam and fissure,
Made each crevice safe from water.
"Give me of your quills, O Hedgehog!
All your quills, O Kagh, the Hedgehog!
I will make a necklace of them,
Make a girdle for my beauty,
And two stars to deck her bosom!"
From a hollow tree the Hedgehog
With his sleepy eyes looked at him,
Shot his shining quills, like arrows,
Saying, with a drowsy murmur,
Through the tangle of his whiskers,
"Take my quills, O Hiawatha!"
From the ground the quills he gathered,
All the little shining arrows;
Stained them red and blue and yellow,
With the juice of roots and berries;
Into his canoe he wrought them,
Round its waist a shining girdle,
Round its bows a gleaming necklace,
On its breast two stars resplendent.
Thus the Birch-Canoe was builded
In the valley, by the river,
In the bosom of the forest;
And the forest's life was in it—
All its mystery and its magic,
All the lightness of the birch-tree,
All the toughness of the cedar,
All the larch's supple sinews;

And it floated on the river
Like a yellow leaf in autumn,
Like a yellow water-lily.
Paddles none had Hiawatha;
    Paddles none he had or needed,
For his thoughts as paddles served him,
And his wishes served to guide him;
Swift or slow at will he glided,
Veered to right or left at pleasure.
    Then he called aloud to Kwasind,
To his friend, the strong man, Kwasind,
Saying, "Help me clear this river
Of its sunken logs and sandbars."
    Straight into the river Kwasind
Plunged as if he were an otter,
Dived as if he were a beaver,
Stood up to his waist in water,
To his armpits in the river,
Swam and shouted in the river,
Tugged at sunken logs and branches;
With his hands he scooped the sandbars,
With his feet the ooze and tangle.
    And thus sailed my Hiawatha
Down the rushing Taquamenaw,
Sailed through all its bends and windings,
Sailed through all its deeps and shallows,
While his friend, the strong man, Kwasind,
Swam the deeps, the shallows waded.
    Up and down the river went they,
In and out among its islands,
Cleared its bed of root and sandbar,
Dragged the dead trees from its channel,
Made its passage safe and certain,

Made a pathway for the people,
From its springs among the mountains,
To the waters of Pauwating,
To the bay of Taquamenaw.

. . . . .

NOTES AND QUESTIONS

Discussion. 1. Of what did Hiawatha make his canoe? 2. Why does Hiawatha call the bark of the birch tree a cloak? 3. What other name does he give the bark of the birch tree? 4. What word tells the sound made by the leaves of the birch tree? 5. What word tells that Hiawatha cut all around the birch tree? 6. Why did Hiawatha ask the cedar tree for its boughs? 7. Read lines that tell why he asked the larch tree for its roots. 8. What other name does he give the larch tree? 9. Why does Hiawatha call the drops of balsam "tears"? 10. Can the hedgehog really shoot his quills "like arrows"? 11. What is meant by "my beauty"? 12. Read lines that tell how Hiawatha decorated his canoe. 13. What did he use for paddles for the canoe? 14. What did Kwasind do to aid the canoeing? 15. Why is the fir tree spoken of as "somber"? 16. Find in the glossary the meaning of: stately, larch, channel. 17. *Pronounce:* horror, hewed, tamarack, fibrous, forehead, balm, balsam, resin, fissure, crevice, bosom, resplendent, supple, veered, swam

Phrases for Study

white-skin wrapper, **341**, 11
oozing outward, **341**, 23
cleft the bark asunder, **341**, 26
summit of the Cedar, **342**, 2
shaped them to a framework, **342**, 8
close the seams together, **342**, 28
robes of darkness, **342**, 32
deck her bosom, **343**, 11
shot his shining quills, **343**, 14
wrought them, **343**, 22
forest's life was in it, **343**, 29
ooze and tangle, **344**, 22

Hiawatha's Wooing

"As unto the bow the cord is,
So unto the man is woman:
Though she bends him, she obeys him,
Though she draws him, yet she follows—
Useless each without the other!"
Thus the youthful Hiawatha
Said within himself and pondered,
Much perplexed by various feelings—
Listless, longing, hoping, fearing,
Dreaming still of Minnehaha,
Of the lovely Laughing Water,
In the land of the Dacotahs.
"Wed a maiden of your people,"
Warning said the old Nokomis;
"Go not eastward, go not westward,
For a stranger, whom we know not!
Like a fire upon the hearthstone
Is a neighbor's homely daughter;
Like the starlight or the moonlight
Is the handsomest of strangers!"
Thus dissuading spake Nokomis,
And my Hiawatha, answered
Only this: "Dear old Nokomis,
Very pleasant is the firelight,
But I like the starlight better,
Better do I like the moonlight!"
Gravely then said old Nokomis:
"Bring not here an idle maiden,
Bring not here a useless woman,
Hands unskillful, feet unwilling;
Bring a wife with nimble fingers,

Heart and hand that move together,
Feet that run on willing errands!"
    Smiling answered Hiawatha:
"In the land of the Dacotahs
Lives the Arrow-maker's daughter,
Minnehaha, Laughing Water,
Handsomest of all the women.
I will bring her to your wigwam;
She shall run upon your errands,
Be your starlight, moonlight, firelight,
Be the sunlight of my people!"
    Still dissuading said Nokomis:
"Bring not to my lodge a stranger
From the land of the Dacotahs!
Very fierce are the Dacotahs.
Often is there war between us;
There are feuds yet unforgotten,
Wounds that ache and still may open!"
    Laughing answered Hiawatha:
"For that reason, if no other,
Would I wed the fair Dacotah,
That our tribes might be united,
That old feuds might be forgotten,
And old wounds be healed forever!"
    Thus departed Hiawatha
To the land of the Dacotahs,
To the land of handsome women,
Striding over moor and meadow,
Through interminable forests,
Through uninterrupted silence.
    With his moccasins of magic,
At each stride a mile he measured;
Yet the way seemed long before him,

And his heart outran his footsteps;
And he journeyed without resting,
Till he heard the cataract's laughter,
Heard the Falls of Minnehaha
Calling to him through the silence.
"Pleasant is the sound!" he murmured,
"Pleasant is the voice that calls me!"
　　On the outskirts of the forest,
'Twixt the shadow and the sunshine,
Herds of fallow deer were feeding,
But they saw not Hiawatha;
To his bow he whispered, "Fail not!"
To his arrow whispered, "Swerve not!"
Sent it singing on its errand,
To the red heart of the roebuck;
Threw the deer across his shoulder
And sped forward without pausing.
　　At the doorway of his wigwam
Sat the ancient Arrow-maker,
In the land of the Dacotahs,
Making arrow-heads of jasper,
Arrow-heads of chalcedony.
At his side, in all her beauty,
Sat the lovely Minnehaha,
Sat his daughter, Laughing Water,
Plaiting mats of flags and rushes;
Of the past the old man's thoughts were,
And the maiden's of the future.
　　He was thinking, as he sat there,
Of the days when with such arrows
He had struck the deer and bison,
On the Muskoday, the meadow;
Shot the wild goose, flying southward,

On the wing, the clamorous Wawa;
Thinking of the great war-parties,
How they came to buy his arrows,
Could not fight without his arrows.

. . . . . .

She was thinking of a hunter,
From another tribe and country,
Young and tall and very handsome,
Who one morning, in the springtime,
Came to buy her father's arrows,
Sat and rested in the wigwam,
Lingered long about the doorway,
Looking back as he departed.
She had heard her father praise him,
Praise his courage and his wisdom;
Would he come again for arrows
To the Falls of Minnehaha?
On the mat her hands lay idle,
And her eyes were very dreamy.

Through their thoughts they heard a footstep,
Heard a rustling in the branches,
And with glowing cheek and forehead,
With the deer upon his shoulders,
Suddenly from out the woodlands
Hiawatha stood before them.

Straight the ancient Arrow-maker
Looked up gravely from his labor,
Laid aside the unfinished arrow,
Bade him enter at the doorway,
Saying, as he rose to meet him,
"Hiawatha, you are welcome!"

At the feet of Laughing Water
Hiawatha laid his burden,

Threw the red deer from his shoulders;
And the maiden looked up at him,
Looked up from her mat of rushes,
Said with gentle look and accent,
"You are welcome, Hiawatha!"
Very spacious was the wigwam,
Made of deerskin dressed and whitened,
With the gods of the Dacotahs
Drawn and painted on its curtains;
And so tall the doorway, hardly
Hiawatha stooped to enter,
Hardly touched his eagle-feathers
As he entered at the doorway.
Then uprose the Laughing Water;
From the ground fair Minnehaha
Laid aside her mat unfinished,
Brought forth food and set before them,
Water brought them from the brooklet,
Gave them food in earthen vessels,
Gave them drink in bowls of basswood,
Listened while the guest was speaking,
Listened while her father answered,
But not once her lips she opened,
Not a single word she uttered.
Yes, as in a dream she listened
To the words of Hiawatha,
As he talked of old Nokomis,
Who had nursed him in his childhood,
As he told of his companions,
Chibiabos, the musician,
And the very strong man, Kwasind,
And of happiness and plenty
In the land of the Ojibways,

In the pleasant land and peaceful.
"After many years of warfare,
Many years of strife and bloodshed,
There is peace between the Ojibways
And the tribe of the Dacotahs."
Thus continued Hiawatha,
And then added, speaking slowly,
"That this peace may last forever,
And our hands be clasped more closely,
And our hearts be more united,
Give me as my wife this maiden,
Minnehaha, Laughing Water,
Loveliest of Dacotah women!"
And the ancient Arrow-maker
Paused a moment ere he answered,
Smoked a little while in silence,
Looked at Hiawatha proudly,
Fondly looked at Laughing Water,
And made answer very gravely:
"Yes, if Minnehaha wishes;
Let your heart speak, Minnehaha!"
And the lovely Laughing Water
Seemed more lovely, as she stood there,
Neither willing nor reluctant,
As she went to Hiawatha,
Softly took the seat beside him,
While she said, and blushed to say it,
"I will follow you, my husband!"
This was Hiawatha's wooing!
Thus it was he won the daughter
Of the ancient Arrow-maker,
In the land of the Dacotahs!
From the wigwam he departed,

Leading with him Laughing Water;
Hand in hand they went together,
Through the woodland and the meadow,
Left the old man standing lonely
At the doorway of his wigwam,
Heard the Falls of Minnehaha
Calling to them from the distance,
Crying to them from afar off,
"Fare thee well, O Minnehaha!"

And the ancient Arrow-maker
Turned again unto his labor,
Sat down by his sunny doorway,
Murmuring to himself, and saying:
"Thus it is our daughters leave us,
Those we love, and those who love us!
Just when they have learned to help us,
When we are old and lean upon them,
Comes a youth with flaunting feathers,
With his flute of reeds, a stranger,
Wanders piping through the village,
Beckons to the fairest maiden.
And she follows where he leads her,
Leaving all things for the stranger!"

Pleasant was the journey homeward,
Through interminable forests,
Over meadow, over mountain,
Over river, hill, and hollow.
Short it seemed to Hiawatha,
Though they journeyed very slowly,
Though his pace he checked and slackened
To the steps of Laughing Water.

Over wide and rushing rivers
In his arms he bore the maiden;

Light he thought her as a feather,
As the plume upon his head-gear;
Cleared the tangled pathway for her,
Bent aside the swaying branches,
Made at night a lodge of branches,
And a bed with boughs of hemlock,
And a fire before the doorway
With the dry cones of the pine-tree.
    All the traveling winds went with them,
O'er the meadow, through the forest;
All the stars of night looked at them,
Watched with sleepless eyes their slumber;
From his ambush in the oak-tree
Peeped the squirrel, Adjidaumo,
Watched with eager eyes the lovers;
And the rabbit, the Wabasso,
Scampered from the path before them,
Peering, peeping from his burrow,
Sat erect upon his haunches,
Watched with curious eyes the lovers.
    Pleasant was the journey homeward!
All the birds sang loud and sweetly
Songs of happiness and heart's-ease;
Sang the bluebird, the Owaissa,
"Happy are you, Hiawatha,
Having such a wife to love you!
Sang the robin, the Opechee,
"Happy are you, Laughing Water,
Having such a noble husband!"
    From the sky the sun benignant
Looked upon them through the branches,
Saying to them, "O my children,
Love is sunshine, hate is shadow;

Life is checkered shade and sunshine;
Rule by love, O Hiawatha!"
    From the sky the moon looked at them,
Filled the lodge with mystic splendors,
Whispered to them, "O my children,
Day is restless, night is quiet,
Man imperious, woman feeble;
Half is mine, although I follow;
Rule by patience, Laughing Water!"
    Thus it was they journeyed homeward;
Thus it was that Hiawatha
To the lodge of old Nokomis
Brought the moonlight, starlight, firelight,
Brought the sunshine of his people,
Minnehaha, Laughing Water,
Handsomest of all the women
In the land of the Dacotahs,
In the land of handsome women.

. . . . .

NOTES AND QUESTIONS

Discussion. 1. Why did Nokomis wish Hiawatha to wed a maiden of his own people? 2. Whom did Hiawatha say he would wed? 3. Find the Falls of Minnehaha on a map. 4. Read lines that tell of Hiawatha's journey "To the land of the Dacotahs." 5. Of what was the Arrow-maker thinking when Hiawatha appeared? 6. Read lines that tell of what the maiden was thinking. 7. Read the words of Hiawatha when he asked the father for his daughter. 8. In what words did the Arrow-maker give his consent? 9. What was Minnehaha's answer? 10. Read lines that tell of the journey homeward. 11. Why did Hiawatha "check" his pace on this journey? 12. What greeting did the bluebird give them? 13. What was the greeting of the robin? The sun? The moon? 14. Read the lines that you like best. 15. Find in the glossary the meaning of: cord, nimble, moor, fallow, swerve, jasper, flags, rushes, basswood, flaunting. 16. *Pronounce:* dissuading, feuds, wounds, chalcedony, plaiting, bade, spacious, benignant, mystic, imperious.

Phrases for Study

feet unwilling, **346**, 30
yet unforgotten, **347**, 17
interminable forests, **347**, 29
moccasins of magic, **347**, 31
heart outran his footsteps, **348**, 1
cataract's laughter, **348**, 3
deerskin dressed and whitened, **350**, 7
neither willing nor reluctant, **351**, 24
wanders piping through the village, **352**, 20
heart's-ease, **353**, 23
sun benignant, **353**, 30
hate is shadow, **353**, 33
mystic splendors, **354**, 4

The White-Man's Foot

From his wanderings, far to eastward,
From the regions of the morning,
From the shining land of Wabun,
Homeward now returned Iagoo,
The great traveler, the great boaster,
Full of new and strange adventures,
Marvels many and many wonders.
And the people of the village
Listened to him as he told them
Of his marvelous adventures;
Laughing answered him in this wise:
"Ugh! it is indeed Iagoo!
No one else beholds such wonders!"
He had seen, he said, a water
Bigger than the Big-Sea-Water,
Broader than the Gitche Gumee,
Bitter so that none could drink it!
At each other looked the warriors,

Looked the women at each other,
Smiled, and said, "It cannot be so!
Kaw!" they said, "it cannot be so!"
    O'er it, said he, o'er this water
Came a great canoe with pinions,
A canoe with wings came flying,
Bigger than a grove of pine-trees,
Taller than the tallest tree-tops!
And the old men and the women
Looked and tittered at each other;
"Kaw!" they said, "we don't believe it!"
    From its mouth, he said, to greet him,
Came Waywassimo, the lightning,
Came the thunder, Annemeekee!
And the warriors and the women
Laughed aloud at poor Iagoo;
"Kaw!" they said, "what tales you tell us!"
    In it, said he, came a people,
In the great canoe with pinions
Came, he said, a hundred warriors;
Painted white were all their faces,
And with hair their chins were covered!
And the warriors and the women
Laughed and shouted in derision,
Like the ravens on the tree-tops,
Like the crows upon the hemlocks.
"Kaw!" they said, "what lies you tell us.
Do not think that we believe them!"
    Only Hiawatha laughed not,
But he gravely spake and answered
To their jeering and their jesting:
"True is all Iagoo tells us;
I have seen it in a vision,

Seen the great canoe with pinions,
Seen the people with white faces,
Seen the coming of this bearded
People of the wooden vessel
From the regions of the morning,
From the shining land of Wabun.
  "Gitche Manito, the Mighty,
The Great Spirit, the Creator,
Sends them hither on his errand,
Sends them to us with his message.
Wheresoe'er they tread, beneath them
Swarms the stinging fly, the Ahmo,
Swarms the bee, the honey-maker;
Wheresoe'er they tread, beneath them
Springs a flower unknown among us,
Springs the White-man's foot in blossom.
  "Let us welcome, then, the strangers,
Hail them as our friends and brothers,
And the heart's right hand of friendship
Give them when they come to see us.
Gitche Manito, the Mighty,
Said this to me in my vision.
  "I beheld, too, in that vision,
All the secrets of the future,
Of the distant days that shall be.
I beheld the westward marches
Of the unknown, crowded nations.
All the land was full of people,
Restless, struggling, toiling, striving,
Speaking many tongues, yet feeling
But one heart-beat in their bosoms.
In the woodlands rang their axes,
Smoked their towns in all the valleys,

Over all the lakes and rivers
Rushed their great canoes of thunder.
"Then a darker, drearier vision
Passed before me, vague and cloud-like.
I beheld our nations scattered,
All forgetful of my counsels,
Weakened, warring with each other;
Saw the remnants of our people
Sweeping westward, wild and woeful,
Like the cloud-rack of a tempest,
Like the withered leaves of autumn!"

NOTES AND QUESTIONS

Discussion. 1. Read lines that tell Iagoo's story of adventures. 2. Where do you think he had seen these things? 3. What was the "bitter" water Iagoo told about? 4. What were the "lightning" and the "thunder" that came from the "canoe with pinions"? 5. Why was his story laughed at as false by the Indians? 6. How did Hiawatha know it was all true? 7. How did Hiawatha say they should receive the white man when he came? 8. What secrets came to Hiawatha in the vision? 9. What "darker vision" did he see? 10. Has Hiawatha's vision come true? 11. What do you think of Hiawatha's character? 12. Which of all the stories in this poem do you like best? 13. Give the reason for your answer. 14. You no doubt enjoyed reading this poem. Can you tell why? 15. Read "A Forward Look," pp. 289-291, and tell why you think Longfellow was a *real* author. 16. You will enjoy reading Eastman's *Indian Legends Retold.* 17. Find in the glossary the meaning of: tittered, hither, counsels. 18. *Pronounce:* pinions, derision, vision, regions, vague, warring.

Phrases for Study

regions of the morning, **355**, 2
shining land of Wabun, **355**, 3
canoe with pinions, **356**, 5
painted white, **356**, 21
heart's right hand of friendship **357**, 19
distant days that shall be, **357**, 25
unknown, crowded nations, **357**, 27
feeling but one heart-beat, **357**, 30
sweeping westward, **358**, 9
cloud-rack of a tempest, **358**, 10

Nathaniel Hawthorne

Nathaniel Hawthorne (1804-1864), a native of Salem, Massachusetts, had the distinction of being born on the Fourth of July. He was graduated from Bowdoin College in the class with Henry Wadsworth Longfellow.

When a mere boy, Nathaniel was crippled by an accident in playing ball. This led him to a life of quiet and to the companionship of books. His vivid imagination made him fond of inventing stories for the entertainment of his friends. When he began to think of a career it was quite natural that he should turn to literature, and that in looking about him for material he should choose his subjects—as Irving did—from those stirring scenes of which he had an intimate, almost personal, knowledge—many of them of his native town, Salem.

Hawthorne pictured New England as Irving did New Amsterdam. He popularized New England history in the form of stories for children, one of which, *Grandfather's Chair,* contains "The Boston Tea Party." He wrote a book, *The House of the Seven Gables,* about the house in which he lived for many years. Soon after he wrote this tale, he wrote *The Wonder-Book,* a volume of stories about Greek gods and heroes, from which "The Paradise of Children" and "The Golden Touch" are taken. Perhaps the best known of all Hawthorne's works is the volume called *Twice-Told Tales.* In this book he collected a large number of legends about colonial life in New England and retold them in such a way as to give us one of the best pictures of early American life that we have. Some of them deal with actual events; others are based on legendary matter. But all of them do for early New England life what Longfellow's *Hiawatha* does for the Indian legends: they preserve the stories and also the spirit of early times. Like Longfellow, Hawthorne was a lover of romance and of the early history of our country. He wrote in prose, not verse, but his prose is as careful and artistic as Longfellow's verse.

The Paradise of Children*

Pandora and the Great Box

Long, long ago, when this old world was in its tender infancy, there was a child named Epimetheus who never had either father or mother; and that he might not be lonely, another child, fatherless and motherless like himself, was sent from a far country to live with him and be his playfellow and helpmate. Her name was Pandora.

The first thing that Pandora saw when she entered the cottage where Epimetheus dwelt was a great box. And almost the first question which she put to him, after crossing the threshold, was this:

"Epimetheus, what have you in that box?"

* See "Suggestions for Silent Reading," page 163.

"My dear little Pandora," answered Epimetheus, "that is a secret, and you must be kind enough not to ask any questions about it. The box was left here to be kept safely, and I do not myself know what it contains."

"But who gave it to you?" asked Pandora. "And where did it come from?"

"That is a secret, too," replied Epimetheus.

"How provoking!" exclaimed Pandora, pouting her lip. "I wish the great ugly box were out of the way!"

"O come, don't think of it any more," cried Epimetheus. "Let us run out of doors and have some nice play with the other children."

It is thousands of years since Epimetheus and Pandora were alive, and the world nowadays is a very different sort of thing from what it was in their time. Then, everybody was a child. They needed no fathers and mothers to take care of the children because there was no danger or trouble of any kind, and there were no clothes to be mended, and there was always plenty to eat and drink.

Whenever a child wanted his dinner, he found it growing on a tree; and if he looked at the tree in the morning, he could see the blossom of that night's supper; or at eventide he saw the tender bud of tomorrow's breakfast. It was a very pleasant life indeed. No labor to be done, no tasks to be studied; nothing but sports and dances and sweet voices of children talking, or caroling like birds, or gushing out in merry laughter, throughout the livelong day.

What was most wonderful of all, the children never quarreled among themselves; neither had they any crying fits; nor since time first began had a single one of these little mortals ever gone apart into a corner and sulked. O what a good time was that to be alive in! The truth is, those ugly little winged monsters called Troubles, which are now almost as numerous as mosquitoes, had never yet been seen on the earth. It is probable that the very greatest disquietude which a child had ever felt was Pandora's vexation at not being able to discover the secret of the mysterious box.

This was at first only the faint shadow of a Trouble, but every day it grew more and more real, until before a great while the cottage of Epimetheus and Pandora was less sunshiny than those of the other children.

"Whence can the box have come?" Pandora continually kept saying to herself and to Epimetheus. "And what on earth can be inside of it?"

"Always talking about this box!" said Epimetheus at last, for he had grown extremely tired of the subject. "I wish, dear Pandora, you would try to talk of something else. Come, let us go and gather some ripe figs and eat them under the trees for our supper. And I know a vine that has the sweetest and juiciest grapes you ever tasted."

"Always talking about grapes and figs!" cried Pandora, pettishly.

"Well, then," said Epimetheus, who was a very good-tempered child, like many children in those days, "let us run out and have a merry time with our playmates."

"I am tired of merry times, and don't care if I never have any more!" answered our pettish little Pandora. "And, besides, I never do have any. This ugly box! I am so taken up with thinking about it all the time. I insist upon your telling me what is inside of it."

"As I have already said fifty times over, I do not know!" replied Epimetheus, getting a little vexed. "How, then, can I tell you what is inside?"

"You might open it," said Pandora, looking sideways at Epimetheus, "and then we could see for ourselves."

"Pandora, what are you thinking of?" exclaimed Epimetheus.

And his face expressed so much horror at the idea of looking into a box which had been given to him on the condition of his never opening it, that Pandora thought it best not to suggest it anymore. Still, however, she could not help thinking and talking about the box.

"At least," said she, "you can tell me how it came here."

"It was left at the door," replied Epimetheus, "just before you came, by a person who looked very smiling and intelligent, and who could hardly forbear laughing as he put it down. He was dressed in an odd kind of cloak and had on a cap that seemed to be made partly of feathers, so that it looked almost as if it had wings."

"What sort of staff had he?" asked Pandora.

"Oh, the most curious staff you ever saw!" cried Epimetheus. "It was like two serpents twisting around a stick and was carved so naturally that I at first thought the serpents were alive."

"I know him," said Pandora thoughtfully. "Nobody else has such a staff. It was Quicksilver and he brought me hither, as well as the box. No doubt he intended it for me; and most probably it contains pretty dresses for me to wear, or toys for you and me to play with, or something very nice for us both to eat!"

"Perhaps so," answered Epimetheus, turning away. "But, until Quicksilver comes back and tells us so, we have neither of us any right to lift the lid of the box."

"What a dull boy he is!" muttered Pandora, as Epimetheus left the cottage. "I do wish he had a little more enterprise!"

THE KNOT OF GOLDEN CORD

For the first time since her arrival Epimetheus had gone out without asking Pandora to accompany him. He went to gather figs and grapes for himself, or to seek whatever amusement he could find in other society than his little playfellow's. He was tired to death of hearing about the box and heartily wished that Quicksilver, or whatever was the messenger's name, had left it at some other child's door where Pandora would never have set eyes on it.

So perseveringly as she did babble about this one thing! The box, the box, and nothing but the box! It seemed as if the box were bewitched, and as if the cottage were not big enough to hold it without Pandora's continually stumbling over it and making Epimetheus stumble over it likewise and bruising all four of their shins.

Well, it was really hard that poor Epimetheus should have a box in his ears from morning till night, especially as the little people of the earth were so unaccustomed to vexations in those happy days that they knew not how to deal with them. Thus a small vexation made as much disturbance then as a far bigger one would in our own times.

After Epimetheus was gone, Pandora stood gazing at the box. She had called it ugly above a hundred times, but in spite of all that she had said against it, it was positively a very handsome article of furniture, and would have been quite an ornament to any room in which it should be placed. It was made of a beautiful kind of wood with dark and rich veins spreading over its surface, which was so highly polished that little Pandora could see her face in it. As the child had no other looking glass, it is odd that she did not value the box merely on this account.

The edges and corners of the box were carved with most wonderful skill. Around the margin there were figures of graceful men and women, and the prettiest children ever seen, reclining or sporting amid a profusion of flowers and foliage; and these various objects were so finely represented, and were wrought together in such harmony, that flowers, foliage, and human beings seemed to combine into a wreath of mingled beauty.

But here and there, peeping forth from behind the carved foliage, Pandora once or twice fancied that she saw a face not so lovely, or something or other that was disagreeable, and which stole the beauty out of all the rest. Nevertheless, on looking more closely and touching the spot with her finger, she could discover nothing of the kind. Some face that was really beautiful had been made to look ugly by her catching a sideways glimpse at it.

The most beautiful face of all was done in what is called high relief, in the center of the lid. There was nothing else save the dark, smooth richness of the polished wood and this one face in the center, with a garland of flowers about its brow. Pandora had looked at this face a great many times and imagined that the mouth could smile if it liked, or be grave when it chose, the same as any living mouth. The features, indeed, all wore a very lively and rather mischievous expression, which looked almost as if it needs must burst out of the carved lips and utter itself in words.

Had the mouth spoken, it would probably have been something like this:

"Do not be afraid, Pandora! What harm can there be in opening the box? Never mind that poor, simple Epimetheus! You are wiser than he, and have ten times as much spirit. Open the box, and see if you do not find something very pretty!"

The box, I had almost forgotten to say, was fastened, not by a lock, or by any other such contrivance, but by a very fine knot of gold cord. There appeared to be no end to this knot, and no beginning. Never was a knot so cunningly twisted, nor with so many ins and outs, which roguishly defied the skillfulest fingers to disentangle them. And yet, by the very difficulty that there was in it, Pandora was the more tempted to examine the knot and just see how it was made. Two or three times already she had stooped over the box and taken the knot between her thumb and forefinger, but without positively trying to undo it.

"I really believe," said she to herself, "that I begin to see how it was done. Nay, perhaps I could tie it up again after undoing it. There could be no harm in that, surely. Even Epimetheus would not blame me for that. I need not open the box, and should not, of course, without the foolish boy's consent, even if the knot were untied."

It might have been better for Pandora if she had had a little work to do, or anything to employ her mind upon, so as not to be so constantly thinking of this one subject. But children led so easy a life before any Troubles came into the world that they had really a great deal too much leisure. They could not be forever playing at hide-and-seek among the flower shrubs, or at blindman's buff with garlands over their eyes, or at whatever other games had been found out while Mother Earth was in her babyhood.

When life is all sport, toil is the real play. There was absolutely nothing to do. A little sweeping and dusting about the cottage, I suppose, and the gathering of fresh flowers (which were only too abundant everywhere), and arranging them in vases—and poor little Pandora's day's work was over. And then, for the rest of the day, there was the box!

After all, I am not quite sure that the box was not a blessing to her in its way. It supplied her with so many ideas to think of, and to talk about, whenever she had anybody to listen! When she was in good humor, she could admire the bright polish of its sides and the rich border of beautiful faces and foliage that ran all around it. Or, if she chanced to be ill-tempered, she could give it a push, or kick it with her naughty little foot. And many a kick did the box (but it was a mischievous box, as we shall see, and deserved all it got)—many a kick did it receive. But certain it is, if it had not been for the box, our active minded little Pandora would not have known half so well how to spend her time as she now did.

GUESSING WHAT WAS IN THE BOX

For it was really an endless employment to guess what was inside. What could it be, indeed? Just imagine, my little hearers, how busy your wits would be if there were a great box in the house, which, as you might have reason to suppose, contained something new and pretty for your Christmas or New Year's gifts. Do you think that you should be less curious than Pandora? If you were left alone with the box, might you not feel a little tempted to lift the lid? But you would not do it. Oh, fie! No, no! Only, if you thought there were toys in it, it would be so very hard to let slip an opportunity of taking just one peep!

I know not whether Pandora expected any toys, for none had yet begun to be made, probably, in those days, when the world itself was one great plaything for the children that dwelt upon it. But Pandora was convinced that there was something very beautiful and valuable in the box and therefore she felt just as anxious to take a peep as any of these little girls here around me would have felt. And, possibly, a little more so, but of that I am not quite so certain.

On this particular day, however, which we have so long been talking about, her curiosity grew so much greater than it usually was that at last she approached the box. She was more than half determined to open it if she could. Ah, naughty Pandora!

First, however, she tried to lift it. It was heavy; much too heavy for the slender strength of a child like Pandora. She raised one end of the box a few inches from the floor and let it fall again with a pretty loud thump. A moment afterwards she almost fancied that she heard something stir inside the box.

She applied her ear as closely as possible and listened. Positively, there did seem to be a kind of stifled murmur within. Or was it merely the singing in Pandora's ears? Or could it be the beating of her heart? The child could not quite satisfy herself whether she had heard anything or no. But, at all events, her curiosity was stronger than ever.

As she drew back her head, her eyes fell upon the knot of gold cord.

"It must have been a very ingenious person who tied this knot," said Pandora to herself. "But I think I could untie it, nevertheless. I am resolved, at least, to find the two ends of the cord."

So she took the golden knot in her fingers and pried into it as sharply as she could. Almost without intending it, or quite knowing what she was about, she was soon busily engaged in attempting to undo it. Meanwhile, the bright sunshine came through the open window, as did likewise the merry voices of the children playing at a distance, and perhaps the voice of Epimetheus among them.

Pandora stopped to listen. What a beautiful day it was! Would it not be wiser if she were to let the troublesome knot alone and think no more about the box, but run and join her little playfellows and be happy?

All this time, however, her fingers were busy with the knot; and happening to glance at the face on the lid of the enchanted box, she seemed to see it slyly grinning at her.

"That face looks very mischievous," thought Pandora. "I wonder whether it smiles because I am doing wrong! I have the greatest mind in the world to run away!"

But just then, by the merest accident, she gave the knot a kind of twist, which produced a wonderful result. The gold cord untwined itself, as if by magic, and left the box without a fastening.

"This is the strangest thing I ever knew!" said Pandora. "What will Epimetheus say? And how can I possibly tie it up again?"

She made one or two attempts to restore the knot, but soon found it quite beyond her skill. It had untied itself so suddenly that she could not in the least remember how the strings had been doubled into one another; and when she tried to recollect the shape and appearance of the knot, it seemed to have gone entirely out of her mind. Nothing was to be done, therefore, but to let the box remain as it was until Epimetheus should come in.

"But," said Pandora, "when he finds the knot untied, he will know that I have done it. How shall I make him believe that I have not looked into the box?"

And then the thought came into her naughty little heart that, since she would be suspected of having looked into the box, she might just as well do so at once. O very naughty and very foolish Pandora! You should have thought only of doing what was right, and of leaving undone what was wrong, and not of what your playfellow Epimetheus would have said or believed.

And so perhaps she might, if the enchanted face on the lid of the box had not looked so bewitchingly persuasive at her, and if she had not seemed to hear, more distinctly than before, the murmur of small voices within. She could not tell whether it was fancy or no; but there was quite a little tumult of whispers in her ear—or else it was her curiosity that whispered: "Let us out, dear Pandora—pray let us out! We will be such nice, pretty playfellows for you! Only let us out!"

"What can it be?" thought Pandora. "Is there something alive in the box? Well!—yes!—I am resolved to take just one peep! Only one peep; and then the lid shall be shut down as safely as ever! There cannot possibly be any harm in just one little peep!"

How Troubles Came into the World

But it is now time for us to see what Epimetheus was doing.

This was the first time since his little playmate had come to dwell with him that he had attempted to enjoy any pleasure in which she did not partake. But nothing went right; nor was he nearly so happy as on other days. He could not find a sweet grape or a ripe fig (if Epimetheus had a fault, it was a little too much fondness for figs); or, if ripe at all, they were overripe, and so sweet as to be distasteful. There was no mirth in his heart, such as usually made his voice gush out, of its own accord, and swell the merriment of his companions. In short, he grew so uneasy and discontented that the other children could not imagine what was the matter with Epimetheus. Neither did he himself know what ailed him, any better than they did.

For you must recollect that, at the time we are speaking of, it was everybody's nature and constant habit to be happy. The world had not yet learned to be otherwise. Not a single soul or body, since these children were first sent to enjoy themselves on the beautiful earth, had ever been sick or out-of-sorts.

At length, discovering that, somehow or other, he put a stop to all the play, Epimetheus judged it best to go back to Pandora, who was in a humor better suited to his own. But, with a hope of giving her pleasure, he gathered some flowers and made them into a wreath, which he meant to put upon her head. The flowers were very lovely—roses and lilies and orange blossoms, and a great many more, which left a trail of fragrance behind, as Epimetheus carried them along; and the wreath was put together with as much skill as could be expected of a boy. The fingers of little girls, it has always appeared to me, are the fittest to twine flower wreaths, but boys could do it in those days rather better than they can now.

And here I must mention that a great black cloud had been gathering in the sky for some time past, although it had not yet overspread the sun. But, just as Epimetheus reached the cottage door, this cloud began to cut off the sunshine, and thus to make a sudden and sad darkness.

He entered softly, for he meant, if possible, to steal behind Pandora and fling the wreath of flowers over her head before she should be aware of his approach. But, as it happened, there was no need of his treading so very lightly. He might have trod as heavily as he pleased, as heavily as a grown man—as heavily, I was going to say, as an elephant—without much probability of Pandora's hearing his footsteps. She was too intent upon her purpose. At the moment of his entering the cottage the naughty child had put her hand to the lid and was on the point of opening the mysterious box. Epimetheus beheld her. If he had cried out, Pandora would probably have withdrawn her hand, and the fatal mystery of the box might never have been known.

But Epimetheus himself, although he said very little about it, had his own share of curiosity to know what was inside. Seeing that Pandora was resolved to find out the secret, he determined that his playfellow should not be the only wise person in the cottage. And if there were anything pretty or valuable in the box, he meant to take half of it to himself. Thus, after all his sage speeches to Pandora about restraining her curiosity, Epimetheus turned out to be quite as foolish, and nearly as much in fault, as she. So, whenever we blame Pandora for what happened, we must not forget to shake our heads at Epimetheus likewise.

As Pandora raised the lid, the cottage grew very dark and dismal, for the black cloud had now swept quite over the sun and seemed to have buried it alive. There had, for a little while past, been a low growling and muttering, which all at once broke into a heavy peal of thunder. But Pandora, heeding nothing of all this, lifted the lid nearly upright, and looked inside. It seemed as if a sudden swarm of winged creatures brushed past her, taking flight out of the box, while at the same instant she heard the voice of Epimetheus, with a lamentable tone, as if he were in pain.

"Oh, I am stung!" cried he. "I am stung! Naughty Pandora! Why have you opened this wicked box?"

Pandora let fall the lid and, starting up, looked about her to see what had befallen Epimetheus. The thundercloud had so darkened the room that she could not very clearly see what was in it. But she heard a disagreeable buzzing, as if a great many huge flies, or gigantic mosquitoes, or those insects which we call dor bugs and pinching-dogs, were darting about. And, as her eyes grew more accustomed to the imperfect light, she saw a crowd of ugly little shapes, with bats' wings, looking very spiteful, and armed with terribly long stings in their tails. It was one of these that had stung Epimetheus. Nor was it a great while before Pandora herself began to scream, in no less pain and affright than her playfellow, and making a vast deal more hubbub about it. An ugly little monster had settled on her forehead and would have stung her, I know not how deeply, if Epimetheus had not run and brushed it away.

Now, if you wish to know what these ugly things might be which had made their escape out of the box, I must tell you that they were the whole family of earthly Troubles. There were evil Passions; there were a great many kinds of Cares; there were more than a hundred and fifty Sorrows; there were Diseases, in a vast number of miserable and painful shapes; there were more kinds of Naughtiness than it would be of any use to talk about.

In short, everything that has since afflicted the souls and bodies of mankind had been shut up in the mysterious box and given to Epimetheus and Pandora to be kept safely, in order that the happy children of the world might never be molested by them. Had they been faithful to their trust all would have gone well. No grown person would ever have been sad, nor any child have had cause to shed a single tear, from that hour until this moment.

But—and you may see by this how a wrong act of any one mortal is a calamity to the whole world—by Pandora's lifting the lid of that miserable box, and by the fault of Epimetheus, too, in not preventing her, these Troubles have obtained a foothold among us and do not seem very likely to be driven away in a hurry.

For it was impossible, as you will easily guess, that the two children should keep the ugly swarm in their own little cottage. On the contrary, the first thing that they did was to fling open the doors and windows in hope of getting rid of them; and, sure enough, away flew the winged Troubles all abroad, and so pestered and tormented the small people, everywhere about, that none of them so much as smiled for many days afterwards.

And, what was very singular, all the flowers and dewy blossoms on earth, not one of which had hitherto faded, now began to droop and shed their leaves after a day or two. The children, moreover, who before seemed immortal in their childhood, now grew older, day by day, and came soon to be youths and maidens, and men and women by-and-by, and aged people, before they dreamed of such a thing.

WHAT HOPE DOES FOR US

Meanwhile, the naughty Pandora and hardly less naughty Epimetheus remained in their cottage. Both of them had been grievously stung and were in a good deal of pain, which seemed the more intolerable to them, because it was the very first pain that had ever been felt since the world began. Of course they were entirely unaccustomed to it and could have no idea what it meant. Besides all this, they were in exceedingly bad humor, both with themselves and with one another. In order to indulge it to the utmost, Epimetheus sat down sullenly in a corner with his back toward Pandora, while Pandora flung herself upon the floor and rested her head on the fatal box. She was crying bitterly and sobbing as if her heart would break.

Suddenly there was a gentle little tap on the inside of the lid.

"What can that be?" cried Pandora, lifting her head.

But either Epimetheus had not heard the tap or was too much out of humor to notice it. At any rate, he made no answer.

"You are very unkind," said Pandora, sobbing anew, "not to speak to me!"

Again the tap! It sounded like the tiny knuckles of a fairy's hand, knocking lightly and playfully on the inside of the box.

"Who are you?" asked Pandora, with a little of her former curiosity. "Who are you, inside of this naughty box?"

A sweet little voice spoke from within: "Only lift the lid, and you shall see."

"No, no," answered Pandora, again beginning to sob. "I have had enough of lifting the lid! You are inside of the box, naughty creature, and there you shall stay! There are plenty of your ugly brothers and sisters already flying about the world. You need never think that I shall be so foolish as to let you out!"

She looked toward Epimetheus as she spoke, perhaps expecting that he would commend her for her wisdom. But the sullen boy only muttered that she was wise a little too late.

"Ah," said the sweet little voice again, "you had much better let me out. I am not like those naughty creatures that have stings in their tails. They are no brothers and sisters of mine, as you would see at once, if you were only to get a glimpse of me. Come, come, my pretty Pandora! I am sure you will let me out!"

And, indeed, there was a kind of cheerful witchery in the tone that made it almost impossible to refuse anything which this little voice asked. Pandora's heart had grown lighter at every word that came from within the box.

Epimetheus, too, though still in the corner, had turned half round and seemed to be in rather better spirits than before.

"My dear Epimetheus," cried Pandora, "have you heard this little voice?"

"Yes, to be sure I have," answered he, but in no very good humor as yet. "And what of it?"

"Shall I lift the lid again?" asked Pandora.

"Just as you please," said Epimetheus. "You have done so much mischief already that perhaps you may as well do a little more. One other Trouble, in such a swarm as you have set adrift about the world, can make no very great difference."

"You might speak a little more kindly!" murmured Pandora, wiping her eyes.

"Ah, naughty boy!" cried the little voice within the box, in an arch and laughing tone. "He knows he is longing to see me. Come, my dear Pandora, lift up the lid. I am in a great hurry to comfort you. Only let me have some fresh air, and you shall soon see that matters are not quite so dismal as you think them!"

"Epimetheus," exclaimed Pandora, "come what may, I am resolved to open the box!"

"And, as the lid seems very heavy," cried Epimetheus, running across the room, "I will help you!"

So, with one consent, the two children again lifted the lid. Out flew a sunny and smiling little personage, and hovered about the room, throwing a light wherever she went. Have you never made the sunshine dance into dark corners by reflecting it from a bit of looking glass? Well, so looked the winged cheerfulness of this fairy-like stranger amid the gloom of the cottage. She flew to Epimetheus and laid the least touch of her finger on the inflamed spot where the Trouble had stung him, and immediately the anguish of it was gone. Then she kissed Pandora on the forehead, and her hurt was cured likewise.

After performing these good offices, the bright stranger fluttered sportively over the children's heads and looked so sweetly at them that they both began to think it not so very much amiss to have opened the box, since, otherwise, their cheery guest must have been kept a prisoner among those naughty imps with stings in their tails.

"Pray, who are you, beautiful creature?" inquired Pandora.

"I am to be called Hope!" answered the sunshiny figure. "And because I am such a cheery little body, I was packed into the box to make amends to the human race for that swarm of ugly Troubles, which was destined to be let loose among them. Never fear! We shall do pretty well in spite of them all."

"Your wings are colored like the rainbow!" exclaimed Pandora. "How very beautiful!"

"Yes, they are like the rainbow," said Hope, "because, glad as my nature is, I am partly made of tears as well as smiles."

"And will you stay with us," asked Epimetheus, "for ever and ever?"

"As long as you need me," said Hope, with her pleasant smile, "and that will be as long as you live in the world, I promise never to leave you. There may be times and seasons, now and then, when you will think that I have utterly vanished. But again, and again, and again, when perhaps you least dream of it, you shall see the glimmer of my wings on the ceiling of your cottage. Yes, my dear children, and I know something very good and beautiful that is to be given you hereafter!"

"Oh, tell us," they exclaimed, "tell us what it is!"

"Do not ask me," replied Hope, putting her finger on her rosy mouth. "But do not despair, even if it should never happen while you live on this earth. Trust in my promise, for it is true."

"We do trust you!" cried Epimetheus and Pandora, both in one breath.

And so they did; and not only they, but so has everybody trusted Hope, that has since been alive. And, to tell you the truth, I cannot help being glad (though to be sure it was an uncommonly naughty thing for her to do)—but I cannot help being glad that our foolish Pandora peeped into the box. No doubt—no doubt—the Troubles are still flying about the world, and have increased in numbers, rather than lessened, and are a very ugly set of imps, and carry most venomous stings in their tails. I have felt them already, and expect to feel them more as I grow older. But then that lovely and lightsome little figure of Hope! What in the world could we do without her? Hope spiritualizes the earth; Hope makes it always new; and, even in the earth's best and brightest aspect, Hope shows it to be only the shadow of an infinite bliss hereafter!

NOTES AND QUESTIONS

Discussion. 1. How long ago did Pandora and Epimetheus live? 2. Find the lines that tell how different the world was then from what it is now. 3. Where did the box come from? 4. On what conditions was it given to Epimetheus? 5. Find lines that describe the box. 6. Why was Pandora interested in it? 7. In what way was it a blessing to Pandora? 8. What led her to open the box? 9. Do you think Epimetheus was at fault? Why? 10. What happened when Pandora raised the lid of the box? 11. How did this affect the Paradise of Children? The flowers? The children? 12. What happened when Pandora opened the box a second time? 13. Why was Hope put into the box with the Troubles? 14. Why are the wings of Hope like the rainbow? 15. What does Hope do for us? 16. What qualities in Epimetheus do you like? 17. What did Hope mean by saying she was partly made of tears? 18. How does Hope "spiritualize" the earth, i.e., make it purer? 19. Tell what you can about the author. 20. On page 291 you were asked to notice the way in which these authors tell their stories. You have no doubt noticed that Hawthorne uses humor and fancy to add interest. 21. Point out examples of his humor. 22. What quaint fancy has he about the way food was provided when the world was young, page 361? 23. By what fancy does he increase our interest in the mystery of the box, page 368, lines 12-19? 24. *Class readings:* Select passages to be read aloud in class. 25. *Outline for testing silent reading.* Tell the story briefly in your own words, using the topic headings given in the story. 26. You will enjoy seeing the pictures in the edition of *The Wonder-Book* that is illustrated by the well known artist, Maxfield Parrish. 27. Find in the glossary the meaning of: caroling, mysterious, whence, pettishly, intelligent (pp. 361-363), babble, combine (pp. 364-365), pried, restore (pp. 368-369), constant, intent, pestered (pp. 371-374), witchery, personage, glimmer, lightsome (pp. 375-378). 28. *Pronounce:* Epimetheus, either, Pandora, threshold, livelong, disquietude, merry, forbear (pp. 360-363), accompany, perseveringly, vexations, profusion, mischievous, contrivance (pp. 364-367), ingenious, merest (pp. 368-369), lamentable, gigantic, molested, calamity (pp. 370-373), grievously, intolerable, hovered, destined, venomous, spiritualizes, aspect, infinite (pp. 374-378).

Phrases for Study

greatest disquietude, **362**, 3
faint shadow of a Trouble, **362**, 6
more enterprise, **363**, 31
unaccustomed to vexations, **364**, 17
wrought together in such harmony, **365**, 6
high relief, **365**, 18
utter itself in words, **365**, 26
roguishly defied, **366**, 6
toil is the real play, **366**, 27
bewitchingly persuasive, **370**, 4
humor better suited **371**, 9
afflicted the souls, **373**, 20
obtained a foothold, **373**, 32
immortal in their childhood, **374**, 12
indulge it to the utmost, **374**, 24
with one consent, **376**, 25
performing these good offices, **377**, 3
much amiss, **377**, 6
make amends, **377**, 13
brightest aspect, **378**, 20
shadow of an infinite bliss, **378**, 21

THE GOLDEN TOUCH*

KING MIDAS AND HIS LOVE FOR GOLD

Once upon a time there lived a very rich man, and a king besides, whose name was Midas; and he had a little daughter, whom nobody but myself ever heard of, and whose name I either never knew, or have entirely forgotten. So, because I love odd names for little girls, I choose to call her Marygold.

This King Midas was fonder of gold than of anything else in the world. He valued his royal crown chiefly because it was composed of that precious metal. If he loved anything better, or half so well, it was the one little maiden who played so merrily around her father's footstool. But the more Midas loved his daughter, the more did he desire and seek for wealth. He thought, foolish man, that the best thing he could possibly do for this dear child would be to give her the immensest pile of yellow, glistening coin that had ever been heaped together since the world was made. Thus, he gave all his thoughts and all his time to this one purpose. If ever he happened to gaze for an instant at the gold-tinted clouds of sunset, he wished that they were real gold and that they could be squeezed safely into his strong box. When little Marygold ran to meet him with a bunch of buttercups and dandelions, he used to say, "Pooh, pooh, child! If these flowers were as golden as they look, they would be worth the plucking!"

And yet, in his earlier days, before he was so entirely possessed of this insane desire for riches, King Midas had shown a great taste for flowers. He had planted a garden, in which grew the biggest and beautifulest and sweetest

* See "Suggestions for Silent Reading," page 163.

roses that any mortal ever saw or smelled. These roses were still growing in the garden, as large, as lovely, and as fragrant as when Midas used to pass whole hours in gazing at them and inhaling their perfume. But now, if he looked at them at all, it was only to calculate how much the garden would be worth if each of the many rose petals were a thin plate of gold.

At length (as people always grow more and more foolish, unless they take care to grow wiser and wiser) Midas had got to be so exceedingly unreasonable that he could scarcely bear to see or touch any object that was not gold. He made it his custom, therefore, to pass a large portion of every day in a dark and dreary apartment, underground, at the basement of his palace. It was here that he kept his wealth. To this dismal hole—for it was little better than a dungeon—Midas betook himself whenever he wanted to be particularly happy. Here, after carefully locking the door, he would take a bag of gold coin, or a gold cup as big as a washbowl, or a heavy golden bar, or a peck-measure of gold dust, and bring them from the obscure corners of the room into the one bright and narrow sunbeam that fell from the dungeon-like window. He valued the sunbeam for no other reason but that his treasure would not shine without its help. And then would he reckon over the coins in the bag; toss up the bar, and catch it as it came down; sift the gold dust through his fingers; look at the funny image of his own face, as reflected in the polished surface of the cup; and whisper to himself, "O Midas, rich King Midas, what a happy man art thou!"

Midas was enjoying himself in his treasure room one day as usual, when he saw a shadow fall over the heaps of gold; and, looking suddenly up, what should he behold but the figure of a stranger, standing in the bright and narrow sunbeam! It was a young man with a cheerful and ruddy face. Whether it was that the imagination of King Midas threw a yellow tinge over everything, or whatever the cause might be, he could not help fancying that the smile with which the stranger regarded him had a kind of golden radiance in it.

As Midas knew that he had carefully turned the key in the lock, and that no mortal strength could possibly break into his treasure room, he of course concluded that his visitor must be something more than mortal. It is no matter about telling you who he was. In those days, when the earth was comparatively a new affair, it was supposed to be often the resort of beings who had extraordinary powers, and who used to interest themselves in the joys and sorrows of men, women, and children, half playfully and half seriously. Midas had met such beings before now, and was not sorry to meet one of them again. The stranger's manner, indeed, was so good-humored and kindly that it would have been unreasonable to suspect him of intending any mischief. It was far more probable that he came to do Midas a favor. And what could that favor be, unless to multiply his heaps of treasure?

The stranger gazed about the room; and when his bright smile had glistened upon all the golden objects that were there, he turned again to Midas.

"You are a wealthy man, friend Midas!" he observed. "I doubt whether any other four walls on earth contain so much gold as you have piled up in this room."

"I have done pretty well—pretty well," answered Midas, in a discontented tone. "But, after all, it is but a trifle, when you consider that it has taken me my whole life to get it together. If one could live a thousand years, he might have time to grow rich!"

"What!" exclaimed the stranger. "Then you are not satisfied?" Midas shook his head.

"And pray what would satisfy you?" asked the stranger. "Merely for the curiosity of the thing I should be glad to know."

Midas paused and meditated. He had a feeling that this stranger, with such a golden luster in his good-humored smile, had come hither with both the power and the purpose of gratifying his utmost wishes. Now, therefore, was the fortunate moment when he had but to speak and obtain whatever possible, or seemingly impossible, thing it might come into his head to ask. So he thought and thought and thought, and heaped up one golden mountain upon another in his imagination, without being able to imagine them big enough. At last, a bright idea occurred to King Midas. It seemed really as bright as the glistening metal which he loved so much.

Raising his head, he looked the lustrous stranger in the face.

"Well, Midas," observed his visitor, "I see that you have at length hit upon something that will satisfy you. Tell me your wish."

"It is only this," replied Midas. "I am weary of collecting my treasures with so much trouble, and beholding the heap so small after I have done my best. I wish everything that I touch to be changed to gold!"

The stranger's smile grew so very broad that it seemed to fill the room like an outburst of the sun gleaming into a shadowy dell where the yellow autumnal leaves—for so looked the lumps and particles of gold—lie strewn in the glow of light.

"The Golden Touch!" exclaimed he. "You certainly deserve credit, friend Midas, for striking out so brilliant an idea. But are you quite sure that this will satisfy you?"

"How could it fail?" said Midas.

"And will you never regret the possession of it?"

"What could induce me?" asked Midas. "I ask nothing else to render me perfectly happy."

"Be it as you wish, then," replied the stranger, waving his hand in token of farewell. "Tomorrow, at sunrise, you will find yourself gifted with the Golden Touch."

The figure of the stranger then became exceedingly bright, and Midas was forced to close his eyes. On opening them again he beheld only one yellow sunbeam in the room and, all around him, the glistening of the precious metal which he had spent his life in hoarding up.

Whether Midas slept as usual that night, the story does not say. Asleep or awake, however, his mind was probably in the state of a child's to whom a beautiful new plaything has been promised in the morning. At any rate, day had hardly peeped over the hills when King Midas was broad awake and, stretching his arms out of bed, began to touch the objects that were within reach. He was anxious to prove whether the Golden Touch had really come according to the stranger's promise. So he laid his finger on a chair by the bedside, and on various other things, but was grievously disappointed to perceive that they remained of exactly the same substance as before.

The Gift of the Golden Touch

All this while, it was only the gray of the morning, with but a streak of brightness along the edge of the sky, where Midas could not see it. He lay in a very unhappy mood, regretting the downfall of his hopes, and kept growing sadder and sadder, until the earliest sunbeam shone through the window and gilded the ceiling over his head. It seemed to Midas that this bright yellow sunbeam was reflected in rather a singular way on the white covering of the bed. Looking more closely, what was his astonishment and delight, when he found that this linen fabric had been changed to what seemed a woven texture of the purest and brightest gold! The Golden Touch had come to him with the first sunbeam!

Midas started up, in a kind of joyful frenzy, and ran about the room grasping at everything that happened to be in his way. He seized one of the bedposts, and it became immediately a fluted golden pillar. He pulled aside a window curtain in order to admit a clear spectacle of the wonders which he was performing, and the tassel grew heavy in his hand—a mass of gold. He took up a book from the table. At his first touch it assumed the appearance of such a splendidly-bound and gilt-edged volume as one often meets with nowadays; but, on running his fingers through the leaves, behold! it was a bundle of thin golden plates, in which all the wisdom of the book had grown indistinct. He hurriedly put on his clothes, and was delighted to see himself in a magnificent suit of gold cloth, which retained its flexibility and softness, although it burdened him a little with its weight.

Wise King Midas was so excited by his good fortune that the palace seemed not sufficiently spacious to contain him. He therefore went downstairs and smiled on observing that the balustrade of the staircase became a bar of burnished gold as his hand passed over it in his descent. He lifted the door latch (it was brass only a moment ago, but golden when his fingers quitted it) and went into the garden. Here, as it happened, he found a great number of beautiful roses in full bloom and others in all the stages of lovely bud and blossom. Very delicious was their fragrance in the morning breeze. Their delicate blush was one of the fairest sights in the world—so gentle, so modest, and so full of sweet composure did these roses seem to be.

But Midas knew a way to make them far more precious, according to his way of thinking, than roses had ever been before. So he took great pains in going from bush to bush, and exercised his magic touch most freely until every individual flower and bud, and even the worms at the heart of some of them, were changed to gold. By the time this good work was completed, King Midas was called to breakfast; and, as the morning air had given him an excellent appetite, he made haste back to the palace.

What was usually a king's breakfast, in the days of Midas, I really do not know, and cannot stop now to find out. To the best of my belief, however, on this particular morning, the breakfast consisted of hot cakes, some nice little brook trout, roasted potatoes, fresh boiled eggs, and coffee, for King Midas himself, and a bowl of bread and milk for his daughter, Marygold. At all events, this is a breakfast fit to be set before a king; and, whether he had it or not, King Midas could not have had a better.

Little Marygold had not yet made her appearance. Her father ordered her to be called and, seating himself at table, awaited the child's coming, in order to begin his own breakfast. To do Midas justice, he really loved his daughter, and loved her so much the more this morning on account of the good fortune which had befallen him. It was not a great while before he heard her coming along the passage crying bitterly. This circumstance surprised him, because Marygold was one of the cheerfulest little people whom you would see in a summer day, and hardly shed a thimbleful of tears in a twelvemonth. When Midas heard her sobs, he determined to put little Marygold into better spirits by an agreeable surprise; so, leaning across the table, he touched his daughter's bowl (which was a china one, with pretty figures all around it) and turned it to gleaming gold.

Meanwhile, Marygold slowly and sadly opened the door and showed herself with her apron at her eyes, still sobbing as if her heart would break.

"How now, my little lady!" cried Midas. "Pray what is the matter with you this bright morning?"

Marygold, without taking the apron from her eyes, held out her hand, in which was one of the roses which Midas had so recently changed.

"Beautiful!" exclaimed her father. "And what is there in this magnificent golden rose to make you cry?"

"Ah, dear Father!" answered the child, as well as her sobs would let her, "it is not beautiful, but the ugliest flower that ever grew! As soon as I was dressed, I ran into the garden to gather some roses for you, because I know you like them, and like them the better when gathered by your little daughter. But, O dear, dear me! What do you think has happened? Such a misfortune! All the beautiful roses, that smelled so sweet and had so many lovely blushes, are blighted and spoiled! They are grown quite yellow, as you see this one, and have no longer any fragrance! What can have been the matter?"

"Pooh, my dear little girl, pray don't cry about it!" said Midas, who was ashamed to confess that he himself had wrought the change which so greatly afflicted her. "Sit down and eat your bread and milk! You will find it easy enough to exchange a golden rose like that (which will last hundreds of years) for an ordinary one, which would wither in a day."

"I don't care for such roses as this!" cried Marygold. "It has no smell, and the hard petals prick my nose!"

The King's Breakfast of Gold

The child now sat down to table, but was so occupied with her grief for the blighted roses that she did not even notice the wonderful change of her china bowl. Perhaps this was all the better, for Marygold was accustomed to take pleasure in looking at the queer figures and strange trees and houses that were painted on the outside of the bowl; and those ornaments were now entirely lost in the yellow hue of the metal.

Midas, meanwhile, had poured out a cup of coffee; and, as a matter of course, the coffee pot, whatever metal it may have been when he took it up, was gold when he set it down. He thought to himself that it was rather an extravagant style of splendor, in a king of his simple habits, to breakfast off a service of gold, and began to be puzzled with the difficulty of keeping his treasures safe. The cupboard and the kitchen would no longer be a safe place of deposit for articles so valuable as golden bowls and coffee pots.

Amid these thoughts, he lifted a spoonful of coffee to his lips and, sipping it, was astonished to perceive that, the instant his lips touched the liquid, it became molten gold, and the next moment, hardened into a lump!

"Ha!" exclaimed Midas, rather aghast.

"What is the matter, Father?" asked little Marygold, gazing at him, with tears still standing in her eyes.

"Nothing, child, nothing!" said Midas. "Eat your bread and milk before it gets quite cold."

He took one of the nice little trout on his plate and, by way of experiment, touched its tail with his finger. To his horror, it was immediately changed from an admirably fried brook trout into a gold fish, though not one of those goldfish which people often keep in glass globes, as ornaments for the parlor. No, but it was really a metallic fish, and looked as if it had been very cunningly made by the nicest goldsmith in the world. Its little bones were now golden wires; its fins and tail were thin plates of gold; and there were the marks of the fork in it, and all the delicate, frothy appearance of a nicely fried fish, exactly imitated in metal. A very pretty piece of work, as you may suppose. Only King Midas just at that moment would much rather have had a real trout in his dish than this elaborate and valuable imitation of one.

"I don't quite see," thought he to himself, "how I am to get any breakfast!"

He took one of the smoking hot cakes and had scarcely broken it, when, to his cruel mortification, though a moment before it had been of the whitest wheat, it assumed the yellow hue of Indian meal. To say the truth, if it had really been a hot Indian cake, Midas would have prized it a good deal more than he now did, when its solidity and increased weight made him know too well that it was gold. Almost in despair, he helped himself to a boiled egg, which immediately underwent a change similar to that of the trout and the cake. The egg, indeed, might have been mistaken for one of those which the famous goose, in the storybook, was in the habit of laying, but King Midas was the only goose that had had anything to do with the matter.

"Well, this is a puzzle!" thought he, leaning back in his chair, and looking quite enviously at little Marygold, who was now eating her bread and milk with great satisfaction, "Such a costly breakfast, and nothing that can be eaten!"

Hoping that, by dint of great quickness, he might avoid what he now felt to be a considerable inconvenience, King Midas next snatched a hot potato and attempted to cram it into his mouth and swallow it in a hurry. But the Golden Touch was too nimble for him. He found his mouth full, not of mealy potato, but of solid metal, which so burned his tongue that he roared aloud and, jumping up from the table, began to dance and stamp about the room, both with pain and affright.

"Father, dear Father!" cried little Marygold, who was a very affectionate child, "pray, what is the matter? Have you burned your mouth?"

"Ah, dear child," groaned Midas, dolefully, "I don't know what is to become of your poor father!"

And, truly, my dear little folks, did you ever hear of such a pitiable case in all your lives? Here was literally the richest breakfast that could be set before a king, and its very richness made it absolutely good for nothing. The poorest laborer, sitting down to his crust of bread and cup of water, was far better off than King Midas, whose delicate food was really worth its weight in gold. And what was to be done? Already, at breakfast, Midas was very hungry. Would he be less so by dinnertime? And how ravenous would be his appetite for supper, which must undoubtedly consist of the same sort of indigestible dishes as those now before him! How many days, think you, would he survive the use of this rich fare?

These thoughts so troubled wise King Midas that he began to doubt whether, after all, riches are the one desirable thing in the world, or even the most desirable. But this was only a passing thought. So pleased was Midas with the glitter of the yellow metal that he would still have refused to give up the Golden Touch for so small a consideration as a breakfast. Just imagine what a price for one meal's victuals! It would have been the same as paying millions and millions of money (and as many millions more as would take forever to reckon up) for some fried trout, an egg, a potato, a hot cake, and a cup of coffee!

"It would be quite too dear," thought Midas.

Nevertheless, so great was his hunger and the perplexity of his situation, that he again groaned aloud, and very grievously too. Our pretty Marygold could endure it no longer. She sat a moment gazing at her father and trying, with all the might of her little wits, to find out what was the matter with him. Then, with a sweet and sorrowful impulse to comfort him, she started from the chair, and running to Midas, threw her arms affectionately about his knees. He bent down and kissed her. He felt that his little daughter's love was worth a thousand times more than he had gained by the Golden Touch.

"My precious, precious Marygold!" cried he.

But Marygold made no answer.

Alas, what had he done? How fatal was the gift which the stranger gave! The moment the lips of Midas touched Marygold's forehead, a change had taken place. Her sweet, rosy face, so full of affection as it had been, assumed a glittering yellow color, with yellow teardrops hardening on her cheeks. Her beautiful brown ringlets took the same tint. Her soft and tender little form grew hard and stiff within her father's encircling arms. O terrible misfortune! The victim of his great desire for wealth, little Marygold was a human child no longer, but a golden statue!

Yes, there she was, with the questioning look of love, grief, and pity, hardened into her face. It was the prettiest and most woeful sight that ever mortal saw. All the features and tokens of Marygold were there; even the beloved little dimple remained in her golden chin. But, the more perfect was the resemblance, the greater was the father's agony at beholding this golden image, which was all that was left him of a daughter. It had been a favorite phrase of Midas, whenever he felt particularly fond of the child, to say that she was worth her weight in gold. And now the phrase had become literally true. And now, at last, when it was too late, he felt how infinitely a warm and tender heart that loved him exceeded in value all the wealth that could be piled up betwixt the earth and sky!

It would be too sad a story if I were to tell you how Midas, in the fullness of all his gratified desires, began to wring his hands and bemoan himself, and how he could neither bear to look at Marygold, nor yet to look away from her.

WHAT KING MIDAS LEARNED

While he was in this despair, he suddenly beheld a stranger, standing near the door. Midas bent down his head without speaking, for he recognized the same figure which had appeared to him the day before in the treasure room, and had bestowed on him this unlucky power of the Golden Touch. The stranger's countenance still wore a smile, which seemed to shed a yellow luster all about the room and gleamed on little Marygold's image and on the other objects that had been changed by the touch of Midas.

"Well, friend Midas," said the stranger, "pray how do you succeed with the Golden Touch?"

Midas shook his head.

"I am very miserable," said he.

"Very miserable, indeed!" exclaimed the stranger. "And how happens that? Have I not faithfully kept my promise with you? Have you not everything that your heart desired?"

"Gold is not everything," answered Midas. "And I have lost all that my heart really cared for."

"Ah! So you have made a discovery since yesterday?" observed the stranger. "Let us see, then. Which of these two things do you think is really worth the more—the gift of the Golden Touch, or one cup of clear cold water?"

"O blessed water!" exclaimed Midas. "It will never moisten my parched throat again!"

"The Golden Touch," continued the stranger, "or a crust of bread?"

"A piece of bread," answered Midas, "is worth all the gold on earth!"

"The Golden Touch," asked the stranger, "or your own little Marygold, warm, soft, and loving, as she was an hour ago?"

"Oh, my child, my dear child!" cried poor Midas, wringing his hands. "I would not have given that one small dimple in her chin for the power of changing this whole big earth into a solid lump of gold!"

"You are wiser than you were, King Midas!" said the stranger, looking seriously at him. "Your own heart, I perceive, has not been entirely changed from flesh to gold. Were it so, your case would indeed be desperate. But you appear to be still capable of understanding that the commonest things, such as lie within everybody's grasp, are more valuable than the riches which so many mortals sigh and struggle after. Tell me, now, do you sincerely desire to rid yourself of this Golden Touch?"

"It is hateful to me!" replied Midas.

A fly settled on his nose, but immediately fell to the floor, for it, too, had become gold. Midas shuddered.

"Go, then," said the stranger, "and plunge into the river that glides past the bottom of your garden. Take likewise a vase of the same water and sprinkle it over any object that you may desire to change back again from gold into its former substance. If you do this in earnestness and sincerity, it may possibly repair the mischief which your avarice has occasioned."

King Midas bowed low, and when he lifted his head, the lustrous stranger had vanished.

You will easily believe that Midas lost no time in snatching up a great earthen pitcher (but, alas! it was no longer earthen after he touched it) and hastening to the riverside. As he scampered along and forced his way through the shrubbery, it was positively marvelous to see how the foliage turned yellow behind him, as if the autumn had been there, and nowhere else. On reaching the river's brink, he plunged headlong in, without waiting so much as to pull off his shoes.

"Poof! poof! poof!" snorted King Midas, as his head emerged out of the water. "Well, this is really a refreshing bath, and I think it must have quite washed away the Golden Touch. And now for filling my pitcher!"

As he dipped the pitcher into the water, it gladdened his very heart to see it change from gold into the same good, honest earthen vessel which it had been before he touched it. He was conscious, also, of a change within himself. A cold, hard, and heavy weight seemed to have gone out of his bosom. No doubt his heart had been gradually losing its human substance and changing itself into dull metal, but had now softened back again into flesh. Seeing a violet that grew on the bank of the river, Midas touched it with his finger and was overjoyed to find that the delicate flower retained its purple hue, instead of undergoing a yellow blight. The curse of the Golden Touch had, therefore, really been removed from him.

King Midas hastened back to the palace and, I suppose, the servants knew not what to make of it when they saw their royal master so carefully bringing home an earthen pitcher of water. But that water, which was to undo all the mischief that his folly had wrought, was more precious to Midas than an ocean of molten gold could have been. The first thing he did, as you need hardly be told, was to sprinkle it by handfuls over the golden figure of little Marygold.

No sooner did it fall on her than you would have laughed to see how the rosy color came back to the dear child's cheek!—and how she began to sneeze and splutter!—and how astonished she was to find herself dripping wet, and her father still throwing more water over her!

"Pray, do not, dear Father!" cried she. "See how you have wet my nice frock, which I put on only this morning!"

For Marygold did not know that she had been a little golden statue, nor could she remember anything that had happened since the moment when she ran with outstretched arms to comfort poor King Midas.

Her father did not think it necessary to tell his beloved child how very foolish he had been, but contented himself with showing how much wiser he had now grown. For this purpose he led little Marygold into the garden, where he sprinkled all the remainder of the water over the rosebushes, and with such good effect that above five thousand roses recovered their beautiful bloom. There were two circumstances, however, which, as long as he lived, used to put King Midas in mind of the Golden Touch. One was that the sands of the river sparkled like gold; the other, that little Marygold's hair had now a golden tinge, which he had never observed in it before she had been changed by the effect of his kiss. This change of hue was really an improvement and made Marygold's hair richer than in her babyhood.

When King Midas had grown quite an old man, and used to trot Marygold's children on his knee, he was fond of telling them this marvelous story, pretty much as I have now told it to you. And then would he stroke their glossy ringlets and tell them that their hair, likewise, had a rich shade of gold, which they had inherited from their mother.

"And to tell you the truth, my precious little folks," quoth King Midas, diligently trotting the children all the while, "ever since that morning I have hated the very sight of all other gold save this!"

NOTES AND QUESTIONS

Discussion. 1. How did Midas think he could best show his love for his daughter? 2. What was his chief pleasure? 3. Describe the visitor who appeared to Midas in his treasure room. 4. What did the stranger ask him? 5. Find the sentence that tells what Midas wished. 6. When did he receive his new power? 7. What use did he make of it? 8. What did Marygold think of the gold roses? 9. Why was not Midas's breakfast a success? 10. When did Midas first doubt whether riches are the most desirable thing in the world? 11. How did he drive this thought away? 12. What made him realize that his little daughter was dearer to him than gold? 13. Find lines that tell what he realized when it was too late. 14. What did the stranger ask when he came again? 15. What was the discovery that Midas had made since the stranger's first visit? 16. How was Midas cured of the Golden Touch? 17. What was he told to do in order to restore Marygold to life? 18. What was the only gold he cared about after he was saved from the Golden Touch? 19. Find examples of humor; of fanciful expressions, such as "day had hardly peeped over the hills," page 384, lines 17, 18; of descriptions that you like. 20. *Class readings:* Select passages to be read aloud in class. 21. *Outline for testing silent reading.* Tell the story briefly in your own words, using the topic headings given in the story. 22. Find in the glossary the meaning of: purpose, mortal, inhaling, induce (pp. 380-384), flexibility, balustrade, burnished, afflicted (pp. 385-387), affright, consideration, perplexity, fatal, agony, infinitely (pp. 390-392), desperate, earthen, conscious, molten (pp. 393-394). 23. *Pronounce:* Midas, calculate, particularly, obscure, tinge, extraordinary, meditated, lustrous (pp. 380-383), composure, blighted (pp. 386-387), hue, cupboard, molten, aghast, admirably, metallic, frothy, pitiable, ravenous, indigestible, victuals, phrase (pp. 388-391), recognized, parched, avarice (pp. 392-393).

Phrases for Study

comparatively a new affair, **382**, 12
woven texture, **385**, 5
wisdom of the book, **385**, 19
cunningly made, **389**, 1
nicest goldsmith, **389**, 2
cruel mortification, **389**, 13
by dint of great quickness, **389**, 29
features and tokens, **391**, 28

GREAT AMERICAN AUTHORS

A Backward Look

A wonderful power lies in the Crystal Glass of Reading—the power to increase your circle of friends and to know intimately people who have lived in distant times and places. Through its power the great heroes of all ages—Joseph, Beowulf, Sigurd, Robin Hood, and our own Washington, Lincoln, and Roosevelt become your companions.

Someone has said that the pen is mightier than the sword, which is another way of saying that great books have had more to do in shaping the lives and fortunes of men than bloody battles. The group of authors whose stories and poems you have just been reading is a company of friends whose thoughts about nature, or about life and its meaning, have been a power in making America what it is today.

Acquaintance with these friends has been made easy for you; you have had placed before you their pictures and interesting facts about their lives, and best of all, you have been able to hear them tell their own thoughts. What authors are in this group? Which of them did you learn to know in Book IV and which were new to you in this book? Close your eyes and see whether your "inward eye" can picture the faces of Franklin, Bryant, Whittier, Irving, Longfellow, Hawthorne. Make one interesting statement concerning each author and his works. Quote lines from poems by Bryant, Whittier, and Longfellow. Make from memory a list of titles of stories or poems you have read from each of these six American authors.

Benjamin Franklin founded the first public library in America; the picture on page 18 shows you what a library must have been like in the old Greek days, and page 288 pictures a view of the Congressional Library at Washington, the home of the complete works of all our American authors. The building is considered one of the most beautiful in the world. Report to the class some interesting facts about this library that you have learned from someone who has seen it.

In the last paragraph of the "Forward Look," page 291, you are asked to notice the way in which authors tell what they have to say. When Franklin was a young boy he was not at all satisfied with his way of writing, so he set himself the task of noticing carefully how a certain English writer, whom he admired very much, expressed himself, and tried to pattern after him. Notice how Franklin made the story, "An Ax to Grind," seem very real by using direct quotations. Where else has he used direct quotations with the same result?

Notice the way Hawthorne added interest to his stories: (a) by touches of fancy; (b) by delicate humor; (c) by apt descriptions. Point out examples of each of these qualities in "The Paradise of Children." Make a similar showing for "The Golden Touch." Compare the two stories in regard to each of these qualities.

Turn to the pictures on pages 292, 297, 302, 310, 321, and 359, and see whether you are able to tell what selection each picture illustrates. You have read many stories in this book that show how fine a thing it is to serve, like Hiawatha, who

> Lived, and toiled, and suffered,
> That the tribes of men might prosper,
> That he might advance his people!

Make a list of the stories you have read in this book that tell about service. Read the lines in "The White-Man's Foot" that describe "the great canoe with pinions." Since you began to use this book, what progress have you made in gaining ability to read silently with speed and understanding?

Glossary

a as in mat	ə as in banana	ä as in father	∅ as in side
e as in bed	ər as in further	au̇ as in loud	ŋ as in sing
i as in tip	ā as in day	ē as in need	ō as in snow
ȯ as in saw	ȯi as in coin	ü as in rule	u̇ as in pull
	ᵊ as in eaten	th as in heather	

a bashed (ə-'basht) ashamed
ab bey ('a-bē) the home of monks
ab bot ('a-bət) head of an abbey
above his for tune ('fȯr-chən) more than he can afford
ab so lute ly (ab-sə-'lut-lē) positively
ab surd in ven tions (əb-'sərd; in-'ven-shənz) made-up stories not believable
a byss (ə-'bis) a space so deep as not to be easily measured
ac com pa ny (ə-'kəmp-nē) go with
ac cost ed (ə-'kȯst-ed) spoken to
ac cout ered (ə-'kü-tərd) dressed
ac cu mu lat ing (ə-'kyü-mə-la-tiŋ) piling up
ac quaint ed (ə 'kwānt ed) friendly with each other
ad age ('a-dij) saying
Ad ji dau mo (äd-ji-'dȯ-mō)
ad mi ra bly ('ad-mə-rə-blē) well
a do (ə-'dü) fuss
a dorn (ə-'dȯrn) decorate
ad vance his people (əd-'vans) help his tribe of Indians to be better
ad vis ers (əd-'v∅z-erz) men with whom he talked
adz ('adz) tool for trimming wood
ae rie ('ar-ē) high nest
Ae sop (ē-säp) a Greek slave who wrote many little stories
af flict ed (ə-'flikt-ed) distressed

af flict ed the souls (ə-'flikt-ed) made people do wrong
af flic tion (ə-'flick-shən) trouble
af fright (ə-'frØt) alarm
aft er math ('aft-ər-math) second crop
a gain (ə-'gen) once more
against all com ers ('kə-merz) with anyone he meets
age of doubt time when people are not ready to believe
a ghast (ə-'gast) startled
a gil i ty (ə-'ji-lə-tē) quickness
ag o ny ('a-gə-nē) grief
Ah meek (ə-'mek)
Ah mo ('ə-mo)
A lad din (ə-'la-dən)
al der ('ȯl-der) a kind of tree
a lert (ə-'lərt) watchful
A li Ba ba (a-lē-'bä-bə)
al lied ('a-lØd) joined
all in their best dressed in their best clothes
all its en dear ments (in-'dir-mənts) everything that makes it dear
al lot ted time ('ə-lät-ed) time granted for doing anything
al ma nacs ('ȯl-mə-naks) small books containing a yearly calendar with little stories
al oes ('a-lōz) a precious wood
al ter nate ('ȯl-tər-nāt) first one, then the other
am bi tious (am-'bi-shəs) eager for
am bush in the oak tree ('am-bu̇sh) hiding place in the oak
am e thyst ('a-mə-thəst) a clear purple or bluish violet; a precious stone
an cient ('ānt-shənt) old; of old time
an ec dote ('a-nik-dōt) a story
a nem o nes (ə-'ne-mō-nēz) wild flowers of pale, dainty colors
a new (ə-'nü) again
animal spirits loud, rough play
An ne mee kee (ən-ə-'mē-kē)
An toine ('an-twan)
anx ious ('ank-shəs) troubled
ape the ways of pride try to copy the actions of proud people
a poth e ca ry (ə-'pä-thə-ker-e) druggist
ap peared con cerned (ə-'pird; kən-sərnd) seemed anxious

apple from the pine pineapple
ap point ed (ə-'pȯint-ed) chosen beforehand for the feast
ap proached (ə-'prōcht) went near to
ap proach the bounds (ə-'prōch) come near the edge
Ar a bic ('ar-ə-bik) language of Arabs
arch and laughing tone (ärch) merry, teasing voice
ar cher y ('är-chər-ē) shooting with bow and arrow
arch ing (ar-chiŋ) curving
arching blue sky
arch of the sun lit bow (ärch; 'sun-lit; 'bō) curve of the rainbow
arch way of rock ('ärch-wā) meeting place overhead of two rock walls
ar ray (ə-'rā) order
ar tif i cer (är-'ti-fə-sər) skilled worker
ash-cakes unsweetened cakes baked on a hot shovel laid on the ashes
as pect ('as-pekt) outlook; state
as pen bow er ('as-pən; 'bau̇-er) thicket of trees, the leaves of which are easily moved by the wind
as pir ing gen ius ('a-spØr-iŋ; 'jēn-yəs) clever person who is trying to rise
as sem bled (ə-'sem-bəld) collected
as sumed the ap pear ance of (ə-'sumd; ə-'pir-əns) looked like
as ters in the brook ('as tərz) reflection of the asters in the water
a stir (ə-'stər) moving around
as ton ished (ə-'stän-isht) surprised
a stride the traces (ə-'strØd) having one leg over one of the straps which fastened the plow to the horses
a sun der (ə-'sun-dər) apart
at ten dance on lev ees (ə-'ten-dəns; 'le-vēz) going to receptions
attend his pleas ure ('ple-zhur) do his bidding
at their glit ter ing best ('gli-tər-iŋ) shining as bright as possible
au di ble ('ȯ-də-bəl) that can be heard
aught but tender any way except kind
au tum nal (ȯ-'təm-nəl) of autumn
av a rice ('a-və-rəs) greed
a vert ed (ə-'vərt-ed) turned aside
a wak en ing of the woods (ə-'wāk-niŋ) the budding of the forest trees
a wry (ə-'rØ) crooked

ay (∅) yes
az ure ('a-zhər) sky-blue; the air
az ure space blue air above

bab ble ('ba-bəl) chatter
bade (bād) told; told to
bal as ('ba-ləs) a kind of ruby
balked (bȯkt) stopped balm
balm (bälm) sticky dried juice
bal sam ('bȯl-səm) same as balm
bal us trade ('ba-ləs-trād) railing
band ag es ('ban-dij-ez) strips of cloth
ban dit ti (ban-'di-tē) robbers
bar ter it all ('bär-tər) trade all that I have gained
bass wood ('bas-wu̇d) wood of the linden tree
bat tle ments ('ba-təl-mənts) irregular top of the high walls of a castle
bay ou ('b∅-ü) inlet
ba zaars (bə-'zärz) shops; market-place
beam ray of light
beaming ('bē-miŋ) shining
bear me ill-will dislike me
bear no mal ice ('ma-ləs) have no ill-will
beast of prey (prā) flesh-eating animal
Beat te ('bē-tə)
beat us holler do things we cannot do
beau te ous summer glow ('byü-tē-əs) lovely brightness of summer time
be calmed (bi-'kalmd) prevented from sailing because of lack of wind
beech en ('bēch-en) of the beech tree
be fall (bi-'fȯl) happen to
be guile (bi-'g∅l) charm
be guiled (bi-'g∅ld) tricked
behold it a fore time (ə-'fōr-t∅m) see it before it arrived
be lated thriftless va grant (bi-'lāt-təd; 'vā-grənt) tardy, lazy wanderer
bel fry ('bel-frē) tower for a bell
be moan himself (bi-'mōn) groan softly
be neath (bi-'nēth)

be nev o lent friendship (bə-ˈnev-ə-lənt) kind and generous acts of a friend
be nig nant (bə-ˈnig-nənt) kindly
be seems his qual i ty (bə-ˈsēmz; ˈkwä-lə-tē) fits his rank
beside himself with joy so happy he did not know what to do
be smeared (bi-ˈsmird) covered
best of cheer things that make one most happy
be trayed (bi-ˈtrād) given me to my enemy by a trick
be wild er ment (bi-ˈwil-dər-mənt) perplexity
be witch ing ly per sua sive (bi-ˈwi-chiŋ-lē; pər-ˈswā-siv) charmingly coaxing
Big-Sea-Water Lake Superior
bil lowed like a rus set ocean (ˈbi-lōd; ˈrə-sət) reddish grass blew like waves
Bish op of Bing en (ˈbi-shəp; ˈbing-ən) Hatto, who starved the poor and was shut up in a tower, where mice devoured him
bi son (ˈbØ-sən) American buffalo
blanc-mange (blə-ˈmaŋ) a dessert of starchy substances and milk
blare (ˈblar) blow harshly
blast (ˈblast) hard wind; loud, long sound
blazing in the sky showing bright against the sky
Ble fus cu (ble-ˈfəs-cū)
blend ed ranks (ˈblen-dəd) mixed lines
blight ed (ˈblØ-təd) withered
blithe (ˈblØth) happy; joyous
blossoming ground earth covered with flowers
blue day day when the sky is clear
blur in the eye tear
boar (bōr) wild hog
bon ny (ˈbä-nē) gay
boom ing (ˈbü-miŋ) hollow-sounding
boon (ˈbün) favor
borne their part (ˈbȯrn) done their share
born to rule the storm naturally able to do anything
bos om (ˈbu-zəm) front part
bound a ry (ˈbaủn-də-rē) marking a division; separating
bound boy boy hired out to work by the year for his board and a small wage
bound by a spell charmed so that I could not move
boundless space the endless extent of the regions of the air

bound to him made them love him
boun ties ('baůn-tēz) generous gifts
boun ti ful trav e ler ('baůn-tē ful; 'trav-əl-ər) generous traveler
Bow doin ('bō-dən)
bow ers ('bau-ərz) lovely rooms
boul ders ('bōl-dərz) large stones
brake ('brāk) valley enclosed by hills
braves Indian men ready to fight
brawn y ('brȯ-nē) strong
break ers ('brā-kərz) big waves striking the shore
break my fast eat my meal
breathed a song sang a song softly
breech es ('brē-chəz) short trousers
bri dled ('br∅-dəld) put the headpiece on
brig ('brig) sailing ship with two masts
bright ened as he sped ('br∅-tənd) grew brighter as he mounted up into the sky
brightest as pect ('as-pekt) look that is most attractive
brin dled ('brin-dəld) having dark streaks or spots on a gray or yellowish brown ground; streaked
bring the hunting homeward carry home what I shoot
broad-faced sun round, cheerful sun.
bro cades (brō-'kādz) heavy silk woven with a raised figure or flower
brood ing ('brü-diŋ) thinking sadly
broom a shrub with yellow flowers
brought to bale ('bāl) made trouble for
buf fet ('bə-fət) slap
bulge ('bəlj) place bent in
bul lies ('bu̇-lēz) teases
bul wark ('bu̇l-wərk) protection; defense
bun ting ('bən-tiŋ) cloth for flags
buoy ('bü-ē) float
bur i al ('ber-ē-əl) act of placing in a grave
bur nished ('bər-nisht) shining
Bus so rah ('bus-ō-rä)
by dint of great quickness ('dint) by acting very fast
by way of sat is fy ing ('sat-əs-f∅-iŋ) in order to quiet the prickings of

ca lam i ty (kə-'la-mə-tē) misfortune
cal cu late ('kal-kyə-lāt) figure up
ca liph ('kā-ləf) an Eastern title
calked ('kȯkt) stopped up
calls but the warders ('wȯr-dərz) only calls the watchmen
calm (kälm) a period of quiet
came into the knowledge of was told
came into the world took part in the business, political, social, etc., activities of the world
can oe with pin ions (ka-'nü; 'pin-yənz) sailboat
cap i tal crime ('ka-pə-təl) a sin so bad that it is punished by death
care is sowing worry and work are making grow
car nage ('kär-nij) killing
car ol ing ('ka-rə-liŋ) singing
car riag es ('kar-ij-ez) carts
Ca sa-bian ca ('ka-zə-'byän-ka)
cast yourself free unroll
cat a ract's laugh ter ('ka-tə-rakts; 'laf-tər) laughing sound made by water falling from a height
catches the gleam reflects the light
ca the dral (kə-'thē-drəl) large church
cau tion ('kȯ-shən) carefulness
ceased their calling ('sēst) stopped singing because they have migrated
cer e mo ny ('ser-ə-mō-nē) formal act
chafe ('chāf) rub, trying to get through
cha grin (shə-'grin) annoyance
chal ce do ny (kal-'se-dᵊ-nē) a beautiful, very hard stone
change ful April ('chānj-fəl) April has sudden changes of weather
chan nel ('cha-nəl) bed of the stream
charg er ('chär-jər) fine horse
charm something with magic power
chas tened ('chā-sənd) with a softer light
Chee maun (chē-'mon)
cheering power of spring how spring makes one glad
cher ished ('cher-isht) lovingly cared for
cherished pos ses sions (pə-'ze-chənz) dearest things he had
Chib i a bos (chi-bə-'ä-bōs)
chief tain ('chēf-tən) one who gave orders

chim ney ('chim-nē)
chore ('chōr) light task
chris ten ing ('kris-niŋ) naming
ci pher ing ('sØ-fə-riŋ) working examples
cir cuit ('sər-kət) round-about trip
cir cum fer ence (sər-'kəm-fern(t)s) distance around the edge of a circle
clam ber ('klam-bər) climb
clap board ('kla-bərd) narrow board
clatter rattling noise
clearings ground where the trees have been cut
cleft the bark a sun der (ə-'sən-dər) split the bark
clog ging ('klä-giŋ) hindering
close couch ing ('kaủch-iŋ) crouching so as to be hidden
close the seams together make the cracks tight
cloud-rack of a tempest flying, broken clouds after a storm
cof fers ('kȯ-fərz) treasure chests
Cog ia Hous sam ('kō-gyä; 'hü-säm)
col lect ed (kə-'lek-təd) thoughtful
collected her thoughts thought quickly
com bine (käm-'bØn) form themselves
come what may no matter what happens
Com mand er of the Faith ful (kə-'man-dər; 'fāth-fəl) leader of those true to the Mohammedan religion. The title is given to the caliphs.
com mand ing look out (kə-'man-diŋ; 'lủk-aủt) place from which the surrounding neighborhood can be seen
com mis sion (kə-'mi-shən) thing to be done
com par a tive ly a new af fair (kəm-'pār-ə-tiv-lē; ə-'fār) a world that had been made only a short time
com po sure (kəm-'pō-zhər) calmness
com rades ('käm-radz) mates
con cealed (kən-'sēld) hidden
con fi dent mood ('kän-fə-dent; 'müd) feeling sure I could do it
con found ed with as ton ish ment (kän-'faủn-ded; ə-'stä-nish-mənt) so surprised that they could not think
con fused (kən-'fyüzd) bothered
con joined of them all (kən-'jȯind) made of all together
con nect ed with himself (kə-'nek-təd) have reference to him
con scious ('kän-shəs) aware

con se quence ('kän-sə-kwens) result
con sid er a tion (kən-si-dər-'ā-shən) reason
con stant ('kän-stənt) regular
con stel la tion (kän-stə-'lā-shən) a group of stars
con sti tut ing ('kän-stə-tü-tiŋ) making up
con sul ('kän-səl) one who lives in a foreign country to look after the business interests of his own country there
con tempt i ble (kən-'temp-tə-bəl) mean
con tracts ('kän-trakts) makes
con triv ance (kən-'trØ-vəns) device
con trived (kən-'trØvd) made
con trive to bur y (kən-'trØv; 'ber-ē) manage to bury
con veyed (kən-'vād) given over
cop pers ('kä-pərz) pennies
cord string of the bow
cor nice ('kȯr-nəs) high molding around the walls
cor po re al sen sa tions (kȯr-'pōr-e-əl; sen-'sā-shənz) coarse pleasures
corpse ('kȯrps) dead body
corse let ('kȯr-slət) armor for the body
council of war ('kaủn-səl) meeting to make plans
counsels ('kaủn-səlz) advice
count all your boasts even though you present your many charms
count like mi sers ('mØ-zərz) count as lovingly as do misers their money
county town town where the business of the county (holding court, paying taxes, etc.), is carried on
cours ers ('kōr-sərz) swift horses; here reindeer
cour te ous ('kər-tē-us) polite
court fa vor ('kōrt; 'fā-vər) good will of the ruler or other high personage
court i ers ('kōrt-tē-yərz) those in attendance at the court of a ruler
cov er ('kə-vər) underbrush large enough to hide behind
cow er ing ('kaủ-ər-iŋ) hovering
cre a tion (krē-'ā-shən) the world
crest fall en ('krest-fȯ-lən) cast down
crest ing the bil lows ('kres-tiŋ; 'bi-lōz) adorning the top of the waves
crev ice ('kre-vəs) crack

crew of gypsies band of ragamuffins
crossbrace the piece of wood between the plow handles
crown of his desire thing he wanted most
cru el mor ti fi ca tion ('krü-əl; mōr-tə-fə-'kā-shən) very great annoyance
cruise ('krüz) trip in a boat
cun ning ('kə-niŋ) tricky
cunningly made skillfully made
cup board ('kə-bərd) a closet for dishes
cur mudg eon (kər-'mə-jən) miser
curt sy ('kərt-sē) bow
cym bals ('sim-bəlz) pair of brass half globes clashed together to produce a ringing sound

Da co tahs (də-'kō-təz), Sioux ('sū)
Daed a lus of yore ('ded-ə-ləs) Daedalus of olden time. The story is that he escaped from prison by flying with wings he had made.
dames married women
Da ri us ('da-ri-əs)
daunt ed ('dȯn-ted) frightened
dawn daybreak
day beds resting places in daytime
death less fame ('deth-ləs) lasting glory
deck her bo som ('bu-zəm) trim the front of the canoe
deems ('dēmz) thinks
deer-skin dressed and whitened skins of deer, which had been cleaned, smoothed, and bleached
de file (di-'fØl) narrow pass
de funct ten ant (di-'fənkt; 'te-nənt) man who formerly lived there but is dead
de ject ed (di-'jek-təd) downhearted
del i cate crafts employ ('de-li-kət) use your skill in cooking
dell small valley
de pos it ed (di-'pä-zə-ted) put away
de ri sion (di-'ri-zhən) mockery
des ert ('de-zərt) uninhabited by man
de sign (di-'zØn) plan
des o la tion (de-sō-'lā-shən) ruin
de spair (di-'spār) hopelessness
des per ate ('des-pə-rət) hopeless

des sert (di-'zərt) fruit pastry, etc., usually served at the close of a meal
des tined to be let loose ('des-tənd) fated to be freed
di a mond ('dØ-ə-mənd) precious stone
di min ished (də-'mi-nəsht) made less
di min u tive (də-'mi-nyü-tiv) tiny
di rect ly (də-'rekt-lē) at once
dis as ter (di-'zas-tər) great trouble
dis clos es (dis-'klōz-ez) lets be seen
dis cov er (dis-'kə-vər) find out
dis mount ed (dis-'maůn-təd) threw down off its mountings
dis put ed (di-'spyů-təd) argued; talked each against the others
dis qui e tude (dis-'kwØ-ə-tüd) uneasiness
dis suad ing (di-'swād-iŋ) advising away from
distant days that shall be time to come but still far off
di ver si fied (də-'vər-sə-fØd) made to have a look of variety
doc ile ('dä-səl) gentle
down of a this tle ('thi-səl) lightest thing you can think of
down tim ber ('tim-bər) fallen trees
dow ry ('daů-rē) gift of a man to his bride
draft ('draft) one drink
dread si lence re pos es ('dred-'sØ-lens; re-'pō-zəz) sleeps quietly, so we fear it
dreamy rec ol lec tion (re-kə-'lek-shən) faint memory
drink your health wish you good health when beginning to drink, usually at a meal
driv en ('dri-vən) blown before the wind
droll ('drōl) laughable
droop ing ('drüp-iŋ) with hanging heads
droop o'er the sod hang over a grave
drought ('draůt) lack of rain
drowned ('draůnd)
dry and dumb ('dəm) dried up and still because there is no water to ripple
du cat ('də-kət) old gold coin ($2.28 [1920])
dun geon ('dən-jən) underground prison
Du quesne (dü-'kān)
dusk y pods ('dəs-kē) dark-colored seed vessels
du ty holds him fast ('dü-tē) he knows he ought to stay
each in its turn the sway one after the other ruled

eager hand ('ē-gər) hand that could hardly wait
earth-bound ties roots which hold it in the ground
earth en ('ər-thən) earthenware
earth was young world had not long existed
Eastern lands Asia and Africa
eaves ('ēvz) edges of the roof which overhang the walls slightly
ech o ('e-kō) say over again
ech o ing cor ri dor ('e-kō-iŋ; 'kȯr-ə-dər) long, empty hall in which they could hear their own footsteps
ei ther ('ē-thər)
elf a made-up creature
ell ('el) forty-five inches
en chant ment (in-'chant-mənt) magic
en cir cled (in-'sər-kəld) wound around
en coun ter (in-'kaůn-tər) meeting
en gines ('en-jənz) implements
en ter prise ('en-tər-prØz) undertaking; willingness to try different things
ep i dem ic (e-pə-'de-mik) a disease which one person takes from another
Ep i me the us (ep-ə-'mē-thē-əs)
eq ui page ('e-kwə-pāj) horses and carriage
ere ('er) before
es teem (is-'tēm) good opinion
e vap o rat ed (ə-'va-pə-rā-təd) passed away from me
ever of fi cious Ton ish (ə-'fi-shəs; 'tō-nish) Tonish, who was always doing too much
ev er y part has a voice ('ev-rē) each stripe and star means something
ev i dent in ten tion ('e-və-dent; in-'ten-shən) plain purpose
E wa yea (ə-wȯ-'yā) a lullaby
ex ag ger a tions (ig-za-jər-'ā-shənz) overstatements
ex cess (ek-'ses) too much
ex ile ('eg-zØl) one away from home
ex plore (ik-'splōr) examine thoroughly,
ex pound (ek-'spaůnd) explain
ex press con sent (ik-'spres; kən-'sent) especial permission being given
ex tend ing themselves (ik-'sten-diŋ) spreading out so as to be at a distance from each other
ex tin guish (ik-'stiŋ-gwish) put out

ex traor di na ry (ik-'strȯr-di-nə-rē) surprising unusual
ex ult ed (ig-'səl-təd) was glad
ex ult ing, glean (ig-'zəl-tiŋ; 'glēn) rejoicing, harvest
eye glass of dew ('∅-glas; 'dū) a dewdrop

fading losing the original color
fail of the fruits have not the fruits
faint shadow of a trouble only a hint of unhappiness
fair voy age ('vȯi-ij) trip without severe storms or accidents
fal low ('fa-lō) pale yellow
Falls of Min ne ha ha (min-ē-'hä-hä) a waterfall near Minneapolis
false es ti mates ('fȯls; 'es-tə-məts) wrong judgment
fal ter ing ('fȯl-tə-riŋ) stopping
fame being known everywhere
fame so be com ing to you (bi-'kə-miŋ) glory that suits you so well
famous roe buck ('rō-bək) fine, big deer
fan tas tic forms (fan-'tas-tik) strange shapes
fash ioned ('fa-shənd) shaped; made
fashioned flutes made pipes from which he blew music
fast in my for tress ('fȯr-tres) held firmly by my love
fa tal ('fā-təl) destructive
fa tigue (fə-'tēg) weariness
fa vor a ble gale ('fā-və-rə-bəl; 'gāl) wind blowing in the direction he wished to sail
feasting his eyes enjoying looking at
fea tures and to kens ('fē-chərz; 'tō-kənz) parts of the face, and expression
feeling but one heart-beat all having the same feelings and wishes
feet unwilling moving slowly without interest
fen lands ('fen-landz) swamps
fer vent ly ('fər-vənt-lē) warmly
feuds ('fyüdz) quarrels
fev ered mart ('fē-verd; 'märt) market place full of excitement
fib rous ('f∅-brəs) made of fibers; strong
filled the night made it all light
fis sure ('fi-zhər) narrow crack
fit ful ly blows ('fit-fə-lē) blows and then stops
fit to be made a tool of suitable to be deceived by flattery to do the work of others

flags long, narrow leaves of a plant
flanking parties riders who were going to stand at the sides
flaunt ('flȯnt) make a great showing of
flaunt ing ('flȯnt-iŋ) waving
flaunting nigh ('nØ) making a great show near them
flecked with leafy light ('flekt) spotted with sunlight shining through the trees
fleck its lonely spread ('flek) show as a dark spot against the great stretch of grass
flesh creeps shudder with horror
flex i bil i ty (flek-sə-'bil-ə-tē) ability to be bent
flight of song where a song goes
flit ting ('fli-tiŋ) flying about
flow in music glide along so as to make pleasant sounds
flow'ry dells little valleys with flowers in them
flut ter ('flə-tər) are in motion
fo li age ('fō-lē-ij) leafy plants
fol ly laughs to scorn ('fälē; 'lafs; 'skȯrn) one who is foolish makes fun of
fond loving
for bear (fȯr-'ber) keep from thy stroke; do not chop it down
for bid ding fur ther pas sage (fər-'bid-iŋ; 'fər-ther; 'pas-ij) keeping them from going on
for bore (fōr-'bōr) held back
ford a shallow place where the soldiers could cross without a bridge
fore fath er ('fōr-fä-<u>th</u>ər) ancestor
fore head ('fōr-hed) upper part of the face
for est fight ers ('fȯr-əst; 'fØ-tərz) men used to fighting among trees
forest's life was in it it was made from the trees and seemed alive like them
forever and a day for all time
for lorn (fȯr-'lȯrn) poor and lonely
former state condition it had been in
for mi da ble ('fȯr-mə-də-bəl) dreadful
fort night ('fōrt-nØt) two weeks
foul footsteps' pol lu tion (pə-'lü-shən) dishonor of the country, caused by an enemy being in it
fowling piece gun for shooting birds
frag ments ('frag-mənts) scraps

fra grant ('frā-grənt) sweet-smelling
frame of mind feeling this way
fran chise of this good people ('fran-chØz) vote of the men of this colony
freight ing ('frā-tiŋ) burden
freight it with ('frāt) load the boat with
fren zy ('fren-zē) joyous madness
fre quent ed ('frē-kwən-təd) visited
fretted tired; teased
frig ate ('fri-gət) light, sailing warship
fringed with trees with a thin line of trees along it
frol ic ('fräl-ik) play
frolic chase game of running after each other
frost ed ('frȯ-stəd) frostbitten, and, as a result, loosened
froth y ('frȯ-thē) having bubbles
frown ing pine for est ('fraün-iŋ; 'pØn; 'for-əst) dark evergreen forest
fu gi tives ('fyü-jə-tivz) horses which were trying to escape
full glory re flect ed (ri-'flek-təd) with all its colors showing
full of in ven tion (in-'ven-shən) good at thinking up plans
fur rows ('fər-ōz) shallow trenches made by the plow
furze ('fərz) an evergreen shrub with yellow flowers

gain said ('gān-sed) changed
gal lant ly ('ga-lənt-lē) bravely
gal lant ly stream ing ('ga-lənt-lē; strē-miŋ) bravely flying
gaunt ('gȯnt) thin from hunger
gauze ('gȯz) thin, transparent stuff
gave me a good char ac ter ('kar-ik-tər) said I was a reliable man
gave myself up for lost stopped having any hope of being saved
genial favorable to growth
ge nial hour ('jē-nyəl) pleasant spring time
gen ius ('jēn-yəs) a person who can do more or better than ordinary people
gen ius a powerful spirit
gen tian ('jen-shən) a beautiful flowering plant, usually blue
ges ture ('jes-chər) motion
ghast ly spec ta cle ('gast-lē; 'spek-ti-kəl) horrible sight
gi gan tic (jØ-'gan-tik) very large
gilt gold-plated metal

gim let ('gim-lət) tool which bores small holes as it is turned
Gitch e Gum ee ('gi-chē-'gü-mē) Lake Superior
Gitch e Ma ni to ('gi-chē-'man-i-tō) Great Spirit
give back the cry answer
give me thought for thought tell me his ideas and listen to mine
glade ('glād) an open, grassy space in a wood
gladness breathes joy seems to come
gleam ing ('glēm-iŋ) light
glean gather
glens little valleys
glim mer ('gli-mər) gleam
glim mer ing o'er ('gli-mə-riŋ) shining brightly over corn and people
glit ter ing ('gli-tə-riŋ) shining
glo ri fied the hill ('glō-rə-fØd) sent beautiful rays of light upon the hill
glory fell chas tened ('chā-sənd) his light at the height of its brightness cast but a soft light
glos sy ('glä-sē) shining
gold en ears before ('gōl-dən) yellow ears of corn taken from their husks and piled in front of the huskers
good ly root ('gu̇d-lē; rüt) the much prized potato
go phers ('gō-ferz) ground-squirrels
gor geous ('gȯr-jəs) magnificent; beautiful
gossip of swallows bird notes that sound like chatter
go the entire round make the furrow around the field
Gov er nor ('gə-vᵊn-ər) the chief man of the colony
gra cious ly ('grā-shəs-lē) with kind courtesy
Gra na da (grə-'nä-də)
gran a ried harvest ('grā-nə-rēd) grain and vegetables stored for the winter
gra ti fy ing his utmost wishes ('gra-tə-fØ-iŋ) giving him anything he might wish for
grave ('grāv) serious-looking
gray of the morning faint light before the sun is up
greatest dis qui e tude (dis-'kwØ-ə-tüd) worst trouble
Great Spirit God
griev ous ly ('grē-vəs-lē) painfully
grim stern; unyielding
gri mace ('gri-məs) made-up face

grip ing landlord ('grØ-piŋ) stingy man who rents houses for high rent
grope ('grōp) feel without seeing
grow into tan gles ('taŋ-gəlz) grow wild as in the woods or fields
guard thy re pose ('gärd; re-'pōz) protect you while you sleep
guid ance ('gØ-dəns) showing him the right course to take
guid ed of my coun sel ('gØ-dəd; 'käun-səl) take my advice
guid ing lines ('gØ-diŋ) reins by which horses are driven
guile less ('gØl-əs) pure in heart
guin ea ('gi-nē) English coin ($5.11 [1920])
gul lies ('gə-lēz) small valleys dug out by water
gush ing ('gəsh-iŋ) freely flowing

hab it a ble ('ha-bə-tə-bəl) fit to live in
had oc ca sion to go out (ə-'kā-zhən) needed to go somewhere in the town
hailed his coming called out gladly when they saw him
half-faced camp shack with three walls and one open side
half-section of unfenced sod 320 acres of unbroken ground with no fence
hal looed (ha-'lōd) shouted halloo
hal low us there ('ha-lō) give us a feeling at home as of sacred things
ham let without name ('ham-lət) few houses near together, but not called a town
ham pers ('ham-pərz) woven baskets
hand i work ('han-di-wərk) what I make
hand ker chiefs ('haŋ-kər-chifs)
hand of art tasteful plan
happily arranged growing in pretty clumps
har dy gift ('här-dē) fruit of the sturdy plant which is given by the earth
har row ing ad di tions ('har-ō-iŋ; ə-'di-shənz) things added that are painful to hear
hart ('härt) male red deer
Ha run al Ra shid (hä-rün´ äl rə-'shēd) Caliph of Baghdad
har vest ('här-vəst) dry seeds
has an ax to grind wants someone to do some hard work without pay
hate is shadow feelings of dislike darken everything
haugh ty ('hȯ-tē) proud

haunch es ('hȯn-chəz) hind legs
haunt ('hȯnt) come back again and again
haunts ('hȯnts) places where one loves to go often
haunts of Na ture ('nā-chər) out-of-doors
hav oc of war ('ha-vək) ruin caused by fighting
hawk-eyed ea ger ness ('hȯ-kØd; 'ē-gər-nəs) watching impatiently and with the sharpness of a hawk
heark en ('här-kən) listen
hearth rug ('härth-rəg) rug in front of the fireplace
heart outran his footsteps wanted to be there before he was
heart's-ease comfort in trouble
heart's right hand of friendship a greeting that shows we feel friendly
heart-strings love
heath ('hēth) land covered with heather, which has a purple blossom
heav 'n res cued land ('he-vən; 'res-kyüd) country saved by God
heavy-rolling flight running with a rocking movement from side to side
heir ('ar) one who takes the property of another after he is through with it
helm ('helm) helmet, a protection for the head; the machinery that steers the ship
he must be cold he lacks feeling
herb age ('hər-bij) grass and other plants eaten by grazing animals
here on earth
he ro ic blood (hi-'rō-ik) descended from brave men
hewed ('hyüd) chopped
Hi a wath a ('hØ-ə-wa-thə)
hid den silk has spun ('hi-dən) threads of down in the pod that resemble those which the silkworm spins
hid e ous ('hi-dē-əs) horrible-looking
hie ('hØ) go; take
high re lief (rē-'lēf) carved so that the features stood up from the box
hire ling ('hØ-ər-liŋ) paid soldier
his prop er sphere (prä-pər; 'sfir) his own place
his rev er ence ('rev-rents) the minister
hith er ('hi-th̲ər) here
hoard ('hōrd) supply of provisions
hoar y ('hō-rē) old and gray

hold ('hōld) lower part of a ship, where cargo is stored

hol lows that rus tle be tween ('hä-lōz; 'rə-səl; bi-'twēn) low, quiet places between large, noisily-rolling waves

home-brew served for wine homemade drinks were used instead of wine

home ly old ad age ('hōm-lē; 'a-dij) common saying

hoodwinked blindfolded

hor ror ('hȯr-ər) great fear

horror of my sit u a tion (si-chə-'wā-shən) great danger of the place I was in

horseplay rude play or jokes

host ('hōst) great number

hot ly pressed ('hät-lē; 'prest) closely followed

hov el ('hə-vəl) small, poor house

hov ered ('həv-ərd) fluttered

hud dled ('hə-dəld) crowded

hue ('hyü) color

hues of summer's rainbow ('hyüz) colors in the rainbow in summer

hu man ('hyü-mən) exactly like man

Hum ber ('hum-bər) a river in northeastern England

hum ble ('həm-bəl) lowly; not proud

hu mor ('hyü-mər) temper

humor better suited to his own mood more like his

hur rah (hə-'rä) a word used as a shout of joy

hur ri cane ('hər-ə-kān) great storm

hush of woods quiet of the forest

I a goo (ē-'a-gō)

Ic a rus ('ik-ə-rus) the son of Daedalus—which *see*

i de as (ø-'dē-əz) thoughts

idle, golden freight ing ('frā-tiŋ) burden of golden-colored autumn leaves

if to windward if the hunter is in the direction from which the wind blows

im ag i na ble (i-'maj-nə-bəl) could think of; possible

im mor tal in their childhood (i-'mȯr-təl) so placed that they would never grow any older

im per i al (im-'pir-ē-əl) royal

im pe ri ous (im-'pir-ē-əs) demanding much

im ple ment ('im-plə-mənt) tool
im ply a share of rea son (im-'plØ; 'rē-zən) suggest some power to think
im press ion con tin u ing (im-'pre-shən; kən-'tin-yü-iŋ) the effect remaining
in a bil i ty (in-ə-'bil-ə-tē) that you cannot
in cal cu la ble (in-'kal-kyə-lə-bəl) cannot be counted
in ca pa ble (in-'kāp-ə-bəl) not able
in cline (in-'klØn) slope
in darker for tunes tried ('fȯr-chənz) they had when they were poor
in dif fer ence (in-'di-fər-ents) not caring
in di gest i ble (in-dØ-'jes-tə-bəl) impossible to digest
in dig na tion (in-dig-'nā-shən) anger against what is wrong
in duce (in-'düs) cause
in dulge it to the ut most (in-'dəlj; 'ət-mōst) be as cross as he could
in fi nite ('in-fə-nət) everlasting
in fi nite ly ('in-fə-nət-lē) much more
in gen ious (in-'jēn-yəs) clever
in hal ing (in-'hāl-iŋ) smelling
in her i tance (in-'her-ə-tənts) a gift from our ancestors
in i tial round (i-'ni-shəl) first furrow around the field
in quir ies (in-'kwØr-ēz) questioning
in such wise so fiercely
in tel li gent (in-'te-lə-jent) clever
in tent upon (in-'tent) interested in
in ter mi na ble forests (in-'tərm-ə-nə-bəl) woods that seemed endless
in ter rupt his lay (in-tə-'rəpt) stop his song
in the largest sense in the broadest meaning
in ti mate as so ci a tion ('in-tə-mət; ə-sō-sē-'ā-shən) close companionship
in tol er a ble (in-'täl-ər-bəl) unbearable
in trud er (in-'trüd-ər) an uninvited guest
in ven tion (in-'ven-shən) schemes
Is lands of the Bless ed ('Ø-ləndz; 'blest) in mythology, islands where people lived happily, after death
isles ('Øəlz) islands

jas per ('jas-pər) a dark, hard stone
jaun ty ('jȯn-tē) gay and easy
jet black
jib ('jib) swing around
joined to such fol ly ('fä-lē) be partner in such foolishness
joy ance ('jȯi-əns) happiness
judg ment ('jəj-mənt) idea; opinion
Jus ti ci ar (jə-'sti-shē-är) chief judge
justs ('jəsts) mock fights between knights on horseback

Kagh ('käg) the hedgehog
keel ('kēl) bottom of a ship
keep support
kept made to go on
khan ('kän) an unfurnished building for the use of traveling traders
king's coun cil ('käun-səl) men who met with the king to advise him
kissed into green ('kist) changed to green when touched by the sun's rays
knight ('nøt) in Great Britain, a man with the title Sir
knights of old men of olden times who went about doing brave deeds
knoll ('nōl) a little round hill
knows full well knows very well
Kwa sind ('kwä-sind)

lady the wife of a knight
lam en ta ble (la-'men-tə-bəl) distressed
lamentable tone sad voice
lan guid ly ('laŋ-wəd-lē) carelessly
lank ('lank) thin
lapsed ('lapst) slipped
larch ('lärch) tree which looks like an evergreen but sheds its needles
lar i at ('lār-ē-ət) long rope with a running noose
laud a ble ('lȯ-də-bəl) praiseworthy
laugh ing ('la-fiŋ)
launch ('lȯnch) get it afloat
lav ish horn ('la-vish) overflowing horn; from the mythological story of the horn that could become filled with whatever its possessor desired

lea ('lē) ground covered with grass
league ('lēg) about three miles
learn ed ('lər-nəd) highly educated
learn ing ('lər-niŋ) knowledge
leave un moved (ən-'müvd) unharmed
lee of the land shelter of the shore
leg ends ('le-jəndz) old stories only partly true
lei sure ('lē-zhər) time to do what he wished
lev ee ('le-vē) reception given by a ruler or his representative
liege ('lēj) having the right to claim service
light and boon bright and pleasant
light some ('lØt-səm) cheery
like a Turk as people do in Turkey
Lil li put ('li-lē-pət)
Lil li pu tians (li-lə-'pyü-shənz)
limes ('lØmz) fruit like lemons, but smaller and more sour
lin den ('lin-dən) made from basswood
list less ('list-ləs) caring about nothing
live li hood ('lØv-lē-hüd) living
live long ('liv-loŋ) whole
loam ('lōm) earth
lone ('lōn) lonely
lone post of death place where he must die alone
looked west er ly ('wes-tər-lē) turned toward the west, the direction in which the wind was blowing before it stopped
loosed ('lüst) set free
lost their labor got no good from the work they had done
love ly to kens ('ləv-lē; 'tōk-ənz) beautiful signs
low er ('lō-ər) darken
lowly thatched cottage small one story house with roof of straw
loz enge ('lä-zənj) a tablet of medicine
lust strong wish
lus ter of mid day ('ləs-tər; 'mid-dā) light bright as at noon
lus trous ('ləs-trəs) radiant
lust y rogue ('ləs-tē; 'rōg) lively little rascal

mag ic arts ('ma-jik) power over spirits
ma gi cian (mə-'ji-shən) one who uses magic arts
magic of his singing charming way he sang
mag nif i cence (mag-'ni-fə-səns) grandeur

Ma ha ra ja (mä-hä-'rä-jä) title of the principal Hindu chief
Mahn go tay see (man-'gō-tā-sē) brave
main tain (mān-'tān) keep
make a mends to the human race (ə-'mendz) make up to people everywhere
make a stand hold out against; fight
man-builded today built by people now
ma neu ver (mə-'nü-vər) planned movement of a large number
man of might strong, important man
man's do min ion (də-'mi-nyən) for the use of people
man sion ('man-shən) large and handsome residence
many a happy return many more
mar i ners ('mar-ə-nərz) sailors
marred ('märd) spoiled
marred the whole scene spoiled the effect planned
mar vel ('mär-vəl) wonderful thing
marveled wondered
Mas sa soit (mas-ə-'sȯit)
match able to win against
matchless having no equal
ma trons ('mā-trənz) married women
mayhap maybe
maze ('māz) confusing number of paths which cross
meads meadows
meas ures ('me-zhərz) melodies
med i tat ed ('med-ə-tā-ted) thought
meeting-house church
mel an chol y ('me-lən-kä-lē) sad
melted them to pity softened their feelings so they were filled with gentle thoughts
mer chan dise ('mər-chən-d∅s) goods
mer chant man ('mər-chənt-mən) a trading vessel
mer est ('mēr-əst) simplest
mer ry ('me-rē) joyous
me tal lic (mə-'ta-lik) of metal
metal true really good iron
me thinks (mi-'thiŋks) it seems to me
Mi das ('m∅-dəs)
mil der ('m∅-əl-dər) glory shone a softer and paler glow cast its light
mil dew ('mil-dü) mold; rust

min gled into one ('miŋ-gəld) so united that one could not be distinguished from the other
min i a ture ('mi-nē-ə-chər) very small
Min ne ha ha (min-ē-'hä-hä)
Min ne wa wa (min-ē-'wä-wä)
mirth ful to ex cess ('mərth-fəl; 'ik-ses) too gay
mis chie vious ('mis-chə-vəs) fun-loving
mis do ings (mis-'dü-iŋz) wrong acts
mis sion ('mi-shən) errand
mists of the deep fog over the water
moc ca sins of magic ('mä-kə-sənz) charmed shoes
mod er a tion (mä-də-'rā-shən) fair way
modest bell bell-shaped flower that hangs over
mol der in dust away ('mōl-dər) lose their form and become earth again
mo lest ed (mə-'lest-ed) troubled
mol ten ('mōl-tən) melted
mon arch ('mä-nərk) ruler
Mo non ga he la (mə-'nōn-gä-hē-lä) river in Pennsylvania
Mon sieur (məs-'yər) French for Mister
moor sandy, wet ground
more en ter prise ('en-tər-prØz) willingness to try to do things
Mor gi a na (mȯr-gi-'ä-nä)
mor tal ('mȯr-tᵊl) human
mortal en e my ('e-nə-mē) man who hates you so much he would like to kill you
mortal fear greatest fear
mor tal ly ('mȯr-tᵊl-ē) so as to cause death
mosques ('mäsks) places of worship in Mohammedan countries
moss ('mȯs) a tiny grasslike plant, very soft
moss-green trees trees with trunks covered by green moss
mount to the sky fly out of sight
mow ('maù) ('mō; here for rhyme) A pile of hay or straw
much a miss (ə-'mis) very wrong
much con triv ing (kən-'trØv-iŋ) making great plans
much fre quent ed ('frē-kwənt-ed) often visited
much in clined (in-'klØnd) having a great liking for
Mud way aush ka (məd-wȯ-'üsh-kä)
multiply his heaps make his piles many times greater
mum mies ('mə-mēz) dead bodies which have been preserved in

a dried state; here, persons whose minds are dry and not open to new ideas

Mun chaus en (mən-'chȯ-zen) a teller of extravagant tales

Musk et a quid (məs-'kət-ə-kwid)

Musk o day ('məsk-ō-dā)

mute ('mūt) voiceless; quiet

mut te ring ('mət-ə-riŋ) saying in a low tone

muz zle ('mə-zəl) nose and mouth

my design my plan

mys te ri ous (mis-'tir-ē-əs) puzzling

mys tic splen dors ('mis-tik; 'splen-dərz) magic brightness

naked sword ('sōrd) sword without a sheath

narrow bound thin wall keeping them out

na tion al con stel la tion ('nash-nəl; kän-stə-'lā-shən) group of stars belonging to the nation

na tive lan guage ('nā-tiv; 'laŋ-gwij) way that is natural to them

nat u ral death ('na-chə-rəl) died without being killed

naught ('nȯt) nothing

nav i gate the az ure ('na-və-gāt; 'a-zhər) sail through the sky

Na wa da ha (nä-wä-'dä-hȧ)

near his cot not far from his cottage

nei ther ('nē-t͟hər)

neither willing nor re luc tant (ri-'lək-tənt) not showing whether she wanted to go or stay

neph ew ('ne-fyü) the son of a brother or sister

nicest goldsmith most skillful worker in gold

niche ('nich) small opening

nim ble ('nim-bəl) quick to do things

no ble ('nō-bəl) coin worth about $1.60 [1920]; man of high rank

No ko mis (no-'kō-məs)

nos trils ('näs-trəlz) the openings in the nose for breathing

note if harm were near to see if there were any danger round about

ob lit er at ed (ə-'bli-tər-ā-təd) taken away

ob scure (äb-'skyür) dark

ob scured their pas sage (äb-'skyurd; 'pa-sij) hid their line of movement

ob ser va tion (äb-sər-'vā-shən) careful notice

ob sta cle ('äb-sti-kəl) something in the way
ob tained a foothold (əb-'tānd) got a start
oc cu pied with her grief ('ä-kyə-pØd) full of sorrow
o cean's breast ('ō-shənz; 'brest) calm surface of the sea
O drug useless thing
o'er shad owed Thanksgiving Day (ōr; 'sha-dōd) brought up sad thoughts on the holiday
o'er the comb ers (ōr; 'kō-mərz) over the long rolling waves
of all degrees of all kinds, large and small
of a se ri ous na ture ('sir-ē-əs; 'nā-chər) of a dangerous kind
of fi cial ly rec og nized (ə-'fi-shə-lē; 're-kəg-nØzd) known and stated
oint ment ('ȯint-mənt) precious salve
O jib ways (ō-'jib-wāz) a tribe that lived just south of Lake Superior
ooze and tangle ('üz) mud and roots
ooz ing outward ('ü-ziŋ) flowing from the tree
O pe chee (ō-'pē-chē)
op en hand ed ness (ō-pən; 'hand-əd-nəs) generosity
op er a tions of the en e my (ä-pə-'rā-shənz; 'e-nə-mē) doings of those fighting against us
op pres sion lifts its head (ə-'pre-shən) people are treated unjustly
o rig i nal (ə-'rij-ə-nəl) first
outlaw one who breaks the laws and flees to escape punishment
overcame this hand i cap ('han-di-kap) got over this disadvantage
Owaissa (ō-'wās-ä)

pack et ('pa-kət) bundle
pack train a number of animals carrying the supplies of the party
pa gans ('pā-gənz) not Christians
painted pul pit ('pu̇l-pit) green and purple over-arching leaf of the jack-in-the-pulpit
painted tribes of light gay, bright flowers of spring
painted white white-skinned, like an Indian's face covered with paint
pale skies gray skies of early spring
pal freys ('pȯl-frēz) saddle-horses
pal i sades of pine-trees ('pa-lə-sādz) tall pines, standing like a wall on each bank
pal pi tat ed ('pal-pə-tā-təd) shook

Pan do ra (pan-'dōr-ə)
parched ('pärcht) dry
par ent ('par-ənt) the giver of life
par take (pär-'tāk) share
par tic u lar ly (pər-'ti-kyü-lər-lē) very
part ners ('pärt-nərz) companions
past will no longer be the past ('past) things that happened long ago will seem as real as though going on now
pa thos ('pā-thäs) sad sweetness
pa tient weath er cocks ('pā-shənt; 'we-thər-käks) patient, waiting for the wind to blow
Pau wat ing (pȯ-'wā-tiŋ) St. Mary's river, joining Lakes Superior and Huron
pay my court ('kōrt) show my respect by visiting you
peace of mind calm thoughts with nothing to disturb them
peas ants ('pe-zənts) lowest class of people
peer ('pir) peep cautiously
pen non ('pe-nən) flag
per form ing these good offices (pər-'fȯr-miŋ) doing these kind acts
per il ous ('per-ə-ləs) dangerous
per i od i cal (pir-ē-'äd-i-kəl) printed matter in the form of a magazine, published regularly (not daily)
per plex i ty (pər-'plek-sə-tē) difficulty
per se vered (pər-sə-'vird) persisted
per se ver ing ly (pər-sə-'vir-iŋ-lē) continually
per son age ('pərs-nij) creature
pest disease which kills
pes tered ('pəs-tərd) annoyed
pet tish ly ('pe-tish-lē) crossly
pheas ants ('fe-səntz) wild birds of delicious flavor
phoe be ('fē-bē) a kind of bird
phrase ('frāz) expression
phys i cal and mor al cour age ('fi-zi-kəl; 'mör-əl; 'kər-ij) bravery of body and mind
phy sique (fi-'zēk) build and health
piece of cov er ('kə-ver) bit of underbrush large enough to hide behind
pierce like a shaft ('pirs; 'shaft) fly through like an arrow
pine-clad hills hills covered with pine trees

pin ion ('pin-yən) wing
pit i a ble ('pi-tē-ə-bəl) sad
place of de po sit (di-'pä-zət) keeping place
plagued the realm ('plāgd; 'relm) made trouble in the country
plague the Abbot ('plāg) annoy the Abbot
plait ing ('plāt-iŋ) braiding
Plan tag e nets (plan-'taj-ə-nets) the English kings from 1154 to 1485
plenty enough of everything
pli ant as a wand ('plØ-ənt; 'wänd) as easily moved as a willow twig is bent
plow had vi o lat ed ('vØ-ə-lā-ted) had been turned up by the plow, and thus spoiled for the small owners
plow share ('plaů-shār) blade of the plow; part which turns up the earth
plun dered store ('plən-dərd) goods he had taken by force
Poet Lau re ate ('lȯr-ē-ət) poet chosen by the king to write on great events of the nation
point to wind ward ('win-dwərd) turn in the direction from which the wind came
poised it in the air ('pȯizd) held it high
po lit i cal bus tles ('pə-li-ti-kəl; 'bə-sᵊlz) activities of politics
pol lu tion (pə-'lü-shən) soiling and making impure
pomp ('pämp) show
pon der ('pän-dər) think
pondering much thinking things over
pon der ous ('pän-də-rəs) heavy
Po ne mah (pō-'nē-mä)
pon iard ('pän-yərd) dagger
por ce lain ('pōr-sə-lən) fine white earthenware
pos sessed au thor i ty (pə-'zest; ə-'thȯr-ə-tē) knew how to control
power of proph e cy ('prä-fə-sē) ability to foretell events
prac tice de cen cy ('prak-tis; 'dē-sən-sē) do the right thing every time
prat tle ('pra-təl) child's talk
pres ence ('pre-zəns) being there
pres ent ly ('pre-zənt-lē) soon
pre vent (pri-'vent) keep from
Pri deaux (prē-'dō)

pried into ('prØd) tried to pull apart
prig one who thinks himself good
prime ('prØm) best
prince ly ('prins-lē) like a prince
pro claim (prō-'klām) show
pro fu sion of flowers (prə-'fyū-zhən) great many flowers
pro ject ed (prə-'jek-təd) extended
proudly we hailed looked at with pride and joy
prov ince ('prə-vənts) one of the divisions of certain countries
pru dence ('prü-dənts) wisdom; sense
Psalm ('säm) sacred song
pub li can ('pə-bli-kən) tax gatherer
pull fod der ('fä-dər) pull up cornstalks by the roots
pulp wet mixture of which paper is made
pump kin ('pəm-kən)
pur pose ('pər-pəs) object; work
pursuit (pər-'süt) chase
put me in mind suggested to me

quail ('kwāᵊl) the bobwhite
quirk ('kwərk) turn
quoit ('kyȯit) ring
quoth ('kwōth) said

ra di ance ('rā-dē-əns) brilliance
ra di ant ('rā-dē-ənt) beaming
raid ('rād) attack made to get something
ram parts ('ram-pärts) protecting walls for defense
rang ers ('rān-jərz) men who live on the range, or prairie
rap tur ous ('rap-chə-rəs) very happy
rar i ties ('rār-ə-tēz) rare and precious things
rav en ous ('ra-və-nəs) very great
rayless disk of red flat, burning circle, not seeming to throw off any rays of light
re ap peared (rē-ə-'pird) came in sight again
rear ('rir) raise
rear ing ('rir-iŋ) standing on her hind legs
re call ing (ri-'kȯ-liŋ) remembering
re ceived in trust (ri-'sēvd) taken, to protect honorably
reck less ('re-kləs) careless

rec og nized ('re-kig-nØzd) saw
re coil (rē-'kȯil) rebound
re cov er ing himself (ri-'kə-vər-iŋ) coming back to his natural state of mind
red-coats British soldiers, so called because of their red uniforms
re deem (ri-'dēm) them buy them back
re dou bled (rē-'də-bəld) repeated
reeds large, tall swamp grasses
re en forc ing (rē-ən-'fōr-siŋ) covering again
re flect ed (ri-'flek-təd) thought
re gions of the morning ('rē-jənz) place where the sun rises; the East
reg u lar or der ('re-gyə-lər; 'ȯr-dər) in straight lines, one behind the other
re lat ed (ri-'lā-təd) told
re laxed (ri-'lakst) loosened; let go
Rel dre sal ('rel-drē-sal)
rem nant ('rem-nənt) few that are left
re mot est corner of Africa (ri-'mō-təst) part of Africa the farthest away
ren der ('ren-dər) give back
re nown (ri-'naủn) fame
re paired to her house (ri-'pārd) went to her house
re pair the mis chief (ri- 'par; 'mis-chəf) make up for the harm
re past (ri-'past) feast
re pel ling (ri-'pel-iŋ) driving back
re pent ance (ri-'pen-tənts) regret
re sem bles (ri-'zem-bəlz) is like
res in ('re-zin) dried sap
res o lute ly (re-sə-'lüt-lē) determinedly
re solved (ri-'zälvd) with his mind firmly made up
re splend ent (ri-'splen-dənt) shining brightly
re store (ri-'stōr) put back
re tired cham ber (ri-'tØrd; 'chām-bər) room away from the main part of the house
re treat (ri-'trēt) hiding place
rev els ('re-vəlz) wild enjoyment
re ver ber a tions (ri-vər-bə-'rā-shənz) echoes
rev er ence ('rev-rens) great respect
richly decked ('dekt) wearing beautiful and costly blankets and other decorations

rich stuffs costly cloth of different kinds
ridges raised lines of ground
ri dic u lous (rə-'di-kyü-ləs) deserving to be laughed at
rills little streams
ring of the same sound of it
rip ened charge ('r∅-pend; 'chärj) precious object in its keeping, now ready for husking
rip pling ('rip-liŋ) blowing in curves
ri val for one hour ('r∅-vəl) equal at the time of greatest beauty
riv et ed ('ri-və-təd) fastened by bending down the end
riveted his attention (ə-'ten-shən) put all his thought
roam ('rōm) wander
robes of darkness blue-black foliage clothing it
roc ('räk) imaginary bird of great size
ro guish ly de fied ('rō-gish-lē; dē-'f∅d) resisted in a joking way
Roha ('rō-hä)
root ('rüt) the potato
ro sy morn ('rō-zē; 'mȯrn) reddish tint of the sky at sunrise
round-tower of my heart safest place for a prisoner
route ('rüt) way
rue ful ly ('rü-fəl-lē) sadly
rue the day ('rü) regret what I had done that day
rug ged ('rə-gəd) uneven
rug ged vales be stow ('rə-gəd; 'vāᵊlz; bi-'stō) rough valleys furnish
ru ined ('rü-ənd) destroyed
ru mi nat ing ('rü-mə-nā-tiŋ) chewing their cuds
run over with joy be wildly happy
rushes coarse grasses
rus set ('rə-sət) reddish brown or reddish gray

Sa chem ('sā-chem) Indian chief
sac ri fic ing ('sa-krə-f∅-siŋ) giving up
sad sea wave ocean seeming sad because you are sad
sage speeches ('sāj) wise remarks
sa lut ed the com pa ny (sə-'lü-təd; 'kəmp-nē) greeted those assembled
san dal wood ('san-dəl-wu̇d) a highly prized, fragrant Asiatic wood from a tree of the same name
sank deep into my mind made a lasting impression on me
sate ('sāt) old spelling of sat

sat in burs ('sa-tin) prickly husks of chestnuts with their smooth, soft lining
sat is fy his mind ('sa-təs-fØ) find out what he wanted to know
save except
sa vor y ('sā-vrē) pleasing to the smell
scaled the wall ('skāld) got over the wall, as soldiers climbed by ladders over the walls of an old-time city
scars of all wars marks left from injuries got in fighting
scope ('skōp) reach
scorched ('skȯrcht) heated until burned
scoured the seas ('skaủrd) hunted over the seas
scour for spoils ('skaủr) hunt for dainty foods
scour ing down the mead ow ('skaủ-riŋ; 'me-dō) sweeping over the grassland
sear ('sir) withered
sea ward glide ('sē-wərd; 'glØd) flow toward the ocean
Se bo wish a (seb-ō-'wish-a)
se cure him a gainst e vil (si-'kyür; ə-'genst; 'ē-vəl) protect him from harm
sedg es ('sej-əz) grasslike plants with tall heads of seeds
se ñor (sān-'yȯr) Spanish for sir
sense of e la tion (i-'lā-shən) feeling of joy
se quin ('sē-kwən) a coin, no longer in use, worth about $2.25 [1920]
se rene of look and heart (sə-'rēn) with a calm face and mind
service liketh us we like to serve
ses a me ('se-sə-mē) a kind of grain grown in the East and used for food
sev ered ('se-vərd) cut off
Sev ern ('sev-ərn) a river in southwestern England
shadow of an in fi nite bliss ('in-fə-nət) hint of happiness that cannot be measured
shanty small, unfinished house
shaped them to a framework bent and fastened them to form the skeleton of the canoe
share *see* plowshare
sheath ('shēth) put into its case
sheaves ('shēvz) bundles of grain
sheer into the river straight down into the water
shift less ('shift-ləs) poorly kept
shil ling ('shi-liŋ) coin worth $0.24 [1920]

shining land of Wa bun ('wä-bən) bright East (Wabun is the East Wind)
shining shoulders bare, wet shoulders glistening in the sun
shipping passage on shipboard
shirk ('shərk) one who tries to get out of work
shivering shock force that breaks its timbers
shoal ('shōl) sandbar
shoot a main have a match
shot his shining quills cast off some of his smooth spines
shoulder your matchlocks take your guns
shroud rope of a ship
shut tle ('shə-təl) tool used in weaving
sieve ('siv) a utensil for separating the coarse particles from the fine
sig ni fy un ion ('sig-nə-fØ; 'yün-yən) mean joining
sin cer i ty (sin-'sir-ə-tē) honesty
sin ews ('sin-yüz) tough strips
singing pine trees pines through which the wind blew with a pleasant sound
sing led out ('siŋ-gəld) chose
sire ('sØr) father
sit u a tion (si-chə-'wā-shən) state in which things were
skil let ('ski-lət) frying pan
skim ming ('ski-miŋ) flying so close as to brush the surface
skirt ed ('skər-təd) walked along the edge of; grew along the edge of
sky ward ('skØ-wərd) cast hung high
slab ('slab) thick slice
slaugh tered ('slȯ-tərd) killed for food
sledge ('slej) a heavy hammer
sleep shall be broken you will be awakened
sleight-of-mouth tricks ('slØt) mysterious disappearances
slow slop ing to the night ('slōp-iŋ) sinking slowly in the west
slui ces ('slü-səz) gates to hold back the water
smiling fields patches of grain growing well
smirk ('smərk) put-on smile
smite the ore ('smØt) hammer the iron into shape
smol dered ('smōl-dərd) slowly burned
Soan ge ta ha (sōn-gē-'tä-hä)
soar ing ('sōr-iŋ) floating in the air
so bered by his ad ven ture ('sō-bərd; əd-'ven-chər) made wise by his experience

soft ly pic tured wood ('sȯft-lē; 'pik-chərd) beautifully colored foliage showing up in soft tints
sol ace ('sä-ləs) comfort
som ber ('säm-bər) gloomy
soothe comfort
sore of heart weary and discouraged
sorry pass sad state
sound of their shock noise when they struck
sov er eign ('sä-vər-ən) ruler
spa cious ('spā-shəs) large
spake with naked hearts hid no secrets from each other
spare yards extra poles used to support the sails
spars ('spärz) masts
speaks sub lime ly (sə-'blØm-lē) has a noble meaning
spec ter like figure ('spek-tər-lØk) person looking like a ghost
spelled down beat in spelling
sphere of gold ('sfir) golden globe
spikes large nails
spire a slender rod, or tower, extending upward from the top of a building; here, for the weathercock
spir it u al izes ('spir-i-chə-wa-lØz-əz) purifies
spir it was grad u al ly sub dued ('spir-ət; 'gra-jə-wə-lē; səb-'düd) she was tamed
splendor dazzles in vain ('splen-dər) bright show of glory does not tempt
splendor wild light rising and falling
spoils of forest free things that come from trees
sported played
spray ('sprā) twig
sprites ('sprØts) fairies
square heaven of blue blue part of the flag
stal wart ('stȯl-wərt) brave
stanch ('stȯnch) faithful
stanched ('stȯncht) checked the bleeding from
standing in for the shore coming toward the land
stand you in yeo man's stead ('yō-mənz; 'sted) be of help to you in your adventures
star-spangled sprinkled with stars
state and person country and the man himself
state ly ('stāt-lē) standing proudly

stature height
stayed my walk stopped me
stay surety be security
stern the back part of a boat
steward man in charge of the food
stick to your sphere do the things you can do; don't try to do those you can't
stiff not to be bent or changed
sti fled mur mur ('sti-fəld 'mər-mər) a low sound not easily heard
stirred their souls to pas sion ('pa-shən) moved their deepest feelings
store large amount
storm still brave stand firm in a hard wind
stoutest bravest
stout fellow gay young man
Straits of Gi bral tar ('strāts; jē-'bròl-tər) narrow waterway between Spain and Africa
strength al lied to goodness ('a-lØd) bodily power added to virtues
strewn ('strün) covered
strick en ('stri-kən) frightened
strife comes with manhood men have to fight
stroked in rip ples ('strōkt; 'ri-pəlz) gently made into little folds
stub ble ('stə-bəl) short stalks left in the ground after grain has been cut
stud ied the sit u a tion ('stə-dēd; si-chü-'wa-shən) thought over the state in which things were
stur dy ('stər-dē) strong; firm
sub lime ly (sə-'blØm-lē) with great nobility and purity
suc ceed ed to the gloom (sək-'sē-dəd; 'glüm) followed the cloudiness
such an old mus tache ('məs-tash) so fierce a soldier
suit a ble to that char ac ter ('sü-tə-bəl; 'kar-ik-tər) such as dancers wore
sul tan ('səl-tən) title of the ruler in some Asiatic countries
sum mit of the Cedar ('sə-mət) top of the tree
sum moned ('sə-mənd) called
sun be nig nant (bi-'nig-nənt) kindly sun
sun is under the sea sun has set
sunshine of sweet looks brightness of expression
sup ple ('sə-pəl) easily bent

sup port ed the dog's chanc es (sə-'pōr təd; 'chans-əz) said that the dog would succeed
sup pressed (sə-'prest) kept down
sure ty ('shür-ə-tē) security
surge's swell ('sərj-ez) waves of the rising sea
sur passed (sər-'past) did better than
swam ('swam)
sweeping westward moving swiftly toward the west
sweetmeats candied fruits
swell the mer ri ment ('mer-i-mənt) make louder the sound of happy voices
swept down into a valley sloped gradually to low land
swerve ('swərv) go crooked
swoon ('swün) faint
sym bol ('sim-bəl) sign
sym bol iz es ('sim-bəl-Ø-zəz) means

tam a rack ('ta-mə-rak) tree that looks like an evergreen but sheds its needles in winter
tang to the spirit ('taŋ; 'spir-ət) fancied taste
Ta qua me naw ('tä-quä-mē-nȯ) river in Michigan
tar nished ('tär-nisht) stained
taught wisdom from the past having learned better things from what had happened before
Ta wa sen tha (tä-wä-'sen-thä) name of a valley in New York
taw ny ('tȯ-nē) yellowish-brown
tax a part of one's wealth given up by law to benefit the public
te di ous ('tē-dē-əs) tiresome
ter race ('ter-əs) a raised level platform of earth
text the subject of a talk
the a ter ('thē-tər) building in which plays are acted
their green re sume (rə-'züm) are again covered with grass
the night is behind us night-time is almost here
there fore ('thar-fōr) for that reason
thick zig zags ('zig-zagz) many paths running this way and that
thinned to a thread grew so narrow she could barely be seen
thongs ('thȯŋz) narrow strips of leather
thresh old (thresh-hōld) piece of timber under the door
thrilled ('thrild) filled with joy
thun der halls ('thən-dər; 'hȯlz) far up, where the thunder dwells

thun der ing down the val ley ('thən-dər-iŋ; 'val-ē) running along level ground with a noise like thunder
thus ac cou tered (ə-'kü-tərd) dressed in this way
thus dis posed (di-'spōzd) so arranged
thwart ed the wi ly savage ('thwȯr-təd; 'wØ-lē) fought against the tricks of the Indians
tinge ('tinj) color; tint
tink ered ('tin-kərd) worked without knowing just how
ti ny ('tØ-nē) very small
tipped with flint having points of flint the hardest kind of stone
'tis meet it is right
tit tered ('ti-tərd) laughed mockingly
titter of winds merry sound of the breeze
toil is the real play work is more fun than playing
toil some ('tȯil-səm) hard
tol er a ble ('täl-ər-ə-bəl) bearable
toll ('tōl) tax; money
took no toll did not rob them
took shipping engaged passage on shipboard
took to his rev els ('re-vəlz) went on with his wild play
tor men tors (tȯr-'men-tərz) flies which bit them
tor tured by their lances ('tȯr-chərd) in great pain from the sharp bites
touch hole ('təch; 'hōl) the place where the powder was lighted
tour ('tu̇r) trip
tour neys ('tu̇r-nēz) meetings where knights fought
to ward ('tō-ərd) in the direction of
tow er ing steep ('tau̇-ər-iŋ) high slope
tow ers ('tau̇-ərz) high parts of the castle
track er ('tra-kər) one who traces the path an animal has taken
trade winds winds which always blow in the same direction
tra di tion (trə-'di-shən) story handed down
traf fic ('tra-fik) business
train those in a company
tran quil ('tran-kwəl) motionless because there was no wind
trans par ent (trans-'par-ənt) able to be seen through
trans port ('trans-pōrt) great excitement
trans port (trans 'pōrt) to remove
trav el ing schoolmaster ('tra-və-liŋ) teacher who went from one place to another
trea son ('trē-zən) attempt to injure the government

tribes of men might prosper all nations might live in better ways
trick ling ('tri-kə-liŋ) of water running in a small stream
trims smooths neatly
tri umph ('trØ-əmpf) victory
tri um phant (trØ-'əmp-fənt) glad of success
tro phy ('trō-fē) prize
troub led spir it ('trə-bəld; 'spir-ət) soul of the dead man which cannot rest
tryst ('trist) meeting place
tur ban ('tər-bən) headdress worn in Mohammedan countries, a cap with a sash or scarf wound about it
tur quoise ('tər-kȯiz) a precious blue stone
tur ret ('tər-ət) a small tower
tusks ('təsks) large, projecting teeth
twin ing ('twØ-niŋ) creeping up and winding about
twinkle of its candle little glow like that from a candle
twinkling moment
ty rant would be lord ('tØ-rənt) cruel master would rule everything

un ac cus tomed to vex a tions (ən-ə-'kəs-təmd; vek-'sā-shənz) not used to any sort of bothers
un an i mous ly elected (yü-'na-nə-məs-lē) given every vote
un apt (ən-'apt) unlikely
un bound ed freedom (ən-'baůn-dəd) state where they did as they liked
un com fort a ble state of af fairs (ən-'kəm-fər-tə-bəl; ə-'fārz) hard way of living
un con scious (ən-'kän-shəs) feeling and knowing nothing
un eas i ness (ən-'ēz-ē-nəs) worry
unequal fight ill-matched struggle
unfolded to your gaze spread out before you
un housed (ən-'haůzd) turned out of their homes
unknown crowded nations great masses of people of different races
unwittingly by accident
upon their kind against other men
use less ('yüs-ləs) without having been made good use of
ut most ('ət-mōst) greatest
ut ter itself in words ('ət-ər) speak its meaning
va grant ('vā-grənt) idle wanderer
vague ('vāg) not clear

vague lisps talk that could not be understood
vales ('vāᵊlz) little valleys
val or ('va-lər) bravery
var ied riches ('vār-ēd) good foods of different kinds
vault ('vōlt) walled-up space underground
vaunt ing ly ('vȯnt-iŋ-lē) boastingly
veered ('vird) turned
ven om ous ('ve-nə-məs) poisonous
ver dant ('ver-dənt) green
vest that is bright red breast
vex a tion (vek-'sā-shən) anger
vex a tions (vek-'sā-shənz) troubles
vict uals ('vi-təlz) food
vil lain ('vi-lən) wicked man
vir gin air ('vər-jən) clear, fresh air of spring
vir tue of vested power ('vər-chü) because of the office to which he had been elected
vi sion ('vi-zhən) dream
vi sions of sugarplums ('vi-zhənz) dreams of candy
vi zier ('v∅-zēr) a high state officer in Mohammedan countries
vol un ta ri ly (vä-lən-'tār-ə-lē) willingly

Wa bas so (wa-'bas-ō)
Wa bun ('wȯ-bən) East wind
Wah wah tay see (wȯ-wȯ-'tā-sē)
wain ('wān) wagon
waist coat ('wāst-kōt) vest
walks of life things they try to do
wand ('wänd) slender stick
wanders piping through the village walks around the town, playing sweet music
wanted nothing had everything he wanted
war ring ('wȯ-riŋ) fighting
war rior ('wȯr-yər) fighting man
wa ry ('wa-rē) easily frightened
was mind ed to try ('m∅n-dəd) felt he would like to test wastes wide stretches of land unfit for cultivation
way side blos som ('wā-s∅d; 'blä-səm) flower growing by the roadside
way side things flowers that grow along the roadside

Wa wa ('wä-wä)
Wa won ais sa (wä-wȯn-'ā-sə)
Way was si mo (wā-'wäs-i-mō)
wea sel ('wē-zəl) a small animal noted for its quickness
wedge ('wej) a tool, thinner at one edge, used for splitting
ween know
well mounted riding on good horses
wend ('wend) go
wheel ing ('hwē-liŋ) circling
whence from where
where the last was bred in the place in which the last sprang
where up on ('hwər-ə-pȯn) after which
wher ev er it list eth ('hywər-'e-vər; 'list-əth) wherever it wishes
white-skin wrapper covering of white bark
Whit sun day ('hwit-sən-dā) the seventh Sunday after Easter
whole round of my isle trip all the way around the island
whose joy is to slay who like to kill
wield ('wēld) use
wig wams ('wig-wȯmz) huts of bark
wil der ness ('wil-dər-nəs) wild country
wildfire jack-o'-lantern gay little man dancing about
willing lands ground ready for plowing
will not eat salt in olden times eating salt with a man (that is, being his guest) bound the guest to do his host no harm, then or afterward
wi ly ('wØ-lē) tricky
winged having wings
winged with feathers ('wiŋd) having feathers at one end, to help them fly
win try hoard ('win-trē; 'hōrd) store of food for the winter
wisdom of the book words which made up the sense
witch er y ('wi-chə-rē) fascination
with in his scope (with-'in; 'skōp) where he could reach it
with one ac cord (ə-'kōrd) with the same idea
with one con sent (kən-'sent) agreeing
without more a do (ə-'dü) not making any objection
wonder ('wən-dər) surprising thing
won drous ('wən-drəs) strange
wondrous birth and be ing ('bē-iŋ) story of the wonderful way he came into the world and lived in it
words cannot paint anything one might say could not describe

work the book out do enough work to pay for the book
wor ship ('wər-shəp) devotion to God
wound ed ('wün-dəd) hurt
wounds ('wündz) old griefs
wo ven tex ture ('wō-vən; 'teks-chər) cloth
wrack ('rak) ruin
wreath ('rēth) garland
wreathed ('rēthd) joyous
wreath ing fires ('rē-thiŋ) flames twisting around
wrought ('ròt) worked
wrought together in such har mo ny ('här-mə-nē) so combined in the carving

Xe nil ('zē-nil)

year ling ('yir-liŋ) an animal one year old
yellow hair the silky threads growing out from the end of the ear
Yen a diz ze (yen-ə-'diz-ē) an idler
yeo man ('yō-mən) free-born man
yes ter ('yes-tər) of the day before
yet unforgotten still remembered
yore ('yōr) olden time
young sun early morning sun